Th

H

Eliza
Bloom

The Two *Hearts* of Eliza Bloom

BETH MILLER

bookouture

Published by Bookouture in 2019

An imprint of StoryFire Ltd.

Carmelite House
50 Victoria Embankment
London EC4Y 0DZ

www.bookouture.com

ISBN: 978-1-78681-683-2
eBook ISBN: 978-1-78681-682-5

For Rachel, who left too soon.

And for my Zaida, who walked along the cherry blossom street with me.

Chapter One

March 2016

As a child Leah would often say, 'tell me about your wedding day.' So I'd get down the photo, and recount the story again.

'Well, you know I was meant to marry a man called Nathan. It was all set. Everything was ready: the dress, the ring, the food. But I fell in love with your daddy instead.'

'Alex!' (Or, when she was really young, 'Awix!')

'That's right. We met when I gave a talk at his work. And so the day of my big wedding to Nathan, me and your daddy ran away together.'

'Running, like in a race?'

'It's an expression. Though actually, we did have to properly run a bit. Anyway, then we got engaged that same day, and soon after, we were married.' I tended to gloss over the gap between us running away and getting married. 'It was a very small wedding. The only people who came were Uncle Kim and Aunty Vicky.'

When Leah was older, nine or ten, she loved the crazy chronology of the thing. 'So you got engaged to Dad on the same day you were meant to marry someone else?'

'Yes, I know! Funny, isn't it?'

Not that anyone at the time had felt like laughing.

But younger Leah just liked looking at the photo: Alex and me, standing beneath a bare-branched beech tree. Me in a long silky red dress and white furry jacket, the only decoration my grandmother's brooch. Standing firm in sensible black lace-up shoes, incongruous with the dress. Him in a dark suit and green tie, his arms round my waist. Our faces close together, our eyes on each other and no one else.

'Your hair is funny.'

'I had long hair back then, and it was pinned up.'

'Wedding dresses are supposed to be white.' A chubby finger pointed accusingly at the photo.

'Not always. Red is a lovely colour. And look, I am wearing *something* white.' I smoothed my finger over the image of the jacket that I'd borrowed from Vicky. I could almost feel its unfamiliar softness. I had never worn anything furry before that day.

'What happened next?'

For little Leah, I'd say, 'We all lived happily ever after.' That pleased her. And for older Leah, I'd bring her own birth into the story, and describe how her arrival made me and Daddy – the happiest King and Queen that ever lived – even happier.

But now she's a stroppy teen, and she isn't interested in that photo any more; she's overheard something I didn't want her to know, found something I didn't want her to find, put two and two together, and correctly made four.

What happened next, Leah used to ask.

It's a good question.

It was adorable, how fascinated she was by our love story when she was little. She still is fascinated in a sense, if last night was anything to go by. Maybe horrified is a more accurate description. Anyway, I don't want to think about last night. I don't want to think about Leah's face as she stood in the doorway, the black eyeliner she favours making her seem even less childlike, looking at me with that cool, clear way she has. I prefer to think about Leah when she was little, and I could do no wrong as far as she was concerned. Not now, when she is fourteen, and angry, and has been missing for five hours.

I was sound asleep when she went out this morning. She was gone even before Alex got up. He says he heard a noise at the front door at about seven, but assumed it was the paper being delivered. Yes, Alex, because that makes a sound *exactly* like someone opening and closing the door.

We've agreed to wait until one o'clock before calling the police. Leah might have just gone out with friends and forgotten to tell us. She's done that a couple of times before. Though never so early. I hope I'm not clutching at straws. But anyway, she's always been back by lunchtime. So we're filling in the wait with an interrogation of me by Alex Symons, Amateur Detective. He's insisting on going over what happened last night when Leah and I were at my brother's. He's hoping to find out something we did or said that might have precipitated her disappearance.

'She didn't eat much at Dov's,' I say, laboriously giving all the boring details, 'so I made her another supper when we got home. She didn't eat that, either.'

Alex dismisses this with a wave of his hand. We both know that her not eating supper is hardly breaking news. He puts the kettle on and stands in front of it as it boils, almost immediately, steam curling around him, because we have not long had tea.

'Steam causes burns, same as boiling water,' I say.

'Worse, in fact,' he says, not moving. 'So what did she do after not eating supper?'

'Made some toast and Marmite.'

'She was all right at your brother's, wasn't she?'

'Of course,' I say. Unsaid words bubble up into my mouth, bang against my teeth. I swallow them down.

Alex didn't come with us to Dov's last night. For various historical reasons, he isn't very involved with my family. He and Dov actually get on really well. But he knew my mum and some of my other siblings would be there who, let's just say, are less simpatico with him.

His phone pings and we both rush for it. But it's only another of Leah's mates who we group-texted this morning, saying she hasn't seen Leah since the end of school yesterday.

'So did anything happen when you got home?' Alex Poirot persists. 'After I went to bed? She was completely normal with me. She was watching YouTube.'

'Nothing,' I lie. I'm too embarrassed to tell him about my conversation with Leah. If she does turn out to have done something crazy, I don't want Alex to blame me for it for the rest of our lives.

His phone rings and he snatches it up. But it turns out to be the mother of another of Leah's friends, who we also group-texted this morning, to say she hasn't seen Leah. Is there anything she can do to help? 'Not really,' Alex says politely, then hangs up, and adds, 'Other than get off the fucking phone.'

Alex never gets in a state. He is the world's most patient father of a teenager. I've only ever once seen him lose his temper.

*

When we got back from Dov's last night, Leah disappeared upstairs. I now realise she'd gone to look for evidence. She's smart as a tack. I'd be proud, under other circumstances, and so would Alex in his new *An Inspector Calls* mode, except I obviously can't tell him.

So it was Friday night, it was late, and Alex, who is a lark to my owl, went to bed. I was emptying the dishwasher when Leah came back down and sprawled on the kitchen sofa, legs improbably long and spindly, like a baby giraffe in tiny denim shorts. She plugged herself into the iPad and I continued with my usual dishwasher reverie. I was vaguely aware that she was sending me dirty looks, but I'm used to that; in her mind, I'm always doing something wrong. I was miles away, I don't know what I was thinking about, perhaps why the dry cycle on the dishwasher never dries the glasses properly, when I realised she'd taken off her headphones and was saying something rather crossly.

'What was that, sorry?' I said.

She muttered a swear word under her breath. She has the mouth of a sailor on shore leave. 'I *said*, what is this, exactly?'

'What is what?'

She held something up. A photo. My heart jumped. I knew what it was straight away, because I'd looked at it earlier this week. I didn't put it back in its safe place; in a hurry, I shoved it into my bottom drawer, making me the biggest idiot in the history of idiots.

'Have you been going through my stuff, Leah?'

She shrugged. She guessed, correctly, that in the hierarchy of bad things, the photo ranked higher than rummaging through my dresser drawers.

'Move up.' I pushed her legs along the sofa and sat next to her. She kept her body held rigidly away from me. I looked at the picture in her hand. A wedding photo. Not the one of me and Alex that Leah used to love examining so much, me in the red dress and white furry jacket, but a different photo.

In this one, the bride is in a white dress, the groom in a suit. They are standing underneath a cherry tree. The bride is me. The groom is not Alex.

The sound of the key in the door is the greatest sound I have ever heard. Alex and I stare at each other, then rush into the hall. As I jump up I knock my tea over, hear the mug crash to the floor behind me. Leah stands just inside the front door, wearing her defiant face and no coat.

'Where have you been?' Alex says, more gently than I would have done.

'Out.'

'Come on, Leah,' I say impatiently, 'we've been going crazy here. You didn't answer your phone…'

'Wasn't allowed to have it on, was I?'

'Why not?'

'*She* knows.' Leah flips a thumb at me. 'I'm starving.' She pushes past us and goes into the kitchen. A second later we hear her wail, 'There's broken stuff and tea all over the floor. Gross.'

'What does she mean?' Alex whispers. 'What do you know?'

I look at him, not knowing where to start. A horrible idea about where Leah might have been is taking shape in my mind.

I say, 'I have absolutely no idea what she is talking about.'

Chapter Two

Summer 1999

'He's turned down even more people than you,' my mother said. Her smile had a slight edge to it. She opened a battered hardback notebook with a blue marbled cover – a book which contained all the possible lives I had been offered, and had rejected. Less poetically, it was where my mother kept details of the potential matches that had been suggested to us by friends and family. She turned to a page quite near the end; the book was nearly full.

'His name's Nathan,' she said, 'and his grandfather and yours were great friends.'

I nodded. My expectations were low. She pushed the book over to me, and I looked at the photo she'd stuck into it, of a pleasant-looking sandy-haired man with a neat beard. Then I glanced at her notes, which gave his age (twenty-eight), his goals in life, his wishes for children, his beliefs about marriage, his level of education, his financial status. I felt like I had read something similar on numerous occasions, probably because I had. The only interesting thing about him so far – that like me, he had turned down lots of introductions – wasn't in the notebook, of course; it would have been unofficial gossip passed on along the mothers' grapevine.

'Your grandfather and Nathan's grandfather were children together, back in the forties in Edgware,' my mother said, and launched into a detailed explanation of the connections between our two families: who knew who, when they knew them, where they lived. I drifted off, started doodling on her notebook. She finally noticed as I was about to colour in Nathan's beard in black biro, and irritably moved the book out of my reach.

'I'd have thought, given everything, that you would be more attentive, Aliza,' my mother said.

'I'm sorry, Mum.' I sat up straight and focused on her. 'I'm looking forward to meeting Nathan. He looks nice.'

I knew I was on borrowed time. While I didn't feel that my mother was particularly in a rush for me to marry, my father was a different story, and Mum always followed Dad's line. He told me regularly that I was too old to be picky; that at twenty-three I was running the risk of ending up a spinster. In the last three years I'd met and turned down six possible matches, an unacceptably large number, apparently. That was before you factored in all the ones I'd not agreed to have an initial meeting with. Only Ha-Shem (and my mother's notebook) knew how many there were of those.

I only had to flick through the pages of the notebook to recall the six I'd formally refused. She'd obviously written their real names and details, but in my head they were:

- Bad-Breath-and-Dandruff (I hoped someone kind would tell him, but it wasn't going to be me).
- 'My Wife Doesn't Need to Work.'
- The World's Shyest Man, who addressed his entire, brief conversation, to my feet.

- Mr Swagger: 'You're a knockout, I'm a knockout – our kids will be gorgeous.' In fairness, he was quite handsome.
- The Pioneer: A man who wanted us to live in Israel and had already paid a deposit for a house in Hebron.
- The Heels: A man who was slightly shorter than me. His opening sentence was, 'Are you wearing heels?' and his second was, 'When we get married, I don't want you to wear heels.'

Nathan came to visit us that afternoon. He and I sat and talked together in the living room, my mother sitting in the corner. It wouldn't do for us to be secluded. There were no surprises – he looked exactly like his photo – and no horrible discoveries of halitosis or obvious personality defects. He spoke quietly, and asked a few questions, but didn't volunteer much about himself. I wanted to ask him about the women he had turned down – how many? Why did he refuse them? Did he give them nicknames like 'Bad-breath-and-dandruff'? – but something about his gentle manner damped down my usual boldness. He didn't ask me about the ones I'd turned down. I looked into his pale-grey eyes but I couldn't read him.

He didn't seem the least bit interested in me, so I presumed I'd be the next 'no' on his list. Like the others, this one will come to nothing, I thought, and this time it won't be my fault. I didn't do anything to make myself particularly charming. I simply nodded, agreed with everything he said, kept my eyes cast down, and didn't give anything of myself away. Being certain Nathan was going to say no, I realised I could safely say yes, and my father wouldn't be able to blame me this time.

When we stood to say goodbye, I saw that we were exactly the same height. He didn't mention anything about heels. Up close, I noticed that his sandy hair, which was rather long, curled on to his collar in a cute way. He said goodbye politely to me and my mother, but he didn't look back as he left the room, and I didn't expect to hear from him again. Once he'd gone, my brother Dov stuck his head round the door and winked. He knew all about Bad Breath and Pioneer and the others, and waggled his hand at me, like a Roman emperor waiting to judge a gladiator – up or down? For the first time, I didn't put my hand down.

My mother was delighted when I said yes, that I was willing to get to know Nathan better, and my father gave me a very rare smile. I basked in the unusual feeling of having done the right thing by them, for once. I was pretty confident that it would go nowhere.

But Nathan said yes.

My stomach lurched when Mum told me this, but I managed to say, 'Great!' rather than, 'Oh no, what have I done?' Us both saying yes meant we were now courting, officially testing out if we felt right for each other. He came round a few days later to take me for a walk, and we smiled in surprise at each other. I guess that he, like me, had wondered if he would ever get to this stage. Walking together was nice. There were a few silences, but a lot of gentle conversation too, and he laughed a lot at things I said. He said I was funny. We started seeing each other every week, then moved to twice a week. We went to cafés, or for walks in the park, always with a relative nearby – in line with modesty laws, we could not be alone on dates. We discussed our families, our interests, our hopes for the future. I sensed that, in his quiet way, Nathan liked me and was ready to settle down. I supposed it was time for me to settle down too. Deborah kept saying I could do a lot worse than Nathan, which was true. Nathan was kind, and attentive, and our grandfathers had been great friends. There was no one better on the horizon, and as my mother said, I would surely learn to love him. His hair curled sweetly on his collar, he smelled of sandalwood soap, and I thought, yes, I can work with this.

Six weeks after the first meeting, we agreed to get engaged. This meant that we were going to get married. In the daytime this was fine. But at night, especially if I woke up in the small hours, I was scared. I asked myself what I had done, agonised over whether I should change my mind, despite the hurt to his feelings and the rage of my father, and worse, my mother's quiet disappointment. But in the morning the night fears seemed foolish. 'I'm engaged, finally,' I told myself, and that felt like I was doing the right thing.

My parents' generation didn't have engagement rings. To give a ring before the wedding would have meant, in their minds, that they were already married, but before all the proper formalities had taken place. Nathan wasn't modern enough to give me a secular kind of engagement ring, but he was planning to follow the lead of many of our contemporaries, and give me a diamond ring, in addition to the gold wedding ring, straight after the wedding ceremony.

'Modern kids,' my father said when he heard about this, 'always think their way is the right way.'

Nathan wanted me to know all about the ring. 'White gold, with a large diamond, and tiny chips of diamond down the sides.'

'And your cousin knows someone in the trade, don't tell me,' I said.

'No, actually.'

'I don't want you wasting your money on a ring, Nathan.'

'My brother-in-law knows someone, not my cousin.' He smiled. 'And I don't regard it as a waste of money.'

*

So, six weeks after we first met, we were engaged.

And four weeks later, I met Alex.

I never saw the ring. I hoped Nathan was able to get a refund.

Chapter Three

September 1999

I'd never understood the phrase 'skipping a beat' till I walked into the room and saw Alex. I honestly thought my heart had stopped, just for a moment. It seemed as if light was shimmering around him, giving a glittering quality to the whole room. Which was odd, considering that we were in a beige conference room at the Hackney Council building in Hillman Street.

I'm tall – five foot nine – but when Alex stood to greet me, I saw that he was several inches taller than me. Not smaller, not the same, but taller; when you're my height, that's quite unusual. His dark hair was a similar colour to mine, but his eyes were a deep mid-blue. His olive skin made me wonder if he was from a Turkish background, or Italian, perhaps. And I realised that I was an engaged woman, wondering things about another man.

The school where I taught was often approached with a request for someone to come and present accessible information about Orthodox Jewish life to groups of children, teachers, or youth workers. Or, as now, local councillors obliged to undergo training in equal opportunities. The head teacher often put me forward – apparently I was a 'good communicator'.

Well yes, usually. But the people in charge of these events didn't usually have such blue, blue eyes.

I could see myself through Alex's blue eyes from the very first moment, and I liked what both of us were seeing. Unlike with Nathan, whose unreadability meant I only knew he liked me because he'd asked to marry me, I knew straight away that Alex thought I was beautiful. He stared into my eyes and then stretched out his hand to shake mine, and though I didn't – couldn't – take it, I found to my amazement that I was thinking how much I *would* like to take it, kiss it, and press it against my heart. He frowned slightly as I failed to take his hand, and the frown produced, between those blue eyes, two faint vertical lines like quotation marks that I could scarcely drag my gaze away from.

To cover my confusion, I addressed the whole group.

'Hello, everyone. The first thing I should tell you about traditional Jews, as your trainer no doubt wishes to demonstrate, is that we have a rule about touching.'

Alex laughed, and sat down. The group turned their attention to me.

I carried on: 'This rule states that people of the opposite gender do not touch each other, including not shaking hands, unless they are brother and sister, or children with their parents and grandparents, or,' and I almost tripped over this last phrase, 'husband and wife.'

After this untypical start it was a relief to go through my talk, and it was lucky that it was a familiar spiel, as I was utterly distracted by those steady eyes on me. It wasn't that I was unused to being watched. There's no merit in false modesty, is there? I knew I was easy on the eye, that in my high-necked top and ankle-length skirt, my long black hair caught in a net at the base of my neck, I looked different from other London women. I'd always been rather proud of that difference. But this was a different kind of being watched, and I was supremely, deliciously conscious of it. I stumbled over my words a couple of times, and when I was listing the three most important roles of a Jewish woman, I caught Alex's eye and completely lost my train of thought, couldn't remember the last one until a few awkward seconds had ticked by.

I managed to finish the talk, and answered the questions as best I could, though I was aware that I'd somewhat lost my focus. Alex turned to thank me, and his smile was the most dazzling I'd ever seen. It lit up his entire face.

By unspoken agreement, we waited in the room till everyone had left, and it was only me and him. I found I couldn't quite reach the end of my breath.

'Miss Bloom. Er.' He coughed. 'Thank you, that was an excellent talk. It would be great to get you to come and speak again. Could we, um, meet soon, to discuss some dates? Tomorrow, perhaps?'

I had the sense of standing on the edge of a cliff, looking down. 'Yes, that would be fine.'

'There's a café near here, Artello's, in Preston Street. Do you know it?'

'I know the street. I can find it.'

'What time could you get there, from school?'

'Probably a little after five. Quarter past?'

'Perfect. I don't suppose you have a mobile phone number, do you? In case you need to change the arrangement?'

'No, we only have a normal telephone, at home.'

'Can I have that number?' Those blue eyes.

'I... don't know.'

'Just so we can arrange, er, other training sessions in future?'

I wrote down my number in his diary, my hand shaking so much that the 3 looked like a 5 and I had to write it out again. Agreeing to meet was one thing; I could easily not go. Giving my phone number was something different. It was making a decision. Stepping off the cliff. Asking to be rescued.

Chapter Four

September 1999

I was unable to eat that evening, or sit still. Mum kept asking if I was all right, and Becca told me I looked 'jittery'. When the phone rang I nearly had a heart attack. I raced to it, but as usual my father got there first. He glared at me as I arrived breathlessly at his side, seconds after he'd picked up the receiver.

'Yes?' he barked into the phone.

There was a pause, then, looking furious, he thrust the receiver at me. 'It's for you.'

I took it from him, scarcely knowing whether I felt more horror or excitement. He didn't move away, so all I could do was turn my back on him and whisper into the phone, 'Hello?'

'Hi, Aliza, how are you?'

I couldn't place the voice. I was sure I remembered Alex's this morning as being deeper, and it was a couple of long, confused seconds before I realised who it was.

'Hi, Nathan.'

'Come on, Kap,' my mother hissed at my father, 'give them some privacy!'

My father reluctantly slunk out of the hall, muttering about young people who always know everything. Nathan talked about his day, and our wedding plans, and the latest news on the flat we would be living in after we married. He'd phoned a couple of times before, for a chat, so it wasn't completely out of the blue, but it took several minutes for my heart to stop racing. He was really sweet, which made me feel bad. I decided that I wouldn't go and meet Alex the next day after all. What had I been thinking? I gave Nathan my full attention, and felt resolved in my mind. I was sure that I had just gone momentarily mad this morning.

But once again, I woke with a start in the night, sweat on my forehead and a dread gripping my stomach like a clenched fist. I could hear Becca and Gila's quiet breathing, sleeping their blameless sleeps, dreaming their innocent dreams. *I've agreed to marry Nathan. Oh god. What have I done?*

In the morning, heavy from lack of sleep and in need of distraction, I told Mum I'd make Zaida's morning tea. I knocked lightly on the door to the annex and went in. Seeing Zaida sitting in his chair always lifted my spirits. This morning it also helped settle my racing heart.

'Aliza! My angel.' His delight at seeing me never wavered. Even though we'd seen each other last night at dinner, as always, he reacted as if we'd been apart for months. I hugged him, and then started to make the tea. He'd boiled the kettle in readiness but he was forbidden by my mother to lift it; he wasn't so strong any more and last time he'd tried, he'd splashed boiling water on his hand.

'I've got to go to work in a minute, Zaida,' I said.

'Ah yes, my granddaughter, the teacher,' he said, with as much pride as if I was chief rabbi or prime minister. 'Have a quick cuppa with me?'

I filled the teapot and sat down opposite him. He was, as usual, smartly dressed in a suit, but his tie had a dark stain on it. 'He isn't getting any younger,' my mother had taken to saying, with a sigh, at regular intervals.

'How's your lovely young man?' he asked me.

'Nathan? He's fine, I think. We're going to go for a walk in Hampstead on Sunday.'

'Ah, lucky young people, at the start of their lives.'

'Zaida?' I handed him a mug of tea, and poured myself one I didn't really want. 'Do you think Nathan is a good match for me?'

'I was great friends with his grandfather, you know, may he rest in peace.'

'I know you were. But do you think...?'

'Aliza, my choochie-face.' He reached out and took my hand. 'You're so smart, so sensible. So bright! I know you'll always make the right decision.'

I looked down at his old, dear hand, warm on mine, and wondered if I would be able to live up to his rose-tinted vision of me.

That afternoon, I finished up at school, got everything ready for the next morning, and walked to Preston Street. The café was easy to find, and I was early. I stood outside for ten minutes, wondering what I was doing, and then trying not to think about what I was doing. When Alex arrived he looked simultaneously as familiar as if I had known him my whole life, and like a complete stranger. I scarcely greeted him, just hurried him to the back of the café in case someone I knew might come in. This was extremely unlikely, but I nonetheless spent several moments looking round anxiously whenever the café door opened.

'Are you all right, Miss Bloom?'

'Aliza. Yes. I'm. I don't want. I don't know.'

The waitress came over and Alex asked what I'd like. I knew there wouldn't be anything kosher here so I said water. He ordered a coffee, and when the waitress had gone, he said, 'Shall we talk about some training sessions you could speak at?'

His face was all lines – those quotation marks between his eyes, lines radiating out from an anxious smile. I could see he was worried that he had misread things between us. The urgency of our situation hit me with a thud; this was no time for coyness.

'Mr Symons, do you really want to talk about training?'

His smile grew wider. 'No.'

'Nor do I.'

There was a pause. And he said, 'That makes me very happy.'

I stopped monitoring the door, and I stopped thinking about anyone else. I let myself become lost in the heat of Alex's gaze. It was fate that we had met. We both felt it.

We met again the following afternoon, same place, same time. In between gazing at each other, he told me a little about his life: his brother, his mum, his dad who'd died, his work as a trainer in equal opportunities and diversity for the local council, his flat in Brixton, his single status. He made particularly sure I knew about his single status.

The third time we met, the afternoon after that, I told him about *my* life: work, synagogue, duties at home, and helping my mother take care of Zaida.

'Is it true what you said in the talk,' Alex asked, 'about not having a telly?'

'Yes. I've never seen television. Telly.' I repeated the word in my head. *Telly.*

He listed some of the other things I'd mentioned. 'No internet, no cinema, no sex before marriage?'

I blushed, and nodded.

'Talking of marriage, you spoke about your own. It sounded like it was happening quite soon.' This was the first time either of us had mentioned it.

'Yes, I'm getting married in December.' As I said it, it felt unconnected to me, as if I was talking about someone else. 'He's the son of a family friend.'

'Did you have any say in that?'

'Of course I did!' I felt protective, all at once, of my life and my family. 'It's an arranged marriage, not a forced one. I didn't have to say yes. I already turned down several others.'

'You look like a magnificent exotic queen of the Stamford Hill desert when you get cross,' Alex said.

'Don't.'

He was silent for a while. I studied his long fingers which were curled round his coffee mug, the lines on the knuckles, the neat square-cut nails. They were headily unfamiliar hands. Then he said, 'Do you ever long for a normal life?'

'I have a normal life.'

'To me, it sounds unbelievably strict. I can see why a child would fall in line, but not someone of twenty-three.'

'I was pretty challenging of the rules when I was a child. Anyway, there are many families much stricter than ours.'

'Really?' Alex poured me some more water. 'On a scale of one to ten, where ten is the strictest possible, what score would you give your family?'

I thought about it. 'We'd be a seven, I guess.'

'My god, what would a ten be like?'

'It's a normal life,' I said, firmly. 'I work. I'm a teacher, I love that. I hang out with my brothers and sisters. I go for coffee with my best friend Deborah.'

'Will you work after you marry?'

'Yes, of course. That's one of the reasons I agreed to it. If I don't marry before I'm twenty-five, my father will take away some of my freedoms. Things like being able to go out to work.'

'That's awful, Eliza.'

'I don't see it like that.' I laughed. 'How else will he get me to hurry up?'

I didn't tell him he'd said my name slightly wrong, as if it was spelled with an 'E' rather than an 'A'. He must have heard it as the secular version when I'd first told him my name. It was pretty close though, and I rather liked the thought of being slightly different, slightly wrong, in Alex's company. It was a pseudonym. I was a spy, with a secret undercover life.

When we met again the next afternoon, I told Alex something I had never told anyone, not even Deb. I told him about the things I was afraid I'd miss out on, if I stayed in my world. Films, music, food – they were only the surface things. 'It's not the specifics,' I tried to explain, 'so much as a general feeling of wanting to see what it's like outside.'

'Outside of your bubble?'

'Exactly! I'm in a tiny bubble and…'

'You'd like to pop it?'

'Yes…'

'Would you like me to help you?'

I didn't say anything.

'Just give me the word,' Alex said. 'I'll be there with a big pin.'

That night, the phone rang, and when Dad thrust it at me with a grumpy, 'It's for you,' I naturally assumed it was Nathan.

'Hi,' I said, breezily.

'Eliza,' Alex said, 'can you talk?'

My heart started pounding so hard I could scarcely think. *Eliza with an E.* I managed to whisper, 'Not really.'

My dad was, as usual, loitering nearby, and shot me a suspicious glance.

Alex said, 'Are you able to say "yes" or "no"?'

'Yes.'

'OK. Listen, I wanted to let you know that I can't make it tomorrow to the café.'

'All right.' I had not even known him a week, so why did I feel so heavy at the thought of not seeing him?

'It's not all right, I'm really sorry. My mum's asked me to take her to a doctor's appointment. I wouldn't miss it for anything, otherwise.'

I wanted to ask if we would meet as usual the following afternoon, but Dad still hung around in the hall. Where was Mum, to tell him to give me some space?

'Eliza? You still there?'

'Yes.'

'I will miss you tomorrow.'

'Yes.'

'I'll be thinking about you. I can't wait to see you. Day after tomorrow, as usual?'

Thank Ha-Shem. 'Yes!'

Dov came down the stairs and took in the scene: me huddled round the phone, my hand cupped secretively round the receiver; Dad a couple of feet away, pretending to go through a pile of post.

I sent Dov a slightly desperate eyebrow semaphore.

'Dad, can you help me with something?' Dov said, picking up my cue immediately.

'What is it?'

'I can't understand this section in the reading we were given today…'

'Let me have a look.'

Clever, lovely Dov. Dad could never resist a chance to show off his Talmudic knowledge. He put his arm round Dov's shoulders and they went into the living room.

'Eliza?'

'I'm here.' I whispered, 'I'll miss you too. Hope your mum's OK.'

'It's only a check-up. Since Dad died, me and my brother take turns to do these sorts of things with her. Anyway, I will be thinking about you the whole time.'

'Will you?'

'I really like you, Eliza.'

I felt a warmth creep over my whole body. 'You do?'

Down the line, he laughed. 'A lot.'

'I like you too,' I said.

Jonny appeared in the hall, and hearing this, whistled at me. He assumed, of course, that I was talking to Nathan.

'I've got to go,' I said, and hung up, quickly, before anyone could grab the phone from me.

The next time we met, Alex gave me a small mobile phone, and showed me how to call and message him on it. This released us from the tyranny of my phone at home, and gave us a great deal of freedom to fine-tune arrangements. Even better, it meant that we could speak regularly outside of the café meetings. I began to rely on him sending me a funny little message every night before bed, and I loved sending him a morning message when I woke up. I hid the phone in my wardrobe, wrapped inside a jumper, and always made sure it was turned off, so Becca and Gila didn't hear it and go looking for it.

I met Alex almost every day for three weeks. Same café, same table. I always arrived at five fifteen, and left an hour later with my head spinning, full of ideas we'd discussed, things I'd learned, new thoughts I'd had. And yes, all right, new desires I'd felt. It was a wonder no one at home noticed how distracted I was. I lied to them every day about why I was late home, juggling excuses of lesson planning, or visiting Deborah. The lying was there right from the start.

I had to tell Deb finally, because Alex suggested we go to the cinema and as soon as he had said it, I couldn't stop thinking about it. I wanted to go to the cinema with Alex more than I had wanted anything in my life. The thought of it made me shiver. I visited Deb on the Sunday, when I knew Michael would be out, and told her the truth. Of course, she was shocked, but I assured her I was committed to Nathan, and that I was trying to get the other man out of my system. Because she knew me so well – she still teased me sometimes about the rebellious child I'd been – she agreed to cover for me.

I met Alex outside the cinema – a big one near Brent Cross, quite far from my house. He was already waiting when I rushed up, late, after getting lost. There were spangles of rain in his hair, like diamonds.

'What will we see?' I asked. I felt sick with excitement.

'You choose,' he said, and pointed to a display of posters advertising the films. 'There are three starting soon. There's *Eyes Wide Shut*, but I think that might be a bit rude. Or,' and he coughed, embarrassed, 'there's *Runaway Bride*.'

I looked at the poster for that film. A girl wearing a white wedding type of dress, her legs bare, was tying the laces of her training shoes. A man smiled smugly in the background.

'Maybe not,' Alex said, catching sight of my expression. 'I think it had better be *The Sixth Sense*. I've heard it has a twist, let's see if we can guess it.'

Seeing that film was one of the most amazing things that had ever happened to me. Walking in together unchaperoned, like everyone else; red soft seats; a huge screen in front of us; the overwhelming volume of the sound which startled me for the first half hour when anyone spoke; the crystal-clear images; the strangeness of the ghost story; and above all, the man sitting next to me in the dark, mere inches away, the sleeve of his jacket so close to my hand that I would barely have had to move to touch it.

When we came outside it seemed extraordinary that the world was still there, the same as it had been before. I turned to Alex and said, 'That was so beautiful.'

'Not as beautiful as you. You're radiant, Eliza.' He leaned forward and his lips gently pressed against mine. It was the first time we had ever touched.

For one magical moment, I kissed him back, as if I was in a dream.

It lasted no more than a second, but it changed everything.

Alex tried to take my hand, but I pulled away, and put myself, my hands and my lips out of reach.

'I want to offer you a different way of life,' he said.

'I can't,' I said, and started crying. I had never felt more confused or overwhelmed, not ever.

'Eliza, I'm ready,' he said. 'Are you?'

'They'd never forgive me,' I said, and I left him, walking away fast. I heard him calling my name and I was so anxious he might come after me that I started running and didn't stop until I was on the tube. I banged and banged on Deb's door and when she finally opened it, looking confused and in her nightgown, I threw myself in her arms. I told her that it – whatever it was – was over.

'Really over?' she said.

'The truth is, I love him, Deb. I love him so much, but I know I can't be with him. So it's over.'

She hugged me tight. 'It's the right thing, Crazy Kid. I know it's hard, but you're doing the right thing.'

I stopped going to the café, and I permanently turned off the phone Alex had given me. I let myself get involved in arrangements for my wedding to Nathan. Gila braided my hair in a new style. Deborah helped me decide on a dress. Uri, my oldest brother, was nicer to me than he'd been for years; like my father, he'd been angered by my failure to agree to a match, but now, he told me how much I'd love being married, and even told me a slightly risqué joke about a wedding night.

Life went on. I made Zaida his tea every morning. I laughed with Dov and Jonny over the funny things the children in my class said. Becca and I helped our mother with the housework like model daughters.

I went round in a daze, but no one seemed to notice.

And that was that.

Something like two months went by, and it was the day before the wedding. I was going through my clothes, planning what to take with me to the marital home, and what to leave for Becca. Then I came across the phone. It wasn't that I'd forgotten I had it, more that I had deliberately put it out of my mind, put it into the closed box marked 'Alex.' Just seeing it made me feel something. Not numb. I knew I shouldn't turn it on, but nothing could have stopped me. There were messages. Lots of messages. I sat on the floor, my back against the door so that no one could come in, and I read them all, from the first to the last, which had been sent earlier that day.

'Eliza, I wish you the very best with your wedding. I know it's tomorrow. I'll be thinking of you all day. In the unlikely event that you read this, please know that I love you, and I always will. All I hope for you is that you are happy and fulfilled. A.'

I snapped out of my daze, and rang his number.

'Eliza?'

'My name's Aliza actually, with an A,' I said, 'and I love you.'

Chapter Five

March 2016

Leah is even more grumpy than usual, presumably a result of her early start this morning. I make her a sandwich and encourage her to go back to bed. Alex mops up the tea I spilled on the floor, while I make some more. Teamwork. I put his mug in front of him, and we sit at the kitchen table, in our usual places.

'Well, go on then,' he says, smiling.

'Go on, what?'

'She said you would know what she'd been doing.' The detective inspector is back.

'Oh, *that*.' I stir the teaspoon round in my tea, though I don't need to; I gave up sugar several years ago. 'I hope she gets some sleep, otherwise she's going to be hell to live with all day.'

'Gotta say, Liza, you are acting a bit suspiciously.' His eyes twinkle at me over the top of his mug, seconds before his reading glasses steam up from bottom to top. He takes them off.

'Look, I don't know anything for sure,' I say. 'It's only a guess.'

'I'm imagining terrible things involving drugs and underage sex, so I would really like you to share your guess.'

I take a deep breath. 'I think maybe she's been to shul. Synagogue.'

'I know what shul means. Why do you think she's been there?' He stops smiling. 'What *did* actually happen at Dov's last night?'

'Nothing! Hardly anything.'

He waits, and I quickly work out a truncated version to tell him. 'This is no big deal, OK? Leah was somewhere in the house with the cousins, and Dov, Mum and I were chatting.'

'You mean your mum was chatting, and you and Dov were waiting politely to get a word in.'

'Yes, pretty much. Anyway, Mum mentioned that she'd, uh, seen Nathan's mother recently.'

Alex raises his eyebrows – Nathan is not a name we lightly bandy about – and I hurry on: 'He's still living in Gateshead. And the big news is that he got married last year.'

'Wow, finally. His mum must be praying her thanks every minute of the day.'

'I expect so.' I cough. 'So, well, Mum was doing that thing she does sometimes…'

'Speculating about how much better your life would have been had you stayed with Nathan?'

'No!'

'Yes, come on.'

Well, not how much better, just how different.'

'And then you wonder why I don't like hanging out with your family.' Alex gets up. 'Going to make us some lunch.'

'It's not all my family. It's only Mum. And Uri. And maybe Becca.'

Alex says nothing, has his back to me, getting food out of the fridge.

'It's not like your family were always massively wonderful,' I say. 'Remember when Vicky, for instance—'

He turns abruptly and snaps, 'Really *not* the time, Eliza. Do you think that before Leah comes down, you could get to the point?'

'OK. Well, Mum started reminiscing about the past, you know.'

'The past is generally what people reminisce about.'

Alex isn't normally this sarky. 'Yes, she was going on about our, uh, lost weekend, and what might have happened if I hadn't been pregnant. Then Dov started hissing, "sssh, sssh," at Mum, and we all realised that Leah was standing at the door. It might be a good idea to use the eggs. I bought too many.'

Alex holds up an egg box with a 'duh' expression on his face. 'How much did she hear?'

'I didn't think she'd heard anything. But back home, she started asking me about it.'

I don't tell Alex that she found the fake wedding photo. He doesn't know I still have it. I was supposed to get rid of it fifteen years ago. I don't know why I didn't. *I don't!* Psychoanalyse it all you like. Feel free.

'How much did you tell her? Do you want cheese in yours?'

'Yes please. I didn't say much. I only said, uh, that after we got married,' and I drop my voice in the hope that no one, including me, can hear, 'I left you for a short while and went back to my family. And back to Nathan.'

'Not *back* to him,' Alex says, in a louder voice than normal, as if to compensate for my quietness. 'You'd never actually been with him. And you weren't with him that second time, either. Where's the virgin olive oil?'

'We've run out. There's the non-virgin stuff in the cupboard.'

'Butter's better than that shit.' He heats the pan, drops in a pat of butter. 'You'd never even kissed him. It wasn't a real…'

'You sure you want to do this?' I stand up. 'Now, after all these years?'

'You're the one who blew it up again,' he says. 'You're the one who told Leah about it. I don't know why I'm splitting hairs anyway: I'm sure you kissed him. I expect you did a lot more than kiss him, after you left me.'

'For god's sake, Alex!'

Why can't Leah walk in now, damn her? This would be the perfect moment for her to interrupt.

'I'm sorry.' Alex cracks eggs noisily into a bowl. 'Two or three eggs?'

'Two please. Al, don't be mad with me.' I walk over to him, take the bowl out of his hands, and nuzzle into his neck. 'You know you're the only man I've ever loved.'

He puts his arms round me and we stand close together. Into my hair, he whispers, 'What's going on, Liza?'

'Nothing,' I say. 'Nothing is going on.'

An unpleasant smell reaches our noses and we break apart.

'Damn it, the butter's burnt!'

Leah doesn't reappear until we're sitting down to lunch. Alex greets her with a quip about her impeccable timing. She really has been asleep; she has crease marks on her face and hasn't touched the sandwich. I make her a plain omelette, the only sort she'll eat, which she grumpily picks at.

'So,' Alex says brightly, 'your mother and I have a bet on. She says you've been to synagogue. I say you've been hanging round the shopping centre. Who's right?'

Leah shrugs. 'Went with Macy to her shul.'

Alex grins at me. 'Mum wins!'

'What was it like?' I ask.

'Dunno.'

'That's it?'

'The rabbi was weird.'

'How was he weird?'

'She, Mum. Rabbis can be women.'

'Not where your mother comes from, they can't,' Alex says. 'You've only gone and found yourself on The Other Side, Leah baby.'

She looks at him, baffled. 'What?'

'Was it the progressive synagogue in Barkingside you went to, by any chance?' he says, openly enjoying this now. I don't for the moment question how he knows where the local shul is, nor how he knows it's a progressive shul.

Leah says, 'Yeah, I guess.'

'Women rabbis, gay rabbis, I bet they let men and women sit together, right?'

Leah shrugs. 'So what?'

'Well, sweetie,' Alex says, forking a tomato and smirking, there's no other word for it, smirking at me. 'Your mum's lot think *that* lot are the enemy, you know.'

'We do not think that.' I don't like the way this is going. 'This omelette's delicious, Alex.' I don't want her to…

'I'm going to ask Uncle Dov if I can go to his shul, anyway.'

Too late. *You bloody idiot, Alex.*

'Listen, sweetheart,' I say, knowing it's hopeless, that whatever I say is going to entrench her more deeply, but unable to not say something. After all, this is my battle, not Alex's. 'There are lots of ways we can explore your heritage, if this is something you want to do. You don't have to do the whole…'

'I want to,' she says. 'I've always wanted to have a religion and you've never let me.'

'Well, that's not true, I never knew you wanted…'

'Everyone else has one. Macy goes to shul, and Omega goes to this church where they sing, like, gospel songs, and Ethan is a Quaker. I could have easily been properly Jewish. You've always acted like I'm not any religion, but if you'd have stayed married to Nathan, you'd have had to bring me up Jewish.'

'Wait, what?' Alex says. He puts his cutlery down. '*Stayed* married?'

'I saw their wedding photo,' Leah says, pointing at me. 'I know everything.'

'No, no, you don't,' I start to say, 'you don't actually know anything,' but Alex is staring at me.

'What the bloody hell, Eliza? How could she have seen a wedding photo? You never married Nathan!' Then it dawns on him. 'Oh, no. No, no, no. Please, don't tell me you still have it.'

There is a silence.

'AWK-ward,' Leah sings, and then the doorbell rings. 'Thank the fuck,' she says, and runs out to answer it.

'You chucked that photo out,' Alex says. He pushes his plate away. 'You told me. Years ago.'

'I'm really sorry. I forgot I had it.'

'You kept it, like an unexploded hand grenade, so it could go off all these years later.'

'Look, Alex. You're being melodramatic. Nothing's gone off. The worst thing we could do now is try and make religion taboo. It will only make her want to do it all the more. She's at that rebellious age.'

'Well, I guess you should know. You were the *sine qua non* of rebellious daughters,' Alex says. I can't tell if he's being nice, or not.

Leah comes back in, a boy hovering nervously behind her. I recognise him vaguely as one of the kids in her posse at school. We're not allowed to call it her posse, of course, but we do amongst ourselves, when she's not listening.

'Mum, Ethan wants to know if I can go into town with him,' Leah says. She has her back to the boy, so he can't see her making an 'I don't want to, get me out of this please' face at me.

'Oh, honey,' I say, picking up my cue, 'I'm so sorry but we have to visit your grandma this afternoon.'

Leah frowns at me – clearly I've chosen the wrong excuse – and Ethan says, 'But you saw her yesterday.'

Leah turns to face him and says, 'Yeah well, she's ill.'

'Oh, I'm sorry. Well…' he stops, not knowing how to extricate himself.

'Maybe another day soon?' I say, and gently steer him out into the hall. Poor boy, with his sagging shoulders, weighed down with unrequited love. I feel sorry for him, and also I see a solution in the puppy-dog eyes that Leah is callously ignoring. As I open the door for him, I whisper, 'Leah's not doing anything tomorrow afternoon, if you want to call by then?'

'OK, thanks, yeah, great,' he mumbles.

I close the door, and take my time going back into the kitchen. My husband and daughter look at me with different kinds of accusations on their faces.

'Lame one, Mum,' Leah says, 'the Grandma defence.'

'That's the last time I help get rid of your suitors,' I say, knowing how wildly annoyed this will make her.

'Oh shut up, he isn't, OK? He's only a mate, not even that, he's boring.'

'I think he's cute,' I say.

Leah gets her phone out. 'I'm going to ring Uncle Dov.'

'He won't answer the phone, Leah, it's Shabbos.'

'I'll leave a message,' she says, and too late, Alex and I realise that she is doing it in front of us on purpose. 'Hi, it's Leah. Just wanted to see if I could come to your shul with you, please. Thanks! Bye!'

She throws us what can only be described as a defiant look, twirls on her heel and stomps upstairs.

'Terrific,' Alex says.

'I was hoping she might go out somewhere with Ethan, get a bit of a different perspective,' I say.

'Well, you killed that one straight away,' Alex says, ignoring the fact that I was doing what she clearly wanted. 'Think I'll go to the gym.'

'I don't know why you're cross with me. I haven't done anything wrong,' I say. 'I know I shouldn't have kept the photo…'

'…and you certainly shouldn't have left it where Leah could find it.'

'No, but it isn't a capital offence, you know?'

'She's at the perfect age to have an identity crisis, and you know what she's like.' He means that she's your classic only-child drama queen. 'She'll be making it all much bigger in her head than it is.'

'I know,' I say. 'I'm really sorry. Look, this won't last. She'll go to shul with Dov, she'll be bored, she'll move on to the next thing. I invited Ethan back round tomorrow.'

'OK.' He stands up, and goes to the door.

I follow him, put my hand on his arm. 'Don't freeze me out, Al.'

'I'm not. I just want to go to the gym.' He gives me a perfunctory hug, and goes out. I start clearing the lunch things away. We need a little space from each other, that's all. I'm sure it will be fine.

Chapter Six

December 1999

I arranged to meet Alex at Seven Sisters station at eleven, a few hours before the wedding. I planned to leave a note in my room and quietly slip out. I deliberately didn't allow myself to think about how everyone would feel. I just knew that I needed to be with Alex, and everything else was going to have to be a very distant second. But I couldn't get a minute to myself to even pack, let alone get out of the house. Either my mum was in my room, or Nathan's mum, or it was one of my sisters fussing around me. Every time I sent one of them away to get me something, another one came in. It was as if they somehow sensed that if they left me alone for a minute, I would change my mind.

It was almost midday before there was a gap between visitors. I sneaked the phone out of my wardrobe and locked myself in the bathroom. I sat on the edge of the bath and rang Alex's number. I could see that he had rung a number of times, and left several messages. He picked up straight away.

'Oh thank god,' he said. 'I thought you'd died.'

I laughed, all the pent-up tension from the morning coming out in one blast.

My mother knocked on the door. 'Aliza, are you all right?'

'Yes, Mum,' I called out. 'Just, er, laughing.'

I could hear her telling someone that getting married turned even the most sensible girl into a meshuggener. Someone, I don't know who, said that I had a head start there. I couldn't hear what Mum said in reply, and I wasn't sure if they'd gone or were hovering outside the door.

'Do you still want to?' I whispered.

'Of course,' he said. 'Do *you* still want to?'

'Yes, but no one's left me alone for a minute. I haven't been able to pack or anything.'

'Shall I come and get you?'

'No!'

'I think I should. In case of any trouble.' There was a pause. 'I can be there quickly, I'm actually already at the station.'

'Well, OK, but hang back then. Don't talk to anyone.' For the first time, I told him where I lived.

I came hesitantly out of the bathroom, but there was no one there. I could hear everyone talking and bustling about downstairs. I ran into my room, which, thank Ha-Shem, was empty, and took a few minutes to throw some essential things into a bag. I left a note for Becca and Gila, took one last look round, then slipped downstairs. I glanced at the annex door, behind which I knew Zaida would be sitting, waiting with great anticipation for my wedding. He wouldn't be able to come out until Uri and Joel went to get him, he was too frail now to walk far without support. He wouldn't have to see whatever was going to come next. I took a breath, grabbed my coat and stepped out of the front door.

All the men were standing in the front garden, smoking and talking. I could see Alex, about fifty yards down the road, sitting at a bus shelter, pretending to be a passer-by. My heart swelled at the sight of him. *He's really here! This is really going to happen.*

He raised his arm but stayed where he was. Showing me he was there, but waiting for me to give the word. I think that might have been the moment when I knew for definite just how much I loved him.

My brothers and their friends swarmed round me, teasing, asking questions. 'What are you doing out here in your coat?' 'What's in the bag?' 'Where are you going?' 'Have you forgotten you've got an important appointment today?' 'Are you off to get Nathan a wedding ring?'

Nathan was there, of course, but he held back a little, stood quietly at the edge of the group. I looked at him, and he smiled shyly at me. The poor man. What I was about to do to him was terrible, and he had done nothing at all to deserve it. I had one thought in my head, which was to act quickly, a quick sharp pain being better than a long, lingering one. I reached out my hand towards him, gestured for him to move closer. My brothers started whooping and catcalling, egging him on to kiss me.

I said, 'Nathan, I am so sorry,' and those few simple words were like a bomb going off. The hubbub ceased instantly, leaving in its place a shattering silence. The men all stepped away from me, as if I was contaminated, and the children on the pavement stopped playing.

In the centre of the stillness, I looked across the road at Alex, and every head turned to where I was looking. Alex stood up.

My mother came out from the house. I don't know if someone had run to get her, or if her instincts had alerted her to the change in atmosphere. She put her arms round me, a dishtowel clutched in her hand. I couldn't tell if it was an embrace, or a restraint.

Then, as Alex said later, it all kicked off. Everyone who'd been inside the house came pouring out to see what was going on, my brothers were shouting, women were berating me, my aunt started beating my shoulder as though to knock sense into me. My father was yelling, though that wasn't news; when did he not yell? My mother clung tight to my arm – hours later, the finger-marks were still there – and she made a terrible keening noise like 'ay-ay-ay-ay-ay' that I would, in the future, impersonate as comedy shorthand for 'I left my whole family for you'. But it wasn't funny yet.

Uri strode past me and walked purposefully across the street towards Alex. I broke away from my mother, pushed through the press of people, and ran after Uri. He and I reached Alex at the same time. Someone back at the house called Uri's name, but he held up a hand without turning round: leave this to me.

I looked at Alex, and he looked steadily back at me.

I'm ready.

'Do you know this man?' Uri asked me.

'Yes. This is Alexander Symons.' All at once, I felt completely calm. 'I'm going to marry him.'

Alex blinked abruptly, and I realised that he and I had never discussed marriage. Well, we were going to have to discuss it very shortly, that was all.

Uri said, 'I'm sorry, that's not possible.' He turned to Alex. 'Please go now. This is a family matter.'

Alex said, 'I'll go when Aliza tells me to.' It was the first time he'd pronounced my name with an 'A'. His voice was a little breathless. I left Uri's side and stood next to Alex. Two against one.

Uri put his hands on my shoulders, the patronising older brother, though I was a good two inches taller than him. 'Aliza. We all go a bit crazy before our weddings. I did, remember? This pretty face has got you all confused.' He made a dismissive gesture at Alex. 'Come, now. Come back inside. We can sort this out.'

There was no time to answer, because Gila hurtled out of the house like a rocket, screaming my name, shoving her way through the crowd of people who were standing outside the house, still and watchful as an audience at a cinema.

'Aliza! No, no, Aliza, don't go!' She ran towards us. I knew she had found my note.

'Stop her,' called Uri, but the people outside the house seemed to have turned to stone.

I shook off Uri's hands, and the next moment Gila was pressed hard against me, her arms tight round my waist, her tears soaking into my coat. I looked over her head at Alex and Uri, and they stared back at me. I realised they were both waiting to see what I would do.

I stroked Gila's hair, and thought about what faced me, if I stayed. Then I thought about what faced me if I left. One was only too obvious, the other completely unknown. I looked at Alex's anxious face, and realised that the decision had already been made, months ago, the night he kissed me.

'I'll see you soon, darling,' I said to Gila. I kissed the top of her head, and hugged her fiercely. 'Look after the little ones for me, Uri.'

Then I turned and walked down the road, fast, away from my home and family. I didn't look back.

Alex ran to catch up with me. He took my bag, and slipped his hand in mine. 'Are you all right, Aliza?'

I didn't break stride. 'Yes.'

We turned right at the end of the street, and now we were out of sight of everyone. But I heard someone running after us. Before we'd had time to decide whether to run or wait, a young man – a boy – rounded the corner. I stepped towards him, my arms held out.

Alex whispered, 'Who's that?'

'Dov, my youngest brother,' I said. Dov didn't move nearer. He shook his head and pointed in the direction in which we were heading.

'You're going that way?' he said.

I nodded. There were two ways to the station from here – left or right. We had just started out on the right. He turned on his heel and ran back the way he'd come.

I'd never thought Dov would betray me, but these were exceptional circumstances, and Dad and Uri could be very persuasive.

Alex looked at me. 'What shall we do?'

'Run!' I said.

We didn't speak again until we reached the station, clattering down the concrete steps out of breath, our legs aching. In the concourse Alex stopped, and rested his hands on his knees.

'Aliza. Last chance to change your mind.'

'They'll be coming for us.'

People swirled round us, but he didn't move. He said, 'Your family back there. They love you.'

'Hurry, Alex!'

'Aliza, I need to know,' he said, and his voice was so quiet and serious that I stopped still to listen. 'Are you ready for this? Are you up for the journey?'

'On the tube, do you mean?'

He smiled. 'No. The journey you're about to take, into another life. With me.'

'Of course I am! Please, we have to go!'

'One more question. Are you sure I'll be enough for you? Just me, on my own?'

I knew he needed to hear it. 'Yes, Alex. You are all I've ever wanted.'

He kissed my hand – in public! – and we hurried down the escalator to the platform, and the tube arrived seconds later, which Alex said was the most magical thing of all. We stood pressed together near the door, and gazed at each other all the way, sometimes laughing, and sometimes serious. One time I thought about Gila's face, and I cried, and Alex took my hand, making me jump. My heart was racing, and I was frightened and excited in equal measure. I felt incredibly alive.

We got out at Brixton, and as we climbed up the steps to the exit, I said, 'Can we get married today?'

'Today?' Alex stood still on the stairs and people pushed impatiently past us. 'Wow, I don't think so. You need to phone ahead, show documents, aren't there banns or something?'

'I don't know.' I felt tired and deflated, like a child who has stayed up too late. 'What are we going to do?'

'Can't we just live together for a bit, see how it goes?'

'Are you serious?' I stared at him. Who was this man, and how little did he know of me? 'Alex, I've tipped up my whole life for you.'

'Christ, Aliza, I know.'

'I have to be married.' I felt desperate. What would convince him of how important this was? 'I can't be with you, I can't have,' I hesitated, '*relations* with you until we are married.'

That seemed to clarify things. 'I'll phone the register office as soon as we get home.'

Alex's home was a two-bedroom flat which backed on to Brockwell Park. He made up the bed in his room with clean sheets for me, saying he'd sleep in the spare room. He emptied several drawers, and suggested I put my things away, though I'd hardly brought anything. Then he went into the kitchen to ring the local register office. Meanwhile, I sat on the bed and rang home on my mobile phone, the one Alex had given me. I knew they wouldn't want to hear from me, but I also knew my mum would be horribly worried about how I was. Maybe she was; I never found out. The call lasted no more than ten seconds.

Alex came back in, singing, 'We're getting married in the morning.'

'Really? Tomorrow morning?'

'Well, no. Not long, though – in sixteen mornings. New Year's Day! An auspicious date, don't you think?' Alex sat on the bed and put his arm round me, deliberately slowly so as not to make me jump. 'Basically, they said you have to wait fifteen days after giving notice, which would mean the earliest we could marry if we give notice today is 31 December, but funnily enough they were completely booked out then.'

'Why?'

'Well, it's the millennial New Year's Eve, of course,' Alex said.

It was the first time I'd heard that word, millennial.

'Very popular day for weddings,' Alex went on, 'but brilliantly, they'd just had a cancellation for the day after, the first of January. Which I obviously accepted. It means we'd better go and give formal notice today, or tomorrow at the latest.'

'Who cancelled? Why did they?'

'I don't know. It doesn't matter, does it? It means we can get married then. They did us a favour!'

He was smiling broadly, but then he looked at me properly, and the smile dropped from his face as though a light had been turned off. 'What's wrong, Aliza?'

'I can't stay here,' I said.

'Really no? Do you not like the flat?'

'It's very nice.'

'Is there not enough drawer space? I can clear this one too, if you like?' Then he realised that I hadn't unpacked at all. 'Look, this is our house now, and your room, well, yours till we marry. You can change anything you like. Maybe you don't like the pictures. Or the wall colour.'

'They're fine. But I can't stay here with you. Us not married.'

'Oh. OK. Does it feel a bit much? Shall I see if you can stay with my brother Kim and his wife? Let me call him.' He was on the point of getting up, then stopped and said, 'Or, what am I thinking! Surely it would be better if we were engaged, wouldn't it? Let's get engaged!'

'Yes, that would be better, thank you.'

But then I put my head in my hands. Alex gently moved them away and smoothed the tears from my face. 'What is it, sweetheart? Do you wish you were still at your home?'

'I just phoned *home*.'

'What happened? What did you say?'

'I didn't get the chance to say anything. Soon as my father heard my voice, he yelled that I was dead to them.'

'Jesus.'

'He said never to go near any of them again, then he slammed the phone down.'

'I'm so sorry, Aliza.' He held me close.

'It's no more than I deserve.'

'No, that's horrible. No one deserves that.'

'Alex,' I whispered, 'what have we done?' But I'm not sure I said it out loud.

'Come on,' he said, pulling me to my feet. 'Let's go out. I'll show you round the neighbourhood.'

*

It was good to be outside, in the air.

'Thus begins the guided tour of your new home-town,' Alex said, stopping outside a café. 'The Roundhouse: this is my favourite place for coffee.'

'What do you like about it?'

'The coffee's good, it's not too expensive, and Marlene behind the counter calls me "handsome devil".'

I laughed. 'Do I need to worry about Marlene behind the counter?'

'Probably, though she's about sixty-five and her tabard is a bit of a tight fit. But man, that coffee of hers.' We walked on. 'Ah, now, here's a lovely bookshop. And next door, look, the Turkish grocers. You can get some great stuff here.'

I sidestepped the overflowing fruit crates outside, and trying to keep my voice light, said 'Where do we get our food from?'

'Wherever you like. There's a kosher store near the station, and we can get everything from there for as long as you want.'

I didn't want to show him how relieved I was, but I rewarded him for his kindness with another squeeze of the hand.

A little further along, we came to a large building, painted bright shades of orange and yellow.

'The best pub in town,' Alex said, 'the Prince Albert.'

'I've never been in a pub.'

'Shall we pop in now?'

'Ohh… no. Maybe later.'

'Are you OK? You look a bit overwhelmed.'

'I'm fine. It's just – all this.' I waved my hand at the whole world. There was so much of it, so many new things.

Alex pulled me past the pub.

'You know what we need?' he said. 'We need a ring.' He held up my left hand. 'Look at this. Naked, so it is.'

I giggled, embarrassed, at the word 'naked'. 'It doesn't matter,' I said. I felt better now we were out of his flat, and the tone of my father's voice had faded a little from my head.

'If we can't get married for another two weeks, we can at least get engaged.' A few yards on, he said, 'Oh look, we happen to be at a jewellers.'

We were outside an old-fashioned shop, with dusty velvet boxes in the window, and a Jewish name over the door. I guessed Alex had chosen it because he thought it would be familiar, comforting.

'I know it's not Hatton Garden,' he said, 'but there's some nice ones here.'

The mention of Hatton Garden, where my father worked, made me wince. Then I looked in the window and winced again, this time at the prices.

'You're a secret millionaire and you've waited till now to tell me, Alex!' I said. 'Seriously, do you have loads of money?'

'Well, not loads, no.'

'I don't want a ring like this. I'd like something with no weight, no pedigree, something I don't have to worry about.'

'Something cheap?'

'Something very cheap.'

'You become my perfect woman even more with every moment.'

I suggested a shop nearby called Accessorize, which had all sorts of pretty things in the window. There was a display of beautiful sparkly rings at the counter, and I knew as soon as I saw them that I wanted one. I chose a delicate filigree silver ring with a large crystal in the centre.

'It's a classic,' Alex said. He slipped it on to my finger and we stood quietly for a moment, both suddenly aware of the significance of the act.

'Ahh, so romantic,' sighed the shop-girl, who had what looked to me to be half the shop's stock pierced through her face.

'Fourteen quid,' Alex said. 'With this cheap crap, I pledge myself to thee.'

I smiled up at him. The shop assistant raised her metalled eyebrows, and the woman in the queue behind us coughed.

Alex handed over his card. 'D'you want a bag?' the assistant asked.

'I'll wear it now,' I said.

We walked on, and when Alex took my hand, I automatically started to pull away, then squeezed his hand instead. We smiled at each other. Hand in hand, we strolled through Brockwell Park.

'The final part of today's guided tour is our local green space,' Alex intoned.

'It's lovely.'

'So are you.'

'Alex?' I felt that I had to ask him, even though I dreaded the answer. 'When we were outside my house earlier, and I told Uri we were getting married, you looked shocked.'

'I'm so stupid. It hadn't occurred to me that you would want that. It's not what most women I've met want. But of course you do, and I'm completely on board.'

'I bet you wish I was more like other women.'

He laughed. 'Let me tell you about the first time I saw you.'

We sat on a bench underneath a large beech tree, and he put his arm round me.

'You walked in that room. It was the end of a long, tiring day. And then I saw you, and I felt wide awake.'

'You did?'

'I never saw a more beautiful woman. Stunningly, gorgeously, unlike any other woman. Tall and elegant, in your long dark skirt and high-necked jumper, all covered up, completely intriguing. Your hair, black as night, coiled at the base of your neck, your huge dark eyes with long spidery lashes like Bambi's, your lips red as Snow White's.'

I had no idea what he was talking about. 'I'll take your word for it.'

'And then you wouldn't shake hands! And you said that cool thing to the group about not touching men, so of course I wanted to touch you more than I'd ever wanted anything ever before.'

'You're making me blush.'

'And I knew you liked me too, because you waited at the end till everyone had gone.'

'Only to be polite.'

'Liar.'

'Maybe.'

'And I had no idea what I was going to say, but I knew you couldn't leave without me saying something.'

'My heart was beating so fast. I wanted you to say something, but I was also terrified you wouldn't. You said, "Miss Bloom. Errr…" Then you had a little coughing fit.'

'Oh my god. I'm never tongue-tied usually. I said, "It would be great to get you to come and speak again. Could we meet tomorrow?" And there was the world's longest pause, and I thought I'd totally misread the situation. Your face was completely blank.'

'I was trying to think what to do.'

'I thought you might storm out. Then you said, "Yes, that would be fine," and it was the best thing anyone had ever said to me. You were blushing your head off.'

I covered my face. 'I know!'

'You wrote your number down in my diary. I watched you, and do you know what I thought?'

'What?'

'I thought, "I could watch that face for the rest of my life."'

'Oh, Alex.'

'Well, Miss Bloom, we've gone and done it now.'

I was half-crying, half-laughing, when he kissed me on the lips, only our second ever kiss. This time I didn't push him away.

After a while, Alex got off the bench, and got down on one knee. 'Aliza Bloom, will you marry me, even though I have mud on my knee?'

'I will, on one condition.' I smiled, so he knew it wasn't anything alarming.

'Name it.'

'Funnily enough, it *is* about names. You know how when we first met, you called me "Eliza"?'

'Yes, sorry about that, I'd never heard the name Aliza before, and it sounds so like it.'

'Actually, I'd like you to call me Eliza from now on.'

'You would?'

I nodded. 'It's a different version of myself. The name of someone new. I like the thought of that, of being Eliza out here.'

'Wow, that's rather profound, Miss Eliza Bloom. It suits you.'

'It sounds exactly the same, the way you say it.'

'Eeee-liza. Better?'

'Better.'

'Well, Eliza, I have to get up, my knee's gone to sleep. So I now pronounce us engaged.' Alex stood up, and pulled me to my feet. 'Are you quite sure that's not enough to legitimise some hanky-panky tonight?'

'If that means what I think it means, then no,' I said firmly. 'Not until we're married.'

'Ah well,' Alex said, and linked my arm through his. 'I guess I've waited thirty years for you. I can wait another two weeks.'

17 December 1999

Dear Deborah

Well, as my fiancé says, 'Miss Bloom, we've gone and done it now.'

I'm really sorry.

I can't even begin to imagine the mess that greeted you when you turned up at our house to help me dress. I'm sorry, sorry, sorry.

You've every right to be furious with me. Not least because I told you it was over. But I didn't lie to you. I thought it was. I was ready to marry Nathan.

And yet. Every night since I said yes, I'd wake, maybe two or three in the morning, and all I could think was, I am making a terrible mistake. And of course that was worse after I met Alex.

You saw Michael, and you just knew. Remember you telling me that, and remember you saying that I would just know?

You didn't tell me what I should do if the person I just knew was a different man to the one I'd agreed to marry.

I didn't lie to you. I was ready to marry Nathan, right up until the day before. That morning, I couldn't stop crying. Gila sat on my bed and cuddled me, and Becca said, 'You're sick with love, that's all.' She thought she was talking about Nathan, but I knew I was sick with love for someone else. And when everyone was out, I phoned that someone else, and now here I am, out in the Real World, adrift, away from everyone and everything I know and love.

Away from everyone, except the man who, when I saw him, I just knew.

I miss you so much, Deb. I hope one day you can forgive me.

Dad told me I was dead to you all. So please send this message from beyond the grave to Mum, Zaida, Dov, Becca and Gila. I love them so much, and miss them, and I'm sorry.

But I didn't want to marry a man I didn't love.

Love,

Your Friend Who Ran Away But is Still Your Friend,

Aliza xxx

Chapter Seven

23 December 1999

Me: 'It's too short.'

Him: 'It barely shows anything.'

Me: 'I'll freeze to death.'

Him: 'Wear tights with it.'

Me: 'You can see my knees!'

Him: 'Charming knees like yours *should* be seen. The whole world should be worshipping these knees.' Alex lifted up the skirt a little higher, and I pushed his hand away.

'Stop it! People are looking.'

'That's the point.' He turned around and addressed the shop at large. 'Roll up everyone, step this way, come and see the greatest knees in London. Possibly the whole of the UK. Kept under wraps for twenty-three years, I kid you not, and only now revealed to the world.'

Though utterly embarrassed, I couldn't help laughing. One or two women smiled vaguely in our direction, but otherwise the shoppers remained indifferent, and continued about their own business. The shop was very busy and loud, and everyone seemed to be moving quickly. A woman grabbed an armful of soft blue scarves from a table next to

Alex and hurried off with them. I saw a man holding a pack of ladies' pants, and looked away.

It was two days till Christmas, and the shelves were decorated with sparkly ribbons in beautiful colours: silver, red, green and blue.

'Tinsel,' Alex told me, and I rolled the unfamiliar word round my mouth. *Tinsel.*

'So, shall we buy it?' Alex said.

'No. I'll try on one of the others.' I darted back into the changing room and took off the skirt. It was a gorgeous colour, a light sunshiny blue, but I couldn't imagine ever feeling comfortable in something so revealing. As I stood in the little cubicle in my top and pants, measuring the lengths of the eight other skirts against each other, Alex stuck his head round the curtain.

'Hey!' I held the skirts up against me to hide my bare legs.

'It's only me,' he said, 'your beloved fiancé. Soon to be your husband, remember?'

He was, indeed, going to be my husband. He'd been my fiancé for one week. In nine days' time, he'd be my husband. Fiancé was a romantic-sounding word. Husband was much more down-to-earth. I wondered if it was made up from two words, 'hus' and 'band', and if so, what a hus was. Hus Band. A band around my hus. He was certainly *banned*, anyway, as far as my family were concerned.

Anyway, even when he was my husband, I wouldn't want him seeing my legs in a public place. I waited till he'd gone, then resumed my task of comparing skirt lengths. Even the longest one only came halfway down my calf, though. I zipped it up and stepped out of the changing room.

'Nice,' Alex said, 'but a bit unfashionable.'

'Where I come from,' I said, 'men don't give women fashion advice.'

'Where you come from,' he said, 'it is painfully apparent that *no one* gives women fashion advice.'

Alex jokingly referred to my usual clothes as, 'your burqas'. They were nothing like as exotic or full-coverage as burqas, but I could see that they looked odd out here. I'd never thought much about them before.

'I am aware of fashion,' I told him. 'I didn't walk round Stoke Newington with my eyes closed.'

'You only had one small bag when you fled the shtetl. You had to leave your smart clothes behind.'

I smiled. I didn't mind him teasing me. It took the sting out of our elopement, somehow. Made it seem more light-hearted. It was true that I'd brought only one small bag when I left, but most of my clothes fitted in it. I didn't own many. Four long skirts: two black, one navy, one dark green. Five long-sleeved blouses, four white and one blue. Three dark high-necked sweaters. In the morning I was accustomed to putting on whatever was clean. It was different out here, in what Deborah used to call, sarcastically 'The Real World'. Women here wore such a wide variety of things, all much more tight or bare than I would wear. And trousers, too, of course. I'd brought a pair of trousers into the changing room to try. But they felt much too strange and I took them off right away. I looked like a man in them, a man with a large backside. The last time I wore trousers was when I was seven years old and put on Joel's clothes. I got into trouble for that.

Alex bought the longer skirt that I liked and, against my protestations, the shorter blue one too. 'You might come round to it,' he said. He also bought several of the shirts and tops I'd tried, some of which had short sleeves. Then we went to get some tights. There were so many different types. Not simply black, but 'barely black' and 'nearly black'.

What was the difference between tan, cocoa, nutmeg, dark caramel and sunset? They all looked brown to me. Then there was the thickness, or rather, thinness: twenty denier, fifteen, even ten. Some were called 'sheer'. The only tights I'd owned till now were made of thick wool.

On our way out we passed a rack of shiny dresses. 'For Christmas Day?' Alex said, holding one up. They had no sleeves, the necks were what Deborah would call 'way down low', and they were covered in what looked like… *tinsel.* Sequins, Alex called them.

'The Real World contains a lot of sparkling materials,' I said.

'It's not always like this, it's just Christmas.' Alex held the twinkling dress up against himself and made a kissing face at me. I shook my head and turned to go, but couldn't remember which direction the door was in. The shop was enormous and there were racks of clothes and people everywhere. I turned back to Alex, he took my arm, and I jumped out of my skin, as I always did when he touched me. Which he did all the time, so I was jumping out of my skin all the time.

Back at his flat I took a pair of tights out of its packet. Fifteen denier, dark caramel. I stroked the tights against my cheek, amazed by their silkiness. Alex laughed and said I was like a GI bride with her first pair of silk stockings. I sort of understood what he meant, though I didn't know what a GI bride was. He saw that I didn't, and said, 'You know what we should do?' He got all excited, ran into his bedroom and returned with a notebook. He sat next to me, and as our bodies touched, I did the skin jump again. I apologised, but he put his arm round me, slowly, so I was prepared for it, and said, 'You leaping in shock at my touch will never get old, Eliza.'

On the first page of the notebook, he wrote, 'FILMS'.

I raised my eyebrows.

'Remember the other day, when I said your eyelashes were as long as Bambi's?'

I nodded, embarrassed.

'You've never heard of Bambi, have you?'

I shook my head, relieved. 'And you said my lips were as red as Snow White's and I had no idea what you meant.'

'You don't have to pretend with me, Eliza,' he said. 'I know there are lots of things you haven't encountered yet.' Then *he* looked embarrassed, and we grinned at each other, me blushing, knowing we were both thinking about some of the interesting night-time things we hadn't yet encountered together.

'OK, so, this notebook can be a kind of cultural "to do" list. We'll put in here some things that you've missed out on, and work through them together.' He wrote 'Bambi' and 'Snow White' under the heading, then turned to the next page, and wrote 'RECENT HISTORY', adding 'GI Brides' underneath it.

'I've missed twenty-three years' worth of stuff, Alex,' I said faintly.

'We need a page on books,' he said, 'and TV, and music – oh god, there's loads of things.' He turned back to the film page. '*Citizen Kane*, of course. Oh, *Apocalypse Now. Singin' in the Rain*, you'll love that.'

He'd been playing me some of his favourite music, and his CDs were spread over the floor. My eye had earlier been drawn to an ochre-coloured disc, with an ink drawing of a black woman's face. Her hair was wilder than mine, but her eyebrows, eyes and mouth were rather like my own. Her CD was called 'The Miseducation of Lauryn Hill'. I liked the rhythm of that word, *miseducation*. I took the notebook and pen from Alex, and on the front cover, I wrote, 'The Re-education of Eliza Bloom'.

'Is this a bad idea?' Alex said. 'I think maybe I'm being patronising. I'm really sorry.' He chucked the notebook on the floor.

'No,' I said, and meant it. This was part of why I was here, after all. I picked up the book and handed it to him. 'I want to know what you like.'

'Are you sure?'

'What have I missed? I want to know everything.'

'It'll be fun,' he said, his eyes shining. 'There's loads of thing I can't wait to share with you.'

'What do I bring?' I asked. 'It sounds a bit one-way.'

'Oh no! Not at all. You bring your own history, the things you have learned along the way, and your beautiful self. Let's start your lists for me in the back of the book.'

He leant over and kissed me full on my Snow White lips, which made me tremble. Literally tremble, as though I was freezing, but the opposite was true. I was boiling hot. I felt sorry for that other girl, Aliza, the shadow self I left behind, left to marry Nathan, milk-and-meat, duty and rules. Sure, Aliza still had her friends and family around her, her reputation, but she didn't have this. I pulled Alex's head back towards me, so he could kiss me again. This was all I wanted, all I needed.

Films

- *Bambi*. His eyelashes are not as long as yours, Eliza. This always makes me cry, by the way – don't tell anyone.
- *Snow White*. My grandfather got taken to this when it came into the cinemas in the 1930s, he was about four, and he screamed so much his mum had to take him out. Scary. Also, rosy lips.
- *Singin' in the Rain*. It's a musical but I'm giving it a pass because it's so funny and it has great dancing. You may fall in love with Gene Kelly.
- *Some Like It Hot*. Probably my favourite film. Even you must have heard of Marilyn Monroe? There's a reason she was so famous and you can see why here. Really funny but also dark.
- *Citizen Kane.* Total classic, on every top ten list there's ever been. (Secretly, I'm not sure I love it, but it's very impressive, esp when you know that Orson Welles was only twenty-five when he made it. What have I been doing with my life?)
- *Roman Holiday*. Audrey Hepburn was my first love. You are prettier, though.

- *Whatever Happened to Baby Jane?* Two total divas acting each other off the screen. Camp classic.
- *The Godfather*. Parts 1 and 2, not 3. Epic, amazing. You will learn loads about the mafia, crossing off a section on the modern history list. Plus, Brando.
- *The Princess Bride*. Bit left-field but something about your sense of humour makes me think you'll like this.
- *Sophie's Choice*. Traumatic, intense. The first film I ever saw about the Holocaust, and I'm not sure I ever got over it. I'll be interested in your take.
- *Star Wars*. Everyone I know likes it. Leaves me cold, but it's a significant cultural thing so you ought to see it.
- *Crocodile Dundee*. This is just sheer fun to watch. And it's a kind of fish-out-of-water thing, which might appeal, given the circumstances.
- *Casablanca*. One of the greats. Bogart and the incomparable Ingrid Bergman. All the most famous lines from movies are in this film, including 'the usual suspects'.
- *The Usual Suspects*. I fell for this hard when I saw it. Clever, twisty, great actors.
- *Apocalypse Now*. One of the greatest ever films. You'll like the backstory about what a nightmare it was to make. Also, crosses off Vietnam War from the history list. And Brando again.
- *Chinatown* – Gotta have a crime movie in there, and there's none better. Shocking at the time, still grips now.

Chapter Eight

December 1999

Today I celebrated Christmas in a Christian house. I couldn't wait till Alex and I were home again, so I could write and tell Deborah. She was always fascinated by Christmas, right from when we were little. You couldn't hide from it, even in our area.

'Trees indoors, oy!' she would say. 'Meshuggeners going crazy in the shops.'

She would have loved to have seen me at Alex's brother's. Well, other than hating that I was with Alex, and at his brother's.

Alex always spoke so fondly and proudly of his brother Kim that I felt terribly nervous about meeting him. I wondered if he would approve of me. But he was lovely from the start. We arrived at his house this morning, and when he opened the door, he was beaming from ear to ear.

'Ah ha! The woman who tamed Alexander Symons!' He made no attempt to hug or kiss me, which I assumed Alex had warned him about; he just smiled at me, before throwing his arms round Alex, and hugging him so vigorously that I took a step back. But that was as exuberant as he got, I discovered. Kim was a toned-down version of Alex: the same dark hair and blue eyes, but not as head-turningly handsome; the same ready smile but hesitant where Alex's was confident; quieter all round.

The house was cosy and glittery with Christmas. Kim's sweet baby Holly even seemed to be named for the holiday. She toddled up to us on her plump little legs, and Alex sat on the sofa and pulled her on to his lap.

They had an indoor tree, covered in sparkles – Deb would have been in heaven. Tinsel hung from every surface, decorations dripped from the ceilings. When Kim's wife came out of the kitchen, wiping her hands on a tea-towel, and she was covered in sparkles too, I felt quite dazzled.

'Ah, here's Vicky,' Kim said, jumping up.

'Every year I ask myself, why do I fucking do it?' Vicky said. It didn't seem that she was addressing anyone in particular, but she was looking at me, so I said, 'I don't know.'

She didn't acknowledge me. 'Gorgeous to see you as ever, Ally-boy,' she said, and reached across Holly to kiss him on the cheek, very near his mouth.

'Vick,' Kim said, 'this is Alex's fiancée, Eliza.'

'You've done well,' Vicky said to me, smiling with all her teeth. 'He never wanted to marry any of the hundred others he's brought round.'

'Vicky!' Kim said.

'What? I'm giving the girl a compliment, aren't I?' She turned to Alex. 'Yes, very pretty, Ally. Well done. Loving her retro blouse. Your mother rang,' she continued, addressing both brothers, 'and she couldn't start the car but it's all right now. Why she had to phone to tell me that when I'm in the middle of basting the fucking potatoes, I have literally no idea.'

'Mama!' Holly said, from Alex's lap. She held up her arms towards her mother.

'I'm busy, Holly,' Vicky said. 'Ask Daddy.' She turned and went back into the kitchen.

There was an awkward pause. 'Sorry about that,' Kim said. 'She finds Christmas a bit stressful.' He picked up Holly and took her into the kitchen; almost immediately we could hear raised voices.

'So, now you've met Vicky,' Alex said, and laughed. He seemed unbothered, so I acted like I was too, but I was actually wondering what the hell I was doing, meeting the brother, the sister-in-law and the mother all in one go.

'I must really love Alex,' I said in my head to Deborah, and imagined her laughing at me. 'Trust you to do something so mad,' she was saying. 'Only you, Aliza, only you.' I knew she wouldn't be so forgiving in reality, but it gave me strength to think of her.

'Is my blouse so terrible?' I asked Alex. It was one of my burqa blouses, it being too cold for one of the new short-sleeved ones.

'You look gorgeous,' he said, which didn't answer the question. I thought about Vicky kissing him, and about the hundreds of other women he'd brought here.

Kim and Vicky reappeared. He was carrying Holly and a bottle of wine, and Vicky was holding four glasses.

'Kim says I was rude,' Vicky said, without preamble. 'Sorry about that. But you'll have to take me as you find, I'm afraid.'

I didn't know how to answer, but they all seemed to be waiting for me to speak. I said, 'Your dress is very pretty,' trying to imagine Deborah's reaction to it. It was made of red sequins, rather like the one Alex had held up in the shop for a joke. The neckline was 'way down low', low enough to see the top of Vicky's lacy bra, which was purple. She looked like one of the women Deborah and I giggled over whenever we were out and about in Hackney, the ones who walked round constantly tugging down their skirts.

'Festive, isn't it?' Vicky said. 'We like to dress up for Christmas.'

The 'we' very much left me, in my non-Christian plain blouse and skirt, out in the cold.

Alex frowned at her, thinking I couldn't see him frowning at her. I honestly didn't think I could feel any more uncomfortable, but there it was: I did.

'Well, duh,' Deb-in-my-head said, 'how were you going to feel anything other than out of place, Crazy Kid?' Of course, she was right. It was Christmas Day, birth of the Baby Jesus. What was I doing here?

Kim handed me a glass of wine, accompanied by a small, 'I'm sorry' smile.

'She probably doesn't drink,' Vicky said. She sat next to Alex and pushed her bosom out so that he either had to let it touch his arm, or move along the sofa. He moved along the sofa, closer to me, but she moved as well. Pretty soon the three of us were squashed together at one end. Planning how I'd describe this later to Deborah was the only thing keeping me going. Then I thought: *But Deborah isn't my friend any more*. I took a big sip of wine.

Deborah was born seven weeks before me, and always liked to remind me that she was older. She lived two doors down, our mothers were best friends, and she was like an extra sister. Not that I needed another one, but she understood me in a way that none of my siblings did, not till Dov came along, anyway. When Deborah married Michael, she and I actually became related – Michael's sister, Esther, was already married to my eldest brother Uri, meaning Deb and I now shared

Esther as a sister-in-law. I don't know what that made us in terms of our relationship, but we liked that we were more than just friends.

Deb was lucky in her marriage; she fell madly in love with only the second man she was introduced to, and she and Michael Lived Happily Ever After. Deb didn't seem to realise that not everyone got so lucky.

'What was wrong with that one?' she'd say, when I turned down another possible match, and I'd explain about not seeing eye to eye, or there being no warmth. 'Ha, warmth you can get from central heating,' she said, but she was being disingenuous. She and Michael adored each other.

'Alcohol is a central feature of Judaism, Vicky,' Alex said, practically sitting on my lap in his attempt to get away from Vicky's roving chest. 'In fact in one festival, Purim, the adults are *expected* to get drunk.' He had clearly been mugging up on my list, the only one I'd written in the Re-Education book so far, which was about Jewish festivals. He put his arm round me, making me jump, of course. My wine splashed slightly out of the glass, and Vicky's eyes followed its trajectory.

'I'll get a cloth,' she said, and shimmied out to the kitchen.

'Christ, Kimbo,' Alex said quietly. 'What the fuck's up with her?'

Kim shook his head. 'She's already had more than her share of alcohol, without the excuse of Judaism.'

'Eliza's feeling bloody awkward enough,' Alex said. 'I'm about ready to take her home.'

'It's all right,' I said.

'It's not all right.' Kim looked at me. 'I'm really sorry, Eliza. She's so anxious about getting everything right.'

'We don't care about everything being right,' Alex said. 'We only want to feel welcome.'

'You *are*, man, you know that. You both are.'

Kim sat next to Alex and the brothers hugged. Then Alex pulled me into their embrace, saying, 'Don't jump, now.' I felt Kim's unfamiliar hand rest tentatively on my shoulder, Alex holding me tight. Then Vicky came in and said, 'Oh how cute, a seasonal orgy,' and we broke apart.

25 December 1999

Dear Deborah

It's late and I think Alex is already asleep in the spare room, but I wanted to tell you that today I had Christmas dinner. I imagine that's not a sentence you ever thought you'd hear from me.

I met Alex and Kim's mother, Sheila, and she was very kind. I wish she'd arrived earlier as Vicky (Kim's wife, she doesn't like me) was a bit more pleasant once she was in the house. Sheila took care to include me in everything. I can see where the boys get their gentleness from. She's not particularly religious, Alex says, just Church of England, but it must still be weird for your son to suddenly marry a Jewish girl. On the other hand, I am definitely nicer than Vicky.

Vicky made a fuss about me not eating turkey. 'Jews can eat turkey,' she said, 'it's not pig, right?' I started to explain about the difference between kosher and non-kosher meat, but when Vicky rolled her eyes I gave up. I ate a potato, even though I suspected it had been cooked in meat juices, and I tried Brussel sprouts, which aren't all that nice.

'Don't tell me,' Vicky said, as I passed round a heavy jug without taking any, 'There's something wrong with my gravy.' I'd drunk three

glasses of wine, Deb, so I wasn't at my most diplomatic. I said, 'I'm sure it's delicious gravy, Vicky, but I'm not used to such riches.' Kim laughed, bless him.

Alex is the good-looking brother. I know you haven't seen him, so you'll have to take my word for it. He's tall, more than six feet. Remember that one boy I was introduced to, who said I'd have to wear flat shoes when we got married? Ha ha, when *we get married, I liked that! Alex is dark, his hair in fact is the same nearly-black colour as mine, but his eyes are an extraordinary blue, almost royal blue. His grandfather on his father's side was Italian, which explains his olive colouring. His father died several years ago, incidentally. Kim is shorter than Alex, a bit podgy, and his face is covered by hair and glasses. He has masses of black curly hair and a huge bushy black beard and the biggest, thickest specs you have ever seen. I told him he wouldn't look out of place in Stamford Hill, with that beard. He thought that was funny.*

I miss everyone so much. I miss Zaida, and Dov, and Mum, and most of all I miss you.

Miss you.

Love,

Your Friend Who Ran Away But Is Still Your Friend,

Aliza xxx

Chapter Nine

27 December 1999

Alex offered to come but I said I wanted to go alone, that it wasn't the sort of thing a man should get involved with. *And*, I said, making more of a case, I hadn't been anywhere on my own yet, since I moved here, and I needed to start finding my own way around. He said he completely understood.

But the truth is, I didn't want a repeat of the shopping experience from before Christmas. It felt too pressurising with him there, trying to persuade me to buy the sort of clothes I wasn't ready for. I still saw that unspeakable image of my backside in trousers whenever I closed my eyes.

The person I really wanted with me, of course, was Deborah. She'd helped me choose the other wedding dress. She was so funny about all the ones I tried on. I spent almost the whole day laughing. Then she stopped being funny when I came out in the dress I eventually chose, the ivory one with the little pearl buttons. 'Oh,' she said, 'you look beautiful.' Deb never normally said things like that.

I wasn't yet feeling confident enough to travel into the West End on my own, so I went to a boutique on Brixton high street, not far from Alex's flat. I didn't have anything in mind, other than I wanted it to be as different as possible from the first dress. I wondered what had happened to it. Perhaps my father would be able to get some of the money back.

The boutique was empty, and the lady left me alone, which was what I needed. I saw several nice things, but then I noticed a long dress of red silk, and knew I had to have that one. Even thinking about choosing something red made my skin prickle. It was another defiant act, though my father would never know about it. I put it on, and stared at myself in the changing room mirror. I could scarcely believe it was me, wearing that forbidden colour. My heart beat so hard I could have been running.

31 December 1999

Dear Deborah,

I don't know if you'll read this, Deb, or if it will go in the bin. Please read it. Please read the others I've sent. Please write back.

This afternoon I went to a pub! And met some of Alex's friends! And they all kissed me on both cheeks! I don't know how long it's going to take me to get used to all this.

We're going out again in a minute, to the park, to watch fireworks. I'm scared of how noisy it will be, but excited too. And tomorrow I get married. I'm scared of that, but excited too. Scared and excited (and somewhat confused) is the way I am negotiating everything in the Real World.

My whole life, I always assumed that when I got married I'd have you to talk to about it, my wise friend, and that Zaida would be there, and Dov and Gila, of course. I don't have any of you, and yes, I know that's my fault, I can see exactly what expression you're wearing as you read this (I hope you're reading this), I know I'm the only one to blame. But.

But I wish you were here.

This is now the longest we haven't spoken since, well, since we met, I think.

Love,

Your Friend Who Ran Away But Is Still Your Friend,

Aliza xxx

PS Happy New Year, as they say round here. Happy New Millennium.

Chapter Ten

December 1999

I held the thin metal stick carefully, and Alex put a match to the top of it. Nothing happened for several seconds, then it flashed into life, fizzing and firing all over the place. It was so alarming I nearly dropped it, but it was also startlingly pretty. Alex lit one for himself from mine, and showed me how to make patterns in the sky. He drew a bright white heart, over and over, then wrote my name. I tried to write his but didn't move it fast enough. Then we turned them round and round, making overlapping circles.

I thought that, in a way, I was like that sparkler. I was dormant, unlit. Then I met Alex, and I burst into life, sparks shooting off everywhere as if someone had thrown a box of sequins into the air.

All too soon, the sparklers sputtered and went out. We dropped them on the ground, and Alex put his arm round me as we walked up the road to Brockwell Park. It was freezing, and I was glad for my old wool coat, which went down to my ankles. When we reached the main road there were lots of other couples like us, heading in the same direction, our breaths making patches in the dark sky.

Tinsel, sequins, sparklers, and now fireworks. The Real World continued to be a very glittery place. In the park we stood in the middle of the crowd and gazed up at the sky at the most incredible light show. All around me people were wincing at the louder bangs, and a few children wore protectors over their ears. But I loved the noise, and the shouts, and the people. It was so quiet being with Alex in his flat. I loved it there, of course I did, but I was used to living in a house with lots of people, and I was surprised how much I missed the clamour and activity.

I felt Alex's eyes on me, watching my reactions to the display. The fireworks were beautiful. I'd never seen anything like them, and I gasped along with everyone else. It was an important date out here, the last day of a century, 2,000 years since Jesus was born. Back home, it was 5760, and not a special date at all. I wondered what they were all doing there.

It was an important date to Alex and me, too.

'It's the night before our wedding!' he said, excited. 'I think these fireworks are actually in our honour, and nothing to do with some boring new millennium.'

'Definitely.'

I was thinking about the other day-before-the-wedding, when I'd made the decision to phone Alex. I wondered how it would all have turned out, if Alex hadn't answered the phone, or if he had said, 'Who is this?' or had told me that, regrettably, he had a new girlfriend and he wished me and my husband well? Once again, I was overwhelmed by the sheer luck of it all. I realised that I had never asked what it had been like for him, those weeks after the cinema and the kiss, when I shut down. In between crashing blasts of coloured lights, I asked him.

'The worst ten weeks of my life, you mean?' he said, grinning. He pulled me closer and rearranged my scarf so it was properly round my neck.

'I'm sorry,' I said.

'You were worth waiting for. Though I didn't realise quite how long you'd keep me waiting. I thought you were just a bit freaked out by the kiss, and the cinema and everything. I thought in a couple of days, you'd get back in touch. So I sent you a message, and left a voicemail. I even called the landline a few times, but your dad always answered, so I had to hang up. After a few days, I thought, maybe she isn't going to contact me again. Well! I wasn't having that, was I?'

An enormous golden firework exploded over our heads and we both said, 'Ooooh!'

'What did you do?'

'Obviously I didn't know where you lived, you'd never told me, but you had told me the name of your school.'

'Oh no! I forgot to phone the school. I wanted to apologise for walking out without any explanation. It went out of my head.'

'I have this feeling that, by now, they've heard all about it.'

'You're probably right. I feel bad, though. I'll call them next week. Go on.'

Pink and purple sparkling sprays lit up the sky.

'Well, they were certainly protective of you. I asked for you a few times, but the secretary always said that you were off sick.'

'Did you actually manage to get in?'

'No, I was stuck outside in the cold, talking into an intercom, begging some unseen harridan to let me talk to you.'

'Oh dear, I'm sorry. She is a bit scary.'

'I waited outside your school every afternoon for a week, which made me pretty unpopular at work but there was no sign of you. I started to think maybe you really were ill, that the stress of meeting me had made you ill.'

'I *was* ill. I couldn't eat, and my mind was so confused. I did take a few days off.'

'Then I went back to our café, five o'clock every day.'

'For how long?'

'Two weeks. You never came.'

'Oh, Alex.'

'I know. What a sap, right? Kim couldn't stop teasing me, and I didn't even care. I thought about you every day. I even lost interest in other women, which hadn't ever happened before, not since I was about thirteen.'

I didn't know what to say to that, so I focused on the fireworks which were now crowding together, one scarcely fading before the next burst into noisy bloom.

'Basically I spent a lot of time at Kim's, being horribly teased, and pointlessly speculating about what you might be thinking.'

'When did you give up?'

People in the crowd started cheering, and looking up, I realised that the fireworks had stopped.

'Eliza, I never gave up.' Alex smiled. 'Weeks, months, I sent you a message nearly every day. And I was right to. December the fifteenth, the day before your wedding, and I was thinking, perhaps I should do that romantic *Graduate* thing – it's a film, I must add it to the list – of rushing into the ceremony and grabbing your hand and getting on a bus. But of course, I didn't know where or when you were getting married. Anyway, I assumed you didn't want an intervention. I sent one more text, wishing you luck. And then my phone rang. I saw it was you before I picked it up, and I was in such a state, I nearly pressed the off button.'

'Do you remember what I said?'

'It's engraved on my heart. You said, "My name's Aliza with an A, and I love you."'

'And you said, "I love you too."'

'And then,' Alex said, and pulled me even closer, 'the shit really hit the fan.'

Midnight, Brockwell Park. We all chanted together: 'Ten! Nine! Eight!' and when we reached zero, everyone screamed and called out 'Happy New Year!' and more fireworks went off overhead. It had got so cold, I couldn't feel my feet.

Alex whispered, 'It's our wedding day!' Then he kissed me. I kept my eyes open but no one was watching us, they were all kissing too. I closed my eyes. It seemed very warm, suddenly, and I let myself melt into the kiss.

Chapter Eleven

1 January 2000

Kim and Vicky were waiting for us outside the register office. Alex threw his arms round Kim. 'Thanks so much doing for this, Kimbo.'

'You're welcome, man, even though I have a hangover the size of the Millennium Dome.'

I leaned in to kiss Vicky on the cheek. After only two weeks living in the Real World I'd learned how much casual friendly kissing went on amongst people who weren't related. Yesterday afternoon, I'd met a group of Alex's friends at the Prince Albert pub, and every single one of them had kissed me, which took ages, and put me on edge worrying about whether they would all do it again when it was time to go (they did). Alex assured me I'd get used to it, and I felt perhaps I was already starting to, as I made the first move with Vicky. But I just got a mouthful of hair as she stepped back.

It was going to be a long slow process to make new friends, and I had secretly been hoping that Vicky could be a ready-made one, despite our shaky start at Christmas. After all, we had the two brothers in common.

'I've met my new sister,' I told myself on the way home from Vicky's house on Christmas Day, hoping that it would feel like that at some point in the future. Today, though, when I smiled at her, Vicky didn't smile back.

'You can't wear that coat,' she said. 'It doesn't go.'

'It doesn't matter,' I said, touching my collar, feeling self-conscious all of a sudden. 'No one will see it.'

The red of my dress looked like fire, but the material was thin, so I was wearing my only coat, the long brown woollen one, over the top.

'Kim's got his camera, you don't want to be wearing that frumpy thing in your wedding photos.' Vicky took off her white furry jacket and pushed it into my arms. 'Something borrowed,' she said.

I took my coat off and put on hers. It was no warmer than mine but was much softer. It smelled of Vicky, of her flowery perfume. I handed her my coat in exchange but she didn't put it on.

'You'll freeze,' I said.

'Not being funny darling, but I'd rather catch pneumonia than wear your granny coat. No offence.'

'Is Mum looking after Holly?' Alex asked, changing the subject.

'Yes,' Kim said. 'She was hoping to come, of course, but with Holly having a bit of a temperature, she kindly offered to stay with her.'

'And let's face it, it was a bit short notice, weren't it?' Vicky said. 'She looks better in my coat, don't you think, Ally? Bit more glamorous?'

I realised she was talking about me.

'Very nice, Vicky,' Alex said, winking at me. 'Well, shall we go in?'

The ceremony was brief, but moving. Alex and I faced each other and held hands as the registrar, a black middle-aged woman with a sonorous voice, intoned the words we had to repeat. I stumbled over 'I know not of any lawful impediment', which made Alex smile. I don't think I'd ever said the word 'impediment' out loud before.

But then Alex had to say, 'I call upon these persons, here present, to witness that I, Alex Symons, do take thee, Aliza Bloom, to be my lawful wedded wife', and his voice cracked on the word 'wife', which set me off. He put a plain silver ring on my finger, to go with the Accessorize ring, and we looked at each other, and smiled. The whole thing passed much too quickly for me, and my eyes were blurry with tears. Kim took photos of us with his new digital camera, and the registrar took some of the four of us. We then went to Brockwell Park to take more pictures, Alex and I standing under a bare-branched tree, but we didn't stay long, it was so cold. We hurried over to the Prince Albert, and I got slightly drunk on red wine while watching Vicky's attempts to flirt with Alex. He constantly rebuffed her, kept drawing Kim and me back into the group, but she persistently tried to exclude us from their conversation.

Later, we relocated to the Roundhouse for chocolate cake. I'd eaten a few items of non-kosher food in the previous two weeks, so it shouldn't have been a problem, but I was churned up thinking about what was to come, and the crumbs dried in my throat. Alex caught my eye, and got to his feet.

'Thanks, guys, you've been stars,' he said, 'but I need to get my tired bride home.'

'It's only four in the afternoon, what's she got to be tired about?' Vicky said, then added, 'Ow!' as Kim elbowed her.

'I think Eliza needs a little lie-down,' Alex said, winking at me.

'Let her go, then,' Vicky said. 'No reason why you can't stay a bit longer.'

'Well, Vicky,' Alex said, 'in fact, both Eliza and I need a lie-down,' and he turned his dazzling smile to me, his new wife.

We laughed about Vicky all the way back to the flat, but once he'd unlocked the front door, we fell silent. He took my hand and led me to his room. For two weeks I'd slept alone in here while he stayed in the spare room. I couldn't stop trembling in his arms as he gently unzipped my red dress, kissing my neck so softly I scarcely felt it. I closed my eyes, so that I felt, rather than saw, my dress fall to the floor. He whispered to me to get into bed and I slid gratefully under the covers in my underwear. I couldn't look at him, kept my face turned away from him as he undressed. When he got in beside me, I knew he was naked.

I took a breath, then turned to face him. He put his arms round me, pressing the length of his body against mine, and I gasped, I actually gasped, from the shock of something so unfamiliar. I couldn't stop shivering, and he stroked my back with gentle fingertips to calm me, softly kissing my face and neck. I don't know how long we lay like this, but my feelings inside of me made it seem that I would burst. We whispered 'I love you' to each other, though I could scarcely say the words as I was breathing so fast, and he seemed to be having difficulty breathing too. He rolled away from me and I couldn't understand why, but then I saw that he was putting something on himself. I knew about condoms, of course – I was sheltered, not stupid – but had never seen one. To my surprise, and his, I was fascinated to watch him slide the condom on. There was so much I had never seen before, until this night: a grown man naked; an uncircumcised penis; my own naked body through someone else's gaze.

To even more of both our surprises, I gently took hold of his penis. How extraordinary it felt, even with the condom over it. Silky and hard and warm all at the same time. I stroked my hand up and down it.

He pressed against me. 'Are you ready to try?' he whispered. 'I don't normally go this fast but I can't wait much longer.'

In answer, I held him tight against me. He slid my pants down and moved across me, and pushed himself into me. It felt like such a tight fit, and then it didn't, and I was barely aware that I was making tiny gasps of surprise and pleasure, my fingers tense against his back. Then he was moving faster, seemed deeper inside me, and then he let out a great yell that I had not expected.

'Oh my god,' he said, kissing me. 'I'm so sorry, that was so quick, are you OK?'

'It was wonderful.'

'Didn't it hurt?'

'A little bit. But it was so… wonderful.' I didn't know how I could ever describe the complex sensations of the heat of his body, the astonishing otherness of him, the flatness of his chest against the curves of my own, the pleasurable warmth in my secret unknown place. 'Wonderful' would have to cover it.

'But you can't even have come.'

'Come?'

'You know. Orgasm.'

I winced, embarrassed, against him. 'No. I don't know how.'

'I'll help you. Give me ten minutes, and we'll try again.'

I laughed, delighted. 'We can do it again, so soon?'

He moved against me, and my whole body tingled. 'We sure can, Snow White.'

Alex's list of food for Eliza

- Cheeseburger and fries. American classic. A good one is a thing of beauty.
- Sushi. I've only recently got into sushi but think you'll like it. There's more to it than raw fish.
- Lamb rogan josh. Curry with yoghurt, which I know is meat and milk. But the meat is cooked for a long time so it's melt-in-the-mouth and probably not that different from lamb you already like.
- Rare steak. OK, here the meat has *not* been cooked for a long time. Yes, Eliza, there might be blood on the plate… but you have got to love the taste!
- Oysters. Well-known aphrodisiac. Also, utterly delicious.
- Bacon butty. The thing that vegetarians dream about. Ultimate comfort food. I know a great greasy spoon, reckon it serves the best bacon sarnie in London.

Chapter Twelve

February 2000

'Cheesy,' Alex said, his face almost hidden behind an enormous bunch of red roses. 'But it's your first Valentine's Day, you ought to get to enjoy some of the clichés.'

He was up and dressed while I was still in bed, slowly coming to the surface. I struggled to a sitting position, and he gently placed the roses in my arms. Then he bent down and kissed me. I managed to jump only a tiny bit. It was barely noticeable, I think.

Red roses weren't a cliché to me. It's not that it was forbidden to celebrate Valentine's Day. We just didn't. My family considered people who did celebrate it, like the Rosens down the road, to be a bit odd. My parents gave each other romantic gifts on Tu B'Av (the Day of Love). I liked it when they did that, it was a rare chance to see my dad being soft. Last year he gave Mum a bunch of cornflowers, wrapped in paper. The flowers were all different colours, not only the usual blue, but pink and white too. Mum saw me looking at them, and gave me some in a jar for my room. I suspect she thought, as I did, that I might never find a man I wanted to marry, might never be given flowers. Neither of us knew that within a few weeks I'd have met both Nathan and Alex.

Mum would be glad to see the enormous bunch of roses today. Well, she wouldn't be glad, of course. She'd be extremely unhappy.

But somewhere deep down, she might be happy that someone loved me enough to buy me flowers.

I laid the roses carefully on the bed next to me and opened Alex's card. He sat on top of the duvet, smiling expectantly. Luckily I'd got him a card too. It was impossible not to notice that Valentine's Day was coming; every shop in town was plastered in hearts. I'd looked at the BBC website, which Alex said was a trustworthy source of information. I was becoming rather reliant on it for navigating my way round the Real World. It told me some Valentine's traditions, such as not signing your name. But when Alex eagerly opened my card, white with a big red shiny heart on the front, his face fell. 'Oh. You haven't written anything in it.'

'It's from your secret admirer!' I said, my own big red shiny heart sinking as I realised I'd made another secular misstep. There were as many rules out here as in my old world, but the ones out here weren't always clear. 'The BBC said not to sign it!'

'Yes, but you're meant to put a message, you just leave off your name,' he said.

Oh.

Alex's card to me said, 'I can't believe that we found each other, against the odds. These two months have been the happiest of my life. I love you.'

Oh, again.

'I was kind of looking forward to finding out what you think of me,' he said.

'You know what I think of you.' I went to put my arms round him, but he stood up and put my card on top of the dressing table. Flat, not standing up.

'No,' he said. 'I don't.'

*

Of all the lists Alex eagerly compiled in the Re-education book, the one I most dreaded us working through was the food one. I'd always been curious about films, TV, and music, and I was enjoying learning some bits of recent history that had been absent from my school curriculum. As for the internet, bring it on! I was becoming addicted to it. Mind you, Alex was rather dismissive of it. 'Cats and porn,' he said. 'That's what the internet is best at. Repeat after me: cats and porn.'

'Cats and porn,' I said obediently.

Porn was also on one of Alex's lists – a blushingly rude list I had only glanced at once, called 'sexy things to try'. I'd have preferred looking at cats, but I resolved to be brave. Try everything once, as Alex said. We looked at a couple of porn sites together – mild ones, apparently, but if that was mild, only Ha-Shem knew what the rest was like. The only thing that stopped me dying from embarrassment was that, most of the time, I had no idea what was going on.

'I've put it in the right order, I think,' Alex said, as I read through the food list. He didn't seem to notice that I was hyperventilating. 'We'll start gently, take time to get you used to things, before we move on to the big guns.'

Start gently? Every item on the list was a total violation of my upbringing. The list made a mockery of everything I hadn't eaten for the last twenty-three years. For all that I considered these items to be edible, he might as well have written:

- Concrete and fur
- Socks
- Leech curry with vomit

- Live baby
- Woodlice
- Bits of my own body

The very first item was a cheeseburger! Made from non-kosher beef, served with cheese, thus mixing meat and milk. Not to mention fries, cooked in who-knows-what oil, possibly even animal fat.

'You shall not seethe a kid in its mother's milk,' I said, trying to smile.

'Does your quoting Genesis at me mean you're feeling anxious?'

'It's Leviticus. I am a bit anxious. But it's fine, honestly. Bring me that damn cheeseburger. Try everything once.'

'Are you sure?' Alex said.

No. 'Yes.'

The day Alex and I got engaged, he asked if I was up for the journey. And he wasn't talking about the journey from North to South London. He meant, was I up for integrating, for leading a secular life? Was I up for trying new things, breaking some of my long-held beliefs, shedding some taboos? Yes, I said, and I meant it. *Yes*, emphatically. I'd spent most of my life feeling out of sync with my own community. I wanted to fit into the Real World, and I'd already missed out on so much.

'I want you to teach me everything you know, too,' he said. 'I want to know what you know.'

But what did I know, in comparison to him? The rules and rituals by which I'd led my life felt limiting, not enriching. Nonetheless, Alex insisted I write some of them in the back of the culture book, so he could learn them. And I did, but they seemed about as useful to our new life together as a blank Valentine's card.

*

'So, let's start the food list,' Alex said, when he got in from work that evening. 'First item: a cheeseburger. There's a McDonald's in town.'

'Alex! I can't go into one of those! Please don't make me.'

He laughed. 'I'm not really going to take you to McDonald's. Not ever, and certainly not on Valentine's Night. What kind of barbarian do you think I am? There's a place in Hampstead that does a great burger, tastes like homemade. I booked us a table. You hungry?'

I shook my head, and he kissed me, and said I would be by the time we got there. Maybe he guessed that I'd put this off for ever, if I could. It had been a big enough deal eating non-kosher cereal, butter and bread. Though that was my idea. Alex made it clear he was happy to shop in a kosher supermarket for as long as I wanted, for ever if necessary, but I knew that if I was going to embrace my new life properly, I needed to eat what everyone else ate.

On the way to the tube, Alex tried to take my arm, but I was bleeding, my second one since we'd married, and I pulled away. The first one had been two weeks after our wedding day and I'd tried to explain then about the need to keep separate from each other, but he looked at me as though I was mad. Until that point I hadn't thought of telling him about those particular laws. It seemed extraordinary that there could be anyone who didn't know about them, who needed to have them explained.

'We're not supposed to have sex,' he'd said, incredulous, 'because you've got your period?'

I recoiled in horror. I had never had a conversation about this with anyone before, let alone a man. 'Not only, er, that thing you said! We're not supposed to touch at all!'

He pulled me close to him, and it took all my willpower not to shove him away. It was the first time since meeting him that I'd not wanted to touch him.

'Look at me!' he yelled to no one (we were in the living room). 'I'm touching the unclean lady! Unclean! Unclean! Where's that bell when I need it?'

'Alex, don't, please, it isn't funny.' I was close to tears.

He let me go, and I saw that he wasn't finding it funny either. 'Don't you think we've had enough enforced separation?' he said. 'I slept in the spare room for more than two weeks after we got engaged! My balls were bright blue by the time we finally… you know.'

'It was important to be married,' I said, sliding my toes underneath the rug, hoping to change the subject back to an earlier, but now-solved, argument.

'This is definitely one you have to get over quickly,' he said, refusing to be deflected. 'I'm way too modern a guy to think of periods as taboo.'

'It's just – those laws are so entrenched in my mind.'

'Eliza, you married *me*.' He pressed his hand against his chest. 'Not an Orthodox guy. Me. I'm trying my best, but I don't know how many more fucking rules like this I can handle.'

I thought quickly. 'I probably need to build up to it, get used to the idea.'

'Try it tomorrow, you mean?'

That was a bit faster than I'd been thinking. 'How about this month, we hold hands. In a couple of months, three or four, we sleep in the same bed. And, er, at some point, we try, you know, the whole thing.'

'We're not sleeping in the same bed because you've got your period?!' His voice rose into a squeak.

I decided it wasn't the right moment to say that I was meant to keep apart from him for seven days after the bleeding stopped, as well. Come *on*, Aliza. If I'd wanted to do that, I should have married Nathan. 'I'll sleep in the spare room.'

'This is absolutely nonsensical.'

I tried to look winning. 'It makes the times we have together more special.'

Alex sighed. 'It's lucky you're worth it.' He leaned across to take my hand, and I jerked away. 'I thought we were holding hands this month?'

'Sorry. Yes, we are.' I let him encircle my hand in his. Resisting the urge to rush and scrub both of us with soap was something I'd just have to come to terms with.

Now as we walked together, a month later, I was still nowhere near used to it. He'd only touched my arm, but all I could think was how unclean he now was. I took a long breath and linked my arm through his.

'Well done,' he said, grinning. 'You look totally relaxed with your teeth gritted like that.'

'I'm fine.'

'I can tell. There's a pulse going in your eyelid. Incidentally,' he went on casually, 'some of the best fucks I've ever had have been with gals on the rag.'

'On the *what*?'

'I had this one girlfriend, Emily, she was really turned on during her period. That's when she most wanted to do it.'

I genuinely thought I was going to be physically sick. I unhooked my arm from his, on the pretext of getting a tissue from my bag, put it to my mouth and breathed into it, nice and slow. There was still so much I didn't know about Alex. In terms of how often we met before we eloped, it was, ironically, not that different from an arranged marriage.

However, I did know him well enough to recognise when he was deliberately trying to shock me. I stored away the information about sexy Emily for another time, and focused on practicalities. 'Doesn't it make a mess?'

'Well yes,' Alex said. 'That's part of the attraction.'

Later that night, he added 'making love during Eliza's period' to the 'sexy things to try' list.

We changed at Green Park for the new Jubilee line, and got out at West Hampstead. Alex led the way to a noisy restaurant full of people. We sat at a wooden table, and he poured me a glass of water which I almost immediately knocked over. A sweet waitress had to come and mop up, and I felt that everyone was looking at me.

It wasn't that I'd never been in a restaurant. We were religious, not hillbillies. I remembered going to a kosher place in Stamford Hill a few times with Mum and Dad before the younger ones were born, when it was just Uri, Joel and me. But going out to eat wasn't something you could do with seven kids, not unless you were Rockefeller. I'd been to cafés, of course, with my siblings, and with Deborah. We used to hang out in Munchies. But we never had more than coffee and a cake.

Alex ordered me a cheeseburger called, rudely, 'The Fat Bastard'. When the waitress had gone, he said, 'I've realised that this a two-taboo deal, isn't it? Non-kosher meat, plus dairy with it. Is it too much?'

All at once it did feel way too much, but I didn't want to back out. I shook my head indecisively, neither yes nor no.

'Would a burger without cheese be better, at least?' he said. 'I'll call her back. Or you can have a veggie burger if you can't face it.'

Him giving me a get-out made me determined to do it. In for a penny, in for a quarter-pounder, *haha*.

'No,' I said. 'This is what I want. I want to live in the secular world. With you.'

He smiled his dazzling smile, the smile I fell in love with. The one that made me leave my life behind, that led to me sitting here, waiting for a cheeseburger to arrive. His smile calmed me, and we talked about non-contentious things: some new films he'd added to the list, my latest letter to Deborah, which other couples were on a Valentine's date. I felt a flutter of panic return, though, when the Fat Bastard arrived. It was well-named; a large disc of meat, with a thick slice of cheese on top, onions dripping from the sides. It was served in a bread bun with seeds on top, which reminded me of platzels, the plaited rolls I ate with Zaida every Sunday, which reminded me who I was.

So, this was really happening. Here I was, embarking on the next stage of my new life: eating non-kosher meat with cheese.

Copying Alex, I picked the burger up with both hands, and raised it to my mouth. It smelled lovely. I took a tiny bite. Don't think about what it is, I told myself. Think about how it tastes. The sensations, not what it actually is. That's how I managed my wedding night with Alex.

And like him, the burger was delicious.

On the way out, feeling buoyed up by the success of the outing, I proposed an idea I'd been thinking about for several weeks.

'Can we go past my parents' house?'

'Really?'

'We're married now.'

'I don't think this is a good idea, Eliza.'

'Dad's changed the phone number and no one's answered any of my letters. I just want to see.'

'OK, if you're sure.'

We got on a train and then changed on to the familiar Victoria line. I stared up at the list of stations, and said, 'It's only two stops.'

'Are you all right?' Alex said.

'I don't know. My hands are sweaty.'

'Let me tell you,' Alex said, 'about the last time I was at Seven Sisters.'

I knew he was trying to take my mind off our ultimate destination, and I was grateful. And he hadn't ever talked much about what it was like for him, the day we ran away; we had focused almost completely on how it affected me.

'Well. You can imagine I was a bit of a wreck, waiting for you at the station, not knowing if you were going to come.'

'Sorry about that.'

'I drank so much coffee that my knee kept jiggling up and down by itself. It was a massive relief when you called. And the truth is, I was pretty keen to get more involved. I was never sure about your low-key plan to meet at the tube. Not what I'd call an elopement.'

'Well, you got your drama then.'

'And then some. So, I pretty much ran to your street, and I spotted the house straight away, because its front door was wide open and people were swarming in and out. There were loads of men in long black coats standing around smoking, women running about with plates and trays, and kids playing outside on the pavement. It looked like a scene from long ago, the kids in their old-fashioned clothes, the boys with those curls at the side of their heads. What is it you call them?'

'Payos.'

Alex laughed. 'At the training session you did, do you remember, someone asked why Jewish men have those long side-curls? And you said, "One theory is that their purpose is to give young men something to fiddle with, to distract them from masturbating."'

'I can't believe I said that. I was feeling very skittish that day.'

'It's no wonder I fell in love with you.'

'You fell in love with me the day we met?'

'I did. Anyway. I sat on one of those uncomfortable slanted plastic benches at a bus-stop near your house, and texted you. Then you emerged from the house in your coat, tall and proud, like Cleopatra in the desert, commanding an empire.'

'Pretty impressive for a Stamford Hill gal, right?'

'You are extremely impressive. OK, we're here. You sure about this?'

I nodded, and we got off the train. We smiled at each other as we walked through the ticket area, where we had, two months earlier, stood and pledged ourselves to each other. But my heart was thumping, and it only got worse as we walked the familiar route to my old home. Alex took my hand, and I squeezed it tightly every time I saw someone coming towards us. But our luck held, and I didn't see anyone I knew.

'Then,' Alex continued, as though we'd had no break, 'the men in the garden started clustering round you. I guessed that most of them were your brothers. One of them was pointing at your bag, and though I couldn't hear what they were saying, I guessed they were asking where you were going. It sounded light-hearted though; they didn't seem to suspect anything was wrong.'

'Not at first.'

'I worked out which one was Nathan.'

I flinched slightly at the sound of this name. 'How did you?'

'Your brothers are all dark. He had light-coloured hair and a kind of rusty beard.'

'Sandy, not rusty.'

Alex looked at me. 'Uh huh?'

'Carry on with the story.' We were getting close to my parents' street now.

'Anyway, I knew it was him because he was holding back, whereas the others were all round you, familiar with you. I thought Nathan was quite nice-looking, by the way.'

'I don't know how to process that. Hurry up, Alex, we will be there in a minute.' For some reason, I wanted to hear the end of the story before we got to my house.

'So Gila was crying, and I looked at you hugging her, and I thought, if this was happening to me, would I have the bottle to go through with it? I felt like I was going to hyperventilate. I thought I might have to fight Uri, maybe even several of them, but I couldn't remember how you actually fight. The last time was when I was eleven and at school, and I got a scratched cheek and torn shirt. Then I noticed how alike you and Uri looked, and I doubted I could even hit someone who looked like you.'

'Heavens, Alex, I had no idea such violent thoughts were going through your mind.'

'I was pretty surprised myself. Then you told Uri that we were getting married, and I thought, we *are*?'

'Yes, you did look a bit surprised.'

'Well, we'd only known each other five minutes, and we'd never talked about marriage. Oh look, here's the legendary bus stop.'

'Let's stop a minute here while I get my nerve up.'

We sat on the bench – Alex was right, it was very uncomfortable – and he continued. 'I just assumed you were talking marriage to Uri to show that we were serious.'

'How little you knew!'

'Too right. Then you straightened up, and I saw on your face the expression I fell in love with that first day, when you walked into that training room: I'm damned if I'll show anyone how uncertain or frightened I am. And when you made it clear that we were going together, I think Uri looked at me with respect.'

'Mmm. His extreme hatred expression is easy to muddle up with his respectful face.'

'Ha ha. Anyway, you suddenly darted off, and I raced after you, and after Dov had followed us you looked at me, and your lovely eyes were glittering, and I thought you were going to say something profound, but you said, 'Run!'

This made me laugh, even though I felt terrified by what we were about to do.

'You were mighty courageous then, Eliza, and you are mighty courageous now.'

'Thank you. I am courageous because of you.'

'Ah, shucks.' He kissed my hand, and we stood up and went over to my parents' house.

I'm courageous, I told myself. Even so, as we reached the door, I was trembling.

'Do you want me to knock?' Alex said.

'No.' I took my hand out of his, and rapped on the door before I could change my mind. Please, I prayed, don't let it be Dad.

The door opened, and Uri stood there. He gaped at me. 'What on earth…?'

Like a scene in a film, there were all at once faces everywhere: my beautiful Gila, Dov, Joel, all saying my name, their eyes flicking from me to Alex. Then, it seemed a second later, everyone disappeared, and my father was standing there. He looked beyond me, down the street, and called into the house over his shoulder, 'There's no one here.'

Then he shut the door in my face.

Alex looked at me. 'Jesus,' he said. 'Are you OK?'

We turned and walked back to the tube. 'Yes,' I said, and I meant it. 'That's it, I'm never seeing them again. I've given them more than enough chances. I'm done with them.'

'I'm sure they'll come round, given time,' Alex said, but he didn't sound too confident.

There was no more talking on the way home. We were talked out.

Back at the flat, while he was annotating the Re-education book, I discreetly retrieved the Valentine's card I'd given him. I wrote in it: 'Thank you for my new life. I love you. Eliza.'

I slipped it on to the mantelpiece and dropped a couple of subtle hints that it might be worth looking at again.

He read it and kissed me. 'You learn fast, Grasshopper.'

15 February 2000

Dear Deborah

Me again. Maybe my last letter got lost. And all the letters before that. I think this is the ninth one, in case you're keeping notes.

How's Michael? How are you? I miss not knowing what's going on with you. I miss not knowing what's going on with everyone.

I want to ask you some things about what happened after I left. Please will you tell me? I would tell you if our situations were reversed. You know I would.

How is my Zaida?

How is Mum?

Has Dov been told not to contact me?

Is Nathan OK?

Love, Crazy Kid, aka Married-Out-But-Still-Loves-You xxx

PS I got red roses yesterday, and a Valentine's card.

Chapter Thirteen

March 2016

As instructed, I wake Leah at seven so she can get ready for 'proper shul', as she is now calling it. Dov knows I'm bringing her over, but it is unspoken between Dov and me that I will be driving. It is unspoken between Leah and me that I will park in the next street and walk her to his house, so Dov's family aren't tainted by my secularity. It is unspoken between Alex and me that I am letting Leah go to the same synagogue I attended, before I burned my bridges in my own spectacular youthful mutiny. Not only letting her go, but facilitating her being there. There is so much unspokenness going on that I feel like yelling out words, any words.

Being the early bird, Alex is the one who always wakes Leah for school, but I can't ask him to get her up today as he doesn't approve of her going to shul. Mind you, nor do I. And it *is* his fault she's insisting on going the whole hog. Not an entirely appropriate phrase, all things considered. If he hadn't teased her about the synagogue-lite that Macy's family go to, she wouldn't have decided she needed to go to the 'proper' one my family attend. However, I appreciate that under the circumstances it's my job to get her up, and to be fair, no one understands as well as I do the lure of the untried option. So I force myself out of bed on a Saturday morning and try to get her moving.

Leah is more bleary-eyed than I am. When she was little she would be up and about in the mornings with Alex, and on weekends they'd often go somewhere for breakfast together, leaving me to have a lie-in. How I loved those lazy mornings, the happy feeling of drifting back off to sleep knowing that my two most favourite people were safe and happy together. By the time they got back, I'd be up and ready with a plan: a park or museum to visit, a toy store or bookshop to browse in, a picnic lunch… But teenage Leah, like me, finds it difficult to get up.

She pulls violently away from my kisses and puts the pillow over her head.

'Leah,' I say plaintively, 'you told me to wake you.'

'Fuck off,' she says.

So I do.

Alex is surprised to see me downstairs; he counts on having at least an hour on a Saturday morning to himself. He politely offers me a coffee.

'A large one please,' I say, opening the Saturday magazine. 'If she really wanted to go, she'd get up.'

'Fair enough, you tried.'

Forty minutes later, Leah bursts in. 'We're going to be late!'

I look at the clock. 'We can still make it if you get dressed quickly.'

'What do I wear, what do I wear?'

'Ah.' I haven't thought this through. 'Have you got a long skirt?'

'Mum, for god's sake, you know I haven't!' Leah regularly gets demerits at school for the shortness of her skirt. If I intervene on her way out, she hitches them up still higher. She has even taught herself to sew so she can turn up any new skirts that are longer than a couple of inches. I'm torn between being cross, and impressed by her determination to show her pants to the world. She isn't even the worst offender.

You should see some of her friends. In fact, you can see almost all of some of her friends, if you get what I mean.

'You can borrow one of mine.'

We run upstairs and I rummage around till I find one of my old skirts, from my pre-Alex burqa wardrobe. I haven't worn it for years, because it reminds me of a certain rather dark period from the first year of our marriage, but I've always kept it, in case. In case, what? I don't know. Leah snatches the skirt and puts it on. She's not quite as tall as me yet, so it reaches her ankles, but that's not the arresting thing, which is that she is wearing it with a vest top.

'Leah! Arms!'

'What about them?'

'They have to be covered! Anyway, it's March. It's cold. Put on a jumper.'

'I'll look hideous.'

'Jumper, or I'm not taking you.'

Leah freaks when she realises that even though we're late I'm *still* not going to park right outside Dov's house. She yells at me, 'It doesn't matter who sees us drive up, why do you even care?' I try to explain my sporadic adherence to the concept of not driving on the Sabbath while trying to find a parking space in one of the most densely populated parts of the entire universe. It's possible I shout a bit more than explain, and anyway, my explanation doesn't make sense even to me. Eventually I dump the car on a double yellow and we run three streets to Dov's. He and his family are congregating on the pavement.

'Ah, here they are!' he says, and hugs us both. 'You look very smart, Leah.'

He means he can't see her legs for the first time ever. I take him aside. 'Dov, no indoctrination now, OK?' He might be a father of four, and a grown man, but to me he's still my darling little brother, meaning I am in charge.

He gives me a goofy grin. 'This is your daughter's idea, not mine.'

'I'm hoping she will get it out of her system quickly,' I say.

Dov never rises to my bait. 'There are worse things she could be into, Aliza,' he says mildly.

His oldest son, Gidon, a year younger than Leah but half a foot taller and darkly handsome, sidles up to her. 'Thought you weren't going to make it,' he says.

'Said I'd come, didn't I?' she says, giving him the full feline eyes, and just like that, I realise one of the key things that has attracted Leah to the idea of shul. I smile at Ilana, Dov's wife, who smiles back in the cautious way she always has, all the years we have known each other. To her, I will always be the crazy meshuggener who married out and shamed my family.

Dov and Ilana lead the children, crocodile style, down the road. It is like watching a cine-film of my childhood. Our family home is only a few streets away from here, where my mum still lives with my youngest sister Gila and her family. We seven kids would file after our parents every week in the same way, in the same direction.

I watch until they have turned the corner, my eyes a little misted, then I remember my illegally parked car and run like the clappers. As I turn into the road I realise with a start that I am in Preston Street, where long ago, Alex and I met illicitly in a café. I slow down, and look at the shops to see if it is still there, and it is! It used to be called Artello's, I remember, and now it's called Armando's, but I peep in through the window and it is recognisably the same place. Ah, those heady, romantic days, before we even kissed, when I was so scared that I'd be caught, when just the sight of Alex walking into the café made my heart melt.

I go over to my car, and shove the inevitable parking ticket in my coat pocket. It's another thing I won't be telling Alex.

He's out when I get home, the gym again presumably, for he is in the full throes of a mid-life get-fit crisis. I decide it's time to tackle the chucking out I failed to do fifteen years ago. The box of secrets is back up on the top shelf of the wardrobe, underneath the jumpers, where it had stayed hidden for so long, until I carelessly left it in a bottom drawer the other week. Anyway, Leah is tall enough to reach up there now. And anyway again, she's already rummaged through the box; this is bolting the stable door way too late.

I tip the box out on to the bed. There isn't much. I only have a few secrets. The first thing I pick up is my copy of the tna'im, the document detailing the engagement between Nathan and me. Why I've kept it, I don't know. I don't imagine Nathan kept his. Folded up inside it is a red paper napkin. Poor Nathan. I shake my head, it doesn't do to dwell too long on the massive mess I made of his life. Not once, but twice.

And here's the main item of interest, to me anyway. The Re-education book, which Alex filled in for me when we first married – lists of things he liked and wanted to share, things he wanted to do with me, or – blush – *to* me. Things he loved about me. I expect Leah didn't even look at this when she was feverishly searching for proof of my hidden past; ironically she would have found out a lot more about me from this than anything else in the box.

Finally, I turn my attention to the fake wedding photo. A couple in their finery, standing under a cherry tree. A couple who never, in reality, stood together like that, under any kind of tree. If Leah had looked at the photo properly, she would have seen that the bride who has my face does not have my body. She is bigger in the bosom than I am, and considerably shorter. In real life Nathan and I were – still are, I suppose, unless one of us has shrunk – exactly the same height. In the photo I am a good three inches shorter than him. The person who Photoshopped the picture wasn't concerned about accuracy. I hesitate, then tear the photo up into tiny pieces. It was made for good reasons, and it served its purpose, but I shouldn't have kept it. Then I rip up the tna'im, and the red napkin from the kosher restaurant Nathan took me to. Stupid, sentimental fool to keep a serviette.

I lie on the bed, worn out by guilt. I wonder how Leah is coping with shul. If you haven't grown up with it, it might come as a shock. Leah won't like being ushered upstairs with the women. She will think it sexist. She won't be able to follow the service as she doesn't understand Hebrew. Anyway, up in the gallery you can barely hear what's going on downstairs; not only are the acoustics terrible, but the women tend to chatter through the entire thing. I try and put myself in her head, but I can't imagine what she's thinking. She is unknown to me, as unknown as a stranger.

Did my mother feel the same about me?

When Leah was younger, say about ten, when she was at her absolute peak of delightfulness, I'd say that I knew 99 per cent of her. She was open, talkative, confiding. She didn't have a phone then, to have furtive conversations on, nor email, Instagram, Snapchat or any of the many ways she maintains a private life. Now I probably know less than 50 per cent of what goes on with her. No, who am I kidding? I probably know less than 5 per cent. I'd blame the phone, but I managed to be just as secretive when I was young, without one. I was a bit older than her, sure, but by the time I was in my late teens there was very little my parents knew about what went on in my head. And by the time I ran away with Alex, at twenty-three, they were as surprised as if it turned out that I was an alien.

The front door slams and Alex calls my name.

'Up here!'

He bounds into the room, full of post-gym vigour, and jumps on to the bed next to me. 'She made it in time, did she?'

'Just about. It was so weird, watching her walk down the road with them.'

'Are you OK?'

I nod. I'm not sure that I am OK, actually. I don't know.

'I ripped up the fake photo,' I tell him.

He looks at his watch. 'Well done, you're only, let me see, oh yes, fifteen years too late.'

'I'm sorry, Alex.'

He rolls on to his side and puts his arms around me. 'I know. And I know that you really don't want her to do this. You're right, though. It's the only way to make it blow over quickly.'

'I think she fancies Gidon.'

'Isn't he a bit young? Anyway, I thought she fancied Ethan. Does she only like boys whose names end in an "n"?'

'She watched a film with Ethan last weekend, but as soon as it was finished she sent him packing.'

'Poor Ethan. Girls were just as cruel to me at that age.'

'I can't believe that. I seem to remember a certain chap boasting about his many conquests.'

'Oh yeah? I seem to remember a certain woman insisting on an actual written list of my former girlfriends.'

'I think I was a bit insecure.' I grin, and say, 'Ay-ay-ay-ay!' This, the sound my mother made when we ran away together, used to mean, 'I left my whole family for you.' But over the years, it has morphed into something more: a checking-in of how far we've come. It reminds us of the difficulties we dealt with in the early years of our marriage, and of the ties that bind me to my past, as well as the ties that bind me to Alex and Leah.

He strokes my cheek, which stirs me; it is often the prelude to love-making. But before I can make my move (stroke *his* cheek), he says, 'It's me who is insecure these days.'

'Are you? Why?' I stroke his cheek now, and he makes his next move – stroking the back of my neck with his fingertips, which used to send me almost crazy.

'I don't know. This stuff that Leah is raking up, I thought it was dead and buried.'

I run my hand down his arm. 'It is. I never think of it any more.'

'But you kept the photo.' He smooths my hair off my face. 'You must have had some reason for that.'

I jump ahead three moves and put my hand on his crotch. 'I wish I hadn't kept it. You're reading way more into it than there is.'

He puts his hand on my breast, the point of no return, and I think at last, now I can relax. I untie the lace of his jogging trousers and slip my hand inside, down into the sweaty depths. He whispers, 'What did happen when you went back? Between you and Nathan?'

'Nothing. You know that.' I close my hand round his penis. Unusually, it is still soft and small, warm as a mouse. I gently coax it, but it doesn't stir. He takes his hand off my breast.

'Actually, shouldn't you be thinking about collecting Leah soon?'

'There's no rush, she can go back with the cousins and have lunch there.'

Alex sits up. 'I need a shower,' he says. 'Do you want lunch before you get Leah?'

'I'm not hungry,' I say, but the truth is, I don't know how I feel.

*

When I get to Dov's, Leah opens the door and hisses under her breath, 'Where have you been? I want to go *now*, OK?'

Dov comes into the hall. 'Hey, Aliza, want lunch? We've got platzels and chopped liver…'

Everyone is offering me food. Leah makes a face at me that says, don't you *dare* think about staying. I take her subtle hint. 'Ah that's sweet, Dov, but we've got to get back. Have you got your coat, Leah? Say thanks to Uncle Dov for taking you.'

'Thank you, Uncle Dov,' Leah says in a robot's voice.

Gidon comes out into the hall and barges up to us. 'You coming again next week, Leah?'

She looks at the floor and says, 'Maybe.' She seems to edge away from him. Has Gidon overstepped the mark with her? He might have; I've never met a more sexually confident kid. He's punching above his weight with Leah and he doesn't even realise.

Leah strides ahead of me up the street. 'Where's the fucking car?'

Luckily I've managed to park a bit nearer this time. She slams into the passenger seat and folds her arms.

'Didn't go too well, huh, sweetie?' I start the car and edge into traffic. I must try not to show how thrilled I am.

'It was good.'

'Was it?'

'I liked it. I'm going to go again.'

'You didn't mind being upstairs with the women?'

'No.'

'Could you understand what was going on?'

'Mmm.'

'Well, great.' Damn. 'But you seem a bit out of sorts. Is everything OK?'

She doesn't answer, turns her head away from me and looks out of the window. We drive in silence for a bit, while I get up the nerve to ask her about Gidon. Then I'll have to talk to Dov. Am I going to have to kill Gidon?

'Were you hanging out with all of the cousins, or just Chanah?'

'All.'

'I suppose Gidon is the closest to you in age.'

'Mmm.'

'Do you like him?'

'He's a twat.'

There, I knew it! I knew he'd done something. 'Why do you say that?'

She starts tapping on her phone. 'Can you drop me at Macy's?'

'Sure, if it's OK with her parents. So, er, did Gidon do something?'

'No.' Tap tap tap.

'Did he say something, then?'

'Mum, I am trying to send a fucking message, OK?'

'There's no need for that.'

'You're going on and on.'

I pull into Macy's street, and Leah almost jumps out before I stop the car. I screech to a halt. 'For god's sake, Leah!'

'Mum, just drop me, OK?'

'I'm going to see you to the door, I need to check what time Macy's mum wants me to collect you.'

'I'm not five! I can walk home or get the bus.'

'Not if it's getting late…' but she has already gone. Muttering dark words, I double-park – this has been the Day of Lousy Parking – and follow her up the path. Macy has opened the front door and is laughing at Leah's clothes.

'Nice look, Leah, didn't know hemlines were long again.'

'Hi, Macy,' I say. 'Can you get your mum for me?'

Both girls roll their eyes but Macy slopes off upstairs, calling lazily for her mother. I grab Leah's arm. 'Leah, please, I'm worried about what Gidon said. Did he say something, er, rude?'

'Get off! You are the most embarrassing person I have ever met. In. My. Life.' She shakes her arm but she is a complete wimp, and I cling on.

'I just want you to tell me if he said anything inappropriate.'

She stops wriggling and looks me straight in the eye, a familiar coolness on her face. 'Yes,' she says, 'he did say something *inappropriate*.'

'I knew it! Are you OK, darling?'

Macy's mother Adina is coming down the stairs, Macy trailing behind her. Leah twists out of my grip with unexpected force, and says under her breath, 'He said Dad isn't my dad.'

'He said *what*?'

Leah grabs Macy's hand and pulls her upstairs.

'Leah, come back here!' I yell, uselessly.

Adina smiles at me. 'Everything OK?'

'Yes, fine. She just said something…' I must get a grip. 'Please can you send her back by five?'

'Oh! But I thought she was staying for a sleepover, that's what she and Macy have arranged.'

The little swine!

'She doesn't have any of her things...' I say, knowing I've been outmanoeuvred by my daughter.

'Oh, we've got spare everything. Toothbrush, pants, pyjamas. We'll drop her at yours tomorrow morning. Macy's had such a lousy week at school with that awful Mrs Bedford, she's really got it in for her. I'm so glad for her to spend time with Leah and put it out of her mind.'

I know when I'm beat. I thank Adina, get into the car, hold on to the steering wheel, and burst into tears.

Eliza's list of food for Alex

- Proper chicken soup with kneidlach (these are white dumplings). No one makes this like my mum, but I will give it a try. Can you get kosher boiling fowls in Brixton??
- Matzo-brei. This is a Pesach (Passover) breakfast dish, a kind of omelette made with matzo crackers. The only thing my dad ever cooked. Stodgy and comforting.
- Chopped liver on bagels.
- Onion platzels (Zaida's favourite).
- Salt-beef.
- Pickled herring.
- Gefilte fish, an acquired taste. Lots of Jews don't like it.
- Honey cake.
- Roast lamb and roast potatoes. Not a traditional Jewish dish; I just really like it.

Chapter Fourteen

Spring 2000

'The best bacon sandwich in London,' Alex said – information which I hitherto had no interest in, and actually still didn't – 'is at Kev's Cabin.'

We were finally at the last, and worst, item on the food list.

But I'm getting ahead of myself.

Following the success of the cheeseburger, we worked our way through Alex's other lists. We spent nights cuddled together on the sofa watching films: *Citizen Kane, The Wizard of Oz, Chinatown*, and *Singin' in the Rain* (my favourite). We both sobbed through *Bambi*, though I felt my eyelash resemblance to the little fawn had been rather overstated. And I enjoyed *Snow White*, and was amused by Alex referring to me as Snow White afterwards. She ended up with a typical Orthodox family, Alex said, loads of kids, wife does all the housework.

London was our playground. We went to art galleries, museums, and the theatre. I tried my first gin and tonic in Alex's favourite café, the Roundhouse, and it became my favourite place too, for Marlene, the motherly waitress, and the cappuccinos (I didn't think much of their gin and tonics, though). We visited a theme park and I went on a rollercoaster and absolutely loved it, screaming as we hurtled down from a great height as though we were about to die. We tried out a few items on the 'sexy things' list, and I screamed as we hurtled down from a great height there, too.

We also worked on non-list parts of my life; specifically about me going back to work. It turned out I'd need further training to be a teacher in a secular school, but they said I could be a TA, a teaching assistant. Alex helped with my applications and I was taken on by a small primary school up the road, part-time, to start after Easter.

It all felt exciting and positive, and it wasn't until we had our first proper argument, over sushi, that I started to question the choice I'd made.

I'd never even heard of sushi, till Alex mentioned it. He said it was quite new in Britain, but now there were Japanese restaurants springing up everywhere. In March we went to a place with exclamation marks in its name, the food trundling round a little train track. I was nervous initially of taking a plate off the track in case I dropped it, or caught my hair in the rails and got dragged round the restaurant against my will. But seeing that some young children near us could manage it unscathed, I tried it. Funny-looking food, it was, a tiny sliver of raw fish on a spoonful of rice, not enough to feed a canary, and 'California rolls', also rice, wrapped in an unpleasant-looking black casing. I could hear Deborah laughing at the tiny, ugly portions. The raw salmon actually tasted quite nice, and was not much different from smoked salmon. I avoided any prohibited seafood such as shrimp and eel.

The only unpleasant incident – until the argument – was when I mistook wasabi for avocado and put a large spoonful into my mouth.

I spat most of it into a napkin but it was several minutes before my eyes stopped watering. Alex kindly didn't laugh, but fussed round with water and tissues to dab my eyes with.

When I'd recovered I tasted the miso soup Alex had ordered, which he claimed was 'like chicken soup'.

'This is literally nothing like chicken soup,' I told him, 'other than it being soup.'

'Isn't it? It's salty, and tangy.'

'Give me that book!'

He'd brought the Re-education book with us so he could tick sushi off. I grabbed it and made a new list in the back, of the foods I'd grown up with that he had to try, chicken soup at the top. But he read it and said, 'Tick, tick, tick. Done 'em.'

'No, you haven't.'

'Well, except gefilte fish. I've seen it, though. Josh had it at his wedding. It smelled gross.'

Josh was Alex's token Jewish friend (apart from me). They'd shared a flat at university, and even though Josh's Reform, watered-down version was as similar to my Judaism as it was to Hinduism, he was regularly wheeled out as an arbiter of Jewish culture. On the one hand, I was grateful to Josh. It was because of him that Alex knew more about Jewish things than the average person. But on the other hand, I was getting tired of hearing about Josh, who luckily now lived a long way away in New York, and who often got things wrong.

'OK, but you can't have had matzo-brei,' I said. 'Unless Josh cooked it for you. It's not a restaurant dish, or a wedding food. It's home food, comfort food. It's matzo crackers, fried with egg.'

Alex looked sheepish, and I expected him to say that he hadn't, of course, eaten this, but instead he said, 'Did I ever mention Rachel, my ex?'

I gazed at the food trundling past us on the track, round and round. 'No,' I said. 'You only mentioned Emily.' Sexy Emily. 'On the rag' Emily. I followed the progress of one plate in particular, a blue one containing what looked like an orange spider on a lump of rice. Surely no one would pick that up?

'Rachel was Jewish,' Alex said. 'Still is, I guess. I haven't seen her for years. We lived together when I was in my early twenties.'

All the plates were different colours. Green, blue, pink and white. I realised that the different colours meant different prices. There was a chart on the wall behind us explaining this. Pink was the dearest. We hadn't had any of those. I wondered what was on a pink plate that made it so special; the food looked no different from the others.

'Rachel made matzo-brei for me one Passover,' Alex said.

I tried to calculate what our six blue dishes and four green ones would add up to. What was six times £2.80, added to four times £3.40?

'Your silence is unnerving me. Please say something, Eliza!'

She made it one Passover? How many Passovers were there? Did you say you were living together?

'I didn't know you had a Jewish girlfriend,' I said. The blue spider-plate came back past, and I picked it up off the conveyor belt so no one would have to eat it. 'I didn't know you lived with someone.'

'God, it was ages ago. I just hadn't got round to mentioning it yet. There's still quite a lot we don't know about each other.'

'No, there isn't, Alex.' He looked at me, his expression anxious, the quotation marks visible between his eyes. 'There's a lot that I don't know about you. But you know pretty much everything about me. There is, after all, very little to know.'

I opened the culture notebook and showed him how many pages he had filled in for me: lots. Then I showed him mine: a page on Jewish customs and festivals, a list of my siblings to help him remember them, and half a page of foods I wanted to introduce him to. Foods he'd already had, anyway, with Josh. And Rachel.

'That's not true, Eliza. You are large and contain multitudes.' He went to put his arms round me, and I moved away. 'You don't like me quoting Walt Whitman?'

'I don't like you doing *that*.'

'Hugging you?'

'Hugging me in public.'

How could he not know by now that public displays of affection made me uncomfortable? Maybe he was right; maybe he *didn't* know that much about me. Not facts and figures and lists, but feelings. Did he think it took just a few months to change your personality so much that you were ready to be groped in a Japanese restaurant?

'Have you had enough food?' Alex asked. 'I'm done. This stuff is small but it's high protein.'

'Where did you live with Rachel?'

'Oh.' He became very busy inspecting the food on the tracks. He picked up a pink plate, then put it back down. 'In, er, in our flat.'

'The flat we live in now?'

'Yes. I, er, well, I bought it with her in 1993, and when we split up I bought her out.'

'You chose it together?'

'Uh, yes. I'm sorry. I was going to tell you.'

'It would have been nice to know I was living in someone else's flat.'

'Hey, Snow White,' he said, touching my arm, 'this isn't like you.'

I shook him off. 'Perhaps you don't know what I'm like,' I said, the heat rising in my face. 'For instance, you still don't seem to know that I don't like being touched when I'm bleeding.'

'I didn't know you were bleeding.'

'I *told* you. It started this morning.' As I said it, I realised I hadn't actually told him – only planned the words I'd use to explain why I wasn't ready to share a bed yet while bleeding.

'Ooh, you know what that means?' Alex said, his eyes brightening. 'This is the third one of our marriage, and you said we could share a bed this time…'

'I didn't say that, Alex! I said three or four months, maybe more. When I've got used to the idea of touching you while bleeding.'

He rolled his eyes. 'Can't you call it your period? Every time you say you're bleeding I'm ready to call an ambulance.'

'It's bad enough I can't go to the mikvah any more, without you trampling all over my feelings.'

'I thought you did your cleaning rituals in the bath. You're certainly in there long enough.'

'It's not the same! For a start, I can barely get the whole of me under the water. It's not exactly a big bath.'

'Is the secret to our married happiness for me to buy you a bigger bath?'

'Well, it would be nice not to have to use *Rachel's* bath.' The words were out before I could stop them.

We looked at each other. Then he shook his head. 'Well, you're not going to like this, but I might as well put everything on the table now, while you're already pissed off with me. It's not really Rachel's bath; the last woman who owned it before you was called Helena.'

'Who's Helena?' My voice was more of a screech than usual.

'My girlfriend after Rachel. The one before you.'

'And she lived in our flat with you too?'

'Yes. Look, I know it sounds awful.'

The weird food sat heavy in my stomach. 'Can we get the bill? Can we just go, please?'

He signalled to the waitress. 'But look, Eliza, I'm thirty years old. This number of partners isn't unusual, in the Real World.'

'Really? Because I feel like I'm married to some kind of International Playboy.'

'I come with baggage. I'm sorry, there's nothing I can do to change it.'

'I'm sorry too, that I am so hilariously unencumbered by baggage.'

I realised that I didn't know, after all, what the secret to our married happiness was. A bigger bath wasn't going to do it. In the story of Snow White, she fell in love, got married and lived happily ever after. But after only a few months, my list of dissatisfactions was growing. It wasn't a list to write down in Alex's book, but it was a list, all the same.

The waitress put the bill down, just as Alex said, 'Eliza, you are the one I love.' He didn't care that the waitress lingered, listening. 'You're the one I waited for. You're the one I want to be with for the rest of my life.'

'I don't know what you see in me. I have no experience. I have nothing.'

Alex put his arms round me, and though this made me feel tense, I didn't protest. He whispered lovely things until I stopped feeling sorry for myself. I apologised, told him I was probably feeling lousy because of bleeding, sorry, because of my period. And because I still hadn't heard from anyone, despite my letters to Deborah, and Dov, and Mum. I didn't tell Alex I'd even written to Dad, asking for forgiveness, which showed how crazy I was. Was Zaida missing me? Was Mum crying for me? Would Dov, or any of my other brothers and sisters ever forgive me?

'I'm sorry, too, Eliza,' Alex said, releasing me at last. 'I promise I'll try gefilte fish, and I'll tell you all about my ex-girlfriends, none of whom, I hardly need to say, should cause you a moment's concern.'

'Why don't you write them down in chronological order,' I joked, handing him his culture book.

He took me seriously. 'Blimey,' he said, picking up a pen, 'this'll take a while.'

April, and we arrived at curry. Homemade curry was best, Alex announced, and no one made it better than his brother. So for the first time since January, I had to see Vicky again. Kim had visited us a few times on his own, which was lovely, but after the way Vicky had been at our wedding, I'd managed to make it clear to Alex, without spelling it out, that I'd rather not spend time with her if I didn't have to. Oh yes, my dear Hus Band might think of me as a naïve and sheltered girl from the backwaters of Lithuania-in-Hackney, but I could spot a predatory woman a mile off. Was Vicky the same when Alex was with Rachel, I wondered? Or Emily? Or Helena, or Joanne – either of the Joannes? Or Nina, or any of the others on Alex's shockingly long list of ex-girlfriends?

In the interests of harmony, I put on a show of enthusiastic agreement about seeing Vicky and Kim. I guess this was what Mum meant when she told me that marriage was made up of endless compromises. Mind you, one of the times I remember her saying that was shortly after Dad had smacked her across the room. Young as I was, I didn't feel that compromise was quite the right word.

So I was back at Vicky's house for the first time since that awful Christmas dinner. While she poured drinks and fluttered her eyelashes at Alex, Kim beckoned me into the kitchen. He closed the door behind us and whispered conspiratorially, 'I wanted to let you know that the lamb is kosher.'

'Seriously, Kim? That's amazing! But how come?'

'I bought it in Golders Green. Blimey, kosher meat's not cheap, is it?'

'No,' I laughed. 'But why did you?'

'Look, I know what my brother's like. He gets these ideas. I think you're very patient with his little education programme, but personally, I think mixing meat and milk is enough of a rule to break at a time.'

'Oh, Kim. You *are* wonderful.'

I didn't tell him I'd already leaped across the meat and milk barrier with the Valentine's Day cheeseburger. I was so grateful for him considering my feelings and going to effort and expense for me that I could cry. Instead, I did something I'd never done before, something that wasn't on the 'New Experiences' list, but should have been: I put my arms round a man who was not my husband or a blood relation. Kim wasn't to know that this was even more of a departure for me than eating un-kosher lamb. He hugged me tightly back, and when I moved out of his embrace I saw something fleeting on his face that made me blush up to my hairline. The bit of his face I could see between the beard and the glasses was red too, as red as my own. We smiled awkwardly at each other. I hoped I didn't look like some kind of bored married floozy in my short blue skirt and short-sleeved shirt. Then Vicky came in, giggling and clinging on to Alex's arm, and I realised I was *not* the married floozy in the house. She was wearing a sheer blouse with six buttons, few of which were done up. Her skirt was half the length of mine. How I longed to be able to turn and wink at Deborah, who would whisper something cheeky in my ear.

Vicky gave me one of her fake smiles. 'You two look like you've been snogging. Caught ya! Nice to see her arms for once, isn't it, Kim?'

Alex jumped in quickly. 'Vicky's been telling me your brilliant news, Kim,' he said, hugging him. 'A little brother or sister for Holly! Congratulations, man.'

Kim said, 'I thought we weren't telling anyone yet, Vicky.' To me, he said, 'It's early days.'

'Family, innit?' Vicky waggled her bosom in Alex's direction. 'Anyway, I thought it might give these two ideas. Not getting any younger, are you, Ally-boy? You're going to want to get on with it.'

'We're still in the honeymoon stage,' Alex said, slipping his arm round my waist, making me jump. 'But it really is wonderful news.'

'Not that wonderful getting all fat again, though, is it, when I've only just lost the baby weight from last time?' Vicky stroked her flat stomach with a superior smile. 'You won't fancy me any more in a few months when I'm blown up, Ally. I told him, Kim, get your dirty hands off me, but he can't help himself.'

I could feel myself smiling stiffly. I deliberately avoided Kim's eye; I didn't want to see him looking embarrassed.

The curry was lovely. You couldn't tell there was yoghurt in it at all, you could just taste the melt-in-the-mouth lamb. Alex asked if the meat was organic, and Kim and I exchanged another smile, not so awkward this time. Vicky drank a great deal of wine, and somehow there seemed to be even more undone buttons on her blouse. She turned her whole body towards Alex when she talked to him, behaving as if Kim and I weren't in the room.

Alex got us out of there as quickly as he decently could; I didn't even need to say anything. I hadn't completely finished eating my dessert (sorbet) when he looked at his watch and said, 'God, sorry, Kimbo, we've got a thing, we had better run.'

Kim knew, I think, but Vicky seemed surprised. 'You've hardly been here a minute!'

'Didn't realise how late it was,' Alex said, helping me into my coat. 'Superb curry, Kim, your best ever.'

We gabbled our thanks and dashed out to the tube, giggling like conspirators all the way back to the flat.

I was hoping to leave plenty of time before seeing Vicky again, ideally years, but in fact the next time was only a week later. It was another important day in the Real World calendar, Easter Sunday, and it was apparently 'our turn' because Kim and Vicky had hosted the excruciating Christmas dinner. Actually it wasn't too bad. Sheila seemed delighted to see me and kissed me on the cheek. I noticed she didn't kiss Vicky, just patted her shoulder. Thankfully, Vicky was distracted by baby Holly, who was being clingy, leaving her too preoccupied to do much more than stroke Alex's arm a couple of times.

Alex made roast lamb and roast potatoes, because I'd put it on my food list. It was completely delicious, though of course it did make me think about the time my father threw a whole plate of roast lamb in the bin.

'It's our first Easter with Eliza,' Alex said at the end of the meal, as we all groaningly pushed half-finished plates of Sheila's apple pie away ('I used marge instead of butter so you can have it without mixing meat and milk,' Sheila told me proudly, though her efforts were undermined by Vicky dropping a large spoonful of ice-cream on to my plate without asking).

'As you all know, ever since Kimbo and I left home, we've had a tradition of getting together with Mum on Easter Sunday,' Alex continued.

'And whichever girl you were shagging at the time, Ally-Boy!' Vicky shouted. Holly had fallen asleep so she was back in full flow.

'Thank you, Vicky,' Sheila said.

'But now I'm married to the beautiful, wonderful Eliza,' Alex said, frowning at Vicky, 'I'd like to add a new tradition. And that is,' and he stood up, and cleared his throat, 'singing "Tradition".'

Kim clapped and whooped, then turned to me and said, 'He can't sing, you know.'

'I know,' I said.

'Eliza will join in, she has a lovely voice,' Alex said. He started blasting out, 'Tradition! Tradition! Come on, Eliza!'

I looked at him helplessly. 'I don't know it, I'm sorry.'

'You don't know *Fiddler on the Roof*?'

'It wasn't really a thing in my family. I've heard of it, but never seen it. I'm sorry.'

'I know it,' Kim said, and broke noisily into what I later learned was 'If I Were a Rich Man'.

Alex joined in and while it was certainly true that neither brother could hold a tune, and their grasp of the words was shaky at best, I was utterly charmed that they were trying to make me feel included. Vicky sat with her fingers in her ears, and Sheila and I hummed along, and the whole thing was considerably more enjoyable than Christmas. But it was impossible not to think about my family sitting down just a few nights earlier for the Seder, the Passover meal, the Jewish foundation of Easter, the meal that is depicted in the Last Supper. Sitting down without me for the first time in twenty-three years, and Gila singing the *Mah Nishtanah – Why is this night different from all other nights?* without me there to hear it. It was always the youngest who sang it. I smiled, thinking of how delighted Dov was the year he handed that baton over to Gila. Alex caught my eye and smiled at me, thrilled at how assimilated I was becoming.

Why was this night different from all other nights? Because I was sitting here with people who I didn't really know. They were kind (apart from Vicky), and welcoming (apart from Vicky), and singing, if you could call it that, but they weren't my people.

My cultural apprenticeship continued. We watched more films, and a lot of TV (I became addicted to *Frasier*), and in May we visited the Tate Modern Gallery which had not long been open. That same month I started my new job at the school, working alongside the Year Three teacher, a kind young woman called Genevieve. Her class – our class – were a gorgeous bunch of funny, sweet little kids, all springy plaits and cheeky smiles. They called me 'Missus Symons' and tugged at my hand to show me their work, and though I was pretty much the only white person in the room, for the first time in a long while, I felt as though I fitted right in.

To celebrate the start of my job, Alex cooked rare steak, the next item on his food list. Well, I say cooked, but the steak didn't appear to have been anywhere near an oven. I put my knife into it, blood oozed out, and I had to leave the room until Alex removed it from my sight. He suggested we skip oysters for now (perhaps mindful of the expense if I reacted similarly), and next time I was ready, go straight for the big one, the bacon sandwich. And I agreed because I wanted the whole thing over.

Now it was June, and we'd been married for six months. We watched tennis on TV which seemed to go on for ever, and listened to five episodes of a not-very funny comedy on the radio that Alex liked.

Though I couldn't pinpoint the exact date at which the novelty of being someone's education project started to wear off, it was around the same time I finally heard from Deborah.

I'd slowed down my letters to her, sending one a fortnight rather than every week. After six months of silence I'd given up on hearing back, and was now writing more as a kind of diary than in expectation of a reply. So when we got back from our disastrous bacon sandwich trip and her letter was waiting for me, it made the day seem even more surreal.

It was 21 June, the longest day of the year. The sort of summer's day when it gets progressively hotter rather than cooling down towards evening. Alex and I met in town after work, and made our way to Ilford on a hot and steamy train. There was something attractively vibrant about the town, with fruit and flower stalls on the pavements, bustling women in saris and hijabs, gaggles of teenage girls toting shopping bags, Asian men smoking on every corner, all backdropped by the heavy, squinting early-evening sunshine. The bustle of the place reminded me of home. There was even a kosher deli. We wandered up one of the side streets off the main road, and the terraced houses were neat as pins, every door painted a different, bright colour. I could live here, I thought. Somewhere new, somewhere that didn't belong to Rachel and Helena.

Then Alex steered me into Kev's Cabin, plunging us into a hell's kitchen dense with the aroma of frying, sizzling pig. The small café was heaving with people, and we had to share a table with two large men, lorry drivers Alex reckoned later. Their heads were bent low over massive plates of sausages, bacon, chips, eggs, and tomatoes and a disgusting-looking object Alex reluctantly told me was black pudding, made from blood. The men nodded at us and kept shovelling in the food, their faces pouring with sweat.

Alex ordered two bacon sandwiches, and sat there with a smug look on his face. Look at me, it seemed to say, I'm getting the Jew to eat bacon. For the first time I wondered about his motivation. Perhaps he was secretly a member of the BNP, watering Jews down, one by one. Maybe Rachel had started out religious, too.

The sandwiches were plonked in front of us, and I swallowed down the sudden rush of bile that flooded my mouth. The bacon sandwich looked nothing like the benign one of my imagination: a thin layer of bacon almost hidden between two thin slices of white bread. The reality of the one on my plate was several layers of piled up meat, barely contained between two thick doorsteps of buttery bread – meat and milk again, on top of everything else!

The joke was that Jews were meant to love the smell of bacon, and still reject it. But I couldn't even stand the smell: cheap, smoky and fatty, it caught the back of my throat.

I shook my head.

'Seriously?' Alex said, two bites into his. He glanced at the lorry drivers, and said in an undertone, 'At least try the sodding thing now we've schlepped all this way.' Given the circumstances, I admired his chutzpah in using Yiddish.

I slowly raised the sandwich to my mouth, Alex watching, an anxious expression now replacing the smug. Jews were allowed to eat pig if they would otherwise die of starvation, I reminded myself. I tried to pretend this sandwich was all that stood between me and death. It wasn't actually all that much of a stretch to imagine I was dying. I'd already been conscious of how hot I was, how hot it was in the café. But now I could feel sweat actually running down my back, and coating my forehead. As the sandwich touched my lips, three thousand years of prohibition came rattling up from my stomach, and I was a bit sick on to the plate. Even as it was happening I knew that I was a ridiculous cliché, the Jew who was terrified of dead pig. But I couldn't help it.

'Christ on a bike,' one of the men said.

The other said, 'You OK, love?'

'She's fine,' Alex said, pushing back his chair. He chucked some money on the table, leaving the remains of his own sandwich, and wordlessly steered me out of the café at speed. We walked back to the station in silence. Though it had gone eight o'clock it was still light, and it crossed my mind with horror that the day might never end.

'I'm sorry,' I said, as we sat on the train.

'It's my fault,' he said. But he didn't look like he thought it was.

The letter was waiting for me on the mat. It was pretty much the first letter I'd had in seven months, other than from my new bank. I saw at once that it was from Deborah. I snatched it up, shut myself in the bathroom and read it.

19 June 2000

Dear Goy Girl

Wow, that's a lot of letters. I thought you might have stopped by now.

Sorry for not replying, but I've been furious. You got that right. First I was furious because you made everyone so upset. What a massive mess you left behind. Remind me to tell you the full story some time. I'll give you one of the highlights: your father throwing a whole platter of bridge rolls across the living room and pretty much redecorating the wall in egg mayonnaise.

Next I was furious because Michael got it into his head that I also might want to bugger off to find my own Goy Boy, because,

I don't know, all the cool girls were doing it this month. It took a hell of a lot of persuading him otherwise, and I'm still not sure he's completely relaxed about it, so thanks for that.

Then recently I popped in to see your mum, and I missed you. It felt so weird you not being there. It didn't help that she kept crying. She made me cry too. She knows you've been writing to them all, by the way, but as you probably guessed, your dad gets up specially early every morning to make sure he gets to the post first – it's his new hobby – and if a letter comes from you, your mum says he makes a rather dramatic bonfire of it in the kitchen sink. She showed me the scorch marks. Did it not occur to you that he would recognise your writing?

If you have *to write, you can write to them care of me. And I must love you a lot, because you know how much doo-doo I'll be in if your dad finds out. Not to mention Michael, who really will think I have something to hide if he sees me with a stack of secret letters.*

To answer your questions, your mum is sad. Dov isn't angry with you, he would never be, but he misses you hugely, all the time. They all do, well maybe not your dad, but everyone else. And surely you don't really want to know the answer to 'Is Nathan OK?' No, you crazy person, you meshuggener, he is very much not OK. He's moved to Gateshead to live at the yeshiva, till he works out what to do with the rest of his life. He loved you, did you know that? I know he wasn't a love-at-first-sight guy for you, but I think you could have made a go of it.

Anyway, what prompted me to write is that I'm sorry to tell you that your Zaida isn't too well. He had a funny turn a few weeks ago on his way back from the cemetery (visiting your Booba). He kind of forgot what he was doing, and he isn't allowed to drive any more. No one was hurt, luckily, but there's a bollard in Filey Avenue that will never be the same again.

Write soon, Goy Girl. Can you get hold of email? I expect you've got one now you're out in the big wide world, probably got yourself a fancy little mobile phone and everything modern. Michael sometimes logs on to my email, so I've set up a new address just for you: myfriendmarriedagoy@hotmail.com

D

There was too much in this letter to process straight away. The bit that hit me right between the eyes was that my Zaida was ill and I wasn't there. And all the burgers and films in the world seemed utterly unimportant, right now, compared to that.

Chapter Fifteen

Summer 2000

From: elizasymons@hotmail.com

To: myfriendmarriedagoy@hotmail.com

22 June

Hey Furious Best Friend, you have no idea how happy I was to hear from you. Thanks for offering to pass my letters on, despite your fury. I posted you three this morning, for Mum, Zaida and Dov. I know I'm asking you to be sneaky around my dad and I'm sorry about that. But as you know, my parents' house is not exactly an easy place to keep secrets in. How is Zaida now? Thanks again for being in touch. Alex set me up this email this morning.

Aliza x

From: myfriendmarriedagoy@hotmail.com

To: elizasymons@hotmail.com

25 June

What's that you say, Goy Girl? Not the easiest place to keep secrets in?! You seemed to manage it well enough when you ran off with a complete stranger on your wedding day and none of us saw it coming.

Beloved grandfather is doing OK, I think. Haven't seen any of your lot for a week or so. Cool new surname you've got yourself there, Mrs Shiksa Symons, and what's with the fancy new English first name? Can't they spell it right out in the Real World?

FBF (which stands for Furious Best Friend but also Former Best Friend)

From: elizasymons@hotmail.com
To: myfriendmarriedagoy@hotmail.com
25 June

I didn't keep any secrets from you, FBF (I prefer the first meaning). You knew I'd met Alex, and you knew I fell in love with him.

Aliza (Goy Girl, sometimes known as Eliza) x

From: myfriendmarriedagoy
To: elizasymons
26 June

Yeah, but you didn't tell me you were going to MARRY him. I thought you were going to marry Nathan. We all did, or have you forgotten that? You stood at my front door and you told me it was over.

FBF

From: elizasymons
To: myfriendmarriedagoy
26 June

I didn't know myself that I was going to marry Alex, till I'd done it. All I knew that day, the day before really, is that I couldn't stop thinking about him, and when I thought about him I felt properly alive, and that meant I couldn't marry Nathan. Do you understand, even a little bit? As we're talking about it, tell me some more about what happened when I'd gone? Please?

Aliza x

PS It is one of the great joys of my life that we are back in touch, Deb. I don't even care that you're constantly nagging me. It's like old times.

From: myfriendmarriedagoy
To: elizasymons
28 June

It's not like old times, Goy Girl.

I don't understand it, no. Not a little bit, and not at all. Why couldn't you have broken things off with Nathan and waited for the next possible husband? Why did you have to shatter your entire family and friends just to make a point?

Anyway, I'm rushing – off to Llandudno tomorrow with Michael's family. Can't wait: a whole fortnight of fending off enquiries about why we still don't have any children. Fun. So I've only got time to tell you one thing. You know how people in the Torah are always rending their garments? That's what your dad did on Black Thursday, except it was your garment, not his. Shame, because it was a nice dress, wasn't it? Those pretty pearl buttons down the back, ivory lace. He ripped it into shreds, told everyone that you were now dead to him. Sure you want to know this stuff?

FBF x

PS I haven't been able to get to your mum's house to hand over the letters yet, sorry. I'll do it when we get back from Wales. No internet there, so this is my last one for a bit.

It was easy to imagine Deb in Llandudno, because when I was little, my family also went on holiday there. We stayed in a hotel right on the beach which catered for the modern Orthodox Jewish family, with kosher food and enormous family rooms filled with camp beds. Uri, Joel and I made sand cars that you could actually sit inside, and one time we collected hundreds of shells and stones and decorated the whole of the car's outside. It took us hours, sticking each shell into place, pressing it into the damp sand. When it was done, Joel and I sat in the car, Uri on the bonnet, and my father took a photo of us. That was, by some way, my happiest childhood memory. My father was as relaxed as I had ever seen him. He didn't shout once on that trip, as far as I remember. When we went back to the beach the next day, the car and the shell decorations had been washed away, but I don't remember being upset about it.

From: myfriendmarriedagoy
To: elizasymons
14 July

Aliza

Got back from Wales yesterday – it rained almost every day – and am quickly sending you this, because I just heard that your

Zaida accidentally set fire to the kitchen in his flat (he's OK, don't worry), and your parents have put him in a care home. I'll try and find out more.

Deb

From: elizasymons

To: myfriendmarriedagoy

14 July

I can't believe my parents would send him away. How could they? He will hate it.

From: myfriendmarriedagoy

To: elizasymons

14 July

Yes, well, sorry dear, but your parents AREN'T EXACTLY AT THEIR BEST RIGHT NOW, remember?

I apologised, and so did Deborah, and she promised to visit Mum and find out how Zaida was, and hand over my letters. I spent the next couple of days fretting about Zaida and wondering which home he might be in (I phoned a few to try to find out if he was there, before realising how many care homes there were in London). Deb must have acted quickly, because only a few days after I spoke to her, a letter arrived. From Dov. I almost snatched it out of Alex's hand as he gave it to me.

'Deborah again?' Alex asked. He knew she and I were back in touch, of course, as he had set up the email address for me to contact her.

'Yes.'

This was the first deliberate lie I'd told Alex since we met. But it was a white lie, to protect him. He'd feel pretty uncomfortable if he knew I was trying to renew contact with my family. He was very aware that they all blamed him for me leaving. Not long after we'd got together, he said, 'I guess your brothers would kill me if they could.'

'Well, Dov wouldn't,' I'd replied, which I guess wasn't entirely reassuring, as my three other brothers were all much scarier than Dov. Uri squaring up to him the day we ran away, was something Alex said still gave him nightmares.

'My family abide by the Ten Commandments, you know,' I said, trying to be more positive. 'Thou Shalt Not Kill.'

'I expect the Talmud has a host of sub-clauses on that one,' Alex said. 'Thou Shalt Not Kill Unless Thy Sister Has Been Taken Away By An Uncircumcised Stranger.'

I ripped open the envelope to Dov's letter. 'How come Deborah's gone back to old-fashioned letter writing?' Alex said. 'What happened to the emails?'

'There's something wrong with her computer,' I said. The second lie. I wanted him to go away so I could read my letter, but he hung around like washing on a line. 'I'll look at it later,' I said, putting it in my bag, and went upstairs, but he followed me, under cover of chatting about which film I wanted to watch tonight. Finally I said I was going to work. When he pointed out that it was one of my non-working days, I told him that a teaching assistant's work was never done, and that I'd promised to help with preparations for Sports Day. That at least was true, though I hadn't promised to help with it today. I walked briskly to the tube, and finally, when I was sitting on a train, I was able to open my letter in peace.

And if you asked me then, as Kim asked me months later, whether I felt as restricted by my marriage to Alex as I would have done in my marriage to Nathan? I might just have said yes.

Oh, the joy of seeing Dov's scruffy handwriting again. His letter was short and to the point.

18 July

Dear Aliza,

Can you visit Zaida? He's at Beis Israel care home in Hendon. I can go there on Tuesday 25 July. Meet me there at 10am.

Dov

PS Can you look like your old self?

No mention of our seven-month separation, but then Dov always was a laid-back chap. I analysed the letter as passengers came and went around me. Dov would have chosen a time for us to meet when he knew my parents wouldn't be there. The most intriguing thing was the request to 'look like my old self'. I wondered what he thought I looked like now. An assimilated secular woman, perhaps, with short hair and red lipstick, high-heeled shoes and a skirt barely covering my bottom, like Vicky.

I looked up and discovered we were pulling into Finsbury Park, meaning I was only one stop away from Seven Sisters. Too close for comfort. I jumped out and got on a train going back to Brixton. There were a couple of frum men in furry shtreimel hats standing on the platform but thankfully I didn't recognise them. Back at Brixton I bought a notepad and pack of envelopes in WH Smiths. I went into the post office, stood at the desk with the leaflets, and wrote Dov a quick reply, care of Deborah. On the way back to the flat I passed a mobile phone shop, and on impulse I went in and bought Dov a phone.

Alex was a morning person. While I struggled to get going, hating to leave the warmth of my bed, he would be up and bounding about. On Tuesday morning though, the day I was to visit Zaida, our roles were infuriatingly reversed. When I started to get out of bed, Alex tried to pull me back down, proposed that we make love. I said no, I wanted to get moving. He clearly couldn't believe it – his eyes actually widened in cartoonish surprise – and actually nor could I. I had never said no before, other than at bleeding times. And lately, not always then. But today, for the first time since we met, I did not find him completely irresistible.

He believed it all right when I shook him off and got up. When I got back from the shower he was still in bed, sitting up, his mouth a sulky pout.

'Do you not want just a little cuddle?' he said in his most winning tone.

'I don't want to make you late for work,' I said. I knew he was only being clingy because he sensed something was up. I don't know how he knew that, nor how I knew that he knew that. It was stalemate. It was layers of lies. In the blink of an eye, I was in the lying marriage I thought I had escaped. Maybe all marriages were like this, regardless of who you chose. Maybe all Hus Bands ended up the same.

I began to dress, my back to him. I couldn't put on my old frum clothes or he would really start to wonder what was up. I slipped them into a bag and put on Real World clothes. Alex finally got up, and I caught a glimpse of his face as he went out of the room. He looked sad, his expression reminding me of the way he looked when we used to meet secretly in the café, and he was never sure if he would see me again. Why didn't I just tell him about Zaida being in a home? About Dov writing to me? I couldn't explain why I didn't tell him; I just knew I didn't want to. I was painfully aware that it was the first crack in our marriage.

I went into the kitchen, where Alex was morosely eating toast.

'We've not been married a year, yet,' he said, 'and already you find me unattractive.'

Underneath the petulance I could see he was genuinely hurt. I had a choice, which was to try and make things better, or walk out and leave a mess. I thought of all the times my father had done that – yelled at Mum, or smashed something, or hit one or other of us, and then left, leaving us shell-shocked and miserable all day.

'I have to get to work soon,' I said. School had actually finished on Friday but I'd told Alex I had to help the teacher with some prepping for the September term. 'So why don't I give you a quick, er, you know' – I made a lascivious gesture with my tongue that felt stagily unnatural – 'and I can still make it in on time?'

Lust scudded across his face. This was the first time I had ever spontaneously offered to do this thing that he liked. I'd tried it once (it was on the 'sexy things' list), but seeing the look on my face afterwards, he hadn't mentioned it again.

We did it right there, in the kitchen. If I didn't have a lot on my mind I'd have felt pretty strange about pleasing him like that, me fully-dressed, the floor hard beneath my knees, him half-naked with his pants round his ankles. He clearly loved it and made wild noises, which excited me, though I knew it was wrong, that I was doing it for the wrong reasons. It was easier than the first time, but I still couldn't swallow the mess. I spat it into a tissue. He cracked the same joke he'd made the first time – 'Must get some of that kosher spunk, so you can swallow' – and then he hugged me tight and told me how gorgeous I was.

We were both slightly stunned by my behaviour, but I managed to push it to one side of my mind and focused on getting out of the house. At the Brixton tube loos I changed into my long skirt, long-sleeved blouse and old sensible shoes. They looked like familiar friends, but once on, they felt more restrictive than I remembered. It was going to be another hot day. I tied my hair up neatly and put a scarf over it. Then I got the tube to Hendon.

I'd learned from the internet that Beis Israel was a small care home for religious Jews. It was a smart-looking building, set back from the road, with a pretty garden in front. I hoped Zaida was happy here, but even more, I hoped it was a temporary thing, until the annex was repaired.

As I walked up the path I saw a man sitting on a bench by a honeysuckle bush. As he stood up and moved towards me, I realised it was Dov. When did he become an adult? We threw our arms round each other and I began to sob, the pent-up strain of the last few months pouring out. He whispered comforting words until at last I spluttered to a stop.

'I'm sorry,' I said.

'What for?'

'Everything.'

'Oh, just everything?' I felt him shake his head against my shoulder. 'Don't worry about it if *that's* all it is.'

We broke apart, and sat on the bench. I looked at his face, that dear face. He had a few worry lines on his forehead that I didn't remember being there before.

'God, Dov, I have missed you.'

He looked shocked. 'You never used to say "god" like that.'

'I guess I'm a bit changed.'

'You look the same,' he said.

'I don't always. I have modern clothes now. A skirt up to here,' I pointed at my knees, 'and tops with short sleeves.'

'I'm glad you look the same to see Zaida.'

He told me some things I already knew from Deborah – that Zaida caused a fire in the annex by letting a pan boil dry. But what I didn't know till now was that this was the third time he'd done something like that. The other times someone in the house heard the smoke alarm and got to him before there was any damage. But this time everyone was out, except for Mum, of course; but she was asleep on the far side of the house.

'It took her a long time to wake up and hear the alarm,' Dov said.

I didn't know what to do with the thought of my always-busy mother sleeping during the day. Dov said gently, 'She's not quite herself at the moment.'

My eyes filled up again. It was my fault my mum wasn't herself, so it was my fault she'd been asleep, and it was my fault Zaida was here.

'The kitchen was a big mess,' Dov said, 'but Zaida was fine. He was a bit muddled about why the fire brigade were there. He kept trying to give them bagels. Mum and Dad had a massive argument. Mum wanted to move Zaida into the main house, but Dad put his foot down.'

There were no spare bedrooms in our house (me moving out only meant one less bed in the room I'd shared with Becca and Gila), but it would surely have been possible to move everyone around and free up a room. But Dad wouldn't consider it. He told Mum that her father needed to be somewhere he'd be properly looked after.

'Dad yelled,' and Dov coloured slightly, '"I will not have another meshuggener in the house."'

'Another?'

He nodded.

'That's a reference to me, I suppose.' I could easily picture the scene with my father, hear his voice in my head, see my mother shrink into a corner, letting him take control. When he was in a rage, no one could stand up to him, not even Uri.

My father must have pulled some strings to get Zaida to the top of the waiting lists. There was a room free at Beis Israel, and in Zaida went, that same day.

'That was two weeks ago,' Dov said, 'and Zaida's very confused. He was starting to lose his memory even before you, er, before you left.'

Zaida was forever mislaying things, or giving you three cups of tea in fifteen minutes because he'd forgotten you'd just had one. But I'd put those things down to his essential Zaida-ness. It never occurred to me it was something that could get worse.

'The whole two weeks,' Dov said, 'he's been in a state.'

My heart ached. 'He can't understand why he's here! He's miles away from anywhere and everyone that he knows.'

'Yes, but also…' Dov hesitated.

'What?' I said, though I guessed what he was going to say.

'He can't understand why he hasn't seen you.'

I closed my eyes for a moment, and he went on, 'He doesn't remember you left. That's why I'm so glad you've come today. He needs to see you, put his mind at rest. He thinks you've died.'

'Well, that's Dad's fault!' I burst out. 'He's the one who told everyone I was dead to him. Poor Zaida.'

Dov politely didn't point out that actually it was my fault to start with.

We rang the bell at the front entrance and were buzzed in. Dov led the way down a long corridor to a sitting room, rather nice, with a high ceiling and slow-moving fans that made the place airy. And there was my Zaida, sitting in the corner fast asleep, his head lolling on his chest. He looked so old, so small. How could I have left him? How could I have thought he would be all right without me?

I knelt in front of him, brushing away a trace memory of this morning's very different kneeling. Dov put a gentle hand on his shoulder to wake him. Zaida's eyes opened, and as he blinked – Where am I? – I put my hands on his.

'Hello, Zaida.'

His face registered astonishment as he saw me, then joy. 'My Aliza.' He broke into his gorgeous smile. 'My angel. My choochie-face.'

My tears dropped on to his trousers with such vigour, I hoped no one would mistake the damp patch for him wetting himself. A care worker came over, beaming, and said to Dov, 'You clever boy.' She put her hand on my arm and said, 'This is the first time Moshe has smiled since he came in, you know. He hasn't stopped asking for you.'

'I'm here now,' I said. 'And I'm not going away again.'

Eliza's Family

- Mum. Miriam. She's kind, she'll help anyone, and she's a great cook. She can be quite funny and chatty, and has strong opinions, but only when Dad's not there. She fades into the background when he's around, lets him decide everything.
- Dad. Kap, short for Kapel, which is a nickname for Jacob. What is there to say? Well, you saw him that time we went round there. 'There's no one here.' If Dad were a colour, he'd be black. If he were a type of weather, he'd be stormy with outbreaks of thunder.
- Uri. He's the oldest of my siblings. Well, you've met him too. He's a bit scary. Takes after my dad. He's married to Esther, who's also a bit scary. Uri's the big scholar of the family.
- Joel. He's the one nearest to me in age, just eighteen months older, and we used to be very close, back when it was just him, Uri and me. He's a gentle soul. Still not married. Like me, he's turned down lots of matches.
- Me. I come next. You know all about me.
- Jonny. He's the funny one, makes us all laugh. Always trying to get out of going to class. He is definitely not a scholar. He's twenty now, but he still seems like a kid.

- Becca. The older of my two sisters. She's the sibling I spent the most time with, doing the housework together. She knows me well, nearly as well as Dov does.
- Dov. I miss him the most.
- Gila. Baby of the family. Fourteen years old, a whirlwind, never sits still. She has such a sweet nature. I really miss her too. I miss them all. Except maybe Uri.
- Zaida. The most gentle, loving person in the world. The person who always used to make everything all right.

Chapter Sixteen

August 2000

Zaida and I were sitting on our usual bench under a copper beech tree. The garden at Beis Israel was a lovely place to sit, full of dappled shade and scented plants. He raised his cup to his lips, spilled half the tea into the saucer, and said, 'Where's that lovely fellow of yours?'

I took the saucer from his unsteady hands and tipped it into the flower bed.

'Which fellow's that, Zaydee?' His memory was getting worse, and I wondered if he meant Dov. He hadn't been immediately sure last time who Dov was, though he retrieved his name after a few moments.

'Your lovely fellow, your husband, of course,' Zaida said. 'Why doesn't he come with you? Busy, busy, I suppose. But it would be nice to see him again.'

Clearly he couldn't mean Alex. He might only have seen him once, the day I left, and in fact, I don't think Zaida was even outside the house at the time. It was all so confused and chaotic. Anyway, even if Zaida had seen him, and even though he was the kindest man in the world, I hardly thought he would refer to Alex as 'your lovely fellow'.

'They don't give you much tea in these places, do they?' he said, staring thoughtfully into his cup. Then: 'His grandfather was my dear friend, you know, when we were at school,' and I realised he was talking about Nathan. He thought I'd gone through with the marriage to Nathan!

Zaida and Monty, Nathan's grandfather, were boyhood friends. Monty died sadly young, in his forties, and after that Zaida always took an interest in Nathan's father, and then in Nathan himself. We didn't see Nathan's family very often when I was growing up – they lived in Edgware, not far from where we were now, and mixed in different circles – but Zaida had known Nathan since he was born, long before he was a twinkle in my father's matchmaking eye. Nathan, unlike Alex, was in Zaida's long-term memory.

Dov arrived then, saving me from having to think of an answer. 'Trains,' he spluttered, red-faced from rushing. Now he had the phone I'd bought him, it was easy for us to liaise about visiting Zaida together, out of sight of the rest of our family. He kissed me sweatily, hugged Zaida, then flung himself into a chair, his impossibly long teenage legs sprawled out in front of him.

'Here he is,' Zaida smiled delightedly, 'My boy. My, er, my boy!'

'It's Dov,' I prompted.

'Yes, of course, Dov. Now, Dov, what do you think?' Zaida sat up straight. 'Why doesn't Aliza bring her husband next time? I haven't seen him for a while, have I?'

'No, Zaida,' Dov said, giving me a look, as if it had been my idea. I shook my head at him. Zaida's keyworker Paulina, a large Polish woman who conversed with him in a mix of Polish, Yiddish and English, came over to ask if we'd like tea.

'I certainly would,' said Zaida indignantly, 'I haven't had any all day.'

Paulina stroked Zaida's hair, and he put his arm round her ample waist. 'Have you met my new lady friend?' he said, and they both laughed. But Dov and I were shocked beyond speech. We'd never before seen Zaida touch a woman, outside of his family.

Later, as Dov and I walked back to the tube together, he said, 'Does your husband know you're coming here?' At least this time I knew which husband was being referred to, though it was no less shocking coming from Dov than from Zaida. This was the first time in two weeks of nearly daily meetings that he'd even acknowledged the existence of Alex.

'Not yet. I'll tell him at some point. He knows he's not exactly the most popular person with my family, so he'd feel pretty awkward that I'm back in touch with some of you.'

'Joel got married,' Dov said.

I whirled round. 'When? Seriously? You're kidding!'

Joel had held out on marriage even longer than me, though of course, that was more OK for a boy than a girl. My brother got married, and I wasn't there! I wasn't invited. I wasn't even told.

'Back in March. Nice girl, Malka Levine, do you remember her? She was a couple of years below you at school.'

I conjured up a fleeting image of Malka, walking along the corridor at our school, her eyes down. A quiet, studious girl with masses of dark curls. 'I can't believe I didn't know that.'

We walked down the steps of the station.

'She's expecting,' Dov said.

'Already?!'

Dov said, so quietly I wasn't sure I heard him right, 'How is *your* marriage going?'

A train pulled in and people swirled round us, rushing here and there. We squeezed on and stood close together near the door. I was near enough to Dov to look right into his eyes, to see the little blemish that he and I alone shared, the small black spot on the brown iris of the left eye. It made us look as if we had a double pupil. Alex called it my eye's beauty spot.

'Good,' I said. 'Really good. Great.'

'I'd like to meet your husband some time,' Dov said.

'You would?'

'I've been thinking…'

'What?'

'I need to think some more before I say it.'

'Go on, you might as well spit it out.'

'Funny expression!'

'I've picked up a lot of weird phrases out here,' I said. But he wouldn't be drawn.

'I'll text you when I've thought about it,' he said.

Dov had taken to the technology like a, well like a typical eighteen-year-old. And he'd managed to keep the phone secret from Dad.

At Euston we got out, and hugged at the top of the escalator where we had to go in different directions. He looked at his watch, and hurried away. I knew he had to study, that Dad would be expecting him home. It felt strange, all at once, that Dad wasn't expecting *me* home any more. Wouldn't expect me ever again.

I headed to my platform, and got on to another hot, packed train. I wondered what Dov was plotting in that funny head of his. I smiled to myself. Things were still far from perfect, but to have him and Zaida back in my life, to get hold of Dov at the end of a phone whenever I wanted, made a huge difference to my state of mind. I felt light and breezy when I got out at Brixton, as if I could float home. I stopped off at the Turkish store to buy lamb chops (non-kosher, of course). I would make Alex a really nice supper. I knew he liked chops, and I resolved that tonight I would try them myself. I bought asparagus, potatoes and a handful of fresh mint, and a bunch of flowers too, cut-price gerberas that had wilted in the heat but looked like they would revive.

I was startled when I let myself into the flat, to find Alex already home, more than two hours before his usual time. I dropped the shopping bag on the floor.

'Is everything OK, Al?'

'We got down-sized,' he said.

'What does that mean?'

'Some bloke with a clipboard was marching round the office. He said the council training department was twice the size it should be. He offered redundancies around like sweets.'

'What did you do?'

'It's voluntary redundancy at this stage. Five people took it. Alan and Liz, three others. It was so weird. They cleared their desks and went.'

'Did you take it?'

'No. He said everyone who stayed would go on part-time hours. They've got me and Katy doing a job-share. She wanted Tuesdays, so I came home.'

'My god, that's all so fast. Are you OK?'

We sat down, and I put my hands round his.

'I'm all right, I guess. Could have been worse. I was thinking on the way home, maybe this is a chance for me to do freelance training on the other two-and-a-half days. That pays pretty well. And I'll be around at home more, which will be nice.'

'Mmm.'

'We can do stuff together on my home days, till you go back to work in September.'

I felt my precious freedom slipping away. Two and a half days each week of my precious freedom, to be precise.

'I texted you when I left work,' Alex said. 'Didn't you get it?'

I pulled my phone out of my bag and saw that there were two texts: one from Alex and a later one, from Dov. The first few words of Dov's message made me catch my breath, but I couldn't look at it now. 'The sound was off, I'm sorry.'

He sat back in his chair and scrutinised me with a raised eyebrow. 'You know, you remind me of a woman I used to know, very religious. Aliza Bloom, she was called. I don't suppose you know her? Conservatively dressed. But hot stuff in the sack.'

I'd been working out what to say while he told me about his work. 'This shirt is actually nice and cool in the heat. And my other skirts were dirty.'

'And the headscarf?'

'I didn't get time to wash my hair this morning.'

He looked so sceptical I wondered if he thought I was having an affair. A weird, kinky sort of affair that required me to wear my frum clothes. I decided to tell some of the truth, leaving out Dov, because I figured Alex would find that far too close to my father and Uri for comfort.

'I heard from Deborah that my Zaida is in a care home,' I said. That at least was true. One point for truthfulness. 'And today I went to see him.' Two points. No need to mention the other times I'd been to see him. 'He's not doing so great.' Three points. I was doing *very* well.

'I'm so sorry, Eliza,' Alex said, his eyes concerned. 'Why didn't you tell me before? Here I am, going on about work.' He put his hands back on mine. 'Is he ill?'

'Not exactly. He's losing his memory, quite fast I think. The care home say it's a kind of dementia, multi-infarct or something?'

'My great-aunt had that. Just awful. So does he recognise you?'

'Yes, thank heavens. He's always so pleased to see me.'

'Always?'

Gah! I needed to slow down, think what I was saying. 'Yes, I mean he always was, and today he was delighted.' All true. I made that a grand total of four truthfulness points.

'So I still don't get it, why are you dressed as a frummer?'

'To show respect to the home.' Minus a point. 'It's a very religious place.' Point back. I didn't need to mention the numerous relatives who wore modern clothes.

'And so your family have no idea that you saw him?'

'My parents have no idea at all,' I said, earning another point.

'Shall I come with you next time?' Alex said.

'Maybe. I don't know when I'll go again. It was pretty upsetting.'

He got up and stood behind me, put his arms round me. I closed my eyes and breathed in his familiar, lovely scent.

'Are you all right?' he said gently.

'Are *you* all right?' I replied. 'You're the one whose job's suddenly been halved.'

'Ah, fuck it,' he said. 'We'll just not spend so much on wine for a bit.' He kissed my neck. 'Talking of which, I'll go get a bottle of fizz to celebrate my exciting new career possibilities. And we can raise a glass to the hopefully lasting health of your Zaida.'

Alex loved fizzy wine, believed it made anything ordinary into an occasion. I smiled broadly till the front door slammed, then grabbed my phone and read Dov's text.

Wedding photo of you and Nathan. What do you think? Too weird? My friend can do a good Photoshop one. Be lovely for Zaida. What do you think about pretending you married Nathan? To make Zaida feel better?

I put the chops under the grill, and got down two champagne flutes. When Alex came back, I was ready. I raised my glass, and made a toast.

'To Zaida. May his last days be happy ones.'

Alex's Exes

- *Joanne 1*. First kiss, when I was eleven. She was a head taller than me. I remember stretching up, but not the kiss.
- *Beverley*. Went out for three weeks when I was thirteen. (I didn't know how much detail you wanted.) Going out just meant sitting together at school. Then she started going out/sitting next to Darren Clarkson.
- *Lisa, Simone, Alison, Nina, Julia*. Girlfriends between ages of fourteen and sixteen. Lost my virginity with Simone. Her mother was French and she (Simone) smoked French cigarettes. She was two years older than me. I thought I was in *Jules & Jim*. NB Must add that to the film list. She dumped me and broke my heart ☹. Went out with Alison on the rebound. She wouldn't sleep with me and chucked me when she realised it was all I ever wanted to talk about. Served me right.
- *Joanne 2*. Everyone was called Joanne in the 1980s. We went out for about six months when I was sixteen. She was a very jealous sort of person.
- *Emily*. First serious girlfriend (and first Jewish one!). We went out from when I was seventeen until I was nineteen. Split up while I was in my first year at university.

- *Jackie + wild times*. Most memorable girl at Liverpool was Jackie, we went out for about four months. But there were quite a few others, much shorter-term things. Most interesting were these two friends, Lisa and Andrea… maybe that's a story for another time.
- *Rachel*. We met in '91 in my last year at university. Bought the flat together in 1993, split in 1995 because she felt I wasn't ready to settle down. She was probably right.
- *Helena*. Had a few one-night stands after Rachel and thought Helena would be one of those, but she was great fun and we stayed together for a couple of years. Yes, she moved in. In fact, that's what finished us off, she turned out to be a bit difficult to live with… She moved out more than a year before I met you.

Chapter Seventeen

March 2016

My school finishes earlier than Leah's for the Easter holidays, so I decide to surprise her, take her out for a treat. I haven't had a chance to talk to her yet about what she said on Saturday, about Alex not being her dad. She got back late on Sunday, having persuaded Macy's mother to let her stay with them till almost bedtime and, claiming exhaustion, went straight upstairs. Monday, I was back to work and she was back to school, and what with her numerous after-school clubs – piano, drama, circus skills – there was never a spare moment.

That doesn't mean I haven't thought about what she said. I've thought about it a lot. I almost called Dov, to tell him that his son's been spreading malicious tales. But I need to talk to Leah first.

I lean against the wall outside her school, the only parent there. I used to enjoy picking her up from primary school back in the day, but that all ends once they go to big school. Their lives become increasingly detached from you, until you have no more idea what they're thinking and feeling than you do about the man in the corner shop. Less, in fact, because when I ask Mr Patel how he's feeling, he tells me, which Leah never does.

Kids start pouring out. Some of them look too small to be at secondary school; they are smaller than the ten-year-olds I teach. Students stream around me as though I was invisible, which I suppose I am, to them. A group of boys pass me, talking animatedly about light years and planets. It's incredible, the amount they learn, the things Leah knows about. Makes me realise how little I was taught at my own school about the world, and also how little I myself knew when I first became a teacher in my late teens.

I recognise a few of Leah's mates, and then there she is, in the centre of a group, laughing and talking. At the exact moment Leah sees me and her face falls, I realise how stupendously embarrassing it might be for your mum to pick you up from school when you're fourteen. Without hesitation I whip up a lie, so that by the time she reluctantly strolls over to me, trailed by her friends, I'm ready.

Before she can open her mouth, I say, 'I'm so sorry to meet you like this, Leah, but your grandma's very ill.' Too late, I spot Ethan in the group and remember that we used that excuse on him just a couple of weeks ago. 'More ill even than before,' I add hastily.

'Oh no,' kind-hearted Macy says, 'that's awful.' I've always liked Macy.

'You OK, Leah?' Ethan asks, his puppy eyes full of concern. I've always liked Ethan.

'Come on, guys,' a girl called Omega says, 'let's go to the mall. Catch you later, Leah.' I've never liked Omega. Stupid name, too. And who says 'mall' in this country?

The kids disperse. When they're out of earshot, I say, 'Leah, don't panic, Grandma is fine.'

'I know,' she says. 'You're a terrible liar, and you only have one lie.'

I laugh. I'm relieved she thinks there's only one. 'I just wanted to hang out with you.'

'You're a terrible role model, Mother, lying to get what you want.' She drapes an arm amiably around my shoulder. She is in a good mood.

Her skirt is ridiculously short and she has a line of holes on the inner seam of her tights, all down the thigh. She sees me glance at them and says, 'Got another demerit for my skirt today.'

'I'm not entirely surprised.'

'Can we go into town? I think I should get some new skirts.'

'Yes, great idea, and some new tights. Though what if we see your friends? They'll know I am a lying mother.'

'Let's go to Brent Cross. We could go to Shipwreck Sushi.' This is Leah's favourite restaurant. It's the one place where I don't worry she's getting an eating disorder. On the other hand, I have to take out a second mortgage to pay for her meal. Nevertheless, I'm so delighted she's being nice I will say yes to anything.

She spends the car journey tapping on her phone, and I heroically don't tell her not to. At Brent Cross, just up the road from the first cinema I ever went to, she takes me into Marks & Spencer, a shop I didn't think was on her radar. We both rummage through the racks, but when I turn to her with four school skirts in my hand, all above knee-length, she is holding one which is almost as long as the ankle-length skirt I lent her last weekend for shul.

Uh-oh.

'What about these?' I say brightly.

'I like this one.' She takes it into the changing room and I wait, expecting her to show me, but a few minutes later she comes out in her old skirt and says, 'It's fine. Can I get two more the same?'

'I was hoping to see it.'

'There's nothing to see, OK? It's just a skirt.'

'It's a bit longer than you usually like.'

'Thought you'd be pleased. You're always going on about how short mine are.' She strides over to the rack and finds two more long grey ones.

'These are the sort of skirts your cousins wear. Chanah and Devora.'

'Can I have them or not?'

We head to the tights section, where she bypasses the type she normally has, and chooses instead a pack of the thickest sort – 100 denier. She's clearly going for the frum-girl look in a big way. I pay for them, then we head to the food hall at the other end of the shopping centre. She sparks up like a string of fairy lights when we go into Shipwreck Sushi, and almost before we sit down she has whipped two plates of salmon nigiri off the belt.

'Starving!'

I order miso soup, which is what I always have. I think of Alex, many years ago, trying to convince me it was like chicken soup, and smile to myself. I wait until she has eaten some more before saying casually, 'So, you know that thing we were talking about the other day?'

She shakes her head, no, her mouth full of food.

'At Macy's,' I persist. 'Gidon said something about Dad not being your dad?'

'Yeah, what about it?'

'Well, Leah, why did he say it? What did he mean?' I keep my voice low, because the twenty-something couple on Leah's other side are not talking to each other. Perhaps they're on a first date? They both look very shy and are focusing intently on their food.

Leah selects another plate, puts a whole California roll into her mouth, and says indistinctly, 'You know what he means.'

'I don't, Leah.'

'Did you know there's a Leah in the Bible? The Old Testament, I mean.'

'Yes, I did know that. Don't change the subject, please. I don't like these terrible accusations being hurled about so lightly. I'm going to have to speak to your Uncle Dov about it.'

As soon as the words are out of my mouth I know I've struck the wrong tone. I can't lay down the law with Leah like this any more. She says calmly, 'If you talk to him, I will never tell you anything personal ever again.'

Well, as Alex likes to say, that escalated quickly. I back down, in the interests of finding out what I need to know. 'I'm sorry, Leah, I'm just a bit upset, it's…'

'*You're* upset? How do you think I feel? To be told your mother screwed around? And everyone except you knows? To be told you're not who you thought you were? How dare *you* say *you're* upset.'

'Leah, don't talk to me like that, and will you please stop shouting.' The couple next to us are openly staring, and I'm sure the man on my other side is texting Leah's comments to a friend; he keeps glancing, smirking, then tapping his phone.

'Oh, are people looking? I'm SORRY.' She raises her voice still louder. 'I'm sorry I have a mother who SCREWED AROUND.'

Everyone who was looking turns away and becomes very busy with their plates. The couple next to her finally start speaking to each other. About us, I imagine.

I put my hand on Leah's arm. 'That's enough.'

'Tell me,' she says, her voice, thank god, at a normal volume. 'Tell me honestly, OK? Is it true that someone else is my father?'

'Wow, I seem to have arrived at an exciting moment,' says Alex, appearing behind Leah. 'Was that you shouting just now?'

I gape at him. 'How are you here?'

'I drove here on the way home from work.'

'You know what I mean, Alex.'

With a flash of his famous smile, Alex gets the first-date couple to move along so he can sit next to us. Everything seems to calm down several notches.

'I texted him in the car,' Leah said. 'Thought it would be nice if we all met up.'

'Yes, great,' I say, trying to ungrit my teeth.

Alex takes a dish of sushi from the conveyor belt and grins at Leah's massive pile of empty plates. 'You full yet, Sugar?'

'Nearly.'

'So, Liza, what did you think of Leah's question?' Alex says. He's smiling at me, but there's something odd about his expression. 'Is it true someone else is her father?'

'You know it isn't, Alex.'

'According to Gidon,' Leah says, all confiding now Alex is here, 'when Mum went back to Nathan she wasn't pregnant. Then when she went back to Dad, she was.'

'QED, clearly,' I say, 'except for two things, Leah. One, I *was* actually pregnant when I left Dad, I just didn't know it. And two, how could I "go back" to Nathan when I was never with him in the first place?'

'I'm not impressed with young Gossiping Gidon,' Alex says. 'Where's he been getting his information from?'

'So for definite, Gidon's wrong?' Leah piles her last few empty bowls on top of the others, making a colourful and teetering mountain. 'You're saying Nathan is totally not my father?'

'That is exactly what I'm saying.' I pour Alex a glass of water from the little tap next to the conveyor belt. 'I'm sorry if it's been worrying you.'

'So can we do a DNA test?'

'Leah, for heaven's sake!' Alex says, finally dropping his super-reasonable tone. 'You can't go shopping for a new father. I'm afraid you're stuck with me.'

'There's no point doing a DNA test,' I say. 'You're Alex's, all right. The dates were completely wrong for you to be Nathan's.'

Oh my god.

I am an utter moronic idiot of the highest order.

Alex puts down his chopsticks. 'Pardon?'

If I could pay a million pounds to cram those words back in my mouth unsaid, I would do it in a blink.

Leah sits up straight.

Ten million.

'Eliza,' Alex says, measuring his words. 'Why would dates have anything to do with it?'

It's like watching a car crash in slow motion. I think of a hundred possible things to say to deflect the impact, but nothing comes. I just sit there, dumb, a stupid, useless bystander to an accident, my mouth opening and closing. Is it too late to lie?

'Al,' I say quietly, 'let's discuss this at home.' I try to indicate with my eyes our small but rapt audience of Leah, the first-date couple, and Texting Man. But Alex doesn't care. He stares at me.

'Dates would only be relevant if you and Nathan had... done anything,' he says slowly, 'But you didn't. Did you?'

Leah looks from Alex to me, as though she's at a tennis match. 'Did you, Mum?'

'We'll talk about this at home,' I say again.

'We'll talk about it *now*,' Alex says, and slaps his hand on the table for emphasis, bringing down Leah's multi-coloured pile of plates. Several fall on to the floor – one actually bounces – and a waitress scurries over and picks them up. The couple and Texting Man both look away; they no longer want to run the risk of catching our eyes.

'Leah, would you mind popping to the loo?' I ask.

'Seriously? Dad?' Leah appeals to Alex.

He says, 'Why should she go? She has a right to know, don't you think?'

'You sound like you have both already decided that there's something to know.' I lean towards him, not quite brave enough to touch his arm, but he leans away.

'Come on, Eliza, you're obfuscating now.'

'The dates don't matter, Alex,' I whisper. 'Leah is yours.'

He takes my hand and looks into my eyes. For a moment, I think everything is OK. Then he says, 'Liza, did you go to bed with Nathan?'

No! Not really. Possibly. Only a little bit.

Yes.

I open my mouth, almost intrigued to see what answer will come out.

Chapter Eighteen

August 2000

'Beautiful,' Zaida said, holding the photo in both hands. 'You look so beautiful.'

I rested my hand on his shoulder and looked at the picture with him, though I had stared at it a hundred times already. I was standing in front of a spreading pink cherry tree heavy with blossoms, a white veil floating dreamily behind my head, my face turned upwards, smiling beatifically. It was my face and head, all right, but it was someone else's body. Whoever she was, she was shorter and curvier than me, with a considerably more impressive chest. The slim man in the dark suit standing by my side, holding my hand, was a good three inches taller than me. I pointed this out to Dov when I first saw the photo.

'Nathan is almost exactly the same height as me,' I insisted.

Dov shrugged. 'Zaida won't notice,' he said, and he was right. It wasn't like Zaida would ever actually see us together in real life, after all. This doctored, Photoshopped picture, put together by some computer-savvy friend of Dov's, was all that there would ever be of Nathan and me.

More of a worry was if Zaida remembered we'd been due to marry in December, and questioned the presence of the cherry tree in full bloom. But he didn't mention it.

Zaida carefully replaced the photo in its cardboard wallet, and I took it from him, telling him I'd put it in his room. I went into the house, leaving Zaida and Dov in the garden, and once out of sight, I slipped the photo into my bag. We couldn't risk leaving it with Zaida. Imagine if Dad visited and saw it, or worse, Zaida produced it proudly. Oy, the hell that would break loose! It was bad enough that Nathan's image, taken from one of our engagement photos, was being used without his knowledge.

My father would consider lying to Zaida to be the ultimate act of duplicity, top of the pyramid of all my many betrayals. But curiously, the care staff had a different take on lying to their patients. They'd explained to Dov and me that they didn't always tell the truth, if the truth would needlessly hurt or upset the resident. The truth is, your wife is dead. The truth is, your favourite granddaughter ran off with a shegetz. The truth is, your son-in-law publicly announced her death.

'What's the point?' the care home manager, Bridie, said to us. 'It only upsets them, then five minutes later they've forgotten the sad news, and you upset them all over again.'

Zaida was convinced that Nathan and I got married, because he remembered that we were engaged and he remembered the run-up to the wedding. He just didn't – thank Ha-Shem – remember what actually happened next. So instead of trying to explain the truth over and over, devastating him each time, Dov and I simply pretended that I did marry Nathan after all.

There were a lot of lies to keep track of, though. For instance, when Zaida asked when he was going to see Nathan, I'd have to say something like, 'Don't you remember, he was here last week?' Zaida would say, 'Oh yes, I think I do remember,' which made me feel awful, except that he looked so happy.

I mentioned to Paulina, Zaida's keyworker, that it would be better if the home didn't let the rest of my family know that I'd been visiting. I didn't go into details, just said that my dad was a bit cross with me at the moment, and she nodded.

'Sure,' Paulina said. 'We all have *tsouris* with our families.'

I went back into the garden and Dov and I got ready to go. When I kissed Zaida goodbye, he held my hand against his cheek and asked his much-repeated question, 'When will your lovely fellow come?'

As usual, I said, 'He came last week.'

But this time Zaida went off script. 'I wanted to ask him something about his dear grandfather.'

Dov and I glanced at each other. Zaida was having one of his rare moments of clarity.

'You know, my memory is so bad. I don't remember seeing Nathan recently at all,' he said.

The look he gave me would have broken my heart, had my heart still been the vulnerable vessel it once was, rather than the tough old boot it had become.

'Zaida's been asking about Nathan a lot,' Dov said thoughtfully, as we walked to the station together.

'Yes, I think the wedding photo has made him even more keen to see him.'

'It's interesting, actually, because Nathan often asks after Zaida,' Dov said, faux-casually, presumably well aware that it was complete news to me that he was in touch with Nathan. 'I bet I could persuade him to come.'

We were taking a shortcut across Hendon Park, past laughing girls in revealing summer dresses, and men in light-coloured trousers and T-shirts. A few young people had taken off some of their clothes and were spread-eagled on the ground, worshipping the sun. How buttoned up and out-of-place Dov and I looked, in our thick wintry clothing. A girl of about twenty strolled past us with her boyfriend, his arm round her shoulder. She was wearing a white dress with yellow flowers on it, the straps no more than thin yellow laces. She was eating a choc-ice, and all at once, I wanted a choc-ice more than anything. I could bring Alex here and we could walk like that, his arm round me, eating ice-creams. These thoughts made me feel disloyal to Dov, who would never be able to casually embrace anyone, even his future wife, in public. Nor eat un-kosher ice-cream, bought from a stand.

We sat on a bench and I said, trying to match Dov's casual tone, 'So, how come you see Nathan? I thought he was at the yeshiva in Gateshead.'

'He was there for a while.' Dov frowned. 'But, well, it didn't work out. He's back home now.'

Nathan was almost five years older than me, so he'd be twenty-nine now. Almost thirty, unmarried, living with his parents. I guessed he probably felt that things hadn't worked out too well. When we got engaged he was already quite old to marry, even for a man. He told me when we were courting that he'd said no to eleven women. This impressed me, as I was considered the wildest rebel in town because I'd turned down six men.

'Why did you say yes to me, then?' I once asked him. I assumed his reasons were similar to why I said yes to him:

1. My father was running out of patience (not that he had much to start with).

2. I was tired of saying no.
3. Nathan seemed decent enough, with a pleasant face (and hair that curled on his collar, till he got it cut a few days before our wedding day).
4. I was ready to move on to the next phase of my life.

But Nathan just smiled and said, 'When you know, you know.'

'Why would Nathan come, though? He can't feel that he owes our family anything, surely?' I asked Dov.

'Well, he is very fond of Zaida,' Dov said. 'And he always asks after you, you know.'

'Seriously?'

Dov nodded.

'But, why? After all, I…' I couldn't say out loud the dramatic words, *I ruined his life*. Instead, I said, 'I assume he hates me.'

'Of course he doesn't hate you,' Dov said, which just showed how young and uninformed he was in the ways of relationships.

On the tube home, I took the fake wedding photo out of my bag. I don't know how long I sat there, staring at it. How happy I looked! It wasn't the first time I'd ever thought about what that other marriage would have been like. But it was the first time those thoughts didn't make me shudder.

Yes, I said. *Yes, I will marry Nathan*. Then immediately I was frightened. I woke with a start that same night, heart racing. I woke with a start every night, from the moment I said yes until the day before the wedding. Every night I woke with a gasp: *What have I done?*

Then I said yes to Alex instead. And for a while, the night anxieties stopped.

But the more time went by, the more the thoughts of my family crowded in, the people I had left behind. My mum, Gila, the boys. Dov. And Zaida.

What have I done to them?

My mum was seventeen when she married my dad. He was a little older, nineteen. She began having babies straight away. My father was always a difficult man. Quick to anger, slow to forgive. Us girls always whispered together that the husbands we chose would be the other way round. Everything that happened in the house, every decision, every conversation, every meal, every anything, was always through the lens of: Will Daddy hate it? Will he disapprove? Will he be angry? If the answer to any of these questions was yes, the decision was made and there was no point arguing.

So, it was no to lighter tights for summer, and no to a smart red duvet cover for Jonny which an aunt once sent, because my father had an aversion to the colour red. He called it 'the Soviet colour'. Seriously. The duvet cover was given to charity, still in its plastic packaging.

It was no to talking about a wide variety of subjects including, but not limited to: British politics, American politics, American anything, literature, any books except Jewish books, any foreign countries except Israel, any criticism of Israeli policies, religions other than Judaism, any criticism of Judaism other than Reform Judaism (criticism of which was very much on the table), art, celebrity, film, theatre, sex, women's rights, fashion and beauty, and a whole host of other topics that we only discovered were not permitted when we raised them.

Despite this, we learned a reasonable amount about the world, thanks to school, and thanks to Mum (when Dad wasn't there), and incredibly, we children carried on raising our voices and insisting on our opinions even when we knew we were going to get a thump for it. We'd clearly inherited Dad's fearlessness and sense of self-righteousness. Sadly, he didn't admire us for it. The only person who got permanently crushed by Dad was Mum.

So it was no, unless he was away, to what later became my favourite meal: roast lamb and roast potatoes. Because he didn't like lamb and roast potatoes.

'Are we Christian?' he roared, the evening my mother discovered this dish was verboten. I would have been about six years old. 'Will we have a nice Yorkshire pudding to go with it, eh, Miriam? Made with milk so we can be properly Christian with our *fleischich* all mixed in with our *milchich*.' Meat and milk.

My fork was clutched tightly in my hand; to avoid putting it down with even a little sound and perhaps drawing his attention to me, I moved my arm down to my side and began to silently scratch a tiny incision in the side of my chair, in the soft wood next to the seat – the apron, I believe it's called. Over the next few years I added hundreds of cuts to it, and to a matching one on the other side, until there were thick grooves for me to put my fingers into. It was comforting, somehow, when there was the potential for volatility at every meal, to place my forefingers in those grooves. Grounding.

Dad picked up the serving dish of lamb, which had the most delicious smell I think I'd ever smelled in my six years. Mum ducked her head, as if she thought he was going to throw it at her. Instead, he tipped the whole thing into the bin, plate and all.

'You know how I hate to waste food,' he shouted, which was hard to fathom when he had just wasted a massive amount of it. He slammed the door and went out and the rest of us ate bread and cream cheese salted with our tears.

Is it any wonder both Joel and I said no to so many possible marriages? Uri, the eldest, was more in Dad's authoritarian mould, and he married young. But Joel and I held off for a long time. Sure, on the one hand, I knew marriage didn't have to be like that. After all, I saw plenty of happy ones. Right on the doorstep there was Zaida, whose long marriage to Booba was widely agreed to have been an idyll. Admittedly, by the time I was old enough to ask any questions about it, Booba wasn't around to give her side of the story. But of course, Zaida was the loveliest man who ever walked the earth. And then there was Uri, whose wife Esther managed the neat trick of being a proper Jewish wife in my father's eyes, despite being confident and fiery, and still holding down a demanding job as a speech therapist. My best friend Deborah fell madly in love with only the second man she was introduced to, and they Lived Happily Ever After.

But on the other hand, there was the dark part of my brain. The part that woke me every night after I said yes to Nathan, with a stuttered cry of *What have I done*?

And then, while I was wrestling with my daytime self (it's going to be fine! Nathan is lovely!) and my night-time self (it's going to be my parents mark two! I'm going to lose my mind! *What have I done?*), I met Alex. And the decision was taken out of my hands.

Chapter Nineteen

September 2000

I saw Nathan before he saw me. Dov intercepted him in the corridor, to pass on some last-minute instructions, giving me a few precious moments to observe him as they stood together. His head was bowed and he nodded as he listened to Dov. His face looked grave. He'd lost weight. He was wearing a blue kippah and a grey suit. That was all I had time to take in before he and Dov were in the room and he was smiling at Zaida and moving towards him. He was very much not smiling at me.

'Ah! Ah!' Zaida, said, getting shakily to his feet. 'Here he is! Here's Aliza's husband!'

He couldn't remember Nathan's name. But he sure as hell could remember he was supposed to be my husband.

'Hello, Nathan,' I said croakily. My legs were wobbly and I couldn't look him in the eye. The last time I saw him was flushed clearly all over my face, a great red residue of shame. But it was fine, because he didn't look at me at all.

'No need to stand, Moshe,' Nathan said. 'You sit now, let me see you. It's been too long.'

Dov shook his head slightly, and Nathan covered up hastily – 'I mean, what has it been, a whole week since I saw you?' – but Zaida didn't notice. He sat Nathan in the armchair on his left, me on his right, him in the middle like a king with his courtiers. He clasped Nathan's hand in his.

'My lovely young people,' Zaida said. He took my hand too, and before either of us could do anything about it, he joined it with Nathan's hand. Touching Nathan was as painful and unreal as getting an electric shock. I don't know what it was like for him, but I presume it was even worse. I didn't dare look at him, but stared straight ahead, signalling with my eyes to Dov to do something. But he, sitting opposite this horror tableau, was powerless to intervene. It was, of course, utterly forbidden for Nathan and I to touch. How upset Zaida would be if he knew he was facilitating such a terrible breach. It was this thought that gave me the strength to pull away, on the pretext of fetching Nathan a cup of tea.

I took my time, letting the urn go through two cycles of boiling and cooling off, so I could also cool off. When I handed Nathan the cup, he still didn't look at me, simply took it without a word. Nothing, just nothing could have made me feel more awful, more guilty, more like the scarlet woman I knew he thought I was, than him pretending I wasn't actually in the room. I sat down again in a state of confusion, almost surprised to find the chair hard beneath me. I felt as not there as a ghost. I wondered if this was what Alex had meant when he described the day we ran away together as an 'out-of-body experience'.

'So, Nathan,' Zaida said, smiling with pleasure as he remembered the name, 'are you enjoying married life, eh? With this pretty one here?'

It hadn't occurred to me – *though why not?* – that this charade would have the potential to be so horribly painful for Nathan. Neither Dov or I had thought it through at all. It was a completely crazy idea. What did I think Zaida would talk about, the weather? I found I couldn't quite catch the end of my breath.

But Nathan handled the question calmly. 'I'm enjoying it very much, Moshe,' he said, though too quietly, so Zaida repeated the whole excruciating question.

'He can't hear you,' I said to Nathan, my shortness of breath making me sound for all the world like an impatient wife.

'I'm enjoying married life very much,' Nathan repeated flatly, but louder.

'Keeps you on your toes, I expect, does she?' Zaida said, turning to wink at me. I smiled weakly back, dying inside.

'You could say that,' Nathan replied.

'Great-grandchildren soon, I hope?' Zaida said. 'Babies?'

My blushing, which had subsided a little after the 'enjoying married life' part of the torture, flared up again. Why was he talking about babies? Would there even be babies, in my future? Alex and I had never talked about it. Would Nathan have children? Had I been the one to put a stop to that, for him?

'You already have great-grandchildren, Zaida!' Dov cried, clumsily trying to rescue the situation. 'Uri and Esther's children, remember? And Joel and Malka have got one on the way!'

'That's true. But don't you agree,' Zaida turned to Nathan, 'that Aliza's babies would be so beautiful?'

Tears started to prickle in my eyes, out of sheer painful embarrassment. Nathan glanced across Zaida at me, acknowledging my presence for the first time. 'Yes,' he said. Then he smiled. 'They would be perfect.'

He still had a very pleasant face.

*

We walked to the tube station, Nathan on one side, me on the other, Dov in the middle. We talked as we walked, facing front on, not looking at each other.

'That was really good of you,' I said.

'I wanted to see him,' Nathan said. 'He's always been so kind to me.'

'I know. Thank you, though. For going along with it. With the silly pretence. We're so grateful.'

My heart was jumping, because I desperately wanted to say something meaningful to Nathan. Something that would explain my awful actions in the past, to try and apologise. But apologising to a man for ruining his life wasn't something I could say in front of my brother. We were at Hendon station before I knew it, and Nathan and Dov were shaking hands. I was going to miss my chance. I barely had time to say, 'Bye,' before Nathan strode off towards the northbound line without a glance in my direction.

Dov and I got on our escalator and I thought fast. As we reached the bottom, I said, 'Blast, I left my mac at the care home.' Actually, it was folded up in my bag. 'I'd better go back.'

'Oh dear,' Dov said. 'I have to get home.'

'You go. You don't want Dad to get cross. Crosser than usual, I mean. I'll be fine.'

I hugged him quickly, then turned and got back on the escalator, waving casually. As soon as Dov disappeared from view I raced up the remaining steps, pushing past stationary people who were standing too far to the middle. I was panting, my legs aching by the time I reached the top, but I kept going, ran on to the escalator for the northbound line, and clattered down it. I rushed breathlessly on to the platform and, thank heavens, Nathan was still there, leaning against the wall down at the far end, his arms folded, staring into space. The indicator board showed that the train was due in one minute.

The last film I watched with Alex was *Crocodile Dundee*. There's a scene at the end where Mick Dundee is on a crowded tube platform and he's trying to reach his girl, but there are so many people in the way, he can't get to her. So he walks across the top of them, held up by their shoulders and hands. I didn't need to do a similar stunt now, though, as the station wasn't busy. As I walked, heart thudding, towards Nathan, I thought of the bit earlier in the film where Mick says, 'That's not a knife. *This* is a knife!' and both Alex and I laughed and tried to imitate it, Alex agreeing that though my Australian accent was terrible, it wasn't as bad as his. I don't know why I was thinking of Alex right now.

When I stood in front of Nathan, he did a double-take. 'What are you doing here?'

'I wanted to speak to you,' I said.

'You already did.' He looked at his shoes.

'Without Dov there, I mean.'

'We can't be alone together. You should go.'

The train came thundering in, too loud to speak across. When it screeched to a halt, Nathan said, 'This is mine,' and quickly got on it. I didn't hesitate, I simply got on too. He looked astonished when he saw that I'd followed him.

'Don't,' he said. He moved along the carriage and stood holding on to one of the poles, though there were spare seats. I stood next to him, holding the same pole, my hand a few centimetres lower than his. He turned his back on me, literally turned away. For a moment I stood still, close enough to breathe in his smell, a soap with a sandalwood scent, which I'd forgotten I even knew. It smelled like the past, of the life I didn't take.

The train started up abruptly, and we were shaken about. Nathan kept his body rigidly away from mine.

'Nathan,' I said. And when he didn't reply, I said more loudly, 'NATHAN.'

A large woman in a tight green coat sitting near us looked up with interest.

'Nathan,' I said again, half-laughing, because I recognised how far I'd come, and I didn't mean how far on the wrong train. I leaned closer and said quietly, 'Please turn round so I can talk to you.'

No movement from him, no acknowledgement that I was there. I took a breath and raised my voice slightly. 'I am a fallen woman. A Jezebel. It would be nothing to me to make a massive scene.' I snapped my fingers. 'I'd do it like that.'

He slowly turned round, the very epitome of reluctant, and looked at me, eye-to-eye. We were of course, as I'd told Dov, almost exactly the same height. I could see the faint freckles on his forehead, the flecks of auburn in his beard, his hair, long again and curling on his collar, the slight caving to his cheeks where he'd lost weight. I wondered if he could see the black spot in my eye, and what he thought about it.

'What do you want?' He could barely bring himself to speak.

I'd imagined this apology scene so often that, now it was here, I didn't know how to start. 'I'm sorry.'

'That's it?'

'No...'

His pale grey eyes bored into me. 'You chased me across a station on to a train so you could say *that*?'

'I know it's inadequate, it's...'

'Inadequate?' He shook his head. 'Inadequate doesn't begin to cover it.'

'Nathan, I'm so…'

'Don't tell me again how, how,' and he ran his hand across his forehead as though his head ached, 'how *fucking* sorry you are.'

I winced, involuntarily. It was so utterly shocking, hearing him say that word. I wondered how often he had said it before. Had he *ever* said it before?

'You walked out on the day of…' He stopped, clearly not able to say the words, 'our wedding.' He spoke so quietly that only I could hear, and me only just, over the noise of the train. The woman in the green coat was watching us intently, unashamedly, as though we were the on-board entertainment. Nathan started to say something else, inaudibly.

'I can't hear you,' I said, and leaned even closer. He put his mouth almost against my ear, his breath hot and unfamiliar. Our bodies were still separate from each other, yet it felt very intimate.

He whispered, 'Our families were there. Everyone saw you leave with *him*.'

The train pulled into Colindale and a large group of under-dressed foreign teenagers got on. The woman in the green coat was blocked from my view as people forced their way into the aisles. Nathan and I were pushed together, and for the first time our bodies touched. He tried to edge away from me and I did the same but it was impossible, we each had people on all sides and there was nowhere to move to. We were closer than we had ever been before, our matching heights making it almost impossible not to look at each other. The noise levels rose higher and higher, the teenagers jabbering at the top of their lungs in Spanish or Portuguese, I didn't know which.

Nathan closed his eyes. I didn't think he would speak again, but when the train started moving, he said something. I felt the words as puffs of air against my face. The train and the teenagers formed a buffer around his voice.

'I can't hear, I'm so sorry. Could you say that again?'

Nathan still had his eyes shut. 'Your voice has haunted my dreams.'

He had been trying to hold himself as far away from me as possible, uselessly, as we were so squashed together. Now he seemed to give up. His body felt heavy against mine; I could feel his warmth, the weight of him. I had no trouble at all imagining how it would feel, him lying on top of me.

'When Dov asked me to visit Moshe, I said no,' Nathan whispered. 'I was worried about what would happen. About the possibility of *this*.'

'But you changed your mind,' I said.

He opened his eyes at last, and looked straight at me. He seemed to have resolved something. 'I need you to get off the train, Aliza.'

'What, here?' I looked outside, the blackness of the tunnel dashing past. 'It's going a bit fast.'

He smiled. 'I can't believe that you can make me laugh, still.'

I smiled back, tentatively, and his disappeared instantly.

'Seriously, at the next stop, please get off the train.'

'OK.'

'You will?'

'Yes. I don't want to make things even worse for you.'

The train started to slow down, and perhaps because he knew I would soon be out of his face, Nathan started talking, fast. 'Your Zaida is a wonderful man. I thought helping you and Dov with him would get rid of some of *this*.' He beat his fist against his chest. 'It doesn't seem to have worked.'

'Nathan, I…'

'Please, Aliza, I can't bear this,' he said. 'I can't bear seeing you. You…'

'I'm sorry.'

'You broke me.'

That, at least, was loud and clear. We pulled into Burnt Oak. 'Can you get off here, please?' he said desperately.

I nodded, shaking free some tears that hadn't yet started to fall. I pushed past the teenagers and stumbled on to the platform, searching blindly for a way out as bodies swirled around me. The train pulled away, and I joined a crowd of people walking up some steps, I didn't know to where. I felt like I had been punched. At the top I stood, my legs shaking, in front of a poster of a tube map till the tears stopped, my blurred vision cleared, and I could work out how to get back to Brixton.

Alex was all smiles when I got home. 'How was your Zaida?' he asked. Then he saw my face.

'Oh no, Eliza, what's wrong?'

He pulled me into his arms, and I rested my head against his chest, trying to think how to explain myself. *Well, Alex, let me tell you about my day.* The man I jilted, you remember him? He was there, and we pretended we were married, then he told me I had destroyed his life, so I'm feeling a bit weird. That should do it.

I managed to come up with something not too far from the truth – that I was very upset to see Zaida today, that his memory was getting worse. Alex was lovely; comforting and sympathetic. He ran me a bath, and while I was soaking and crying, he ordered a new item from the food list: Chinese take-away. We had hoisin duck which came with little pancakes, and though I couldn't eat much, it was delicious. I barely even thought about the duck being unkosher. We watched another film from the culture list, which I picked: *Sophie's Choice*.

'Are you sure?' Alex said. 'It's really sad, you might prefer something light tonight.'

But I welcomed it. I wanted an excuse to cry. I couldn't help reading rather too much into the film about my own situation, and was absolutely wrung out afterwards. But when Alex wanted to make love, I did. I felt I owed him that much.

The next day was Monday, one of Alex's work days. After he left, I put on my old clothes. I wanted to see Zaida again, without the tainted feeling of Nathan being there. I hadn't been able to focus on Zaida yesterday, and that wasn't fair to him. I texted Dov as I walked to the station, and asked if he was able to meet me there.

Zaida was, as always, absolutely thrilled to see me. In no more than a couple of seconds his face went from blank to lit up. I threw my arms round him and kissed the top of his head, sat down beside him and put my hand over his.

A familiar voice behind me said, 'So it *is* true.'

A horribly familiar voice.

I turned slowly round. 'Hello, Dad,' I said.

Chapter Twenty

September 2000

My heart was still racing when I got out at Brixton. My legs were shaking too much to walk to the flat; instead I went to the Roundhouse and the red-haired waitress, Marlene, brought me a coffee. When I picked it up my hands trembled so much I had to put it down again before I scalded myself. I could still feel the aftershocks of seeing Dad in full flow. I'd somehow forgotten how terrifying he was.

I bent my head to the cup, to avoid having to pick it up, and inelegantly managed to sip some coffee, which helped calm me down. When my hands were steadier I texted Dov, asking if he was OK. He would even now be getting the brunt of Dad's rage, and I knew, with a leaden feeling in my stomach, what that would be like.

When I told Alex that he knew everything about me, I had of course been talking nonsense. I realised that now. Here at last was a list from me to him that would come as a surprise: Things Alex didn't know about my life before I met him. I wondered if I would ever be able to share it with him.

My father used to hit us children when he was angry, and he was angry most of the time. Though he didn't often hit Mum, she was far more frightened of him than the rest of us were. She was brave, though, always standing up to him when he went for one of us.

I remember when I was fourteen, two representatives from Jewish Women's Aid gave a talk at the synagogue about domestic violence. They were laughed out of the building. I remember a girl turning to me in disbelief and saying, 'How can they think that a Jewish man would ever hit his wife? What a joke.' Becca and I followed the speakers out to the street and as we casually walked past, Becca put out her hand for one of their leaflets. I hid it down my skirt and later we gave it to Mum, but she set fire to it over the sink for fear that my father would see it. We never spoke of it, not at the time and not afterwards.

I was seven when my father first smacked me; or at least, that's the first time I remember. I'd been growing increasingly bored in the upstairs section of the synagogue, set aside for the women, far away from the action. So I decided I was going to be a boy. I borrowed some clothes from Joel and stood with my brothers in the men's section. I would have got away with it too, if it wasn't for that pesky Uncle Ben. (Alex would be pleased to see me quoting from *Scooby Doo*, one of the shows on his 'TV Classics' list. I enjoyed it, but Alex said it was the same plot every time. We only watched two episodes but it looked like he was right.) Uncle Ben, always a joker, winked when he realised it was me. I thought the wink meant he'd keep it a secret, but after the service finished and everyone was milling about, he said loudly to my father, 'See you've got another boy, Kap. What a blessing.'

'What are you talking about?'

My father turned to where Ben was pointing, and there I was in Joel's trousers and shirt, prayer-cap on my head, my hair pinned up, more or less, with dozens of Mum's hairclips. My father didn't say anything, not in front of everyone, but he said plenty later.

'I don't like to smack you,' he shouted, smacking me, 'but you're old enough to know right from wrong.' Maybe he was trying to smack my nature right out of me. I bet he wished later that he'd been able to. I sometimes wish he had, too.

The worst part was that Joel got into trouble too, because he'd let me borrow his clothes. Joel was the brother I was closest to, until Dov came along. This was the last time I remember him doing anything naughty. Not me, though. My parents often despaired. My father assumed my troublesome side was inherent to my personality, but my mother worried that it was something she had done. She once said, 'Where did I go wrong with you, Aliza? The others are so obedient, but you…'

That was when I was young, way before I rejected every possible suitor she put in front of me. I didn't act up to upset her, in fact I hated it when she was upset, but my father, well, that was a different story. I was always frightened of him, but couldn't respect him; and the disrespect always triumphed over my terror, meaning that I carried on disobeying him whenever I could.

Zaida was my safe place. It was about the time of the boys' clothes incident that I began going to see him every day after school, and every Sunday, and every time my father started yelling. My dad would try and whack me before I got to the annex, but once actually in there, I knew he wouldn't come after me. I'd creep into Zaida's living room, or at times run in breathlessly, having only got away by the skin of my teeth, and Zaida would greet with me a hug and a whispered, 'Hello, choochie-face.' Then he'd settle me in the armchair, and tell me a story.

All his stories started the same way.

'Once there was a little girl called Aliza, who was very…' and then the story would revolve round what the 'very' referred to. 'Once there was a little girl called Aliza, who was very brave' would mean a story about Aliza taming lions, or fighting in a war, or sailing a ship. 'A little girl called Aliza, who was very funny,' would be an adventure about running away to be a circus clown. 'A little girl called Aliza, who was very kind,' would be about Aliza setting up a home for lost cats, or poor orphans. I did secretly envy those orphans, with their blissful fatherless state. As Zaida told his tale, my heart gradually stopped hammering and my breathing steadied back to normal.

Neither Zaida or I ever said anything about my dad, but I knew that he knew. My siblings took refuge in the annex too, of course, when things got rough in the house, but I was the only one who went every day. Zaida loved all of us dearly – he was a man with a huge capacity for love – but I always told myself that he loved me best. And along with Dov, he was the person I loved most in the world.

Zaida never asked questions, he was always just there. And I would be there for him now, whatever happened. Beis Israel had in some ways replaced the annex as my safe space. Now my cover had been blown, I was worried I had lost that safety. I shivered all over again as I thought of Dad shouting, his face contorted, spit flying, waving his fist at me, the carers trying to calm him down. But I wasn't going to let him stop me seeing Zaida. I imagined a scene in which Dad told the staff not to let me in, and could imagining them agreeing for the sake of a quiet life. The thought made me feel sick.

Alex was at work, thankfully, when I let myself into the flat, so I didn't have to come up with what to tell him this time to explain my tear-stained face. Telling the truth meant telling him I'd seen my father; and even though Dad had been vile, I didn't want Alex to start worrying about my increasing contact with my family, and what it might mean for us.

I sat at the computer and emailed Deb.

From: elizasymons

To: myfriendmarriedagoy

11 September

Dear Deb

You'll soon hear that I've caused a bit of a scene. Yes, yes, I know: another one. Maybe you've already heard. I imagine the Stamford Hill bush telegraph is buzzing like crazy by now. Someone told Dad I'd been visiting Zaida, and he caught me. It must have been Nathan, I suppose, though I'm shocked he'd be so mean. You probably think I deserve it. Luckily it being a public building, Dad couldn't kill me. He settled for yelling the place down instead. The old folk were all gaping at him, and Zaida kept clutching my arm and saying, 'What's the matter with Kap?'

It took three male carers to get Dad out of the lounge, and he was still screaming as they dragged him out. I tried to get Dov to come back to Brixton with me – we both knew it was going to be way worse for him than me – but he said he might as well get it over with, that he'd have to go home sometime. Then Zaida needed the toilet, and because all the male carers were handling Dad, Dov and I took him out into the corridor, just in time for Dad to come hurtling out of wherever he'd been taken. He roared liked a jungle beast when he saw us, and kind of charged at us, raising his fists at me. You have never seen anything like it. Zaida shouted, 'Don't you touch my Aliza', and that did stop Dad in his tracks, but then he started shouting at Zaida, awful things, calling him a stupid useless old man and much worse. Dov stood between them, on the optimistic assumption that Dad wouldn't actually hit him in front of everyone. As soon as the carers stepped in to intervene, Dov pushed me and shouted, 'Go, go!' and I did. I ran past Dad, past the carers and gawping residents, and out on to the street. I didn't stop running till I reached the tube.

My life is one drama after another.

I know it's a big ask, but I'd be so grateful if you'd keep me posted about Dov. He may not want to get back in touch with me after Dad's given him hell.

Aliza xx

I sent the message and checked my phone again: still nothing from Dov. I hoped he'd been able to keep his phone a secret, because Dad would grind it into the earth with his heel if he found out about it. I left Dov a trembly voicemail asking him to call me, then moped around the flat, not able to settle to anything.

Why *was* Dad so angry all the time? I couldn't remember a time when he wasn't, apart from that day on holiday when we made the sand car with the pretty shells pressed into it. I had no idea. Now I was away from home, I realised I didn't really know much about him. I didn't even know what he did all day. He worked some of the time as an accountant for a small chain of shops in Hatton Garden; and some of the time he must be at the kollel, the religious centre for married men. But what else did he do? His parents were both long-dead. I never knew his mother, and only vaguely remembered his father, Levi, a thin man sitting in a chair, his beard white, looking as old as Father Time. Dad's brothers and sisters were not close to him and we rarely saw them. I remember Alex asking, some time back: what did my dad like doing? Who were his friends? I teased him for thinking he could bond with my dad by learning about him, but now I realised that I hadn't answered because I didn't know. It was strange to have this distance from my father, reflect about him as a person, separate from the shouting bullying man who flitted in and out of the house. A disappointed person, perhaps. Someone whose life hadn't worked out the way they hoped.

I had a secret life. Maybe my father did too.

When Alex came in, he knew, as usual, that something was wrong. I still hadn't worked out what to tell him, but Alex handed me the solution.

'Oh god, Eliza, has something happened to your Zaida?'

I could just say yes, that Zaida had taken a turn for the worse, and I would get the comfort I needed, like I did yesterday over Nathan, without having to mention my dad, or Dov. That wouldn't be the right thing to do, though. I should tell Alex the truth. Tell him I was being pulled back into my family. Tell him that my father's fury was oddly cleansing; that if I truly was dead to him, he wouldn't have behaved like that. You don't go yelling at a dead woman. Tell him that, despite everything, Dov loved me as much as he ever had. That Zaida would never stop loving me.

I looked into Alex's trusting eyes, and felt strangely detached. I loved him, of course I did, but it didn't feel like I was completely here, any more. Part of me was sitting at the big table in Springfield Street, my fingers resting on the sides of my chair, in the grooves I made with my fork years ago. My mum stroking my hair as she passed, Gila plonking herself heavily on to my lap, Dov telling me something he'd heard,

Deb popping round for tea and staying for hours. Dad out and not coming back till evening.

'Yes,' I said, 'Zaida has gone downhill.'

'I'm so sorry.' Alex wrapped his arms round me. I leaned against him, feeling the warmth of his body, and closed my eyes against myself.

In the morning I turned on my phone to find three missed calls from Dov. I gave silent thanks that Alex was already up and getting ready; he was catching the early train to Cardiff for work. In fact he was staying overnight in a B&B there. He was thrilled to have got this freelance job, and was easy to bundle out of the door with many kisses and good luck wishes.

As soon as the door shut behind him, I rang Dov back. I'd never heard him more excitable.

'Dov! Are you OK? Was Dad horrible? Slow down, I can't understand what you're—'

'Wait till you hear! You're not going to believe it.'

'What?'

'Are you sitting down?'

'Yes.' I sat down hurriedly.

'Mum. Told. Dad. Off.'

'You are *kidding* me.'

'I'm not. Everything's topsy-turvy here. It's like the world's gone mad, owls hooting in the middle of the day—'

'What happened?' I interrupted. 'Tell me!'

'So you know when you ran out of Beis Israel? You run pretty fast, by the way.'

'Thanks.'

'For a girl.'

'Get on with it, Dov!'

'So Dad was still roaring and frothing away, then the care home manager marched out of her office and told Dad to stop yelling *immediately*.'

'What, Bridie? Seriously? Wow, that's so brave.'

'I know, she's only tiny. She's Irish, did you know?'

'Yes, Dov.' When was he going to get to the point? 'Go on.'

'Dad just stopped, his mouth hanging open in mid-shout, and she ordered him into her office and had a massive go at him. We could hear her going on and on. He didn't get a word in. She didn't even raise her voice – unluckily for us, because we couldn't hear what she was saying.'

'I'd love to have known what she said!'

'Wouldn't we all. While Dad was in there, Paulina told me Bridie was absolutely furious that Dad had upset Zaida, and the other residents. When Dad came out he looked like a small boy who's been told off by the teacher.'

'This is absolutely incredible. But listen, Dov, what about Mum?'

'I'm getting to it. It's all part of it. So me and Dad got in the car, he yelled at me all the way home, but you know, I'm used to it, it didn't bother me.'

I knew what he meant. We'd all become adept at tuning out Dad's rants. You had to, or you would lose your mind.

'Then at home, Dad told Mum what had happened, expecting her to be on his side as usual, and *she* went mad too!'

'What do you mean?' Mum had never 'gone mad' in her life.

'It was like she had taken on Bridie's personality! She *shouted* at Dad.'

'Say that again.'

'Honestly! I taped her on my phone, I'll play it to you some time. She shouted, how dare he yell at Moshe, her father, an old man who'd done nothing wrong, who was already so upset about being sent away from us and in a home.'

'I honestly can't picture it.' I was holding the phone so tight against my ear that my wrist ached.

'Nor can I, and I was there! She went on for ages, saying how good Moshe had been to all of us, and how he was her only remaining parent, and remember the Fifth Commandment, and Dad didn't say anything, and then she stood up and she said, wait for it, she said, "You were wrong, Kap."'

'This can't have happened. You must have misheard.'

'We all heard it. Uri was there, and even *he* told Dad he was in the wrong! And Joel said Dad shouldn't even be angry with *you* because it showed that you were still part of the family if you were visiting Zaida.'

Ah, my brave Joel.

'And then *everyone* stood up to Dad and was telling him off,' Dov went on, 'and he looked like he was going to crumble into a hundred pieces. He looked as old as Zaida. I don't even feel scared of him any more, it's like a switch has gone off. I don't know how long it will last, but it's been off all last night and this morning, and I feel the same.'

'Honestly, I can't believe it.'

'One more thing. When Dad finally managed to get a word in, and told Mum you'd given me a phone and we'd been in touch, he thought she'd be furious with me and you. He *wanted* her to be cross with us. Instead, she asked me, *in front of Dad,* to call you on my phone and see if you will come over.'

'She wants to see me?'

'Dad said, "Is that what you want, Miriam?" all quiet and hurt. And she said, "I want my Aliza."'

I want my Aliza.

This couldn't be happening. Tears spilled out on to my cheeks.

'Aliza? Are you still there?'

I swapped the phone to the other side. 'She really said that? She doesn't think I'm dead to her?'

'She never did, silly.'

'Oh, Dov.'

'Dad said, if that's how you feel, I won't stand in your way. He went out, didn't even slam the door, and we all just looked at each other. Oh, hang on! Gila wants to talk to you!'

I had barely a moment's silence to think about what it meant. I could go back. I could see my family. I hadn't thrown everything away after all. Then Gila's wonderful high-pitched voice was squealing at me. 'Everyone's gone crazy! Me and Becca have been using your bed as a sofa but you can have it back.'

'Gila, darling.'

'Aliza, you are coming home, aren't you?'

The question I never thought I'd hear. I wanted to answer, but my voice caught in my throat.

Dov said Dad would surely be out all morning, maybe all day, so I decided to go right away. I ran upstairs and pulled off my skirt and T-shirt. I stood in my underclothes for a moment, the Eliza between two worlds, then I dug out my old long skirt and shirt, and transformed myself back into the Aliza my family knew. I carefully washed modern Eliza off my face: the mascara I had only recently learned to use, the blusher, the lip-balm. I tied a scarf round my hair, and tried to see myself through my mother's eyes. Did I look like the person she remembered? Without make-up, without the softening effect of my hair round my face, I looked younger, plainer. I looked like someone else.

I wasn't going to overthink it.

Before I left, I hurriedly checked the computer to see if Deb had emailed me back. There was one line from her, sent last night:

From: myfriendmarriedagoy@hotmail.com

To: elizasymons@hotmail.com

11 September

Wow, you've really done it this time, Crazy Girl! My mum can hear your parents yelling from her house!

I walked quickly to the station and got the tube to Seven Sisters. I wanted to bring Mum cornflowers, but the stall at the station didn't have any, so I bought roses instead. Though it had only been nine months, it felt like years. I saw everything through an outsider's eye. The people looked pale, and overdressed in the sunshine. The shops which had seemed so enticing looked scruffy, not at all special. The streets I'd walked up and down thousands of times, thinking they were the only streets, were just ordinary. This was not the whole of the world, any more.

As I walked towards my house, I saw some of my family standing outside on the pavement, waiting for me. I blinked at the memory of the last time I'd seen them all standing there, and started running towards them. Gila saw me first and came full-pelt at me, into my arms, hitting me like a train. The others ran to me too, as though we were enacting the Prodigal Son, a story I now knew from the New

Testament. Uri and Joel weren't there, of course; they'd be at kollel. Dov should have been at yeshiva with Jonny but he'd clearly taken the morning off, and stood there grinning at me, as though he'd made the whole thing happen, which really, I guess he had. Becca flung her arms round me, and she and Gila pulled me into the house, into my mother's kitchen. Mum was waiting, standing by the table nervously as though expecting an important guest. She didn't have her apron on. There were homemade biscuits on a plate.

'My girl,' she said, smiling and crying at the same time. She held both my hands and looked me up and down. 'You've lost weight,' she added, inevitably. Then she pulled me closer and held me tightly, as if she was never going to let me go.

Things Alex Didn't Know About My Life Before I Met Him

- My father used to hit us children when he was angry.
- Sometimes, he hit Mum.
- Becca and I gave Mum a leaflet about domestic violence but she burned it.
- The first time I remember my father smacking me, I was seven.
- The last time he hit me, I was fourteen. I yelled at him not to hit Dov, who was only eight, and he hit me instead. Pretty soon after, I grew taller than him, which might be why he stopped.
- My Zaida was always my safe place. That's why I need to be there for him.

Chapter Twenty-One

March 2016

Given the shipwreck of our family at Shipwreck Sushi, it's not the ideal time for the longest bank holiday weekend of the year. It's also not the ideal time to be having a family lunch. But Alex's family have an unbreakable tradition of Easter Sunday lunches, and this year it's our turn to host. Alex has an unbreakable tradition of singing songs from *Fiddler on the Roof* at these lunches, which he started back when we first got together to make me feel more included, but which didn't work for two reasons: 1) he's a lousy singer, and 2) I'd never seen *Fiddler on the Roof.* I have of course seen it now, and can join in, if pushed.

Alex's family have another tradition, less explicit, of couples who've split up staying in touch and being all friendly. So we have his brother Kim, and Kim's ex-wife Vicky, their kids, and Vicky's new partner Tony (though he's not that new, they've been together for five years), and their baby. I'm just hoping this divorced-but-friendly tradition isn't one I'll soon have first-hand experience of.

I'm peeling potatoes and wanting to talk, while Alex is preparing a chicken and ignoring me. Leah is hiding in her bedroom. She lit the blue touchpaper, and then retired.

'Al, please can we talk?'

'They'll be here in an hour.' He has a glass of wine on the go, and takes a slug from it. 'I don't want to start a big thing and then have to pretend everything's OK.'

Aren't we pretending everything's OK anyway?

Alex shoves a lemon and an onion up the chicken's behind with more force than necessary. 'Where's the garlic?' he says.

'We've run out.'

'We always run out of the fucking stuff I need.'

'How come we're having chicken, anyway? We always have roast lamb on Easter Sunday.' I try not to make it sound like a complaint, but he throws me a look.

'I wanted a change,' he says.

From the look of the wine bottle, he is already on a second glass. I put down the peeler and wrap my arms round him, as he stands with his back to me, fiddling with the damn chicken. He leans back into my embrace. He doesn't know how not to. We always lean into each other.

'It won't be any good without garlic,' he says.

'Are you crying? Alex, what the hell?' I try and turn him to face me but he is fixed fast. I scoot to the side and say, 'Don't cry, honey, don't cry. I can borrow some from next door.'

'I'm not crying.' He wipes his eyes on the apron. 'It's the onion.'

'Are you sure?'

'It's the fucking onion, OK?'

I let him go and he puts the chicken in the oven, then blows his nose.

Kim arrives first, with Holly and Freya, his kids with Vicky. Holly's a couple of years older than Leah, Freya just a few months, and they have always got on well with her. Leah's all smiles as she finally shows her face downstairs. But Holly has inherited her mother's judginess about appearance. When I met Vicky, almost the first thing she said to me was something unfavourable about what I was wearing. And the instant Holly claps eyes on Leah, she blurts, 'Wow, Leah, you look like a Muslim.'

The adults all look puzzled. I suppose Holly means that Leah is uncharacteristically covered up – she's wearing one of her new long school skirts and a long-sleeved T-shirt with a crew-neck.

'No she doesn't,' Kim says. 'You look lovely, Leah.'

'Oh, so Muslims can't look lovely?' Holly says.

Kim and I exchange weary smiles. Who'd be the parent of a teenage girl? Seriously, who? The kids go upstairs and we take Kim into the kitchen and give him a glass of wine. I'm slightly shocked, as I pour it, to find it leaves almost nothing in the bottle. How many glasses do you get from a bottle? Is it four? Five?

'Vicky's bringing Mum,' Kim says. He's comfortable in our house, and he potters about, peering into saucepans and stirring things. He and Alex both fancy themselves as good cooks. 'Roast potatoes? Excellent, my favourite. Hey, listen, I read a brilliant thing the other day that Jamie Oliver does with them, he gets salt and he…'

'We've done them,' Alex snaps. 'They don't need salt, or anything else.'

'All right, man! No need to bite my arse off.'

Alex moves him aside, not gently, so he can open the oven. Kim mouths at me, 'What's wrong?' and I shake my head.

The doorbell rings and Kim goes to answer it. I hiss, 'Alex, pack it in. Kim's going to wonder what's going on.'

'Let him.'

'Ah please, love. Let's just get through this, shall we? We can talk after.'

'You lied to me.' He slurs slightly, and my heart sinks. Alex doesn't usually drink, and he doesn't hold it well.

'I didn't! Not really. I—'

'Welcome back, Miss Fickle,' he says, this awful nickname another tradition that I thought had lapsed long ago. It stops me in my tracks, and I am still trying to think of a reply when Kim comes back in with Sheila, Vicky and Tony. Tony is carrying George, their baby, who's fast asleep. Everyone kisses everyone, even Vicky and Kim. I'm impressed by their cordial relationship, though baffled by it as well. How can you love someone so intensely, then break up, and yet still be friendly? It's the right and sensible thing to do, of course, especially when there are children involved, but I do find it incredible.

I get everyone drinks and, true to form, Vicky mentions my clothes, though this time she is complimentary – I'm wearing a new grey dress which suits me. We all cram round the living room table. There isn't quite enough space – it seats six and we're nine, plus the baby on Vicky's lap, so everyone keeps banging their elbows and being slightly ratty about it. I wonder if they've picked up the tension coming off Alex and me.

'So how *is* everybody?' says Sheila, who always wants things to be all right.

She gets a bland chorus of 'fine' and seems satisfied. 'So, Eliza,' she goes on, politely, 'it's normally Passover around now, isn't it, as well as Easter?'

'Yes, it is.' I don't keep track of the festivals any more, but Sheila always asks me about them, so I check if I know I'm going to see her. 'It's late this year, and Easter is early.'

There is a too-long silence following my fascinating fact, which Tony politely breaks by telling me how delicious the chicken is. I thank him, and tell him that actually Alex did the cooking. Alex nods, and drinks some more wine, his face a study in gloom. *For god's sake, Alex! Everyone will think you don't want them here.* I must look desperate, because Kim, who has always been very sweet to me, says, 'So, who wants to hear my interesting news?'

'Me!' I say with relief.

'You don't, Aunty Eliza,' Holly says. 'It's gross.'

'Dad-dy's-got-a-girl-friend,' sings Freya.

'Oh yes?' Vicky says. 'And when were you planning to tell us?'

'Now,' Kim says, 'I was planning to tell you now.'

'Oh, Kim, that's wonderful,' I say. 'Isn't it, Al?' I wish I was near enough to Alex to kick him under the table.

'Yes, great,' Alex says, pancake flat. I have never ever seen him lose it like this in public. I mustn't panic. I catch my breath. I wonder how quickly I could get everyone out of the house if I faked an illness.

'Well, tell us more, Kim, we're agog,' Sheila says.

Poor Kim, I don't think he had any intention of telling us but was trying to save the lunch.

'It's very early days, Mum. I wouldn't call Sarah my girlfriend, not yet, OK, Freya?'

'Well, Kim, you shouldn't introduce her to the children until you know she's going to be a permanent fixture,' Vicky says primly.

'I haven't introduced her to them yet, Victoria,' Kim says.

'Where did you meet Sarah, Kim?' I ask, and watch the embarrassment spread across his face like a blind being pulled up. Oh god, I'm only making the whole thing worse. I pretend I didn't say that, and start gathering up plates. 'Er, we have two desserts, everyone: Alex's famous strawberry cake, or Sheila's legendary pavlova.'

'How is pavlova different to strawberry cake? They both have strawberries, right?' says Holly. I am rapidly going off Holly.

'Daddy met her online,' Freya pipes up. 'And we helped make his profile.'

'Oh, *that's* appropriate,' Vicky says. 'Get your kids to pimp you out.'

'Vicky,' Tony says, in a warning voice. He's a man of few words, but he makes them count. She listens to him in a way she never did with Kim. Talking of Kim, the poor man is now hiding his face in his hands and groaning.

'Everyone meets online these days, I believe,' says good old Sheila. 'I was reading about it in the *Express*. There's no stigma any more. That's right, isn't it, Alex?'

Alex is normally the life and soul of family gatherings, and Sheila must be wondering what's going on. Ordinarily, a tasty titbit like Kim's new girlfriend would be his idea of a fabulous day of banter, he'd be all over it. But he's simply sitting there, brooding. Everyone else's plates are in a pile, waiting for me to take them to the kitchen, but his is still half-full, his knife and fork crossed ambiguously in the middle of a potato.

'Alex,' I say gently, 'are you done?'

He looks at me as if only just noticing I'm there. 'Yes, I'm done,' he says, and pushes his plate over. To my ears it sounds like an awful portent.

'Isn't it, Alex?' Sheila continues gamely. 'Online dating is all the rage?'

'It's weird,' Alex says, and it must be obvious to everyone how drunk he is. His words run into each other. 'Because I always assumed Kim was too much in unrequited love to go round dating anyone.'

'Is that so?' Kim says. 'Well, mate, you couldn't be more wrong. Vicky and I came to a natural end.'

'We totally did, Ally,' Vicky said. 'I admit that he was a bit less into separating at the time than me, but you know, it's been eight years, he has really come a long way, we both have, and now we…'

'I wasn't referring to you, Vicky,' Alex slurs. 'I was referring to Kim's longstanding and until now unacknowledged love for my wife.'

'Oh, Alex!' I say this in chorus with Sheila and Vicky. It's possible that Tony and the kids say it too, I can't be sure.

'That's utter bullshit,' Kim says, his face ablaze.

I'm so tempted to point out that the only time there was the slightest hint of impropriety between us two couples, it was a certain incident on Brighton pier, and Kim and I were not involved. But I sense I'm not going to do myself any favours by bringing that up now.

'I'm so sorry, Kim,' I say. 'Sorry, Sheila. He's had way too much to drink. Alex, you need to apologise and you need to stop drinking.' I reach over to take his glass away, but he grabs my hand, so I'm stuck, stretched across the table, across Kim's plate.

'In vino veritas, though, don't you think, my sexy Yiddisher Mama?' Alex says, kissing my hand. 'My Bathsheba? In vino veritas.'

Baby George starts wailing. I know how he feels. With a yank, I pull my hand out of Alex's and turn to Leah, Holly and Freya, who are variously looking appalled, delighted and puzzled. 'Girls, please can you take the dirty plates in for me, and then go watch a movie. We'll have a little break before dessert.'

I say it so authoritatively that no one argues; they jump up, grab the dishes and scuttle out.

'What's going on?' Sheila asks. She is close to tears. She looks from me to Alex, and back again.

'Everything's fine, Sheila,' I reassure her.

Tony stands up and says he'll take George for a nappy change. Whether the baby needs it or not, I am grateful for Tony's tact. The door closes behind him.

Kim says, 'It's one thing to take the piss out of me, man. You've done it all your life. But don't you go dissing your wife in public. It's not cool. I don't give a shit how pissed you are, you don't do it.'

Alex laughs. 'Good to know, little brother. Good to know the etiquette. What does your manual say about mooning round after someone else's wife in public, eh?'

'Please stop it, Alex,' Sheila says.

'Alex, for your mother's sake, if not mine and Kim's, please pack it in.'

'See how easily she says "me and Kim",' Alex grins. 'It trips off her lying tongue.'

Kim stays admirably calm. 'Alex, when you have sobered up we will have a proper conversation about this.'

'Christ, Alex,' Vicky says, and I hope she's going to offer something useful. The triumph of hope over experience, I know. But she says, 'Never seen you like this. You've always been such a pushover when it comes to Eliza.'

'Not any more, brash little ex-sister-in-law of mine,' Alex says, showing his teeth. 'No more Mister Nice Guy.'

'I think maybe we should head home,' Sheila says, dabbing her eyes with her napkin.

'Al, just because you're angry with me, that's no reason to be so nasty to your family,' I say.

'No, you're right.' He smiles. 'How about they all stay, and *you* go?'

I stand up. I don't have any idea what to do.

Kim says, 'Why don't you come back with me, Al? The girls are going with Vicky, so after I've dropped Mum home, you and me can have a nice brotherly chat, you can shout at me for whatever it is you think I've done, and in the morning I'll give you a lot of coffee and send you back to apologise to Eliza.'

'Fuck off, Kim.'

'That really is the giddy limit, Alexander,' Sheila says, and pushes her chair back. 'Kim, I would like to go now, thank you.'

'Sure, Mum.' Kim stands up, and says, 'Sorry, Eliza.'

Alex gets up and, swaying slightly, says, 'I will come with you actually, Kimbo.'

'You certainly will not,' Sheila says. 'You can't speak to us like this and then expect favours. You are out of line.'

Alex starts to say, 'Mum, I—' but Sheila leaves the room. Kim scurries after her, giving me an apologetic look as he goes.

Eventually it's agreed that Alex will go with Kim after all, and Vicky will take Sheila home. I have never seen Alex's mother looking so stony-faced.

Vicky calls the girls, and shoots me an intrigued look as she and Tony round them up. For the first time in sixteen years, I am of interest to her. She even kisses me goodbye.

'But I didn't get any pavlova,' I hear Holly complain as they're outside.

Kim gets his mum into the car – she moves slowly and with difficulty these days – and Alex and I face off at the door.

'I fucked up, right?' he says, smiling.

'We'll tell them you have a brain tumour,' I say.

He leans in to me, bends down a little so I get the full force of his boozy breath in my face. 'Tell me, honestly, Liza. Just tell me. Did you like fucking Nathan?'

'Al, let's talk about this tomorrow, when you're sober.'

'Was he better than me? Please,' he says, putting his hands on my shoulders, I think mainly to help him balance. 'Please tell me. It's killing me.'

I take a breath. 'No, he was not. Alex, I'm sorry. I wish I hadn't done anything with him, and if I could turn back the clock, I would.'

He reels away. 'You loved it. You wish you'd stayed with him.'

'Of course I don't! It didn't mean anything. It was only one time, and a terrible mistake. And you know what?' I'm starting to get fed up with being placating, and with Sheila's quietly furious comment 'you are out of line' in my head, I go on, 'I can't believe you ruined lunch for this, that you thought it was OK to humiliate me in front of your family over one insignificant f-fuck from so long ago.'

'Ac-tu-all-y, it's not the fucking,' he says. I feel like both he and I have said the f-word more in the last five minutes than in the last five years. 'It's the fucking lying. It's always the fucking lying with you.'

Kim comes back to the front door to ease Alex away. Kim says, 'Don't worry, sweetheart, everything's going to be all right.' I nod, then realise he's not addressing me. Alex and I turn to where he is looking, behind us, and see that Leah is sitting on the stairs, her face a picture of misery.

'Darling,' I say, and hold out my arms to her. She comes over and tries to hug both Alex and me at once, like she used to when she was little. But Alex pulls away.

'You know what, Leah,' he says, 'I think you might be right. I think maybe I'm not your daddy after all.'

He weaves out into the street, and Kim, ashen-faced, follows him. I shut the front door, and sit on the stairs. Leah comes back over and sits next to me. I put my arm round her, smooth her hair, and tell her over and over another lie, Kim's lie. 'Don't worry, sweetheart. Everything's going to be all right.'

Chapter Twenty-Two

September 2000

It felt completely wrong being in the annex without Zaida there. Even though Mum had asked me to fill in for her, it felt like trespassing. I quietly laid out breakfast things, glancing uneasily every few minutes at the closed bedroom door. The bedroom led right off the kitchen, something Zaida often joked about ('I like to be as near food as possible, even when I'm asleep').

I sliced bagels and poppy seed platzels, spreading some with cream cheese and leaving others blank. I made both tea and coffee, to be on the safe side. I chopped up strawberries, raspberries and watermelon, and put Greek yoghurt in a bowl. I poured a glass of orange juice and stood back, admiring my work.

It was 8.30 a.m. I sat down at the table to wait. Waiting patiently was very much not my strong suit. My thoughts crowded in like ants, thousands of them, crawling towards the centre of my brain. I brushed them away over and over, but they started up again, undeterred, more numerous than ever. My head felt incredibly heavy under the wig.

My heart felt heavy too. Zaida should still be here. Sure, Beis Israel was pleasant enough, but this was where he belonged. He'd lived here my whole life, first with his wife, my Booba. She died when I was two, and I barely remember her. She died in the room that Nathan was sleeping in now. I didn't expect Nathan knew that. I probably wouldn't mention it.

Booba was already ill when my parents' marriage was arranged, and they knew from the start that she and Zaida would live with them. My father agreed to have his new in-laws to stay, as long as they had a separate space. This house was chosen specifically because of the annex, or 'granny flat', Mum said the previous owners had called it. The annex was tiny: one bedroom with an ensuite bathroom, and a kitchen-cum-living room. But my Zaida would sit on the squashy armchair, snuggle me on his knee, and say, 'I have everything I need, right here.' Even when I was very little, I was never in any doubt that he meant me.

It was impossible to think of Zaida, the strong, confident man who welcomed me in after school every day with a bagel and cream cheese, as being the same person as the confused, shrunken old man sitting idle in a home.

When the bedroom door opened I was so lost in my thoughts that for a moment I expected Zaida to walk into the kitchen, but of course it was Nathan. He was wearing a dark suit and tie, his hair combed, his beard neatly trimmed. He looked rather handsome. He must have been surprised to see me – or horrified – but he didn't show it. He stood in the doorway and waited for me to speak.

'Good morning,' I squeaked. Not quite ready to look him in the eye, I focused on the table. 'I hope it's OK, I've made you breakfast.'

I wondered if he was thinking about us on the tube two days ago. *Your voice has haunted my dreams.* If he was, he gave no indication. 'I heard someone moving about,' he said. 'I thought it was Miriam.'

'Mum asked me to stand in for her. She went to Joel's first thing, Malka isn't having a very good pregnancy and Mum's gone to help. I hope that's OK.' I realised I was gabbling.

'You can stop asking if it's OK. It's fine. I don't actually need anyone to get my breakfast, though. I'm not helpless.'

'I know. I'm sorry. I'm just trying in a small way to say thank you for, you know. Pretending, the other day. For Zaida.' I didn't, you'll notice, say that I also wanted to apologise for my following him and forcing a scene, because now I knew he must have told Dad that I'd been visiting Zaida at the home. This rather usefully stopped me feeling so bad about him. Anyway, it looked like he'd unintentionally done me quite a favour there.

Nathan sat at the place I'd laid out for him. 'Is there coffee?'

I jumped up to get the cafetière, and poured coffee into his cup.

'Is there any cream left?' he asked.

'Only milk.'

He grunted. 'Milk's fine.'

I passed the carton to him but he didn't take it, just gave a slight shake of his head. Then I remembered that he couldn't risk brushing my hand, accidentally touching me. I'd only been away a few months and I was already starting to forget important things. Though of course, we'd not only inadvertently held hands the other day when Zaida connected us, but brushed against each other on the tube. For some reason that thought made me feel even more unsettled, reminded me of how I felt lying in my room last night, in my old bed. I put the carton down next to him and we sat in silence while he added milk and stirred in sugars. Three. I made a mental note for next time I made him coffee. (Also, wow, three sugars; what sort of state were his teeth in?)

'So, you're probably wondering why I'm here,' I said.

'You told me. Blah blah Miriam, blah blah Malka.'

'I mean, why I'm back at my parents' house.'

'I heard about it from Dov last night when I got in.' He was trying to look bored, but I suspected it was put on.

'Blah blah Dov, was it?' I said, and watched as he started to smile, then switched it off as soon as he saw me looking.

'Something like that,' he drawled, hiding behind his coffee cup.

When I came over yesterday, there was so much to catch up on that I didn't think about getting back until late. Alex was away in Cardiff and I didn't fancy travelling to Brixton in the dark, letting myself into an empty flat.

'Can I stay over?' I asked Mum. 'Maybe in the annex?'

'Oh.' She looked embarrassed. 'There's someone staying there at the moment.'

'It's Nathan,' Gila burst out. She was so excited about me being there, that even though I could see she'd been sworn not to tell me, she wasn't able to help herself.

I looked at Mum. 'Uh, Nathan is staying in Zaida's flat?'

'Yes. Just temporary, you know. Till he gets on his feet.'

'I thought he was at his parents'?'

'He wasn't doing too well there,' Mum said evasively. 'He might restart at Gateshead in a few weeks, after Rosh Hashanah.'

'Stay with me and Becca in our room. Please, please,' Gila squealed. 'Your bed's still there. I've got a couple of things on it, but I'll quickly move them.' She ran upstairs.

Dov laughed. 'She's got everything she owns on your bed.'

Becca, who till now had said very little, looked at me. 'Every night for months, Gila would pray, "Dear God, when I wake up please let Aliza be back in her bed." Tomorrow morning her prayer will finally be answered.'

I felt my tears start, and put a hand on Becca's. 'I'm sorry, Becs. It must have been horrible for you.'

She took her hand away. 'You've honestly no idea,' she said.

Clearly, Becca was going to take a while to forgive me. I went up to help Gila move her stuff, and made up my old bed. Dov came in and lounged on Becca's bed, and when Jonny got back he came running upstairs and gave me a massive hug. The evening was a miraculous playing-out of all the times I'd ever imagined being back, the prodigal daughter. Then Uri and Esther came round.

Gila had told me that it was Uri who really took Dad on after the shouting at Zaida incident, and I whispered, 'thank you,' to him, but he didn't answer, didn't even look at or acknowledge me in any way. Esther was slightly less frosty and gave me a small smile. Dad was still out, so the only tension was from Uri and Becca. But even she melted a little by the time we went to bed.

We lay in the dark, us three girls, on our backs, same as always. It felt weird, but also utterly familiar, as though it was only a few days since I'd last been here.

'Will you stay for ever?' Gila asked.

'I can't. I'm married, sweetheart.'

'Not really, though.'

'Yes, really. Properly legally married.'

'Not in shul. Not to a Jewish man.'

'This is all I've heard for months,' Becca sighed. She mimicked Gila's voice. 'It's not a real marriage, so she'll soon be back.'

'Alex is lovely,' I said to Gila, but also to Becca. 'I'd like you to meet him one day.'

'Does he know you're here?' Becca asked. She always did have a knack of asking the difficult questions.

'Not exactly. Well, he's away for the night. Working.'

'Maybe he's with his family,' Gila said. 'He could stay with them, and you could stay here.'

'It's lovely to be here,' I said, 'but I don't live here now.'

The girls didn't say anything else, and after a while I knew from their breathing that they were asleep. I stayed on my back, making out the old stains on the ceiling, the map of Africa, the flower that looked like an eye, as familiar to me as my own hand. I thought of Alex, in a B&B in a Cardiff suburb, surviving, as he had texted me earlier, on a microwaved chicken chow mein from a corner shop. Then I thought of Nathan, lying chastely in the annex in Zaida's bed, and to my astonishment, my body prickled. I had never before had such feelings about Nathan. To hush my treacherous body, I rested my hand lightly on my private area, and fell asleep in that position.

Faced now with the real, daytime Nathan, those feelings seemed ridiculous. He was mildly handsome, pleasant-looking without being attractive, I decided. The frisson when I thought about our bodies pushing against each other on the tube had passed. I twisted the wedding ring on my finger, and tried to think of something to say. Would asking him how he slept be considered too salacious? Probably. I was about to say something about the post-fire redecoration of the kitchen, to stop the silence yawning on, when Nathan said, 'How was Kap, when you showed up?'

'He wasn't home. I haven't seen him since our little disagreement at Beis Israel.'

I waited for Nathan to confess that it was because of him that Dad had known I was there, but he didn't.

'I think everyone's made him feel pretty bad that he yelled at Zaida,' I continued, hoping to make Nathan feel bad too.

'He's a hot-tempered man, is Kap. And you're…' Nathan petered out.

'I'm what?'

'Nothing.' He shoved a spoonful of fruit salad in his mouth and said, 'Mmm, delicious.'

'Don't stopper your mouth with strawberries, Nathan! What were you going to say?'

Nathan smiled. 'It's so easy to remember the bad things about a person who's hurt you. I'd forgotten the things I liked about you.'

To my astonishment, the prickling night-time feeling fluttered inside me. I stared at him, the colour rising on my cheeks. I felt utterly wrong-footed, and he looked a bit taken aback himself. We stared at each other for a moment, then both looked away.

From some distance, I heard him say, 'Will this be a regular thing?'

'I don't know,' I said. Which 'this' did he mean? Encountering each other? The making of breakfast? Me hanging about in the annex? The banter? Or the frisson that shivered between us?

He drained his coffee and stood up. 'I've got to go.' He'd eaten nothing but a few strawberries.

I stood too, and moved to the door with him in his wake. He put on his hat and coat.

'I could quickly wrap a couple of bagels for you,' I said.

'Yes, OK. Thanks.' He stood waiting while I rummaged around for cling-film and a sandwich bag. I held the bag out to him, but he did another tiny shake of the head, and I put it down on the table next to the door. He picked it up and put it into his briefcase.

'Bye then,' he mumbled.

'Bye.'

'I quite like muesli,' he said, his hand on the door.

'You do? What sort? I can get some easily. With nuts, or the fruit kind?'

'Any, I don't mind.' He looked as if he wished he hadn't said anything. 'Well, bye.'

As he opened the door, he looked at me, at my hair particularly, and gave another headshake. That could get annoying pretty quickly. Then he went out.

I walked over to the mirror. The wig – the sheitel – that Mum insisted I wear, one of hers, was completely squint, tilted over to the left and showing a considerable expanse of my own hair. Christ! I served him breakfast looking like a crazy drunk woman. I let out a blast of laughter, relieving some tension, and took the sheitel off. There were droplets of sweat all round my hairline. I wondered how my mum managed, wearing hers all the time. Or Deborah. She wasn't exactly averse to complaining about most aspects of her life with little prompting, but I couldn't remember her ever mentioning it.

Mum hadn't let me go into the annex without it. 'You are a married woman, and your hair is a private matter between you and your husband.'

It was too confusing to start arguing that my husband couldn't care less whether other men saw my hair or not. Mum didn't lay down rules as regularly as Dad, but once she did, there was never any point arguing. In her own quiet way, she'd always been as hard to defy as Dad. It was amazing, really, that I had managed to disobey them both so thoroughly.

I sat down and worked my way through Nathan's breakfast. The platzels made me think of my Sunday mornings with Zaida. I came to the annex every day, but Sundays were our special day. Sundays meant onion platzels. Bagels he ate the rest of the week, or pitta bread, but for some reason platzels were special.

Even on a Sunday, no matter how early I arrived, Zaida would be up and dressed. I never saw him in anything other than a full three-piece suit and tie. Dov and I used to speculate that he wore a tie with his pyjamas. He was still in his suits at Beis Israel, though he must be boiling in them, the heat of that place.

On Sundays he might already have been to the bakery up the road by the time I arrived. Not Grodzinski's, he thought their staff were unfriendly, but Sharon's, where the platzels were five pence more expensive but the man who served him was 'a mensch'. If he hadn't been yet, we would walk there together, and he would let me carry the warm paper bag back.

My Zaida preferred onion platzels to any other kind, and I learned to love them too, to delight in the sweet taste of the translucent onions, which were stuffed into the little hole on the top of the roll. These platzels had a design flaw, for the onion would fall out as you ate. I once pointed this out to Zaida, but he, eternal optimist, knew how to spin anything into a positive.

'That's the best bit, choochie-face,' he said, beaming at me. 'You spread the cream-cheese on the platzel, you eat the platzel, and then, just when you think you've finished, you find these little bits of delicious creamy onion to nosh.'

I wish I could see the world as he used to see it: a place of continuous and unfolding delight. I wish he still saw it like that.

New Experiences

- Go on a rollercoaster – You have embarked on a metaphorical rollercoaster with me, so let's go on a real one too.
- Swim in the sea – I know you said you did this as a child but it's something we should do together soon. Exhilarating in this country; wonderful in warmer places.
- Go abroad – You've been to Israel but there's a whole world out there. Where shall we go?
- Football match – I'm not mad about football but there is something exciting about a live match. I prefer cricket but I won't make you sit through a game, they go on for days.
- Theatre – Let's see something brilliant in London. You choose.
- Drink a pint in a pub – I know you've already been to the Prince Albert, but this is the next frontier: drink a pint of beer. Well, let's start with a half. It's an acquired taste.
- Gig – There's a few big ones later this year that we could think about: Van Morrison at the Albert Hall, Lou Reed (Albert Hall again), Bob Dylan at Wembley (tough one to get tickets for), or for something a bit different, Shirley Bassey at the Festival Hall (you might like her – big diva, like your good self).

- Meditate – I can teach you. It's brilliant for emptying the mind (I know yours sometimes feels a bit busy).
- Watch a film in the back row of the cinema – The traditional place for kissing and holding hands.
- Jeans – Buy and wear a pair. A derriere like yours shouldn't be hidden away.
- Ice-skating – I haven't been since I was a kid. I think you might like it.
- Play a slot machine in an amusement arcade – A great thing to do at the seaside. Hours of fun for a couple of quid.
- Try on a Wonderbra – I admit this one is probably more for my own benefit.

Chapter Twenty-Three

October 2000

My favourite festival when I was little was Sukkot, the Feast of Tabernacles. I loved it because we'd build a shelter in the garden, from wood slats and branches. This took several days. Dad and Uri always did the bulk of the building, and when it was finished we younger ones would crowd in and decorate it, inside and out, with leaves and flowers.

In Springfield Street they'd soon be getting ready to celebrate Sukkot. Meanwhile, in the Real World, Alex and I were in Brighton with Kim and Vicky. I'd secretly decided to actively avoid Vicky, for the rest of my life if possible, and had managed not to see her since Easter. But a few days ago, Kim had come over and asked Alex and I to join him and Vicky on his birthday outing.

'I want to go on the Turbo Coaster on Brighton pier, but Vicky's too pregnant to go on it.'

'Isn't life with Vicky enough of a rollercoaster for you?' Alex said.

'I'll come on it with you, Kim,' I said.

'Really? Awesome!'

'Yeah, Eliza's a veteran of these things,' Alex said. 'Well, she's been on one, anyway.' His voice sounded angry, but he looked normal. I stared at him but he wouldn't catch my eye.

'Yes,' I said, 'at Thorpe Park.'

'Did you like it, Eliza?' Kim asked.

'I loved it.'

'She screamed the whole way,' Alex said. 'I like a woman who screams.'

Kim flicked a glance at me. He was clearly wondering why Alex was being so rude to me. I pretended nothing was up. 'I'd like to go to Brighton,' I said. 'My family went there once when I was little, but I don't remember much about it.'

'It's the perfect place for a birthday outing,' Kim said. 'Rollercoaster, chips on the beach…'

'Bit fucking cold for chips on the beach, isn't it?' Alex said.

'You old grouch,' Kim said. 'You up for it, Eliza?'

'Definitely.'

'There's some things on the "New Experiences" list you could do while we're there,' Alex said, brightening. 'Slot machines, swim in the sea…'

'Hang on,' Kim said. 'How come it's too cold to eat chips on the beach but not too cold for Eliza to swim?'

'She can dip her toes in.'

'I have swum in the sea, you know,' I said.

'Not since you were a kid.'

I shivered at the thought of it. 'I might save that one for next summer.'

Kim got up to go. 'Your birthday next month,' he reminded Alex, as he shrugged on his leather jacket. 'What are you going to do?'

'Dunno. Something grown-up, I should think. Dinner and a movie. Not candyfloss.'

'Oh yes, you're so mature.' Kim gave Alex a playful push, and Alex gave Kim a considerably more forceful shove back. 'See you Saturday, guys.'

When Kim had gone, I raised my eyebrows at Alex.

'What?'

'You were a bit weird with Kim.'

Though I said this, I knew that his mood wasn't anything to do with Kim. For a few weeks, I had been living a double life. I wasn't ready to tell Alex about what I was up to, for fear of worrying him. I didn't want him to think I wanted to go back to my old life. So since reconnecting with my family I'd had to invent outings with Genevieve from work as an excuse for some of it (she *was* really nice, but I didn't see her socially), and visits to Zaida for other times (that at least was true). I regularly found myself changing clothes in the toilet at the station, or telling Alex I had to get in early to work. A couple of times I'd even had to eat two suppers when I forgot to coordinate things. On the plus side, Becca was far more friendly now, and Nathan and I had moved past some of our initial awkwardness. For Dov and Gila, it was like I'd never been gone.

The downside was that Alex was getting a bit fed up with how absent I was.

'I was normal,' he said. '*You* were the one who was fucking weird. "Oh yes, Kim, I'll come and sit on your lap on the rollercoaster."'

'That's silly.'

'Is it?' He went out of the room, and we avoided each other for the rest of the day.

Things still weren't right between us when we met Kim and Vicky at Victoria Station a couple of days later. Alex and Kim's mum was taking care of Holly, and Kim seemed to have taken over the role occupied by a child – 'I love my birthday!' He was delighted by the gifts Alex and

I gave him: a selection of CDs and books that we knew he wanted, each one individually wrapped, so that it took him quite a lot of the journey to get through them all.

It was sunny but cold, and Vicky was wearing her fluffy white coat, undone because the buttons wouldn't reach across her pregnant tummy. Her bust seemed to have doubled in size, a fact of great pride to her.

'I got quite titty when I was preggers with Holly,' she told me and Alex, mostly Alex, 'but nothing like this.'

The creamy upper slopes of her breasts were on display in one of her almost-no-buttons shirts and I was sure Alex must be finding it difficult to look away; I know I was. Kim behaved as if Vicky wasn't there, an uncomfortable experience made more so by him directing most of his conversation to me. It was a relief when we arrived at Brighton and walked down the wide busy street to the pier. I was dazzled by the noise, the lights, the crowds of people, the sickly smells of doughnuts and waffles. Thorpe Park was much bigger, but here it was all contained in a small place: the dodgems were right up against the Haunted House, the rollercoaster directly above our heads. I watched it loop round and plummet, the screams of the passengers ringing in my ears.

'Who's in?' Kim shouted, his eyes flashing with excitement.

'Not me,' Vicky said, stroking her tummy.

'Me and Alex!' I cried. I could see that there were seats for three.

'You're all going to leave me on my fucking own, then?' Vicky said. She folded her arms, did a mock pout, but I could see she was feeling genuinely left out.

'I'll stay—' I started to say, but almost at the same time she said, 'You'll keep me company won't you, Ally-Boy?'

Alex looked from me to her, and said, 'Sure. It'll be a pleasure.'

'Oh, Ally, you are a true gent.' Vicky fanned her hands in front of her face. 'You're making me cry!'

I started to protest, to say that the brothers should go together and I'd stay with her, but Vicky was already dragging Alex away to buy candyfloss, and Kim was in the queue, calling me. We clambered into our seats and Kim had to help me with my seat belt, which caused us both embarrassment when his hand brushed my lap; he yanked it away as though it was radioactive. We then had to wait a while as others took their seats, and there was an awkward silence.

'Are you having a good day?' I asked.

'Brilliant,' he said, smiling down at me. 'Are you?'

'Oh, yes.'

'Alex seems in a bit of a bad mood, though. Again.'

I'd hoped Kim wouldn't have noticed. I didn't want his birthday to be spoiled. But there was no point pretending as he clearly knew something was off.

'I'm not sure why,' I said. 'He's been a bit cross with me lately.'

'I don't know how anyone could be cross with you, Eliza.'

Embarrassed again, I blurted, 'Well, I've been going out a bit more, and we've had less time together.' I hadn't intended to say anything but Kim's soft eyes on mine made me uncharacteristically outspoken.

'Does he not like you going out?' Kim said. He shook his head. 'That's a bit bloody much.'

'Oh, no, I don't mean that. I mean…'

What did I mean? And why was I talking about my husband like this, to his brother? His brother, who I was aware had certain tricky feelings? I tried to turn his attention away from me. 'Does Vicky mind when you go out?'

'Christ no, she can't get me out of the house enough. Mind you… ooh, here we go!'

The mechanisms began clanking, the tinny music started up again, and we were slowly raised into the air.

'Mind you,' Kim continued, 'I'm pretty happy for *her* to go out. More often the better.'

'I suppose with her pregnant,' I said, feeling ever more awkward, 'and a little one in the house, it can be a bit stressful…'

The coaster climbed up and up, until we seemed impossibly high above the rest of the fairground, the sea sparkling a long way down.

'Oh, look how far up we are!' I said.

'Shouldn't have married her,' he said.

I turned to look at him; his face was serious. 'Oh, Kim, no, you can't mean that?'

We suddenly plummeted down, headfirst, at immense speed. I felt my hair whip back behind me. I screamed at the top of my lungs, and Kim grabbed my hand, and for a few moments I honestly thought we were going to die. Then with a teeth-shattering jerk, we pulled up and began moving slowly towards a loop.

'Oh my god, this is much scarier than the one at Thorpe Park!'

Kim was still holding my hand and I didn't know how to extract it, other than to rudely pull it away, and anyway we were now moving into the loop, which meant we would shortly be upside down… I screwed my eyes shut and held his hand even tighter. I couldn't stop myself screaming again as we went round and round the loop: right way up, upside down, then whisked the right way up again, as though we were beetles being cruelly flicked by a bored child. It seemed for ever before we levelled out and there was a breathing space as we began a slow climb again. I managed to pull my hand away.

'Alex has always had a strong personality,' Kim said.

'I guess so.' My breath was short, and I was anxious about the next plummets, in both the rollercoaster and the conversation. 'He has lots of ideas, and knows what he likes doing.'

We had to stop talking then, as we plunged at extraordinary speed down on to another track. Kim grabbed my hand again. My throat felt raw with all the screaming.

'He always called the shots when we were kids,' Kim said. He seemed unperturbed by the sudden nosedive we'd just come out of. 'It made me feel, I don't know, a bit hemmed in.'

I didn't know what to say. 'Oh.'

'What about you, Eliza?'

'What about me?'

'Well.' He looked away. 'You didn't marry…'

Again we lurched downwards, and his words were drowned out by the noise of the coaster and my own shouts.

'What?' I yelled, as we pulled into a slow uphill section.

'You didn't marry someone else back then. You wanted to avoid a restrictive marriage.'

'That wasn't the only…'

'I wondered if you feel restricted now?'

'What do you mean, restricted?' I gripped the bar at the front tighter. We were speeding up, and I could tell we were shortly going to…

'With Alex?'

'What? I can't hear…'

Down, down, we went, and it seemed that we would surely crash this time. It felt that we were horribly close to the ground and I closed my eyes.

'With Alex!' he shouted. His ability to keep talking while plunging to certain death was incredible.

'What do you mean?' I managed to say as we avoided the pier at the last minute and started a groaning, clunking climb.

'You can't do what you want? He tells you what you should do?'

My heart started thudding. What *was* this conversation? 'Sometimes, maybe.'

'I don't think he gives you enough freedom,' Kim said. '*I* would.'

I chose to ignore the second part. 'I have plenty of freedom,' I said. 'Much more than if I'd stayed in Hackney.'

His answer was lost as we went into another loop. I could hear everyone else screaming along with me.

'Are you scared?' Kim said as we levelled out.

'Yes! No! I love it and hate it at the same time.'

'A good description of marriage,' he said. 'Well, not mine.'

In a level moment before the next drop, I looked down at the sea, sparkling blue in the sunshine, and at the pier. We were almost at the highest point of the climb again, and I could see little people down below like dolls. None of them were taking their lives in their hands like us. None of them were doing anything so daring. Presumably none of them were having a conversation like this, either. I saw Alex and Vicky standing by the railings at the side of the pier. I recognised her white-coated arms around his neck and his dark head bent towards her before I registered that they were kissing. I lost sight of them almost as soon as I'd seen them, as we went into a final speed-of-sound drop that made my teeth rattle in my head. As we came out of the dive and slowed down ready to stop, I twisted round trying to pick them out but couldn't get my bearings. I looked at Kim but he clearly hadn't seen anything amiss. Which side of the pier had they been on? It was impossible to work it out. We at last came to a halt and I felt so confused, it didn't even feel awkward taking my hand out of Kim's.

'Thank you, that was brilliant,' I said, and before he could say any more intense stuff I was out of the belt, out of my seat and back on the ground. Vicky and Alex were standing waiting for us, leaning against the coconut shy, quite separate from each other. I walked towards them on wobbly legs.

'Did you get a picture?' Kim asked Vicky, out of breath.

'Oh no, I forgot,' she said. 'Sorry. We were busy.'

'Doing what?' I asked, looking at Alex, at the frowning quotation marks between his eyes. They came out when he was anxious, or angry. Which was it?

'Looking for candyfloss,' Vicky said. 'Can't fucking find any.'

'There's some right there,' Kim said, pointing to a stall behind her.

Vicky laughed. 'Couldn't see for looking,' she said. She pulled Kim over towards it, and Alex put an arm round me. I could smell Vicky's perfume on his jacket.

'Was it good?' he asked.

'It was great. Was it good for you?' I replied, my stomach feeling even more hollow than when I'd been on the rollercoaster.

'I didn't go on it,' he said, looking puzzled.

'I know.' I decided not to say anything now. It was Kim's day. Vicky was decorating his eyebrows with candyfloss and he was laughing.

'Shall we go on the amusements?' Alex said. 'I'll show you the 2p falls, they're my favourite.' He pulled me closer and pressed his lips against my cheek. 'I really love you,' he said. 'Don't ever forget it.'

We walked on the pebbly beach, and I tested the water with my hand. It was so cold, I resisted all Alex's entreaties to take my shoes off and have a paddle. He went in up to his knees, though only for a few seconds before he came running out, or more accurately staggering, on the stones, laughing about how freezing it was. Vicky told him to sit and she'd rub his legs warm, but he said he would soon be fine if we kept on walking. We got fish and chips and ate them on the beach, their warmth welcome as the sun went down.

'This was a brilliant birthday,' Kim said as we sank into our seats on the train home. He put his arm round Vicky's shoulders.

'That's not comfortable, Kim,' she said. 'You're making my neck ache.' She moved his arm, and he grinned across at me. 'Told you, she thinks I'm a pain in the neck.'

Back in the flat, Alex kicked off his shoes and said, 'I'm going for a bath. I'm still a bit cold from the sea.'

I made some tea, and took it into the bathroom. He was lying in a deep bath, no bubbles, his long body stretched out under the water. Even after all these months, it still seemed extraordinarily shocking that I could see a naked man whenever I wanted to. And sometimes when I didn't want to. I put his tea on the edge of the bath.

'Ah, this will warm my insides, thank you,' he said.

I opened my mouth to tell him what I'd seen, then closed it again. I felt too silly, like I was trying to be someone in a film. I thought instead about Gila and Dov, draping bunches of sage over the roof of the sukkah.

I said, 'Genevieve rang, and asked if I can go shopping with her tomorrow.'

'On a Sunday?' Alex said. He sat up and took a gulp of tea. With his wet hair slicked back, he looked like a man I'd seen on a poster on the tube, advertising something, I didn't remember what.

'Well, the big shops are open.'

'I mean, we normally do things on Sunday. You and me. Together.'

'It's only for a couple of hours in the morning. I'll be back in the afternoon.'

He splashed water on his face. 'OK, sure.'

When Dad and Uri saw me coming into the back garden, they both quietly disappeared. This was what they did every time I showed up at the house. Gila threw her arms tightly round my waist, more than making up for it, and Dov said, 'Ah, great, you can put some of this stuff on the roof, my arms are aching.'

'Isn't this young lady helping you?' I asked, swinging Gila in my arms.

'She claims to be too short still,' Dov said.

'I am! Look!' Gila stood on tiptoes to try to reach the top of the sukkah.

'One more year, I reckon,' I told her. I took some branches and spread them across the roof myself. The simple action took me back, far back, to when I was younger than Gila, watching Uri doing the same thing. Dov and Gila, meanwhile, took on a side of the sukkah each, twisting fronds in and out of the wooden supports. It took us quite a long time to cover the structure, and when we finally stepped back to look at it, I was impressed.

'Wow, we've surpassed ourselves. Isn't it bigger than usual?'

'Yes, Nathan built the frame,' Gila said blithely, not realising the effect on me of her casual naming.

'We'll have to get him to do it every time, this one's miles stronger than we've ever managed before,' Dov said. 'Let's go inside.'

We crowded together in the centre of the structure, sunlight flitting through the leaves on the roof to cast patterns on our faces. I breathed in deeply, loving that scent of foliage, of childhood freedom. Mum put her head in and asked if we wanted our lunch in there, and we chorused 'yes' as though we were little children. She handed through plates of sandwiches, and the three of us sat on the ground to eat them, enjoying the annual novelty of being in an outside house.

Dov pushed his hand against a wall. 'Solid as a rock. Do you remember that year it fell down the minute Jonny put a branch on the roof?' He started laughing at the memory, and Gila joined in, though she was, I was sure, too young to have been there.

'Weren't you in it at the time?' I said to Dov, and he – doubled up and now laughing too much to answer – nodded.

'I've got a confession,' I went on. 'I did lean on it a bit to encourage it to collapse on you.'

'No!' Dov, still laughing, grabbed my arm and gave me a weak Jewish burn, a pinching thing we used to do as kids. 'I can't believe you would suddenly confess to that after all these years!'

'Aliza's full of surprises,' a voice said from outside, and moments later Nathan was squashed in with us too. He made sure to sit next to Dov, not touching Gila or me, but he still seemed very close, almost as close as he had been that day on the tube.

'Like it?' he said, and it felt that the question was directed at me.

'It's the best ever,' I replied, colouring. Were we talking about the sukkah?

'We were saying,' Dov said, 'that we must get you to build this every year. We have never managed one so big that actually stayed up.'

'Well, who knows where I'll be next year?' Nathan said, smiling. 'A lot can happen in that sort of time, isn't that right, Aliza?'

'I guess so,' I said. 'I'll, er, go and see if Mum needs some help.' I wriggled past Nathan and got out of the sukkah before my face burned up.

Mum was washing up and roped me into drying. It was a lovely familiar thing to do, and I quickly got back into the old rhythm. We talked about neutral things: the sukkah, Gila's school, the illnesses of various older relatives.

'Are you staying for supper?' she asked, as I put away the last of the dishes.

'I'd love to, but I said I'd be back early afternoon.'

'It's nearly three,' Mum said.

'Oh no, is it? Sh—' I almost swore. I kissed her hurriedly instead, and grabbed my things. 'Sorry, Mum, I'd better run.'

She looked at me oddly. 'See you soon.'

'Al, I'm so sorry, I lost track of time.' I burst into the flat, breathless from running.

Alex was sitting on the sofa reading a book. He didn't look up, or say anything.

I sat next to him and tried to get him to look at me. 'We can do whatever you like. I really am sorry.'

'No, *I'm* sorry. Sorry that I'm not as much fun to hang out with as *Genevieve*.'

'Don't be daft!'

I put my hand on his shoulder, but he shook me off. 'Honestly, Eliza!' He slammed his book shut. 'You said you'd be a couple of hours, so I've been hanging round waiting for you. Kim invited me over, and I told him no, because I thought you'd be back.'

The mention of Kim reminded me that Alex didn't have a leg to stand on. How dare he start on me, after what he'd done? The anger inside me bubbled up to the surface. 'Yes,' I said, 'I'm sure it was disappointing for you, missing out on Vicky today.'

'Eh? What's that supposed to mean?'

I folded my arms. 'I saw you.'

'Saw me what?' His voice was innocent but I could see from his face that he knew.

'You and her. Yesterday. On the pier.' He didn't say anything, just stared at me. I took a big gulp of air. 'I saw you kissing her.'

He laughed, which struck me as highly inappropriate. 'Actually, you saw her kissing me.'

'Why the hell are you laughing, Alex? What difference does it make who kissed who?'

'A lot! Look, I should have told you straight after—'

'Yes, you damn well should! Why do you think I didn't want to be here today?' I was shouting, and couldn't seem to stop. 'It isn't funny, it's horrible. Why *didn't* you tell me? There's only one possible reason that I can think of, and that's because you liked it, and hope it will happen again – and maybe more, who knows.'

'Eliza!' Alex took hold of my arm, not painfully, but firmly, like you'd hold someone who was about to cross the road against the lights. 'That is emphatically not the reason. The truth is, I didn't tell you because I was too embarrassed. I don't know how long you were watching, but if you'd hung around with your binoculars for a little longer, you'd have seen that she pounced on me and that I pushed her away almost immediately.'

'Almost, huh?' I stood up, and walked over to the window. I didn't want Alex to see that I was crying.

'Christ, Eliza! It took me a moment to realise what was happening. Then I told her to fuck off.'

'She didn't behave like you'd rejected her, when me and Kim showed up,' I said. I rubbed a mark off the window with my thumb. The whole place was dirty, it seemed to me.

'She thought the entire thing was hilarious. She said she'd tell Kim I kissed her, and then said she was only joking when she saw how angry I was.' Alex came over to me, and tried to take my hand, but I pulled it away.

'If that's all it was, then I can't understand why you didn't say anything.'

'You're right, it was stupid not to tell you. I would have done soon, anyway. I was just wanting not to think about it for a few days. It wasn't a particularly pleasant experience.'

He appeared to be genuine, but I couldn't shake the image of those white sleeves round his neck.

'Eliza? Come on. Don't cry. She's not worth a single one of your tears. How could you think I'd kiss someone like her when I'm married to someone like you?'

'You find her very sexy.' I turned to face him, my arms still folded, a barrier between us.

'I find her very tarty. *You're* the one who's very sexy.' He stroked the back of my neck. It didn't work its usual magic, and I realised that I couldn't remember the last time that his touching me had made me jump, the way it did when we first met. When he leaned in closer, I moved away.

'I can't. I just feel so weird and upset about you and her.'

'There *is* no me and her.'

'I don't know.' I shook my head. 'She'd love the chance to be with you.'

'Maybe she would. But I do have a say in it, you know. I don't fancy her, Eliza. I don't even like her. I think Kim could have done a lot better. And even more importantly, I love *you*. I want to be with *you*.'

'You should have told me. And I think you should apologise,' I said, surprised at my own daring.

'You're right. I'm sorry,' he said. His eyes looked worried. Worried that I wouldn't believe him? Or worried that I had found him out? I knew he was a player once: all those girlfriends, that long, intimidating list of them. He might still be. I looked into his eyes; could I trust him? I thought about Nathan's steady pale eyes.

Then I thought: *Can Alex trust me?*

Chapter Twenty-Four

March–April 2016

After Kim took Alex away from our nightmare Easter Sunday lunch, Leah and I spent a weird bank holiday without him. We watched a film together that evening – *The Princess Bride*, always our go-to film to cheer us up when she was younger. It worked some of its old magic, as I think we both felt a little less wrung-out afterwards; it was also a good thing to do as we didn't have to try and make conversation. On Bank Holiday Monday she went out with her friends, and I stayed in and worried, and ate most of the chocolate Alex had bought for Leah. I didn't hear from him, but neither did I try and get in touch with him. I thought it was good, grown-up, that we were giving each other space. Kim, always thoughtful, texted a couple of times to say that Al was OK and they were chatting and chilling.

Alex came home late on Monday evening. He was quiet and apologised briefly for making a scene, but apart from that, he most definitely did not want to talk about it. And I was happy not to, either. Then he plunged headlong back into work, and so did I, and Leah went to stay at Sheila's for a few days over the school holidays, and when she came back she did her own thing a lot while Alex and I worked, and I thought we'd settled back into normality. Evenings

Leah would often be out at a friend's, and Alex and I would eat supper, watch TV, and not talk much. He conspicuously didn't drink more than one glass of wine in an evening. We certainly didn't talk about anything important. Every time I thought about raising it, I thought about his face when we stood in the hall, him saying, 'It's not the fucking, it's the fucking lying.'

The last time we'd made love was Maundy Thursday.

Two days after the end of the holidays, Leah's friend Macy comes round after school. I look behind her up the street but there's no sign of Leah. Then I remember that she's at after-school drama.

'Is everything OK, Macy?'

'Yeah.' She stands there, hesitating.

'Well, Leah's not back yet. Do you want to come in?'

She does so, looking worried. 'Don't tell Leah I came, she'll kill me.'

'What's going on? Have you two fallen out?'

'No. Yeah, maybe.'

I make her a coffee and eventually she tells me, with much coaxing, that Leah has been skipping after-school activities and going off somewhere unknown. That she's become secretive, seems anxious; that she isn't hanging out with Macy or her other friends. I'm paraphrasing – Macy does her best to express herself but her teen-speak isn't up to the subtleties she wants to get across. She's concerned, I can see that, but struggling to explain why. I have to do a reasonable amount of Alex-style detective cross-examination to get even the smallest snippets.

'How long have you been worried about her?'

'From before Easter.'

'And you don't have any idea where she goes when she's not at the clubs, Macy?'

'No.'

'Any thoughts at all on what's going on?'

'No. Well. I think it's something to do with. Well.'

'Something to do with… her dad and me?'

Macy nods, relieved I've spelled it out for her. 'I think maybe sometimes she meets her cousin. The boy?'

That little shit, Gidon!

'I'm very grateful to you for letting me know, Macy.'

'Don't tell her.'

'I won't.' I wonder *why* Macy has told me. It definitely flouts some teen code of honour. A cold feeling stirs in my gut. 'Are you really worried about her?'

She frowns. 'I think she might do something crazy.'

'Oh my god, what do you mean, hurt herself?'

'Oh, no. Not that. Something. Nothing, probably.' She gulps down her coffee. 'Better go.'

I see her to the door and thank her again. She steps out on to the path, and over her shoulder, she says, 'She wants to find her real dad.' Then she breaks into a run.

At the exact time that Leah would have got back home had she been to drama, I hear her key in the door. She's in school uniform, her school backpack absolutely bulging with god knows what.

'Good day, darling?' I ask, my voice light.

'Yeah.'

'I've got you a cupcake,' I say. She trails into the kitchen, and sits on the edge of her seat, so she can keep her suspiciously full backpack on. I guess it has non-school clothes in, so she can hang round the shopping centre without drawing too much attention to herself.

'The school rang this afternoon,' I say, not thinking ahead too far because I can't bear to guess where it might go.

Her head jerks up. 'Why?' she says, mouth full of cake.

'They said you haven't been going to your after-school clubs.'

'Fucking liars.'

'Leah...'

'Oh fuck off, Mum.' She puts the cake down and storms upstairs.

I make supper, listening to the stomping and loud music upstairs, a parody of stroppy teen behaviour. When Alex comes in I pour him a (small) glass of wine, and tell him what Macy said. I am completely unprepared for his solution.

'Our situation's having a bad effect on Leah,' he says.

'What does "our situation" have to do with it?'

'She's devastated that we've been fighting.'

'Well, other than that lunch' – I can't bring myself to say 'Easter Sunday', as it's associated with such an awful feeling – 'we haven't been fighting at all.'

'That's because we've barely been speaking.'

'Let's speak now, then.'

'I'm not ready.'

'You're still so angry with me?'

He shrugs. 'I'm working through it.'

'Christ, Alex!' I sit down. I feel very tired. 'I know it was bad, but it was one time, fifteen years ago.'

'You lied to me about it for fifteen years, Eliza. If Leah hadn't have started digging I would never have known. You would never have said.'

'You don't have to know everything.'

'Can you hear yourself?' He sighs. 'I do sometimes wonder if you are a bit stunted, psychologically, when it comes to relationships.'

'What an absolutely appalling thing to say!' My eyes fill with angry tears.

He pushes his glass of wine away, untouched. 'Liza, I don't want to fight any more. You're tired, I'm tired. We need to put Leah first.'

'I thought we always did.'

'We haven't lately.'

'So, what do you want to do?' I play my trump card. 'I don't know if I can bear to have counselling, but I will if you want.'

'I'm already seeing a counsellor,' he says, taking the wind right out of my sails.

'You are? Since when?'

'Since after I went to Kim's, the Easter weekend.'

'How often have you seen him?'

'Her. Twice a week for the last three weeks.'

'Oh. What does she think?'

'Counselling isn't about what the counsellor thinks. It's about what I think, it's about working it through.'

'So what do *you* think, Alex?'

'I think we need a little space from each other for a bit.'

'God, what are you saying?'

He goes over to the sink. With his back to me, he says, 'The counsellor thinks I'm too angry with you to have a proper discussion right now.'

'You just said it wasn't about what the counsellor thinks.'

'OK then, *I* think I'm too angry to have a proper discussion right now.'

'Don't you think it would help you stop being so angry with me if we could talk about it?'

'I'm not ready.'

'Please, Al, will you look at me?'

He turns round, and his face is so sad. Perhaps I've made him more miserable during our marriage than I'd realised.

'So how do you think we should facilitate this "little space"?' I say, trying not to emphasise the inverted commas.

'Last time our marriage was in trouble,' he says, 'I went back to my family.'

'Er, yes. We both did. What's your point?'

'I went first. This time, it's your turn.'

'Pardon?'

'Just for a short while.'

'We take *turns* to leave each other?!'

'Let me handle Leah for a bit,' he says. 'She's rebelling against you much more than me. And she's furious with you for not being straight about whether Nathan could have been her father.'

'Nathan is not her father, OK? And you're the one who's furious, not her!'

He gets up. 'I'm going to go talk to her.'

I let my head sink into my arms, and listen to him going upstairs. I stay like that for ten minutes, not really thinking about anything at all. Then I go upstairs too, and pack a bag. When I hear Alex come out of Leah's room and go back down, I tentatively knock on her door. She is standing at her dressing table, the drawers all open. She turns round and pulls her backpack closer to her.

'Leah,' I say gently, 'I'm going to go away for a few days.'

She turns big, wet eyes on me. 'Why?'

'I just need a little break. A holiday. I haven't had one for ages.'

'Is it because of me?'

'Oh god, no darling!' I move towards her and she steps back. I sit on the bed so she doesn't think I'm going to pounce. 'The fact is, me and Dad need a bit of space from each other. We're getting on each other's nerves.'

'Will you come back?'

'Yes, of course!' I make my voice sound as definite as possible. 'Want a hug, Leah?'

This time she does come to me. She moves into my arms and I hold her tight.

'I'd like a little holiday too,' she says.

'Would you? But you're not long back from Granny's.'

'I want to go somewhere I've never been. Like somewhere up north.'

'Well, you know what, let's do that soon. May half-term, maybe?'

She nods, her head moving up and down against my neck. Finally, she breaks away, and goes back to her dressing table. 'Text me.'

'Of course. Text me back?'

There is no such flowery send-off with Alex. He tells me he'll rearrange his work for the rest of the week so he can be around properly for Leah. Flexibility is, as he has often said, one of the perks of running his own business.

'I'll talk to her about sagging off her after-school commitments, though I'm not that bothered about it,' he says.

'Me neither, but I think it's a symptom of something else,' I say. 'Could you try and dig a bit around whatever is going on in her head about…' I hesitate, 'her "real dad"?'

'Shame we can't get her real dad to lend us a hand with the parenting, eh?' Alex says.

He walks me to the front door, as if he is actively seeing me off the premises. It feels all a bit over the top, but as I start to say something, he says, 'Bye, Eliza,' and walks back into the house, leaving me to close the front door behind me. Vicky's words to Alex come into my mind: 'You've always been a pushover when it comes to Eliza.' Is Alex trying to show that he isn't a pushover any longer?

I was going to go to Dov's, the obvious first port of call. But my feelings about him are less crystal-clear than usual, muddled up with thoughts of Gidon and Nathan. I ring Deborah instead. *Yes, yes,* she says. *Come now.*

Chapter Twenty-Five

November 2000

Alex once told me about Carolyn, a girlfriend of Kim's, who he was involved with long before Vicky. It turned out that Carolyn was addicted to gambling, but Kim didn't realise. He knew she liked fruit machines, the sort I played on when we were in Brighton. If Carolyn went anywhere that had one, she always had to have a go on it. But Kim didn't know that when she wasn't with him, she was in an amusement arcade, putting in endless coins, using up all her money. It got worse and worse, till she didn't care that he knew, till she lost her job, till she was even stealing money from him. It ended when she was arrested for stealing from someone she didn't know: she took a woman's purse out of her bag in a supermarket. I was so shocked when Alex told me. I couldn't understand her behaviour at all, how she could have got so out of control.

But I ought to have felt a bit more sympathy towards her, because I was in the grip of a compulsion myself. It was no less strong than the one I'd had a year ago, when I first saw Alex and knew I had to be with him. My compulsion now was the exact opposite: I was being pulled back into my old life. But I didn't think of it in that way, not till Alex accused me of becoming addicted to leading a double life.

Then I remembered Carolyn, and wondered if we weren't as different as I'd thought.

The day I came back late from building the sukkah, Alex finally showed how upset he was by my mysterious absences, though his concerns got sidelined by the much bigger Vicky-kiss row. I vowed to myself then that I would slow things down. But the truth was, I couldn't seem to help it; after that, my going out actually increased. I was out nearly every other evening, and much of the weekend. I added an evening class in history to my roster of Genevieve outings and Zaida visits – I got the idea from Genevieve herself, who was the one actually doing the class. And on Alex's work days I'd go to the annex early, to make Nathan breakfast.

Things were much more relaxed between Nathan and me; he even allowed me to pass him various breakfast items now he knew I'd make sure not to accidentally touch him. Our conversations were still a little stilted, but I reckoned that would improve, given enough time.

On Sunday, when I told Alex that Genevieve had asked me to go see a film with her, he said irritably, 'Seriously, again?'

'She's split up with her boyfriend.' The lie came easily. 'She wants someone to do things with.'

'She must have some friends other than you. We haven't done anything together for ages.'

'I thought you'd be glad I'm building up my social life.'

'I am, of course I am. But I want us to do things together, too. You're out so much, I feel I've barely seen you properly for weeks.'

We agreed a compromise; I'd go out with my 'friend' in the morning, and spend the afternoon with Alex. I saw Zaida, had lunch with Mum and some of the others; I avoided Dad completely; and then I came back in good time, and Alex and I watched the next film from his list, *Some Like It Hot.* Afterwards, we made love.

It was a memorably good day, because it was the very next one that things were blown apart.

I left the flat at my usual time, but on the way, I phoned work and said I was sick. I really wanted to spend as much time as possible with my family. I didn't think about it any more deeply than that. All I knew was that when I was back in my parents' house, I felt whole again, in a way I hadn't felt for a long time. I changed into my old clothes at Brixton tube loo as usual, got to Mum's shortly after eight, and borrowed her sheitel. I was getting better at putting it on straight, and even starting to get used to the heat of it. It felt less hot, anyway, now that we were properly into autumn. I went through the connecting door into the annex to make Nathan breakfast. But he was already sitting at the table. That was new.

'Oh! You're up. Shall I get you some coffee?'

'No thank you. Please sit down, Aliza.'

His voice was quiet, but surprisingly commanding. I sat opposite him. He looked directly at me, and try as I could to maintain eye contact with him, I had to look away.

'Do you think you made a mistake?' he said.

I looked at him then, all right. 'Pardon?'

'A mistake, when you didn't marry me?' His voice shook a little, but he still looked straight at me.

I studied my hands. 'I think it was the right thing at the time.'

'It was scarcely more than ten months ago. Are you that changeable?'

'I haven't changed! I'm still very much in love with Alex.' My voice wavered saying Alex's name out loud. It was the first time I had said it to Nathan. It felt like the most intimate thing I had ever said to him.

There was a silence, then he said, 'Well, in that case, Aliza, I don't know why you're here.'

I didn't answer. I was struggling to explain it to myself, let alone to him. Why was I here, more mornings than not? Why was I was making him breakfast like the subservient Jewish wife I had so spectacularly failed to be? Was I trying to make amends for jilting him? Was I worried about his post-jilted state and trying to make sure he ate a good breakfast, at least? Was there more to it? He had a right to know what it meant. If it meant anything.

'Well, if it comes to it, I don't know why *you* are here either,' I said, playing for time.

He laughed, and rubbed his hand across his brow. 'I have been wondering that myself rather a lot, lately.' His face went back to its habitual serious expression. 'I gave up the flat we were going to have. You and me.'

'I'm sorry.' I'd never seen this flat, which Nathan had found for us, a few streets away from his family.

He waved his hand, to say that was the least of it. 'I went back to the yeshiva after we… I thought I could resume my life back there, but it didn't work. They said I'd had a breakdown and they sent me back to my parents.'

'Oh, Nathan. I'm…'

'You're sorry. Yes, I know. I couldn't stand it with my parents, though. I couldn't bear the, the, the, scrutiny. The pity.' He wiped his mouth with a tissue. 'Your mother is wonderful, and leaves me to myself.'

'She *is* wonderful.'

'So, that's why *I'm* here. Why are you here, Aliza?'

I stared down at the table. I wished the answer was written there. 'I... I'm not really sure.'

'Did you get scared, out in the big world?' His voice was mocking. 'Being a secular girl not working out how you hoped?'

'I missed my family.'

'I'm not your family, but you seem to be spending a lot of time with me. Playing house. Fussing round me.'

'I'm sorry if it's seemed like fussing. I was trying to show how sorry I was that I wrecked things.'

'Don't flatter yourself, Aliza. I'll bounce back. I'm not wrecked. Which is more than I can say for you.'

I remembered him saying, *you broke me*. I didn't think he could have got mended so quickly. I stood up. 'I was only trying to be nice, Nathan.'

'I thought I'd find some peace here.' He raised his voice. 'A quiet flat, be on my own, try and work out what I'm going to do next. And then you turn up, wafting in and out like this is your house, like I'm your husband. I'm not your husband. I wanted to be, but you, you, you...' He didn't finish the sentence, but instead bowed his head and closed his eyes, shutting me out.

'I'm sorry I disturbed your peace.' I felt desperately sorry for him. I looked down at him, at the top of his head, at the blue skull cap nestled in his hair, the curls on his collar. I felt sorry for myself, too. 'But you did choose to stay in the house of the family whose daughter... You weren't exactly keeping your distance.'

His eyes snapped open. 'I didn't know you'd be here, did I? Your father sat *shiva* for you. You are meant to be dead.' He spat out the last few words, and then he stood too. We faced each other across the table. Same height. Eye to eye.

'Well, I'm here,' I said, and that, at least, was unarguable.

'We both seem to be having difficulty letting go,' he said. He walked over to me, stood close enough that I could feel his breath on my face, and for one crazy prickling moment I thought he was going to kiss me. Then he walked past me, took his coat from the hook by the door, and left.

I'd eaten an emergency platzel to calm my nerves, and was sweeping up the dropped bits of onion when my phone rang. I put down the dustpan and looked at the screen.

I made my voice as casual as possible. 'Hiya, Al!'

'Hi,' he answered. 'You left very early this morning.'

'Oh, yes, I had a planning meeting. Everything OK?'

'Where are you, Eliza?' he said.

'I'm at work, of course.'

'Eliza, seriously, where are you?'

Oh, god. 'What do you mean? I told you, I'm at the school.'

'There's only one of us at your school, and it's not you. *I'm* at your school. I dropped by to bring your travel card. You left it on the shelf in the hall.'

Oh, GOD. 'Oh yes, I had to pay for a ticket. Damn nuisance.'

There was a silence.

'Eliza, if you're not at work,' Alex said, his voice very quiet, 'do you think you might be so kind as to perhaps tell me where the actual fuck you are?'

The next day was Alex's birthday. I gave him a card with a penguin on the front. Inside I wrote, 'I'd be lost without you'. And I bought him a subscription to a film club which sent out a surprise DVD every month. I was pretty pleased with myself, but I was the only one who was.

'Very thoughtful,' he said. 'Films for me to while away the empty evenings.'

'Oh, Alex, please.'

He read the card, and raised his eyebrows. 'Lost without me, huh, Miss Fickle? Surely not. You know exactly where you'd go without me.'

I was Miss Fickle now, after my about-face with regard to contacting my family. I wished I had been less 'that's it, I'm never seeing them again' when we first married and my father slammed the door in our faces.

So I was 'Changeable' to Nathan, and 'Miss Fickle' to Alex. They had even more in common than they knew.

Unpleasant though it was, at least Alex was talking to me. After the 'where the actual fuck are you?' phone call, he'd insisted I come straight back to the flat. He was there waiting for me – he'd called in sick himself – and we had the mother of all rows. We both cried, he kept saying, 'I don't understand,' and I confessed everything. I told him about reconnecting with my family, and that I hadn't really been doing an evening class or seeing Genevieve. Well, I didn't tell him quite everything. I left Nathan out of it, because he wasn't relevant. Even without any mention of Nathan, Alex was absolutely furious. He went on and on about trust and lying and honesty. I tried to explain how much I'd missed my Zaida, but he didn't even let me finish.

'Look, I'm not pissed off because you wanted to reconnect with your family. That's natural. I think some of them were shits to you, so I'm not entirely sure why you want some of them back, but hey, that's families for you. I'm pissed off, Eliza, because you lied to me.'

'Well, while we're talking about trust, what about you and Vicky…' Most of me knew that this wasn't fair, that mine was the greater crime, but there was a small part of me that thought, *well you kissed someone else.*

'You're not seriously comparing that to this, are you?'

'You hoped I wouldn't find out about it, Alex. It's not that different.'

'Yes, it is completely different! I didn't tell you because I didn't want you to get the wrong idea, for heaven's sake! While you didn't tell me because you didn't want me to get the right idea.'

'I'm sorry.' It seemed that all I was doing lately was apologising.

'I don't understand you, Eliza! There was absolutely no need to lie. I wonder, were you sort of loving the deception? Addicted to leading a double life? All that crap about going out with Genevieve, and saying I couldn't come with you to see your grandfather, and pretending to go to work. Why did you do that? Am I an ogre? Are you terrified of me?'

I shook my head. I didn't know now why I'd lied. I thought of Carolyn, the gambling addict who Kim dated, unable to stop herself. Was he right, was I hooked on my secret life? I suppose I hadn't told Alex because I didn't want him to be angry. Maybe that's how Carolyn felt. Pretend there's no problem, nothing's going on, in the hope that the people you care about won't yell at you. There was also something fluttering at the edge of my brain about Nathan, but I batted it away.

Now Alex put down my birthday offerings, and looked at his watch. 'Well, Miss Fickle, don't you have places to go?'

'It's not one of my working days.'

'No, but isn't it one of your return-to-the-fold days? Oh wait, that's every day, isn't it?'

'This is why I didn't want to tell you. I knew you'd react badly.'

He blew out an exasperated puff of air. 'Well, go on then.'

'Go on, what?'

'Go and see them. I'm going to do some work today, make up for yesterday.'

'But… it's your birthday. I thought we would do something together.'

'Thirty-one, it's nothing special,' he said, and went out of the room.

I waited for a bit to see if he'd come back to make up, but he didn't. So I got up and put on my frum clothes. Where else was there for me, if my husband rejected me? My legs were heavy as I trudged to the station. I felt that I could sleep for a week. In fact, I did nod off on the tube and startled awake only as we pulled into Seven Sisters.

Mum asked if I'd mind giving the annex a tidy. She said Nathan was out, so I didn't put on the sheitel, but when I pushed open the door he was there, standing in the kitchen, his back to me, wearing nothing but a bath towel round his waist.

'Oh!' I said, backing out. He turned round, a strange unsettling expression on his face.

'Hang on a minute,' he said.

I stood in the doorway, holding my hand over my hair, as though that would hide it. 'Mum said you were out.'

'I was, but I came back.'

'I was going to do a bit of cleaning. I'll leave it for now. I don't have my, uh,' I gestured to my hair.

'I'm standing here half-naked, Aliza. I think the time for modesty is over, don't you?'

I'd never heard Nathan talk like that before. My breath caught in my throat. Without thinking about what I was doing, I stepped inside and closed the door.

Chapter Twenty-Six

April 2016

Deborah's house is full of cushions. She loves them the way some women love shoes. I curl up in a huge armchair fat with cushions, and weep all over them. She hugs me, hands me tissues, and brings me tea and squares of honey cake at regular intervals.

'Why am I eating so much honey cake?' I finally ask, when I have stopped sobbing.

'I've a freezer full of it,' she says. 'Everyone made honey cake last Rosh Hashanah.' The Jewish New Year. 'I made one, Mum made one, Pearl made one. I have three days to get rid of it all.'

'I used to love helping Mum get rid of the cake.'

This was one of my favourite rituals as a child, the ridding the house of chametz (leavened food) before Passover. For eight days you're only allowed to eat food that contains no wheat, barley or oats. You have to ensure the house is free of every crumb of that stuff, which is achieved partly by cleaning but mainly by getting your children to eat it all up – a great job. I loved watching Mum unpack the boxes of Passover crockery and cutlery, a whole other set to replace the usual ones. The Passover plates had patterns of ferns on them, and they seemed festive and special when I was young.

'Eat up, now you need to help *me* get rid of the cake.'

'Surely the kids will help?'

Deb and Michael's twins, Eli and Noam, are still very little – three years old. She and Michael were married a good few years before starting a family, a modern move in our circles.

'They are sick to death of honey cake. And I put some more in their lunch boxes today for nursery, so they'll be cross with me when they get home. Eat, eat,' she says, parodying our mothers, 'you're so thin, skin and bone.'

Deborah hasn't asked many questions yet about my domestic travails, has just said that of course I can stay with them, as long as I want. I know Michael doesn't approve of me, never has, though he is always perfectly pleasant. But Deb has mellowed out over the years. The woman who grudgingly wrote to me all those years ago – signing her emails 'Former Best Friend' – to tell me my Zaida was ill, has become someone altogether more generous, more forgiving. Getting older has improved her all round. She looks terrific, has given up on the wigs and now covers her hair with beautiful silk scarves, leaving her fringe peeping out, which makes me think of Julie Christie in *Dr Zhivago*. I suspect the reference will be lost on her, but tell her anyway.

'I think I did see it, years ago,' she says. 'I remember it was very long.'

She and Michael have a television, something which would have been unthinkable when we were children.

'So,' she says. 'Want to tell me what's up, Goy Girl?'

Her using my old nickname makes me teary again.

'I'm going to be forty next month, Deb.'

'So? I'm already forty, and apparently I look like Julie Christie.'

'But forty! And I'm still making the same mistakes I made in my twenties.' I dab at the tears under my eyes. 'I should never have married out.'

'This again! I thought we were years past that.'

'Have I told you about Leah's new obsession? She's been going to shul with Dov and Ilana, and she made me buy her long skirts. She's stopped eating bacon-flavoured crisps.'

Deborah laughs long and loud. 'Talk about the chickens coming home to roost! I almost wish your dad was here to see that, *alav ha-sholom.*'

'I know, I know, I deserve it. I shouldn't have locked it away from her.'

'Ah, I'm starting to realise that whatever you do with kids, you can't get it right.'

'God, if you think that now, Deb, wait till they're teenagers.'

'I'm looking forward to it,' Deborah says, 'in the same way I look forward to the mikvah. It will be cleansing.'

Cleansing is right. I take a breath, and tell Deb the whole sorry story. 'Tell Auntie Deb all about it,' she used to say. I start with Leah finding the fake wedding photo, and move on to Showdown at Shipwreck Sushi, and the Easter Endgame. It all pours out. Her eyes get very wide when I tell her about my night with Nathan. By the time I finish, my coffee's cold.

'So, that's something you never told me... that there was more than a kiss between you and Nathan.' Deb raises her eyebrow at me, as she's always done when I've been naughty.

'You guessed, though, didn't you? When you gave me that massive telling off about mistreating Alex? You quizzed me so closely I almost caved and told you.'

'We're going to come back to your little fling with Nathan, don't think we're not.' She wags her finger at me. 'But first, I have to say I can't believe Dov would have told his child all the gory details about when you and Alex separated.'

'Nor me. I think it must be something Gidon has overheard.'

But as I say it, I realise I haven't dwelt on this at all, about how Gidon had even heard of Nathan, or why Dov would have been talking about it. Nathan has, as far as I know, lived in Gateshead since 2001. And Dov has always been the most reliable constant in my life, my dearest brother, my dearest relation, in fact, now Zaida is no longer with us. Dov is the only one who never turned his back on me.

'Anyway, back to you-and-Nathan,' Deb says, ignoring my expression. 'I did wonder at the time. If I remember correctly, I gave you quite a large opening to tell me. Why didn't you?'

'Oh, I was so messed up. I suppose I thought I'd made the mistake of my life with Alex, and that I could make it right by going back to Nathan. But it was a disastrous idea. You can't suddenly choose not to be in love with someone. And you can't suddenly choose to love someone else.'

Deb looks thoughtful. 'That's very true.'

'I loved Alex. I still love him. When Nathan and I… well, let's just say that even as I was… getting involved, I knew my heart wasn't in it.'

'So, what are you going to do now, GG?'

'I don't know.' I cuddle a soft velvet cushion. 'I'll give it a couple of days, then talk properly to Leah. Alex thinks she will be less confused and strung out if me and him aren't in the same house together, being upset with each other.'

'Personally, I think it's a lousy idea,' Deb says. 'Not that you're not super-welcome here, of course. But I don't think you should have let him send you away.'

I shrug. 'I messed up, and I'm being punished, and I think that's right.' The tears threaten to return, and I force them back. 'I *did* lie to him in the past, and I didn't tell him the truth when he asked me about it afterwards.'

'But "in the past" is right. It's been and gone. Everyone makes mistakes.' Deborah shifts in her seat. 'None of us are perfect, Aliza. Not even Alex.'

'I know. There isn't anyone perfect. Except you, of course, Deb.'

She laughs. 'You'd be surprised.'

I keep up my usual work routine while I'm staying at Deborah's, going to school every morning. It's a schlep from her place, though, and it reminds me horribly of when Alex and I had our 'lost weekend' back in 2000. Back then I had to travel from my parents' house to the school I was working at in Brixton, just a short walk from the flat Alex and I first shared. Now it's Deb's place to Stratford, and I'm a deputy head not a teaching assistant, but the feeling of dislocation, of being in the wrong place feels unpleasantly familiar. On the other hand I feel utterly relieved when I walk into school and see everyone, because then normality kicks in. It's a full and busy day, and I have lovely colleagues and (mostly) terrific kids. There are whole minutes at a time when I forget what's happened.

The first evening, going home, I walk with my teaching assistant, Pam, to the station as usual, and automatically follow her on to the platform. It's only when the train comes whooshing into the station that I remember.

'Oh, Pam, I'm on the wrong platform,' I say, and burst into tears. She heroically gives up the train and sits with me on a bench until I get a grip.

'I think Alex and me have split up,' I tell her.

'But you're the strongest couple I know,' she says.

I used to think that too.

Every evening on the way back to Deborah's, I phone Leah and chat to her about her day. She is reticent, but occasionally tells me something that has happened. She has rebuffed my suggestion to meet and talk several times, and so, trying to be where she's at, I don't ask any awkward questions. I tell her that I love her. I hang up, have a little cry, get over myself, and by the time I get to Deb's I'm ready to help her with the children, read to them and play with them. We eat together, usually with Michael, and make uncontroversial pleasantries, then when I go to bed I phone Alex. If he answers, which he doesn't always, he gives me an anodyne account of his day, which consists of work and the gym and trying to get Leah to do her homework. He asks after my day, and I tell him in the same quick and insipid style. Then I text Leah good night, tip the many cushions off the spare bed, and try and go to sleep.

Deb and Michael invite me to join them for the Seder, the celebration of the first night of Passover. The other guests are Michael's father, and Deb's unmarried sister Pearl, who drinks the spare glass of wine put out for the Angel Elijah when Michael's not looking. Deb's kids run round in hysterics looking for the afikomen, the hidden matzo, and we sing the songs I remember, word for word, though I haven't sung them for many years. Eli and Noam are too little, really, to take on 'Mah Nishtanah', though they are the youngest, and Pearl steps in as the next youngest, singing it in a high, clear voice that reminds me of Gila's. *Why is this night different from all other nights?* Because I am not home, where I should be. My heart aches, thinking about Alex and Leah, and wondering what they're doing.

In the morning I make Deborah and the kids a traditional Passover breakfast after Michael's gone to shul. Jews aren't meant to cook on the Sabbath but that's a prohibition I shrugged off years ago, and Deb's not complaining. She calls me her Shabbos Goy. You're not permitted to do *any* work on the Sabbath, including one I'd forgotten about till I go to the bathroom: tearing off pieces of loo roll. There's a neat pile of squares of paper, prepared the day before by Deb's fair hand. It makes me smile, thinking about what Alex would say about that.

As I cook the matzo-brei, I remember my first big argument with Alex, when I discovered he had already eaten it, made by someone else, one of his exes. Ah, those fraught early days of our relationship! And ah, the fraught later days of our relationship now. I have never made matzo-brei for him, and that might have been just as well, because I burn the first one and have to throw it out; the second is rubbery, though Deb says it's nice.

Chapter Twenty-Seven

December 2000

I was rushing about getting my things together when Alex came in from work. Things had settled down between us since the return-to-the-fold argument, but weren't quite back to normal. We were slightly wary of each other, our interactions a little more formal than before.

'Hi!' I waved across the room. 'I'm off to see Zaida.' I needed to get there early, before Shabbos.

He nodded, went to the sink and poured himself a glass of water.

I glanced at the clock – I thought I'd be long gone before he got back. It was only 12.30; Fridays were his half-day but he usually worked till 2 p.m.

'You're back early, Al. Are you OK?' I put some grapes in a plastic tub. Zaida loved them and they didn't seem to have much fruit at the home.

Alex drank down the glass in one go and filled it again. 'I don't feel well.'

'Oh, I'm sorry. What's wrong?'

'Don't know, I feel like shit.' He drained a second glass, then slumped into a chair.

Though I wanted to get going, I went over and put my arms round him.

He leaned against me. 'I just…' he began, then stopped.

'What?'

He pulled out of our embrace. I looked at him properly. His skin was pale and there were deep black circles under his eyes. I sat next to him, and he put his hand on mine.

'What's the story, Eliza?'

'What story?'

'Come on, you know. What's going on? You're never here when I'm here. You're always running out the door. You'd have been gone if I'd come back at my normal time.'

'Is this why you're "feeling ill"?' I felt bad as soon as I said it. 'Sorry. I didn't mean it.'

He shook his head. 'No, it's a fair question. Maybe. I've felt out of sorts for weeks.'

'Since I started seeing my family again?'

He nodded.

'But that's so unfair, Alex! You've got all your family around you. You have no idea what it's been like to be on my own.'

'Eliza. Darling. You aren't on your own.'

'It felt like I was.'

He blew out his cheeks. 'Wow, that makes it sound like I don't count at all.'

'Well, after that thing, you know, at Brighton, with Vicky, I didn't feel so welcome here.'

'Ah Jesus, Eliza! You know Vicky means absolutely nothing to me. Less than nothing!'

'And I miss my family.'

He drank some more water. 'Look, I'm totally supportive of you making peace with them.'

'It doesn't feel like it.'

'Of course I am. I want you to be happy. But you're there all the time. You're never here.'

'That's not true!'

He shook his head. 'You've stayed over there three nights this week. Sunday, Monday, and Wednesday.'

'Wow, I didn't know you were keeping notes.'

'I've missed you. Surely we can sort out a compromise? Can you maybe stay there a couple of nights a week or something?'

'I didn't see them for nearly a year, and now you want to restrict me?'

'I don't want to restrict you. I just want to spend time with you. *And* your family. I'd like to meet them.'

'You'd like to meet my dad?'

'Well, maybe we could start with the easy ones. Your Zaida. And Dov, he sounds great.'

'I don't know, Alex.' The thought of my two worlds coming together made me feel panicky. Trapped. I was two different women now, and I didn't know whether I could merge them. 'A bit later on?'

'Perhaps you're ashamed of me.'

'Of course I'm not!'

He gave an odd little smile. 'It's our first anniversary next week.'

'No, we married on January first.'

'December sixteenth was the day we ran away together, the day we were engaged. The happiest day of my life. But I think perhaps you regret it now.'

'Don't be silly. I only want to see everyone at home.'

'For Christ's sake!' Alex shouted, and thumped his fist on the table, knocking over his water glass and making me jump. Making me remember that I used to jump when he touched me. How had things deteriorated so fast? I had never before seen him lose his temper. I automatically slid my hands down to the sides of my chair but of course, there were no grooves to rest my fingers in, no safety in the storm. I got to my feet, grabbed a cloth from the sink and started mopping up the water.

'Just fucking leave it, will you?' he said, pulling the cloth from my hand.

'Why are you so angry?'

'You called your parents' house "home".' He crumpled the cloth into a ball and hurled it in the direction of the sink. 'You never call this flat home.'

'Well it isn't my home, is it?' My own resentment, as suppressed as Alex's, flickered into life. 'It's *Rachel's* home, and *Helena's* home.'

'You don't really think that, do you?' The anger was gone from his voice.

'I'm probably just passing through, like they were. I expect Vicky will be the next one along.'

'Ah seriously? *Vicky*?'

I thought of them kissing. Probably he hadn't really pushed her away. It was nothing to him. 'I'm just another one on your long, long list.'

'Jesus, Eliza, we're *married*. I love you. If that's how you feel, that this isn't your home, let's move house. I can't bear for you to feel like that. We can start looking for somewhere else today.'

'I can't.' I stood up. 'I'm going to see my family today.'

'Oh, god.' His shoulders sagged. 'I feel lousy. I'm going to go and lie down.'

'That's a good idea. I'll leave you to it.'

Were those tears in his eyes? I looked away.

'Are you coming back tonight?' He said.

'Well… it's tricky, because it's the Sabbath, so I can't really travel back.' I mumbled this, because I knew he wouldn't like it, but he heard me fine.

'Because those are laws you're starting to keep again?'

'I can come back if you really want me to,' I said.

'I want you to really want to,' he said, and went out. I heard the bedroom door close.

I felt furious he'd made it seem as if reconnecting with my family was a bad thing. He should be happy for me. I snatched up my bag, and walked briskly to the tube. To push Alex out of my mind, I focused instead on that day a month ago, when I came into the annex, bareheaded, and Nathan stood there almost naked in his towel. His expression as he stepped towards me, caught hold of my hand and raised it to his lips; the heat of his breath on my hand. The thrill of the forbidden touch shook through me. Scarcely knowing what I was doing, I pulled my hand away, and we stared at each other. There was a moment when something else could have happened, but I was too afraid. I mumbled something about returning later, and backed out of the annex without waiting for his reply.

I hadn't been able to stop thinking about it.

First stop was to visit Zaida, who was delighted to see me, though he seemed vaguer than last time, and then I went to Mum's. I was pulled straight away into the little family dramas, and though I'd only intended to stay over on Friday, I decided to stay on Saturday night too. I left Alex several answerphone messages, but he didn't pick up. Still, a bit of time apart would do us good, cool things down.

On Sunday morning I went into the annex to make Nathan's breakfast. Though I'd seen him numerous times since the bath towel incident, it had all been formal and proper between us. But today I felt antsy and unsettled, and he seemed to be the same. I dropped a bowl, and he had a choking fit after some water went down the wrong way, and it was all very odd. The tension stretched out, and I began to feel reckless. So when he asked after Zaida, I decided to show him that I knew what he'd done.

'Zaida's OK,' I said. 'But you know, I don't think he's ever been the same since that awful scene with Dad. He still flinches, you know, if anyone raises their voice.'

'I'm so sorry to hear that.' Nathan clicked his tongue sympathetically, the phoney. 'That poor man.' He clearly believed in his own sympathy, which made me absolutely furious.

'Oh, come off it, Nathan!'

'What?' He was quite the actor, pretending to be all baffled, his spoon halfway to his mouth.

'Don't act all innocent. I know it was you who grassed on me to Dad that I'd been visiting Zaida.'

'Grassed?' Nathan put the spoon down. 'Do you mean told? It wasn't me.'

'Of course it was! How else could he have known?' I stood up, unable to sit still any longer, and started clearing the table, though he hadn't finished. 'There's no way that Dov would have told him.'

'I don't know how Kap found out, Aliza, but I swear, it was nothing to do with me.'

'Bull*shit*.'

'Nice mouth you've got on you, since you went out there.' He gestured to the Real World outside the house. 'You really think I would do anything, anything at all, to hurt Moshe? That lovely man?'

'You bloody hypocrite!' I slammed empty plates on top of full ones, till I couldn't hold any more. 'You didn't expect it would backfire on to Zaida, you were just hoping to get me into trouble. Well, let me tell you—'

Nathan stood up, and in one fluid movement he leaned across the table, across my armful of crockery, and kissed me full on the lips. There was no warning at all. I was so shocked, I kissed him back. For a few astonishing, suspended-in-time seconds, we were kissing. I can't say, even now, how it happened or what it was like. It was as if it was happening to someone else, in a film. The image of Alex kissing Vicky flickered into my head, but before I could even think of anything more, Nathan pulled away.

'What was *that*?' I said, gaping at him.

'I needed to stop you shouting and swearing at me,' he said. To my astonishment, his eyes were twinkling. 'You are your father's daughter, all right.'

'I'd like to see you kiss Kap to shut him up,' I said.

'Hmm, maybe not.' He got up and put on his coat. I didn't want him to leave, but I couldn't think of something to say to stop him. Then he turned at the door, and said, 'I didn't tell your father, Aliza. For some reason, it matters a great deal that you believe me.'

'Who did tell him, then?' I refused to believe Nathan, despite his seeming sincerity. There wasn't anyone else it could be. I couldn't bear to think that Dov might somehow have blurted it out. No, he never would have.

'I have no idea. I'm going to visit Moshe later, about two, if you want to be there at the same time so he doesn't worry about where your "young man" is.'

He went out, and I stood there, staring at the door. After a few moments, I shook myself, dumped the plates in a heap on the table, and sat down with a thud. My mind was churning, the ant-like thoughts crawling all over it. Everything was so confusing.

In many ways, I was the happiest I had been for a long time. Perhaps ever. Mum, Dov and Gila were thrilled to have me back in their lives. My other brothers were more respectful of me than they'd ever been. Dad was not his old self at all, and that could only be a good thing. Sure, he wasn't talking to me. But he wasn't yelling or hitting me – or anyone – either. Joel's description, a good way of putting it, was that Dad had been 'de-fanged'.

Here was the big ant that kept running round in my mind. The biggest one – the Queen Ant. This was the first time I'd even been able to articulate it to myself: had Ha-Shem sent Alex so I could find out what my family meant to me? And now I had found that out, what did it mean for me and Alex?

After a morning helping Mum and Becca clean the house, I was late to what I now thought of as my appointment with Nathan. I rushed down the corridor at Beis Israel and burst into the living room in time to hear Nathan say, 'She'll be here soon, Moshe.' He looked up, and broke into a grin. 'See, what did I tell you? I conjured her up.'

I threw my arms round Zaida, and over the top of his head, mouthed 'thank you'. The two of us sat on either side of Zaida while he chattered away, reminiscing about the past and about our wedding, which he was now convinced he'd been to. Luckily for me, he didn't mention the fake photo – I wasn't sure how far Nathan's new understanding persona would go if he discovered there was a pictorial record of our non-existent marriage. Zaida nonetheless embarrassed us both hugely by asking if there were any little ones on the way – 'Not yet,' Nathan said, his face the colour of pomegranate seeds – but he didn't try and join our hands together again. I kept thinking he might.

Dov wasn't able to come today, so Nathan and I left together, with no one to chaperone us. It felt subversive walking through the front garden of the home, even though we were several feet apart from each other. Nathan held open the front gate to let me through, and as I smiled at him, I saw Alex standing across the road. I came to a complete standstill and Nathan almost walked into me.

'What is it?' he said, then followed my gaze. 'Oh.'

I called Alex's name, but he turned and walked away as if he hadn't heard. I hesitated. Should I run after him? Why had he come here? What did he think when he saw Nathan and me come out of the garden?

'Are you going after him?' Nathan said.

It was a simple question, and also a line in the sand. Was I going to go after Alex? Or was I going go back to my parents' home? With Nathan?

*

It was still early in the morning – only seven or so – when I let myself into the flat. I'd spent Sunday night tossing and turning, causing Becca to complain that I was keeping her awake. I wanted to see Alex before he went to work. You couldn't help who you loved. I knew that Nathan was starting to reignite his feelings for me, but I also knew that I loved Alex. I loved him, and there was nothing I could do about it. I knew I needed to tell him that, and tell him clearly.

I crept quietly about in the kitchen making breakfast, a funny echo of my morning stints in the annex. I thought the smell of coffee would wake Alex up, but he didn't appear, so after everything was ready, I went into the bedroom. The curtains were still drawn, and still Alex didn't stir; odd as he was usually such an early riser. I opened the curtains a little. I wanted him to wake gently and lovingly. I went over to the bed and whispered his name. It took me longer than it ought to realise that he wasn't in the bed. I couldn't quite believe it. I patted the lumpy duvet but it was just rucked up. There was no one inside it. I turned on the light and now I could see that the wardrobe was open, his clothes gone.

There was a note for me on the table next to my side of the bed. It was sitting on top of the Re-education book.

Eliza, I've gone to stay with Kim and Vicky for a while. Please take the Book with you, it makes me sad to see it. Love you, always. Alex.

It made me sad to see it, too. The Book was the symbol of all that was new and exciting, and wrong and difficult, in my short-lived marriage. I picked it up and cried, tears which felt as if I'd been waiting to shed them for weeks, maybe months. I lay down on the bed and let it all out. And after I couldn't cry any more, I packed a bag, and went back to my old life.

Chapter Twenty-Eight

April 2016

I've been staying at Deb's for a week when she tells me her secret. When I finish work and get on the Victoria line – no confusion any more, Pam no longer needs to remind me of my correct platform – I find her harassed and yelling. Michael's out and the children are fretful and whingey. I take over with them, and of course, because I am not their mum, they are quickly fine, and soon settle down to some drawing. Deb looks like she has aged ten years since this morning. She crashes about in the kitchen for a while till she calms down ('I nearly walloped the little blighters, lucky you came in when you did!'), then we feed them and get them into bed.

'Glass of wine?' Deb says as we creep downstairs, and seeing my astonishment says, 'I'm bloody having one.'

'Things sure have changed since I left the faith, Deb. I would never have imagined you having a drink like this.'

'I don't know if things have changed,' she says, taking a bottle of wine out of the fridge, 'but I have. Tell me this doesn't last for ever.'

'This stage is very tiring,' I say, 'but it goes quicker than you think, and then you're into the next thing. Teenagers are exhausting too, in a different way.' I think of Leah, and her grunting at me while staring at her phone, yelling furiously that she is perfectly capable of talking to me and texting at the same time. I really miss her.

She slugs down her glass and pours another one. 'When they're teenagers, I'll come and stay with you and Alex for a bit.'

'I hope there will be a me-and-Alex to stay with.'

'There will, this is just a blip.'

'Shall I make something to eat?' I say. 'You don't want to get too pickled.'

'Pickled, like a cucumber.' She giggles, in a pickled way.

'I think you were so smart, Deb, not to have kids for a few years. Alex and I were barely together before Leah came along. You and Michael built up a solid base before you let the little intruders in.' Deb starts laughing, so I join in, then I realise that actually she's crying. 'Hey, love, what have I said?'

Deborah isn't one for crying. She must be even more wrung out than I thought. 'They're gorgeous kids, wait and you'll see,' I tell her. 'They're just at a tricky age, and twins are hard enough in anyone's books. When they get a bit older they'll…'

'They're not Michael's, you know.'

'What's that?'

'Michael can't have kids.'

I stare into her big blue wet-lashed eyes. 'Deb, why didn't you tell me? So you did IVF? Was it awful?'

'Yes.'

'I'm sorry. I wish you'd told me.'

'I am telling you. In fact,' she takes another gulp of wine, 'I'm going to tell you what *really* happened, and nobody in the whole world knows that. Apart from me.' She slurs slightly. 'You said we were sensible to wait to have kids. Well, we didn't want to wait. We tried and tried, from the moment we married.'

'Oh, love. You never said.'

'Don't get me wrong,' she gives me a watery version of the old Deborah grin, 'it was fun trying. For the first few years, anyway. If I could ignore his mother going on and on, *alav ha-sholom*, may she rest in peace, although not too much peace.'

'Ah, she was awful. Do you remember how vile she was that time we were helping at Ezra's bar mitzvah?' I smile. 'It was the first time I ever heard you say the word "bitch".'

'It was a word that came in handy several times subsequently. Always about her.'

'It must have been really painful if you did want kids, Deb; I just assumed you were happy to wait.'

'That was the story we told everyone. When nothing happened, we saw doctors. Can you imagine how long it took to persuade Mikey that we should see someone? Anyway, they said it was unlikely, that his sperm count was pretty low. Well, he wouldn't consider IVF.'

'I thought you said...'

'He wouldn't do it, because we'd need to have a donor.'

'I'm a bit confused.' I put my glass down and lean forward. 'You said yes when I asked if you had IVF.'

'Nuh-uh. I said yes, it was awful.'

I gestured for her to go on.

'We had terrible arguments. I was desperate for a baby. Bit ironic now, as I would give anything for an afternoon off.'

'I'll give you an afternoon off. You will fall in love with them all over again when they get out of the Terrible Threes, honestly.'

She waves a hand, to hush me. 'So I was desperate. I was nearly at the baby-snatching stage. And you know what it's like round here, these are *big* families. Some of those frummers with two or three babies in prams all at the same time, barely nine months between them, I thought to myself, would they really notice if there was one less? Might they even be secretly relieved?'

'That isn't what you did, is it?'

'Yeah, I stole the tiny Baby Pinkus from his mother's arms.' She smiles. 'Of course not! I kept on at Michael, begging him to consider IVF. But he refused. We nearly split up.'

'Deb, all this time, you never told me about this.'

She mimics my voice: 'Aliza, all this time, you never told me about sleeping with Nathan.'

'OK, OK.'

'Look, you were busy, you had your own little family, yada yada.'

So, uh, what happened?'

'Finally, Michael said, "Do what you have to do."'

'What does that even mean?'

'Who knows? He said, "Do what you have to do, I don't want to know about it."'

'Oh my god, how annoying!'

'I know, right? So at first I was going to do IVF by myself. They gave me the fertility drugs, you know the ones that make multiples more likely. Believe me, that is not a myth.'

'Hang on a minute. You were going to do IVF *at first*?'

'Then I thought, well, there is a less medical way…'

'Deborah, what are you saying?'

'I will have to kill you if I tell you.'

'How is this going to work, then?'

'You can have ten guesses. I will only answer no. If I don't reply, you can draw your own conclusions.'

'Did you have sex with another man?'

No reply. She pours herself another glass of wine and smiles enigmatically.

'Christ, Deb, no wonder you drink.'

'I drink because three-year-old twins are hard work.'

'Is the father someone I know?'

'No.'

'Is it someone you're in touch with?'

'No.'

'Is he Jewish?'

'I didn't ask.'

'Does he know you got pregnant?'

'No.'

'Did you meet him online?'

'No.'

'The zoo?'

'Now you're being silly. You've had seven questions. Look, it doesn't matter where, OK?'

'I can't picture you going off to a singles bar and picking someone up.'

She says nothing. There is a strange look on her face.

'There's so many things I want to know.'

'You can have three more questions, then we will never speak of this again.' Her face is deadly serious. 'I mean it.'

'Does Michael know they're not his?'

'We have never discussed it. I hope he assumes we finally got lucky. Thank Ha-Shem, they look like me.'

'Do you have any regrets?'

'No. Not now they're asleep, anyway. Last question. Michael will be back any minute.'

'Are you completely happy?'

There's a long silence. Then she says, 'Is anybody completely happy?'

'Wow, Deb. I'm so,' the word in my mind is 'shocked', but I say instead, 'so honoured that you told me.'

The front door slams – Michael coming in.

Deb says, 'So you know you liked Pearl's shoes that she was wearing at the Seder the other night?' She puts the wine bottle back in the fridge, and her glass in the dishwasher, seemingly unhurriedly, but she is sitting back down alcohol-less by the time Michael comes in. It looks as if only I'm drinking. 'She gave me the name of the shop – they're not cheap, though. Oh, hello, darling.'

'Hello, ladies,' he says, and I see him clock my glass. That outrageous Deborah. I look at her, and she looks innocently back at me.

'Have you two not eaten yet?'

'We got lost in conversation,' Deborah says, jumping up and taking a Tupperware out of the fridge. 'Do you want some, darling?'

'Yes please,' he says. 'I'll just pop up and look in at the kids.'

'He's a great dad,' Deborah says, heating a casserole in the oven, and that's the end of it.

Deb's spare bed is another surface that she's covered in cushions. I remove nine or ten and pile them up on the floor before I can get into bed. I text Leah good night, as usual, but she doesn't reply. Maybe she's already asleep. My head's absolutely whirling with what Deborah told me, and I have to admit, though I know this doesn't reflect well on me, that I am relieved. Relieved that I am not the only one who messed up. Relieved that other people's lives, not just mine, are full of secrets, compromises, and ambiguities.

It takes me an age to get to sleep, and it feels only minutes later when my phone rings, calling me up from the depths. I fumble for the phone and drop it, luckily on to a safety-net of cushions. I answer it moments before it goes to voicemail.

'She's gone,' Alex says. He is breathing hard, and his voice is much higher than usual.

'Leah?' I sit up, wide awake. 'Gone? Where?'

'I don't fucking know, do I? I got up and she's not in her bed.' There is panic in his voice.

'Have you checked everywhere? The bathroom? The kitchen?'

'Eliza, the front door's unlocked. Her school bag's gone. She's even taken her coat.'

I squint at my watch on the bedside table: 6.30 a.m. Leah would know that in order to sneak out before Alex got up, she'd have to be very early. For her to do that, she who can barely function before 10 a.m., it must be something she is absolutely desperate to do.

'Have you phoned her?'

'Yes, and left five voicemails. Plus loads of texts.'

Alex has waited a while to call me, then. Presumably he hoped he could sort this out without me ever knowing.

'I'm so sorry,' he says, and starts to cry. This is not crying that can be passed off as being caused by an onion. This is full-on sobbing. I have never known him do this, and I grip the phone tight, saying soothing things.

'It's going to be OK, Al. It's all going to be OK.'

When at last he calms down, he says, 'Do you know where she might have gone?'

'I have an idea,' I say.

Chapter Twenty-Nine

January 2001

Six in the morning. I slipped out of the annex into the main house, hoping not to see anyone, but Mum was of course bustling about in the kitchen.

'Have you already been in to make Nathan's breakfast, Aliza? It's terribly early.'

'Er, yes, he said he wanted it first thing today.'

She looked at me oddly. 'You went in without the sheitel? And you're wearing the same clothes as yesterday?'

'Just rushing, Mum. Right! Better get ready myself.'

'It's Sunday, you don't have work.'

'No, I'm, er, I'm going to Deborah's.' I hastened out of the door, but her voice followed me upstairs.

'At this hour?'

I slipped into my room, but unfortunately Becca was awake, lying in bed and reading. Gila was snoring gently. Becca regarded me with an ironic expression.

'Where have you been, Aliza?'

'Got up early to do Nathan's breakfast, that's all.'

'Sure you did.' She propped herself up on an elbow. 'So early you didn't actually bother going to bed in the first place.'

I glanced at my bed which clearly had not been slept in.

'Well, no, I, uh, you didn't wake up when I got up, I made my bed before I—'

'Save it, Aliza.' She turned back to her book, but not before throwing me the filthy look of the century. 'I don't care what you do, any more.'

I hid in the bathroom, and as soon as it was a decent hour, I rang Deb and begged her to let me come over. Since Alex and I broke up, a month ago, I'd gone over to hers at least three times a week. If she was getting sick of me, she didn't show it, and today, more than ever, I was grateful to her for being there. My mind was in such a mess, the ever-persistent ants crawling all over it, an army of thousands.

Deb was dependable, but other than her, everything was odd and different in my life. Living in my parents' house didn't feel the same as before I married Alex. I'd been out in the Real World, seen and done things none of my family could imagine. And they didn't trust me not to disappear again. The simplest action – such as walking from one room to another, or into the hall, or heaven forbid, towards the front door – ignited everyone's attention. One of my siblings would say, 'Where are you going, Aliza?'

If I said I was going out, they'd say, 'Where? Does Mum know?' They all did it, even Dov and Gila. Especially Gila. She was a complete pain. If I admitted that no, I hadn't told Mum, but I was in a rush, she would race through the house, yelling, 'Mum! Mum! Aliza's going out!' It was very annoying.

Actually, lots of things were annoying, about being back home:

*

1. Sharing a room. Of course, I'd shared with Becca and Gila all their lives. Almost all my own, too – I could barely remember a time before Becca came along, when I must have had the room to myself. But since marrying Alex, I'd got used to my own space. Alex was never an invasive presence the way my sisters were. As they had the same daily goal (to avoid Dad) as me, and as Dad never went in the girls' bedroom, they were mostly to be found in our room, lying on their beds, keeping up a running commentary. I must have once been used to this, but now it set my teeth on edge. 'Oh, is that a new top, Aliza?' 'Can I come with you to visit Zaida, Aliza?' 'Have you seen Nathan today, Aliza?' 'Where are you going, Aliza?' 'Where have you been, Aliza?'

   It made me want to scream.

2. The food. Everyone seemed so conservative, but of course, it must have always been like this. *I* must have always been like this. I slotted back into taking my turn at cooking the evening meal, alternating with Mum and Becca. Everyone comprehensively rejected any attempts I made at innovation. My lamb curry, for instance – kosher lamb, with kosher coconut milk instead of yoghurt – was only eaten by me. Everyone else pushed theirs aside. You should have seen the face on Jonny. Dad threw his in the bin, along with the plate it was on, just as he'd done all those years ago with the roast lamb. I'd have asked him what his problem with lamb was, but it didn't seem quite the right time. Also, he wasn't speaking to me.

   The curry was really nice. Alex would have loved it.

3. The assumptions. It would never have occurred to Mum or Becca to ask why it was us who did the cooking, rather than Dad or any

of the boys. It hadn't occurred to me, either, *before*. Now it was absurdly obvious. I felt too uncertain of my place in the house to raise it. But I did notice it.

4. The looming presence of Dad. On the positive side, he was still thoroughly shaken by the berating everyone gave him after his outburst at Zaida. It was the first time in decades that any of us had challenged him about anything: no wonder he was shocked. Dov told me that Dad was consulting a lot more with Mum and Uri about decisions than he'd ever done before. Some things, such as allowing me to come back home, had naturally not been Dad's wish, but he had deferred the final ruling to Mum, or she had insisted on it, no one was sure. Either way, that was how it came about that I was able to move back in.

Dad hadn't had a complete personality shift, of course. He was forced to sit with me at meals, but otherwise he would silently remove himself from my presence, which was obviously a bit unpleasant but preferable, as Dov pointed out, to him staying there. But as the weeks passed, and he – and everyone else – got used to me being back, he began to stay in a corner of the room, glaring at me. It was funny at first, then it wasn't.

Along with the glaring, he began to address the occasional snide remark at me under his breath. 'How's your *momzer*, Aliza?' meaning bastard, and then 'Oh, I forgot, you left him.' Or 'You've put on weight, haven't you?' Actually there was some truth in that: with Mum on a mission to feed me up, my clothes had started to feel tight. Of course I understood Dad was deeply offended that I was back in the family home. Having told everyone that I was dead to him, it not only completely undermined his authority, but also made him look very silly. I was no longer as terrified of him as I had once been, but it was horrible being on the receiving end of his little bombs of rudeness. He'd drop them in the middle of several days of silence, with no warning. I simply got back into the habit of avoiding him, like my sisters.

Alex would be pleased to know I'd started to categorise things into lists.

5. Alex. I just missed him. One night a couple of weeks ago… oh, why pretend to be vague? It was 1 January, the day of our first wedding anniversary, and missing him had become unbearable. I took out the Re-education book for the first time since I brought it back from the flat. I read the first page, and it was so soothing. I got into the habit of looking at it last thing every night, lying in bed. I waited till Becca and Gila were asleep, then quietly clicked on my torch and read under the bedcovers. I rationed myself to one list per night, to make them last. I found it comforting to think about which of the things we'd done on the list, and which we hadn't. But the thought that we probably wouldn't ever do those ones now gave me a hollow feeling in my stomach, like homesickness. I traced Alex's handwriting with my finger, round the funny loops of his y's. I thought about his face as he wrote the lists, his look of concentration, his smile.

*

So home was odd; the annex with Nathan rather than Zaida in it was downright weird; and as for synagogue, I only went once, a few days after I came back, and it was like a scene from a film I saw with Alex, where the stranger walks into the bar and everyone stops talking. Afterwards I told Mum I couldn't go back, which I thought would be difficult for her, shul being such a huge part of our lives, but she seemed relieved. Me being there reminded everyone, including her, what a scandalous mess I'd made of everything.

Work was a respite, despite the forty-minute schlep from Hackney to Brixton, and so, most of all, was Deb's house – the only place from my old life that felt the same.

Sure, she didn't hold back with the forthright remarks, but that was one of the things that was familiar. That was just Deb. I knew she loved me. And the more time I spent with her, armed with my painfully acquired new insights about relationships, the more I began to realise that she wasn't quite as content and sorted as I'd assumed. The perfect bubble I'd always pictured her living in was, it seemed, as imaginary as my marriage.

Marriage. Proposals. Last night. Don't think about it.

Deb and I sat together, one at each end of her enormous sofa, part of her impressive cushion collection propping up our backs, coffee mugs in hands. Legs up, our bestockinged feet meeting in the middle, sole to sole.

She teased me about how early I'd called. 'Can't get enough of me now, can you, Goy Girl?'

'Making up for lost time, FBF,' I told her.

Deb was looking nice today, her light brown wig a good match for her colouring, far better than the heavy chestnut one she sometimes wore.

I've been meaning to ask you for ages,' I said. 'How come you have never once complained about wearing a sheitel?'

Her hand went automatically to her hair. 'What made you think of that, you meshuggener?'

'I've been wearing one, a bit.'

Deb put her head on one side. 'Uh huh?'

'On and off. Last few months.'

'How come I haven't seen this?'

'Well, I, er, I just wear it to, er, when I serve Nathan breakfast, you know.'

I was already regretting starting the conversation, even though I knew I had to talk to someone about what had happened last night. And Deb was the only one I could tell.

Deb smirked at me. '*Oh, I just put on a sheitel to serve Nathan breakfast*. For Ha-Shem's sake, Aliza, you are *transparent*.'

'Honestly, it's only to help Mum out.'

'How thoughtful.' She took a gulp of coffee. 'So do you stay over with him to save your mum having to make the bed each morning?'

'That is beneath you, Deb.' But horribly close to home.

'I expect you help him undress so your mum doesn't have to go collecting his laundry.'

I laughed. 'Anyway, tell me about you, Deb. Tell me about sheitels.'

'Mrs Changey-the-Subject. Answer me one question, then I'll talk sheitels till the cows come home, if you want.'

I sighed. I might as well get this over. 'Go on, then.'

'What's going on with you and Nathan?'

'Nothing?' I said it too quickly, and with an uncertain inflexion that I hadn't meant to put in.

'Oh, the sort of nothing that means something!'

'Look. It's truly nothing. Not really.' I coughed. 'We just went out for a meal last night, and… well, nothing.'

'You went for a meal on your own? On a Saturday night? Oy vay!' Deb sat up straight, spilling coffee on her skirt. 'Ouch! I can see from your face that something happened.'

'Nothing happened.'

'Will you stop saying "nothing"! And you waited till now to tell me! This is why you've come round at the crack of dawn on a Sunday morning, and yet you let me sit here talking about *wigs*!' She threw a cushion at me. 'And?' she shouted. 'And? What happened?'

'I'm really embarrassed,' I said. How much should I say? I desperately wanted to talk about it, but I knew I couldn't tell her all of it.

'How did you get away with going out on your own together? Your mum would never agree to it.'

'She didn't know.'

'But they're all over you, you said. They always want to know where you're going... oh.' She clocked my sheepish expression. 'You told her you were coming over here, didn't you?'

'Sorry, Deb.'

'That's all right, I might need you to do the same for me one of these days. If Michael invites his mother to stay for a week again, for instance, I'll be the one needing an alibi.'

Deb was what passed in these parts as a woman of the world, but I knew she'd be horrified if I told her everything. She would judge me, and I couldn't blame her; I judged myself. I didn't want her to see me in a horrible new light, especially since she had only recently managed to get over the horrible new light she saw me in when I ran away with Alex.

'So, Nathan wanted to buy me dinner as a thank you, for doing the breakfasts and things...'

'What things?' Deb jumped in.

'Just the breakfasts, I mean.'

'Go on.'

'And. Well, it was nice.'

'Dinner was nice. That's it?'

'Yes.'

Deb studied my face. 'What is it, I wonder, that you're not saying?'

'Nothing.'

'I see our old friend, Mr Nothing, is back. Well? Does Nathan still like you?'

'No?' I said, and Deb laughed.

'I'm going to get this out of you if it's the last thing I do.'

'There's nothing to get,' I said, examining my cup.

'So let me ask you another question, hon. When are you going back to your husband?'

I shook my head. 'He left me, Deb.'

'I thought he was back in your flat now.'

That was true. Alex had sent me a text two weeks ago to let me know that he'd moved back in. He said he didn't want to leave the place standing empty.

'Maybe he's waiting for you there,' Deb said.

'No. He just didn't love me as much as I loved him.'

'Why on earth would you think that?'

I'd been making this particular list in my head for months. I ticked the items off my fingers. 'One: he left me. He didn't exactly put up much of a fight for me. Soon as things got tough, he left. Two: he didn't even want to marry me.'

'Of course he did!'

'He really didn't. He wanted to live together. It was only because I forced him that we got married.'

'Oh.' Deborah was silent for a moment. 'I didn't realise that, Aliza.'

'Three: he's had hundreds of girlfriends. I was just the next one along. Seriously, Deb, I'm talking loads. He even lived with two others before me. In the same flat.'

'Ugh.'

'He even, he even kissed another woman practically in front of me.'

'What?!'

I told her about the Vicky kiss, the pier, the white coat, him not admitting it till I confronted him. I didn't bother her with the weird conversation I'd had with Kim on the rollercoaster. Thinking about that made me feel a little uncomfortable.

'And he said she'd kissed him and he'd pulled away almost straight away, but, you know. What sort of idiot would believe that?'

'Well,' Deb said, 'Vicky does sound the sort who might do something like that. Didn't you say she'd always been keen on him?'

I thought about Vicky at Christmas, Alex trying to get away from her on the sofa.

'OK, well, maybe the kiss wasn't his fault, though I'm not sure he'd have told me about it if I hadn't mentioned it. But there are lots of other things. Number four: he was always trying to change me, get me to do different things. You don't change someone, do you, if you love them?'

'Well... I'm always trying to get Michael to eat less like an animal.'

'That's different. He tried to change the way I dress, the food I eat, everything. And five...' I trailed off, because I couldn't remember number five.

'We need more coffee.' Deb swung her legs off the sofa. I followed her into the kitchen and leaned on the counter while she bustled about.

I rubbed at an imaginary mark on the fancy marble worktop. Anyone else would have thought this a perfect room but Deb was planning to rip everything out and start again.

'When are you getting the new kitchen fitted?'

'Excuse me, Crazy Kid. If you think I'm going to allow you to deflect this fascinating conversation, you have another think coming.'

She rinsed out the cups, and said casually, her back to me, 'So how was the meal with Nathan?'

'Very nice, thank you.'

'You're missing something out. I *know* you. What happened?'

'Nothing.'

'Enough with the nothings already. No little searching glances? No mad passionate kisses?'

She was joking – it was utterly verboten for an unmarried couple, or even a married one come to that, to kiss in public. But her saying 'kiss' made my face heat up, and she saw this, and spread her arms wide in an 'ah ha!' gesture.

'I can wait all day if I have to,' she said.

I needed to tell her something. More than that, I wanted to. It was threatening to burst out of me.

'All right, but if I tell you…'

She pressed her hand to her heart. 'It will stay locked in here for ever, I promise.'

'You can't even tell Michael.'

'Michael?' Deb snorted. 'He's the last person I'd tell.'

'Why's that?'

'Stop stalling, Crazy Kid.'

'Nathan kissed me.'

'Excuse me?!'

'You heard.'

'Where?' She gasped. 'Not in the restaurant!'

'In the taxi on the way back.'

'You meshuggener! On the lips?'

I nodded. 'I knew it!' Deb said, and pressed her hand to her heart. 'My god, your life, Aliza.'

'I know.'

'And so… and then…?'

'That was it.' I could see that this was more than enough for me to reveal. The rest would have to stay locked up inside me.

'That was it?' Deb said.

'No confessions of love, no reconciliation?'

'We got back to the house, agreed it had been a mistake, he apologised, and we parted on perfectly good terms,' I lied.

'Seriously?'

'That's all,' I said, firmly. 'I'm just going to the loo,' I added, taking my betraying red cheeks out to the bathroom for a douse in cold water.

When I rejoined Deb on the sofa, I prompted her again to tell me about sheitels, before she could ask anything else.

She raised a sceptical eyebrow and passed me my mug. 'OK, I'll allow it. *For now*. Though I suspect there's more you're not telling.'

'Your lack of trust in me is shocking, Deb.'

'Oh yes? Well, I remember a certain person meeting a certain Goy Boy and not telling me anything much about that until it was, "Oh, by the way I love him – bye, everyone!"'

'I can't think who you're talking about.'

'You are quite a secretive person, Aliza Bloom. Sorry, Aliza Symons. Eliza Symons. What actually *is* your name? Who *are* you?'

'Sheitels, Deborah Shapiro.'

She sighed. 'All right. Well, in fact, I have complained plenty about wearing sheitels. I just didn't complain to you.'

'Why not?'

'I suppose it's one of those things you don't discuss with people who haven't had the experience. Like none of my other friends will talk to me about having children.'

'Ah, Deb. I haven't got kids either. Talk to me about that.'

Her face clouded over. 'I've nothing to say on the topic.'

'I'm sure it will happen for you soon.'

'Neither Michael nor I want them yet.'

'Well, that's fine then, isn't it?'

'Maybe you could tell Michael's mother that it's fine. You wouldn't believe how many times she can mention our lack of offspring in one short visit.'

'I'm so sorry. What are you going to do?'

'Continue to ignore her. And what are you going to do about your many men?'

'Who's Mrs Changey-the-Subject now? I don't have many men, do I? I don't have any. I've lost two in the time most people take to find one.'

'Is it really all over with you and… Alex?'

The tiny hesitation before his name made me realise it was the first time she'd said it out loud to me. She usually referred to him, if at all, sarcastically, as 'Goy Boy'.

'Yes, I think it is all over,' I said. 'I think we were like a sparkler that burned brightly, and then fizzled out.' I burst into tears, and Deb took the shaking mug out of my hands. She scooched round so she could put an arm round me.

'It's about time you told Aunty Deb all about him.'

And I did. For the first time, other than with Kim on the roller-coaster, I talked to someone about my marriage. The excitement at the start, the way Alex made me feel, the newness, the tenderness between us. She laughed when I told her about the Re-education book.

'Such a good idea! I could do lists for Mikey, like "Things You Don't Understand About Me" and "Reading Between the Lines" and "Ten Ways to Tell Your Mother 'No'".'

'He just wanted me to know the stuff he liked, to share it with me.'

'That's kind of cute, really. So, come on then, what went wrong? Did he not want you to see your Zaida?'

'Oh, no. He was lovely about it. He offered to come with me.'

'Well, what then? He didn't want you reconnecting with the Blooms, I suppose.'

'Not exactly. He kept complaining that I was at Mum's too often, staying over there too much. Went on about how he never saw me any more.' I felt indignant all over again. 'Then after we had a big argument he saw me coming out of Zaida's home with Nathan. I suppose he'd come to check up on me, and when he saw Nathan I guess he thought we…' I stopped, because Deb was once again giving me her classic eyebrow raise.

'You know who else does that?' I said, pointing to her brow, in the hope of deflecting her from whatever she was going to say. 'Roger Moore!'

'Who?'

'Actor. Used to play James Bond. He raised one eyebrow at a time, like you.'

'Who's James Bond? Listen, meshuggener, this is crazy even by your own high standards. You can't split up over *that*.'

'What do you mean?'

'You were staying away from him! Overnight! A lot! What husband – or wife – would put up with that? I certainly wouldn't. Imagine if Michael decided to start staying over at his mother's house three times a week!' She shook her head. 'Alex probably just turned up at the home because he wanted to apologise after your row.'

That interpretation hadn't occurred to me and I said nothing, which gave her the chance to ram the point home.

'You were wrong,' she said, jabbing me in the chest, 'and he was right.'

'I can't believe you, Deb. You know how much I wanted to reconnect with my family.'

'Maybe. But it also seemed to be your chance to play housewife with Nathan. I hope Alex didn't know about all those cosy breakfasts!'

'You've never defended Alex before!' I wriggled out of her arms and moved back to my end of the sofa. 'You're *my* friend! You should be on my side.'

'You know me, Aliza – I only call it how I see it. To me, it looks like you had a try at life outside, then ran back when it got hard, and thought you'd have another crack at Nathan.'

'My god, Deborah, that is a terrible thing to say.' I could feel the traitorous red spread across my cheeks yet again.

'Sorry, hon, you can tell me it wasn't like that if you want.' Deborah shrugged.

'How is it,' I said, my voice trembling, 'that you find it so easy to have a confrontation with me and yet you can't even say boo to a goose at your mother-in-law?'

'Mother-in-laws are a special case.' Deb had the chutzpah to laugh. 'And you're crying out for a confrontation, Crazy Kid.'

'I didn't want to try again with Nathan.' I stared at my knees, willing my face to cool down. I would never tell Deb, or anyone, ever, the truth about my disastrous night with Nathan.

'I believe you hon; thousands wouldn't. Thousands *won't*.' She went on, undeterred: 'But you know, there was no reason you couldn't have split your time between your family and your husband. It's called "compromise", Aliza, it's what couples do. I know your mum does all the compromising in your family, but your parents are old-fashioned.

Modern couples both have to do it. Michael would get mad, rightly so, if I spent as much time as I wanted with my sisters, so I see them when he's out, or at work. I don't suddenly say, Oh, by the way, I'll be staying with Pearl four nights this week.'

'It wasn't only that, though.' The unfairness of Deborah's accusations made me want to cry. I needed her to understand that it wasn't my fault. 'There were too many cultural differences. I didn't fit into his world.' Echoing words Nathan had said last night, I added, 'Mixed marriages never work out.'

'Didn't exactly give it a lot of time, though, did you?'

'Deb, I thought you were supposed to be cheering me up.'

'Sorry, hon.' Deb shifted back along the sofa so we were feet-to-feet again. I think she could see that I'd had enough. 'Let me think of something uplifting. Oh yes, I know. You can help me with the catering for Ez's bar mitzvah this weekend.'

'How is that uplifting?' I forced myself to engage with this new topic. 'And why are you involved with the catering? They've hired some fancy-shmancy company.'

'Oh, but *she's* asked me to supervise the waitresses. *She* doesn't trust them, apparently, because the company *she* always uses got a few new staff. *She* squeezed a discount out of them, but you know, there's no reassuring her.'

She was Esther, Michael's intimidating older sister. She was married to my brother Uri, which meant that Ezra, the bar mitzvah boy, was both my and Deb's nephew. Even I found the family connections confusing. Deb and I were some vague variant of sisters-in-law, a couple of times removed. We'd known Esther all our lives; her family lived at the other end of Springfield Street. She terrified us when we were kids.

'Why did she ask you to help?'

'Story of my life. Until I have kids, I'll be the one roped into all these things. "You've got time on your hands, Deborah,"' she whined, imitating Esther's nasal voice.

'Why didn't she ask me, then?' Seeing Deb open her mouth to tell me exactly why, I waved her down. 'No, it's all right, I know, I'm the meshuggener who ran away. She'll probably put me at a table in the kitchen.'

'Aw, hon,' Deb said, softening. 'Look on the bright side. Now you've returned to the fold, everyone's got such low expectations of you. Rock-bottom low. You were the golden girl, and now you've chucked that away. All you have to do is manage not to kill anyone, and they'll all think you're doing brilliantly.'

Sexy Things to Try

- Drunk sex.
- Play strip poker (or Scrabble, or whatever game you like – whatever game you're not very good at, Eliza!).
- Go out together, with you not wearing any underwear.
- Sex in the shower.
- Sex standing up.
- Watch porn together (only mild, I promise).
- Oral sex – Alex to Eliza.
- Oral sex – Eliza to Alex.
- Sex outdoors (in Brockwell Park?).
- Make love during Eliza's period (sorry, 'bleeding').
- Some light S&M (I will explain this when we get to it).

Chapter Thirty

January 2001

Here's what I didn't tell Deborah.

Yesterday morning.

As usual, I was in the annex, getting Nathan's breakfast things together. And as usual, he was watching me and saying very little. I'd got used to his steady gaze over the past few weeks. I quite liked it. All right, Deb-in-my-head, I liked it a lot. But when he cleared his throat and asked me out to dinner, I was startled. I think he was too. His eyes were wide, as if he couldn't quite believe that he had said it out loud. It was a baffling request, whichever way you looked at it. Going out to dinner was not something unmarried people did, especially not ones with our history. But even as I was working out a polite way to say no, by invoking impropriety and my parents' disapproval, I knew I would say yes. We had both already travelled so far outside impropriety that he would know it was a nonsense. As for my parents' disapproval, I didn't exactly have a track record of caring about that. And the truth is, the memory of his lips on mine still sent a warmth across my body every time I thought about it.

My silence seemed to rattle him, and he said in a rush, 'No big deal. Just to thank you for all you've done since you moved back home. The breakfasts, and the cleaning. And everything.'

'There's no need, Nathan.'

'I want to.' His surprised eyes held mine, and I blinked more heavily than usual and looked away.

'That would be lovely,' I said, knowing that I was allowing an already-ambiguous situation to become even more uncertain.

Last night.

We met at the restaurant at seven o'clock. It goes without saying that we couldn't leave together from my parents' house. As Deb guessed, I told Mum I was going to her place.

It also goes without saying that we couldn't eat anywhere local where people might know us. Nathan chose a kosher place on the other side of North London which wasn't easy to find. I was slightly late, and he was waiting for me outside the restaurant.

'Aliza!' he said, and we stood there, me slightly breathless and him slightly awkward. 'I thought you might not come.'

'Will they think we are married?' I asked. I was still wearing my Accessorise engagement ring and the silver wedding band.

'I don't care what they think,' Nathan said, and pushed the door open.

We were greeted by an unsmiling waiter, who I felt was judging us, though he knew nothing about us. Nathan chose a table in the middle of the room, rather than a more obviously nice one in the window. Despite his bluster, I guess he was worried that we might be seen. I felt absurd and shy, and studied the menu. It wasn't as comforting as

I'd thought it might be, even though it was a list of food in which everything was familiar. I pushed away the thought of Alex sitting in various restaurants opposite me, the same position where Nathan sat now, smiling, offering vegetarian alternatives to the things we had come to try, soothing my many anxieties.

I began to worry about what Nathan and I would talk about, and after we'd ordered, there was an awkward silence. Then the waiter brought a bottle of wine that I hadn't heard Nathan request, and we both quickly drank a glass, as if by agreement. Things were easier after that, and easier still after a second bottle that, like its predecessor, seemed to turn up unannounced. I remember us both laughing at the huge pile of red napkins the waiter brought, as if we couldn't be trusted to eat tidily. We managed to talk about our families, and the things we had done since our abortive engagement, without either of us becoming upset or angry. To start with, I kept apologising, and Nathan kept asking me not to, but after a while it did genuinely feel as if we had moved forward into a place of forgiveness. He even said that he found my rebellious streak exciting.

'Is that why you said yes, after we first met?' I asked him. It felt like a perfectly natural question to ask, right now, even though part of my mind was aware that at any other point I'd have died rather than talk about our courtship. But he seemed not to mind, and responded:

'Ah, I didn't know you were rebellious then. I only knew you'd turned down a few others, but I thought that was because they were unsuitable.'

'They were!'

He waved his wine glass at me. 'You were my twelfth introduction, and I have to admit, my expectations were low. I vaguely remembered seeing you when we were children at some family thing, I was about fifteen and you were maybe ten.'

'I don't remember that at all.'

'You were just a little kid. But now, I walked into your parents' stuffy living room, and I saw a beautiful woman.'

'My mother is holding up very well,' I said, to deflect my embarrassment.

Rightly, he ignored my joke. 'The light from a table lamp fell across your face, and you were... well, you were glowing. There was something about you that touched my heart.'

'Oh, Nathan.'

'I knew that finally, it was time to say yes.'

'Nathan, I'm so sorry I wrecked all that for you. That's beautiful.'

'You're beautiful, Aliza. More beautiful even than when I first saw you.'

I didn't know what to say, so I did this stupid fanning thing with my hand in front of my face, I have no idea why but I'd seen Vicky do it when she was pretending to cry.

'And you said yes to me,' he said. 'You have no idea what that meant to me. Why did you?'

The reason at the time, of course, was that he had been the best of a bad bunch. But the man sitting opposite me was a good man, a kind man, and he deserved better than that.

'There was something about you, too. I liked the way your hair curled on your collar.'

He laughed, and touched his hair. 'I had better let it grow a bit longer, in that case.'

The conversation moved on, and I found myself talking about Alex, about our missteps and difficulties, and how he had walked out on me. Nathan listened carefully, smiling and nodding. He looked more relaxed than I had ever seen him.

'It's so difficult,' he said, dabbing his mouth with a napkin, 'to be with someone from a different culture. Mixed marriages never work out.'

'Don't they?' Maybe he was right. Mine hadn't, after all.

'You can't go back.' He signalled to the waiter.

'What do you mean?' I tried to process his words in my head, but found it impossible.

'I mean one can't go back. Not just you. Once one's done something irreversible, there's no going back.'

I glanced at my watch, and was astonished to see that it was past eleven o'clock. Where had the time gone?

'I came back, though,' I said.

'You never really left, though, did you,' he said, smiling. He glanced at the bill, and put down a pile of notes.

'Halvesies,' I said, but he shook his head. Then he smoothed out two red napkins and handed one to me. 'Let's keep one of these each. A reminder of a wonderful evening.'

I put the napkin in my bag. 'Thank you for a lovely dinner.'

'No, thank you. Thank you for your extreme honesty and openness tonight.'

Had I been so honest and open? I wasn't too sure, now, what I had said. Had I revealed too much? I stood up to go to the ladies, and was shocked at how drunk I was. I couldn't walk in a straight line to the bathroom, and my face seemed blurry in the mirror. I nearly tripped over when I came out of the cubicle. I was giggling about this when I got back to Nathan, and he firmly steered me to the door and into a black cab that was waiting. I practically fell into the back seat and he sat very close to me, and as the taxi moved away, he pulled me close and kissed me, long and hard on the mouth.

*

It was one thing to kiss him. It was quite another to sleep with him. Being drunk, feeling reckless, worldly, tainted: these were terrible reasons to do something.

And yet here we were, lying side by side in Zaida's bed, facing each other. I knew I was more experienced than him, and that the things I knew would make him blush. He looked absolutely petrified. I stroked my fingers up the length of his penis, and he moaned in horrified pleasure. It was slightly longer than Alex's, but thinner, and in its circumcised state it looked vulnerable. I felt sorry for it.

I knew I had to get it over with and climbed on top of him; he lay under me, pale and unsure. Whatever had happened in the cab, I now felt no desire at all. I guided him into me with my hands, and moved up and down against him in what felt like a horrible parody of the times I had made love with Alex. I didn't even think about condoms, but let him come into me with a shout that would have wakened the dead. As I rolled off, knowing I wouldn't come – that was something I would only ever allow myself to do with Alex – I caught a glimpse of the disgust on Nathan's face. I knew that to him – and to myself – I would always be damaged goods.

I woke, heart thudding, mouth dry as the Sahara, glad to emerge from a confused, frightening dream full of nameless chasing creatures. I stared at my watch until my eyes adjusted to the dark enough to allow me to read it: 4.45 a.m.

Carefully, desperate not to disturb him, I untangled myself from the sheets and slid out of bed. I pulled on my shirt, the only item of clothing I could find, and tiptoed into the kitchen, closing the door behind me. I stood at the sink and drank my weight in water.

I didn't turn on the light. The darkness was friendly. I didn't want to look myself in the eye. What wouldn't I give for the ability to not think about anything at all? To have a perfectly blank mind? Alex told me about meditating, about emptying your mind, but it was just another of the many things on his lists that I hadn't got round to. I sat at the table, the ants crawling frantically through my brain. If only the Brixton flat was still empty, I could go now, could get a night bus. But Alex was back there. I had no place to go other than back to my parents' house, but I couldn't creep in there now. I'd been meant to be out at Deb's, but should have been back home and in bed hours ago. If I went in, and anyone woke up… I shivered at the thought. No, I'd have to stay here till I heard him stir – he usually got up around seven – hide in the bathroom till he'd gone, then grab my things and go into the house then. Pretend I'd been preparing his breakfast as usual.

But moments later the bedroom door opened.

'Sorry I woke you,' I said, turning. I could see only his outline. 'I tried to be quiet.'

He snapped on the overhead light, and I covered my eyes with my hand.

'I wasn't sleeping too well,' he said. 'Too much wine.' He sat next to me, gently drew my hand away from my face. 'Aliza, look at me.'

'It's too bright.'

'Aliza, I think we should get married.'

'I'm already married!'

'Not properly. Not in the eyes of Ha-Shem.'

I covered my eyes again.

'I know what people are like, out there,' Nathan said. I peeped through my fingers at him, watched him waving his arm, dismissing the secular world in a 'they're all the same' gesture, the way I might once have done. 'They get divorced all the time.'

'They don't, not really.'

'You hear about it. Married for a few months, then get divorced.'

'That's famous people, actors and musicians. Not real people.'

Nathan put his hand on my arm. Though he had, just a few hours ago, put his hands on far more intimate places, I still jumped in shock.

'You've got a second chance, Aliza,' he whispered, 'and so have I.'

I stared at him, my thoughts careering wildly, the ants out of control on a rollercoaster. Up they went – *I can't marry Nathan*! And down they came – *maybe I can*! How much easier everything would be, if I could. Second chance! Maybe the whole Alex thing was just a dream! Up again – *but it was a lovely dream…* Down – *but I've woken up now…* up and down it went.

I don't know how long I stared at Nathan, but it was too long, because he said, 'It's disconcerting when you don't say anything, Aliza.'

It felt unbearable to hurt him again, but I knew what the answer was the moment he said, 'I think we should get married.' I knew from the moment he kissed me.

Two nights ago, I had read the next list in the Re-education book. It was 'Poetry' – Alex's favourite poems. He'd even written out some verses in his tiniest writing, so it all still fit on one side.

Let me not to the marriage of true minds
Admit impediments. Love is not love
Which alters when it alteration finds,
Or bends with the remover to remove.
O no! it is an ever-fixed mark
That looks on tempests and is never shaken.

By the time I'd reached the end of the page, my face was wet with tears.

You can't help who you love.

'Nathan,' I said. I couldn't bear to see the hope that was written across his face. 'I really want to thank you for your kind offer…'

'It wasn't meant *kindly*, Aliza.' His expression darkened.

'I know, but it *is* unbelievably kind of you to give me another chance,' and in a rush, my stomach weighed with guilt, 'I'm so sorry but I'm going to have to say no.'

'But…' he looked as if I had whipped the floor out from under him, 'you came back.'

'What do you mean?'

He spread his arms wide. 'You ran off, you married out, we thought that was that. When you came back, I assumed… Jesus.' He put his head in his hands.

'You assumed… I came back for you?' The heavy weight in my stomach felt as if it had doubled in size.

'I am such an *idiot*,' he groaned, his face still hidden.

'You aren't.' I put a hand on his shoulder, but he shook me off. 'I'm the idiot. You're a great man, a good, kind man…'

'I'm a total *fucking* idiot.'

'You are *not*. You will make some lucky woman very happy. But it can't be me, Nathan, because I don't feel as I should towards you. It wouldn't be fair.'

'Fair?' He took his hands away from his face and laughed, a short bark. 'Since when do you care about fair? You only care about yourself. Always have. You've always been wayward. Selfish. No sense of duty.'

I bowed my head. I deserved it.

'That day,' he said.

'What day?' I said, quietly.

'*That* day. I was too early. I couldn't sit still at home, so I went to your parents' house. There was nothing for me to do. I stood outside with your brothers. Joel teased me about whether I'd be able to keep you in line. Do you know what I said? "I like that she has a mind of her own." Well, that came back to haunt me pretty quickly.'

'Nathan…'

'When you came out of the house in your coat, I thought you were going to visit a friend, maybe Deborah, to talk about whatever women talk about the day of their wedding. I wasn't worried at all – there were still more than three hours till the ceremony. I smiled at you, but you didn't see me, and I realised you were looking somewhere else. At someone else.'

He seemed as if he was right back there, outside my house, watching me looking down the street at Alex.

'Nathan, let's not do this.'

'I want you to know what it was like. From my point of view, I mean.' His voice was quiet, calm. 'I heard you say that you were sorry. Then you weren't there any more, and your mother and little sister were screaming. I couldn't understand what was happening. I don't know how long it was before you walked off up the street with *him*. I knew I had to get away from everyone, and I started to walk away too. But I got pulled back and people were telling me you'd gone crazy, you'd been abducted, they would catch him. Dov was there, out of breath, telling everyone which way you'd gone, and several of the men went racing off after you. I tried to stop them.'

I blinked away the tears; it was his pain to feel, not mine.

'I was surrounded by women clucking and soothing and tutting. My mother said, "She'll be back, don't worry. Sooner or later, she'll be back. But she doesn't deserve you."'

'Your mother was right, I didn't deserve you.' I knew I must sit here and listen. He needed to say this, and I needed to hear him.

'And you did come back, and I went out on a limb for you,' Nathan said, his voice getting louder. 'Broke all the rules. What was it for? What was all this business with making my meals, fussing round me? Why did you do all that?'

'I don't know. I was trying to be helpful.'

'Well, that worked out well. The only good thing in this is poor Moshe will never have to know what you did to me.' Nathan spat out the word 'did' as though it was a curse. 'Anyway, I don't feel as I should towards you, either.'

We both pretended to believe him.

'That's fine,' I said. 'I just wanted to give you my answer straight away. I don't want to mess you about.'

'Unlike last time.'

This felt like the most honest thing he'd said to me since our encounter on the tube.

'Nathan, If I could put the clock back, I would, and I don't even know how far I'd turn it. I've ruined everything. For both of us. I'm sorry, and it's time for me to stop behaving as if we have a chance. I think you're a wonderful man, but if I can't repair my marriage to Alex, I can't be with anyone.'

'Lucky him,' Nathan said. His face was more sad than angry now, but it was impossible to tell if he was being ironic or not.

'Well, I shouldn't think he feels very lucky at the moment.'

Nathan stood up. 'I won't be needing you to make my breakfast any more,' he said. He walked over to the bathroom. 'To be honest, you make a lousy breakfast.' The door slammed behind him.

*

I stayed at Deb's as late as I decently could; she pretty much had to throw me out. I barely spoke to my family when I got in, and went straight to bed. It was a long wait before Becca and Gila were asleep, but at last I turned on my torch and opened the Re-education book. The next list was 'sexy things'. Reading the first couple of items made me shiver, and I quickly glanced across at Becca's bed to double-check she was asleep.

Alex and I hadn't done everything on the list, but we'd done one double, as Alex called it: we combined 'make love outdoors' and 'go out in public with no underwear on' in one glorious night.

Brockwell Park was always a special place to us, and one sunny September evening, we made our way to a secluded part far away from the popular area near the lido. I was so nervous of being caught, but the nerves and the excitement jangled together until I could barely think straight. Alex's hand was clammy in mine, and I knew he was wildly excited too. I brushed a hand against his jeans and felt that he was already hard. Neither of us were wearing underwear.

He grinned at me. 'Let's walk a little faster,' he said, and we picked up speed, so that we were almost running. We reached a secret place we had scouted out a few days earlier, far back in a clearing of a small copse of trees. The evening light dappled through the leaves high above our heads. Alex laid out a blanket he'd brought in his rucksack, and still breathless, we kissed. As the kissing became more intense, he gently moved on top of me, stroking and kissing until I felt I was hallucinating.

'Shit,' he whispered, 'I forgot the condoms.'

'It doesn't matter,' I said. We were both too far gone to care.

He pushed up my skirt and with no underclothes in the way he was immediately inside me. I was soaking down there, as wet and turned on as I had ever been. He filled me up, whispering sweet words, and the flickering light gave me the feeling of being in a dream. My arms round his neck, I pulled him closer still, further into me, as deep as he could go. His teeth gently bit my neck and that was all it took, and I came, crying out so loudly he put a hand over my mouth, for I had forgotten where I was, even who I was, far less that we were in a public place. He came straight after, with a long shuddering breath, and we lay together for what felt like hours, he still inside me. I gazed up at the canopy of leaves above us, like a sukkah, safe and enclosing.

I don't know how long we'd been there when we heard voices. They sounded as if they were quite near.

'Oh no,' I whispered. Alex again put his fingers on my lips, and the echo of the earlier time he'd done that, the repeat of that unfamiliar movement, roused me. I clenched myself against his soft prick and felt it respond. I looked into his startled eyes, saw myself reflected there.

'Yes?' he whispered. I nodded, and he quietly raised himself on to his elbows and began moving in and out of me once again. At first I could barely feel him, just the sensation of his body against mine, then he hardened and my hips raised to hold him tightly inside. We could still hear the voices, people right outside the copse or perhaps even walking through it, but it made it even more erotic. I came again, quickly and hard, and I wouldn't have cared if an entire coach party had turned up to watch.

As we finally lay still, and shadows began to darken our hideaway, the voices grew more distant.

'That was fucking amazing,' Alex said. He smoothed damp hair from my forehead. 'Less than a year ago you were terrified of being seen with me in a café. You've surprised me, Eliza.'

'I surprised myself,' I said.

I closed the Re-education book and slipped it under my pillow. I could hear Becca and Gila's steady breathing. I turned on to my side, and felt a tear slide down my cheek.

Chapter Thirty-One

January 2001

'Brace yourself,' Deborah said. 'They're coming!'

The waitresses stood to the side, and Deb and I followed suit as a distant babble of voices and clatter of heels signalled the imminent arrival of the guests, all doubtless more than ready to eat and drink and gossip.

Esther was first in, ahead of her guests. 'These doors need to be kept open, Deborah,' she said as she rustled past me in her noisy peach taffeta two-piece, a mother-of-the-bar-mitzvah-boy outfit par excellence with its matching bow the size of the catering budget on her hips. Her sheitel was an enormous pile of blonde candyfloss.

Deborah fixed the doors into place and winked at me behind Esther's back. It was the first time since I'd returned that it really felt like us, me and Deb, versus the world. Esther nodded at me stiffly, looking rather anxious – what did she think I might do? – and bustled off to greet the guests as they began pouring into the hall. Deb and I stood to attention with the waitresses, ready to help. The waitresses didn't need any supervision, but they kindly let Deb and me behave as if they did. Actually, they were so very much *not* in need of help that I suspected it was Esther's way of keeping Deborah and me occupied.

Probably Esther had told Deb to ensure I was out of the way. I didn't mind at all, though. I was happy to have something to do. I'd got to see Ezra do his reading, and then Deb and I had left before the prayers to get to the hall and move piles of plates from one counter to another.

As the hall began to fill up, Deb and I stepped forward, offering to guide people to their seats. I got *the look* from several women, but I was expecting it. Then Esther and Michael's mother came into the room in a grand entrance kind of way – make way for the grandmother!

'Do you know where I am sitting?' she snapped, sweeping her gaze over me in a brilliantly overdone manner. Joan Crawford came to mind.

'I'll show you,' Deborah said, moving forward.

'This one is perfectly capable of it, I'm sure,' Mrs Shapiro said.

'This one is, indeed,' I said, with a smile at Deb. 'I'll take you to the top table.'

I started to weave my way round the people and tables, Mrs Shapiro following close behind, talking in a low voice. 'I'm surprised to see you here, Miss Bloom.'

'Are you?'

'Were you invited, or are you working for the caterers?'

I carried on walking towards the top table. I didn't want her to see my face, to know that she was rattling me. 'Ezra is my nephew, as you know. And Esther asked me to help out.'

'I imagine she meant for you to stay in the kitchen, though? It's not so nice for everyone else.'

It was the first time since I got back that someone had been so rude, other than Dad, and it certainly stung. But I guess it was just what a lot of them were thinking. At least Sadie Shapiro had the nerve to say it to my face. I thought about another woman who always spoke her mind: Vicky. I decided I was going to channel her.

'I'm sure everyone will cope with seeing me, Mrs Shapiro.' I flicked an imaginary cigarette. 'After all, I give them something to gossip about.'

'You really are a silly little girl, aren't you?'

Thank heavens, we had reached the table. I stopped so abruptly, she walked into the back of me, rather ruffling her calm. 'Oops! Here we go, Mrs Shapiro. Your seat is right here.'

Deborah had been following us at a distance, and now she caught up and said, 'Aliza, can you help me over here?'

Esther's mother put a hand on my arm to stop me moving away.

Deb hissed at her, 'Sadie, Aliza and I have things to do.'

'*Feh*, Devorah,' Mrs Shapiro said. '*You* may not know how a mother feels, though I pray one day you will. But I do, and this one here has broken her mother's heart.'

Deb rolled her eyes, and I started to giggle.

'Oh yes, it's so funny. Everything's so funny to you. Listen, *bub-beleh*,' and she prodded her finger into my shoulder, 'if you marry out, you don't get to swan back in whenever you feel like. It doesn't work that way.'

'I'll bear that in mind, next time I want to swan in,' I said, shaking her off. Deb grabbed my hand and pulled me away.

'Your poor, poor mother,' Mrs Shapiro called after us. 'Silly girls!'

We moved hastily to the front of the hall. My heart was beating fast.

'Are you all right?' Deb said. 'You handled that well.'

'Your mother-in-law really is a…'

'She's a total bitch, yes.'

'Deborah!' I couldn't remember hearing Deb ever use that word before.

'Well, *honestly*. She's already found time this morning to tell me about three people she knows whose daughters-in-law are having babies.

I don't want to ruin Ezra's big day, but I'm this close to grinding her face into the profiteroles.'

'Well, if you change your mind I'll hold her down while you do the grinding.'

The two of us went back to showing people to their seats. I kept a lookout for Zaida, and at last he appeared, walking very slowly, supported by Uri and Dov on either side.

'My best girl!' he cried as I approached him. He hugged me tight with one arm that he'd pulled free from Uri. He wobbled a bit and we guided him quickly into a chair. Looking down at him I could see how sparse his hair was, the pink scalp showing between every strand.

'Where's that lovely young man of yours, er…'

'Nathan?' Dov prompted.

'Er, yes, Nathan,' Zaida said, looking confused, and I realised that it was *my* name he wasn't able to remember. I saw with a sudden clarity that there was no going back for Zaida. He wasn't going to get better; there was only one direction this could go in. He would never be capable of living on his own again. He would never again greet me in the annex with a plate of love disguised as a cream cheese bagel.

'Nathan? What do you…' Uri started to say, and looked astonished when Dov and I both waved our hands at him. 'What? What's going on?'

I shook my head at Uri, who continued to look baffled. 'Nathan's moved back to Gateshead, Zaida,' he said in his loud, clear voice. I hadn't known this, having avoided the annex religiously for the last week, since the second marriage proposal.

'Where? Gateshead?' Zaida said, his head swivelling between Uri and me. 'What's the meshuggener want to do that for? He can't leave his wife.'

'His wife…?' Uri said, the dumb fool.

'He's not left permanently,' Dov said, laughing as if it were all a misunderstanding. Which I guess it was. 'Just for a few days. Isn't that right, Aliza?'

'Yes, of course.' Over Zaida's head I did a hand-across-the-throat gesture, meaning to kill a conversation. I'd picked it up from the Real World, but Uri got it and, shrugging and shaking his head, moved away to be congratulated on his son's achievements by the rest of the guests.

Zaida beamed up at me. 'Where's your lovely man?' he asked again.

'He's popped out for a minute,' I said, to avoid any further confusion.

'Oh yes, that's right,' Zaida said, but clearly he had already forgotten what he had asked. He began to look agitated. 'Is Paulina here?' Before I could ask what he wanted, she materialised right next to us.

'Want the loo, Moshe? OK, up we get.' She smiled at Dov and me, and smoothly got Zaida up and on to his feet, gently placing his hands on a walking frame. 'Come on then, my lamb,' she said, and they walked out together. He didn't look back.

'Can we sit?' I said to Dov. The room was full of people, but he was the only person I felt I could bear to be with.

He led me over to the outcasts' table at the far end of the room, by this time filling up with the oldest and dustiest of the aunts. Esther was a ruthless table planner. I already knew I had been seated here, but to my surprise, the place setting next to mine had Dov's name on, written in Becca's swirling calligraphy – she was always asked to do the place-cards for fancy occasions.

'How did you manage this?' I smiled at Dov. 'You're meant to be at the top table.'

'Oh...' He looked a bit shifty. 'Uri asked me to help arrange chairs and tables in here yesterday.'

'Who did you swap with?'

He grinned. 'Uncle Ben.'

How I loved Dov. I was surrounded by all these people, feeling their judgement radiating at me. But with him, I was not alone. And it was going to be fun to watch the top table – Uncle Ben would keep Esther and her mother on their toes up there.

Dov and I sat and clinked our empty glasses together. The wine waiters were a long way from our table.

'Did you know Nathan moved back to Gateshead?' I asked.

'Yes, he went a couple of days ago.'

'I didn't think he'd go so soon.'

'I think it's good news, don't you?' Dov looked at me with his clear, shrewd eyes. I was saved from answering by a waitress plonking a jug of water in front of us.

The noise and activity in the room was intense: more than a hundred and fifty yammering people, calling to relatives across several tables, standing up to greet friends, making loud complaints about the food, impassive waiters and waitresses gliding round with drinks and starters. I glimpsed Deborah hurtling from one table to another, her face anxious.

I thought of Nathan going back to the yeshiva to start again. I thought of the day I chased him across the station and he told me to get off the train. The way his face looked in the early hours of the morning as he told me how he'd felt about being jilted. Before I knew it, I started to cry, that out-of-control crying that sneaks up when you least want it to.

A woman on my left, in a bright red skirt suit, sausage tight, one of Esther's distant relatives, asked if I was all right. I nodded, then turned my body towards Dov so she couldn't see my face.

'I had some tissues but Mum used them up in the car on the way here, crying about Ezra,' he said, patting his pockets fruitlessly. 'First grandson bar mitzvah-ed and all that.'

My eyes blurring, I rifled in my bag and pulled out a tissue, but found it was stuck, embarrassingly, to an old sanitary towel. As I shoved them both back into my bag, I thought: *When was the last time I used a sanitary towel?*

'I should have told you about Nathan going back,' Dov said, handing me a napkin. 'I'm sorry.'

I dabbed my eyes. It was a paper napkin but was nonetheless monogrammed with EB, Ezra's initials. Esther would be able to re-use any left over, for they were her initials too. I wondered if she'd already thought of that. Probably.

'It's not your fault, sweetie. It's me. I'm such a mess.'

'You are not,' he said, loyally.

'Did you think I might get back together with Nathan?'

He nodded, staring at the table.

'So did I,' I said, admitting it to someone – and myself – for the first time.

'But you stopped making his breakfasts.'

I laughed weakly. 'Yes, it was causing confusion. For both of us.'

'Anyway,' Dov said, pouring me a glass of water, 'you still love Alex.'

'What?' I sat upright.

The waitresses finally reached our next-postcode-along table and served us beetroot-cured smoked salmon starters. The sausage-suit woman beside me said, 'My lord, I thought we'd been forgotten,' and began vigorously attacking it with a fork. Her husband, a saggy man, shrunken in a suit that was too large for him in about the same amount as his wife's was too small for her, said 'Is it meant to be purple? Why is it purple?'

'Miss,' the woman opposite me called out to the waitress, holding up her plate, 'I don't eat fish. I said I was vegetarian months ago.'

This was exactly the sort of issue I was meant to be helping stage-manage, but all I could do was stare at Dov. 'How do you know I love Alex?'

'You just look sad all the time. Since you came back.'

'I'm not the sort of fair-weather vegetarian who eats fish,' the woman said to no one in particular. The waitress removed her plate without making any promises. The saggy man shovelled in his salmon in one go and struggled to deal with it, a piece of chive sticking out of the corner of his mouth as he chewed.

'Didn't I look sad before?' I said.

'Not when you came to visit Zaida those first times, when you were still with Alex. You looked completely happy.'

My eyes misted up again. 'I think my marriage is over,' I said.

'Is it really?' Dov said.

'Not eating yours, dear?' The sausage woman pointed at my starter.

'You have it,' I said, pushing the plate towards her.

'I don't suppose I'll get anything now,' the vegetarian woman announced. 'Always at the bottom of the pile.'

'The salmon's very nice,' the woman next to me told her.

'I don't eat fish!' the vegetarian exclaimed.

'Salmon's barely fish,' the woman next to me said, mildly. 'It's smoked. No bones.'

'I thought Alex looked kind,' Dov said.

'When did you see him?'

'The day you ran away with him.'

Of course he had. The film of Alex and I running towards the end of the road – walking very fast, anyway – unreeled in my head.

'There's a reason there aren't purple foods in nature,' the saggy man said.

'Aubergine's purple,' his wife said instantly, as if this was a conversation they had a lot. 'So is purple sprouting broccoli.'

I tried to tune them out. 'Yes, he is kind. Was kind. And he did love me. But it wasn't ever going to work, was it? Him and me. We are from such different places.'

The waitress returned and put a plate of bread in front of the vegetarian. 'We've run out of the veggie starters, sorry,' she said.

The woman stared at her. 'Is this some kind of joke?' She picked up a piece of the bread and waved it around at the table. 'Bottom of the pile!' she shouted. Then she started to eat it.

'Do you remember when you wore Joel's clothes?' Dov said.

'A bit random, but yes, of course. You don't, though. You weren't even born.'

'Everyone told me about it. That Aliza, that sister of yours, she's such a rebel.'

'I actually own some trousers now. Well, I did. I left them behind. Probably Alex has chucked all my stuff out.'

'Then there were all the possible matches you refused. Uri said he'd never heard of any other girl turning down so many.'

'I know, I know. Too fussy for her own good. So what's your point, Dov?'

'Nothing really.' He shuffled his feet. 'I suppose – I can't picture you living a life like Mum or Malka, or Esther. Or even Deborah. I could never picture it, even before. When you went away, it made a sort of sense. I hated that you'd gone, but I did understand it.'

'Dov, I wish I could see myself through your eyes.'

Those same grey eyes held my gaze. I looked at the black spot on his iris. Was he looking at the matching one on mine?

A big hand clapped down on Dov's shoulder, making us both jump. 'Dovvy, mind if I sit here for a few minutes?' Uri always managed to make a question sound like an order.

'Sure!' Dov jumped up, the way all of us jumped for Uri. He was our father's natural heir. Uri sat in Dov's seat and waved him away.

'Mazeltov, Uri,' I said, looking into his craggy, forbidding face, trying to get in ahead of whatever berating he was planning to give me. 'What a blessing, your boy a man. You must be very proud.'

'Mazeltov, Uri!' all the dusty aunts chorused, echoing me. He smiled round at them and held up his big meaty hand in acknowledgement.

'I am very proud of Ezra,' he said. Then quietly, just to me, he added, 'I'm not so proud of myself.'

'Pardon?'

'I did it for the right reasons.'

'Did what?'

He pushed his chair away from the table slightly, and moved his mouth close to my ear. He whispered, 'I told Dad about you visiting Zaida.'

'You? No you didn't, it was Nathan.' Even as I said this, I knew it made more sense for it to have been Uri.

'Aliza, it was me.'

'How did you find out?'

'Esther's Aunt Liv.' Uri pointed discreetly to an elderly woman at our table, next to the vegetarian. 'Her husband's in Beis Israel, and she saw you when she was visiting him.'

The woman, feeling our gaze on her, looked up and gave us a friendly little wave.

'She doesn't even know me,' I said.

'Aliza, everyone knows you.'

Of course they did – the Scarlet Woman of Hackney E5.

There was no sense asking Uri why he'd told Dad. I knew why. Because he was furious with me. For leaving, for challenging the rules he had always abided by without question, the rules he had grown up with and then established with his own family. He was a more benign father than ours, but still, he had that same iron will. The interesting question was, why did he feel bad about it now?

I said, 'I'm sorry I made you so angry.'

Uri laughed. 'Angry? That's not the half of it.'

'Really, I need to thank you, for allowing me to reconnect to you all. I don't suppose you meant it to work out like that when you told Dad. But thank you.'

He briefly closed his eyes. 'I thought Dad would frighten you into leaving Zaida alone.'

'You didn't think how it might make Zaida feel?'

Uri picked up a glass, but finding it empty, stood up and bellowed across the room. 'Deborah! We have no wine here!'

I couldn't see Deb but imagined her scurrying to grab some bottles.

He sat down again. 'I hadn't anticipated quite what would happen, no.'

'It's a family trait,' I said, 'not being able to predict the outcome of our actions.'

Deborah appeared, looking flustered. She put two bottles on the table, muttered, 'Thanks for your help, GG,' and darted away.

Uri poured red wine for us both. 'GG?'

'Goy Girl.'

'You don't mind her calling you that to your face?'

I raised my glass to him. 'Maybe we would all be better off if we said what we really thought? Rather than hide behind rules and duties and excuses?' I would never have dared to speak to Uri in this way before, but he had never seemed so human before.

He clinked his glass against mine, then drank the contents down in one blast. 'Ez doesn't want to go to the yeshiva, you know,' he said.

His first-born son not wanting to follow in the religious life – I knew how painful that must be for Uri. 'What does he want to do?'

'Chemistry.' Uri made it sound like a swear word. He filled his glass again.

'Will you let him?'

Uri shrugged. 'If I give him his way, will it stop him being as meshuggener as you?'

I laughed. 'Perhaps. Though I don't think I am quite as meshuggener as I used to be.'

I was standing in front of the mirror in our room, sideways on, when Becca came in. I moved quickly but she'd seen. She looked straight at me. 'Are you all right?'

'Fine.'

'Have you realised?'

'Realised what, Becca?'

Before she could say anything more, Gila burst in. She threw herself on my bed, and shouted, 'Wasn't that the best day ever?'

Gila adored all family occasions, and had always been close to Ezra who, despite being her nephew, was only a year younger. As Gila started reciting her favourite things about the day, which centred on the amount of cake she'd eaten, Becca gave me worried looks, and tilted her head to invite me to join her outside the room. I shook my head.

'What are you two making faces about?' Gila said.

'Nothing.' I sat on the bed next to her, and stroked her hair. She was really over-excited: the food, people, and dancing, had made her a little crazy. She leaned back against my pillow and complained, 'There's something hard here.' She reached under it and pulled out the Re-education book.

'Give me that!' I said, but she clutched it tight to her chest and jumped off my bed. I grabbed at her arm, but she pulled away and ran over to her own bed. She opened the book. '"Poems I like,"' she read out. 'What is this?'

'It's private, Gila. Give it back, please.'

Gila ignored me. '"New experiences." Whose writing is this? "1. Go on a rollercoaster. You have embarked on a meta, a meta…" I can't read this word.'

'Give it back to Aliza now,' Becca ordered.

I leapt over and dived on to Gila's bed. I managed to grab hold of a corner of the book, but curiosity gave her strength and she clung on. I realised that my reaction was only making her more determined, so I returned to my own bed and gritted my teeth.

'Never mind,' I told Becca. 'She won't find it that interesting.' I could only hope that she didn't land on the 'Sexy things to try' list.

Gila turned over some more pages. '"Modern history." Boring. "Internet sites." Wow, there are so many. "My favourite books." "My favourite poems." "Best 90s TV programmes." Hey, this one looks good: "Things I love about Eliza." Your name is spelled wrong. "Number one: Her skin smells of peaches." Aw, that's so dreamy. "Number two: Her laugh makes me feel…'

'What's that?' I bounded back over and held out my hand. Something about my expression made Gila give up the book without a fight.

I took it and went downstairs. I could hear Gila wailing, 'Where are you going, Aliza?' as I went, and Becca scolding her.

I pushed open the connecting door to the annex. After only a few days, there was no trace of Nathan. It was like he'd never been there; the annex felt safe again. I curled up in Zaida's armchair, the one he and I used to sit in together when I was small enough to fit on his lap. I was uncomfortably aware that I was not only big now but getting bigger. Sitting with my feet under me made me realise more forcibly than ever just how tight my skirt was. Yes, Becca, I'd realised. My heart fluttering, I did some quick, frightened calculations in my head, but I already knew, thank Ha-Shem, there was only one possible explanation.

I turned to the end of Alex's lists. The last one I knew he'd written was places he wanted us to visit together. But after that, there was a list I'd never seen, the one Gila had stumbled upon. I wondered when he had written it.

'Things I love about Eliza.'

It had taken me a long while to realise what the book really was. I'd thought it was just a book of lists. Sometimes fun, sometimes patronising, sometimes challenging, sometimes irritating. I now saw it for what it was: a book of love. Alex's lists were one long love letter to me. Everything he adored, he shared with me in the lists. Because these things made him happy and he wanted me to be happy too. Because he loved me.

Now there was a love letter that wasn't in disguise, and I cried as I read it.

At the end, there was a scribbled note in a different colour pen, added later. 'I hope she phones me when she reads this.'

I closed the book.

*

'You can't go back,' Nathan had said.

But maybe sometimes, you could. I rang Alex's number, and he picked up on the second ring.

'Hey, you,' he said.

'Hey.'

'How are you?'

'I read your last list.'

'Ah, finally.'

'There's one item you missed.'

'Really? I thought it was pretty comprehensive.'

I could hear the smile in his voice. I pictured him, sitting in the living room, maybe on the sofa, his long legs stretched out in front of him.

'You missed: "I love Eliza because she will be the mother of my baby."'

I heard him gasp. 'Are you…?'

'Yes.'

I waited. It was up to him now.

'Are you coming back, Eliza?'

A younger Eliza would have pointed out that I hadn't been the one to leave; that it was him who'd gone. But I was older now. Re-educated. I knew that though he'd been the one to physically leave, I had left emotionally long before that.

I said, 'Do you think we could move somewhere else? Make a fresh start?'

'That's a brilliant idea.' I could hear the relief in his voice. 'Anywhere in particular that appeals to you?'

Swishes of saris, brightly coloured piles of oranges and apples, delis with cheese piled high, neat-as-pin homes with bright front doors and no history.

'Ilford is nice.'

'Great plan. It'll be handy for us to get our bacon sarnies at Kev's Café every morning.'

'You're so funny.'

'When are you coming home?'

'Let me look at my diary.' I rifled through a few pages of the Book of Love. 'You know what? I seem to be free right now.'

Things I love about Eliza

- Her skin smells of peaches.
- Her laugh makes me feel that everything is going to be all right.
- She is kind.
- She has been very patient with me.
- She doesn't know how beautiful she is.
- She's one of the bravest people I know.
- She is very funny, not always intentionally.
- Her willingness to try anything once.
- The way her face glows when she sees me (well, it did when we first got together, anyway).
- That little black beauty spot on her left eye.
- The way she used to jump when I touched her.
- Her lovely hands.
- The thoughtfulness on her face when she doesn't know I'm watching.
- The way I feel I will never completely know her. But I am ready to try.
- She makes me feel like the best version of myself.

I hope she phones me when she reads this.

Chapter Thirty-Two

April 2016

Dov and I race up the M1 in his enormous Renault. He drives fast, which I normally hate, but not today. He's had his foot to the floor since he collected me from Deborah's, and we've been lucky with the traffic, but we're still three hours away, maybe more.

We set off less than an hour after Alex rang me to tell me Leah was missing. Alex and I agreed he'd stay at home in case I was wrong and Leah would be coming back. I rang Dov to get some information about addresses and he immediately said he'd come with me. When I told him it was too much for him to drop everything, he insisted. I wondered if he was feeling guilty about his part in it all.

Dov pulls into a service station so we can get petrol and coffee. As we wait in the queue, I say, 'How much of a head start do you reckon Leah has on us?'

'Not much, probably,' he says. 'Depends on when she got the train.'

'*If* she got the train. Maybe she got a coach instead.'

'In which case we're way ahead of her.'

'That's if I'm right, of course,' I say.

We take our coffees to the car and set off again.

'I wonder how she knew where to go,' I say, fishing. I want him to acknowledge that it's his fault she's gone, that it's his son who gave Leah the idea in the first place. When we were kids, Dov always had this ability to stay silent in the face of trouble, something I never learned how to do. He could stand up to our dad ranting and raving without ever trying to answer back and defend himself. I admired it then, but now it seems little more than a massive evasion of responsibility.

Dov, true to form, doesn't say anything.

'Oh come on!' I explode. 'She only knew about me and Nathan because of Gidon!' I manage not to call him 'that little shit-stirrer Gidon', but it's a close thing. 'Gidon must have told her where Nathan lives.'

'He doesn't know, though,' Dov says calmly. 'Like I told you, we don't have Nathan's address.'

'I find that hard to believe, Dov. His family have been friends with ours for ever. You were pretty matey with him back in the day.'

'Yes, but since you and he… well, look, I haven't seen him for years. I didn't even know he was married until Mum told me. She's still friendly with his mum.'

There is a silence, and I know the same thought has occurred to both of us. *Mum*.

'Do you think…' Dov says.

'Yes, I bloody do.'

'But why would she?'

'That is something I intend to ask her,' I say firmly, 'once I have brought my daughter home. But for now, I am merely going to ask her for the address.'

I call Mum, and after some prompting she reads out Nathan's address, slowly and clearly, spelling all the words, even 'Avenue'. She doesn't ask why I want it. When I ask if she has already given it to Leah, she becomes a bit less clear.

'Oh, I don't know, Aliza.'

I relay this to Dov, and he laughs. 'Classic Mum, going a bit vague when she realises she shouldn't have done something.'

'What's going on?' Mum asks. 'Is Dov with you?' She must have heard him laughing.

'Yes, Mum. We're heading to Gateshead to see Nathan.'

'Oh, that's nice. Say hello from me.'

'Mum, I'm afraid I've got some worrying news. Leah's run away.'

'Oh no, oh no…'

'I'm going to have to get the police involved,' I lie.

'The police! Ay-ay-ay-ayy!' I can practically hear her clutching her heart over the phone.

'Well, you know, Leah's never travelled further on her own than to see you in Hackney. I'm very worried. But before I call the police, it would be useful to know if she might have gone to visit Nathan.'

'Oh, I remember now! My memory, honestly. I think she did ask for the address. Let me think… oh yes, she did! Lucky you reminded me.'

'Thanks, Mum.' I hang up, and even though I'm worried about Leah, I have to laugh. Partly with relief that my hunch was right, and partly at the bizarre machinations of my mother's mind.

'Well played,' Dov says. 'She is an outrageous meddler. Look at what she was like at Gidon's bar mitzvah last year. She moved all the place cards round so she could prevent our family from mixing with Ilana's.'

Mum has a long-standing but mysterious feud with Ilana's mother which dates back to the 1960s. It makes me laugh that even though Dov did the right thing and married young into a good Jewish family, Mum still isn't satisfied. Without Dad around to express displeasure in a more obvious manner, it's far clearer that she is a person of strong opinions herself.

'You weren't above moving place cards yourself, once,' I remind him, thinking of us sitting together at Ezra's bar mitzvah. I start laughing, remembering Esther's mum's face when she discovered she was sitting next to Uncle Ben – slightly smelly and prone to inappropriate jokes and gestures. Him, not her. Though actually I found her fairly inappropriate too.

I tell Dov, and he starts laughing too. 'And what about Esther when Ben stood up,' he says, 'and started to give a speech to Ezra about the natural urges of young manhood!' We both giggle again, thinking how quickly Uri had rushed to Uncle Ben's side, urging him forcefully back into his seat.

'Well, that was very naughty, Dov. You're in no position to judge Mum,' I say primly, half-laughing.

'Ah, that was only one swap, though,' he says. 'Mum rearranged the entire seating plan.'

'I suppose she's bored now most of us have left home. And Dad's not there to fight with any more.'

My eyes are heavy, and I'd love to lie on one of the two back seats in this crazy-big car and shut everything out, not think about stuff for a while. But I have too much marching about in my head, a whole colony of ants. I think back to other times Mum's meddled in our lives, in her quiet way. Perhaps all those years ago, when she encouraged me – insisted, really – to make breakfast for Nathan every morning. I haven't thought about that for a long time. And I need to put it aside now, while I find out just how Mum-like Dov's involvement in this whole business has been.

'OK, Dov, I have to ask.' I fold my hands tightly together. 'How did Gidon get the idea that Nathan might be Leah's father?'

'I don't know. He has a very inquiring mind,' Dov says.

Nice try, Dov. 'I thought there were only two people who knew that Nathan and I had, uh, had relations.' I have reverted to coy language in front of my upstanding little brother. 'Me, and Nathan. I never told anyone. But somehow, a rumour clearly started. And now it's blown up in my face. So, are you going to tell me, or do I have to give you a Jewish burn?'

There's a silence, and I think he's not going to talk, and I start trying to remember how you do a Jewish burn. Do you twist the skin in two different directions?

But then he says, 'Nathan told me.'

'NATHAN told you?!'

'There's an echo in here.'

'But he – but he—' I can barely get my brain to articulate the thought. 'He was furious with me. And it was completely taboo to him, he was disgusted by what we'd done.'

Dov's ears are red, and he is very much focusing on the road in front of him. It may not be possible to grip the steering wheel any tighter than he is right now.

'Sorry. Dov. Too much information, as Leah would say.'

'I don't know about furious, or disgusted. But he was certainly completely miserable. He thought he'd got a second chance, and then you left him *again* for Alex.'

'How come you never told me he spoke to you?'

He laughs. 'Do you have any idea how taboo the word "Nathan" was for you? Even a few weeks ago, you went white as a sheet when Mum mentioned he'd got married.'

Fair enough. 'Go on, then. What happened?'

'It was a few days before Ezra's bar mitzvah. Nathan was in a bit of a state. He told me that he'd asked you to marry him again, and you'd said no, again, but he thought the signals were a bit mixed. He asked if I thought he should try again, said he kept thinking, "third time lucky". He said did I think it was over between you and Alex, that he didn't care about being second best. He was sure you could come to love him.'

'Good god!' After our terrible love-making, and after I'd already turned him down twice. I couldn't decide if he was astonishingly brave, or supremely arrogant. 'What did you say?'

'That I believed you really loved Alex,' Dov said, 'and I was pretty sure you would go back to him. I also pointed out that, given your nature, you probably wouldn't make Nathan a terrific Jewish wife.'

I was so moved that Dov, young as he was then, would have stood up for me in that way. I blinked hard, and said, 'I think I would be an excellent Jewish wife, you cheeky so-and-so.'

'You wouldn't, and you know it. Could you imagine being like Mum? Martyring yourself? Thinking about the next meal all the time? Stuck with a difficult, violent man, not feeling you could leave?'

'That's not Jewish wifehood, that's Mum. Ilana's not like that. Deborah's not.'

'I know. Though I do think Nathan would have been more like Uri and Dad than, say, me or Michael. But anyway, there was still Halacha, all the laws. Even when you were tiny, Uri said, you were always asking why, why, why, and breaking every rule you could.'

'A questioning attitude is not incompatible with being a Jewish wife.'

'This is irrelevant,' he says, flicking on the indicator and moving into the exit lane for Gateshead. 'You chose not to be a Jewish wife, and we have all finally got used to that. Anyway, do you want to know the really interesting thing Nathan said, back then?'

'Of course I do.'

'He told me he was going to fight for you. He was going to go after you, and tell you that it was a mistake going back to Alex.'

'Seriously?' I couldn't imagine Nathan even thinking such a thing, let alone saying it out loud. Not after our final conversation. Brave, romantic, over-confident Nathan! I conjure up his earnest expression, and then Alex's smile flashes into my mind. Poor old Nathan; such a grand gesture would have made no difference at all.

Dov slows down at a roundabout. 'So, to finish the story, and answer your question, which was so long ago you've probably forgotten. Nathan was halfway out the door, thinking he would be dashing after you, so I told him you were pregnant. For his sake, as much as yours.'

'Hey, hang on a minute! How did you know? I didn't realise myself till the evening of Ez's bar mitzvah.'

'Becca told me.'

'Christ, how did *she* know?'

'Well, she shared a room with you. She said, er, she had seen you when you were undressed.'

I suppose Becca always was the most worldly one of us sisters, despite me being the one who emigrated to the Real World. We were never particularly close but I have a sudden urge to see her, though she and her family live inconveniently far away, in Bournemouth.

'God, I really was in denial back then.'

'Just back then?'

'Ah shut up, Dov. So go on, back to Nathan. You told him I was pregnant – wow, you were brave. And what did he say?'

Dov coughs. 'He looked like he was going to faint. He stared at me, and sat down on a chair like he had fallen on to it. At first I thought he was shocked because you were pregnant and separated from your husband.'

'Oh god.'

'Then he said, "But how can she know so soon? We only made love two days ago."'

'Oh, *god*.'

So *that's* how Dov found out I'd slept with Nathan. Poor Dov. He was only eighteen. He had to process the fact that his sister had slept with the fiancé she'd previously jilted, while pregnant by her gentile husband. And then he had to explain to her ex-fiancé that her gentile husband was in fact the father of the baby, not him.

The embarrassment of it all hits me like a freight train, fifteen years too late, and I cover my face, making wincing noises.

'I'm sorry, I'm sorry, I owe you one, Dov. God, how awful.'

I realise that Nathan must have packed his bags and returned to the yeshiva the next day. I'd always assumed he left because we'd made love and I'd rejected him, but there was even more to it than that. What a big, stinking mess I made back then. And how lucky I had my little brother to clear up after me.

Hang on, a minute, though… I uncover my face, as Nathan follows the satnav instructions to turn left, then take the second right. 'So only you knew. How come Gidon found out?'

'This is the point at which you realise you don't owe me one after all,' Dov says. 'Gosh, Gateshead is bigger than I thought.'

'*You told Gidon?*'

'Of course not! But…' Dov coughs, 'he might have overhead me saying something to Ilana. We were discussing it after we heard that Nathan was getting married.'

'Ilana knows about me and Nathan too?'

'Yes, we don't have any secrets from each other.'

'You mean *I* don't have any secrets from Ilana!'

So *that's* why she's always been so weird with me. Now I just need to find out that Dov has told Vicky too, and all the strange relationships I have with my sisters-in-law will be completely explained.

It doesn't take long to find Nathan's house, but when we knock on the door, my heart in my mouth, it is a woman who answers. She's younger than I expected, and pretty, an attractive scarf framing her face. Lucky Nathan, at last. She holds a baby in her arms, and has a pregnant tummy heralding the next one.

When Dov asks if we can see Nathan, she says with a nervous smile, 'Everyone is looking for him today.'

'A young girl?' I ask. 'Tall, long dark hair?'

'Yes,' she says. 'About an hour ago. She told me she might be his daughter. Is she? He never said anything to me about a daughter.' Now I see that her eyes are red, her face tense. Her settled, safe world has the potential, all at once, to be turned upside down.

'She is definitely *not* his daughter,' I say.

'I told her he would be at the yeshiva. I hope that was all right.'

We thank her, then Dov drives us to the yeshiva, a large redbrick building stretching across a part of one street and into another. I wonder how Leah will find it from Nathan's house. Dov thinks they're about two miles apart, and I look out for her all the way there, but don't see her.

With Dov doing the talking, it takes only a couple of minutes to pass the security checks at the yeshiva and be admitted through the gates, into a reception area. I sit while Dov goes up to ask if we can speak to Nathan. The man at the desk asks some questions that I can't hear, and nor do I catch Dov's quiet answers, but whatever he says works because finally the man picks up a phone and mumbles into it. Minutes later, a door behind the reception desk opens and a man walks towards us, a man with a familiar face, his hair a bit thinner on top but otherwise recognisably himself. When I stand up to greet him, I am short of breath. He hugs Dov and they slap each other's backs.

'Dov, it's been too long,' he says. When they release each other, he looks at me, and nods. 'Aliza,' he says. 'You look well.'

'So do you.' We look each other in the eye, and I remember anew that we are almost exactly the same height. 'We met your wife,' I say, quickly, so he doesn't think I'm here for another go at him. 'She's beautiful.'

'Thank you. She is. So,' he looks at Dov, 'what can I do for you?'

Dov invites him to sit with us, and he quietly explains about Leah 'getting the wrong end of the stick'. As it dawns on Nathan what Dov means, his face darkens. He glares at me.

'Why can't you just leave me alone?'

Well, the social niceties didn't last long.

'Nathan, I'm sorry, it wasn't—'

'I can't believe this! At last I've managed to find peace in my life, I have a lovely wife and a child, and you burst in again. What *is* it with you? Why do you have to keep bothering me?'

I haven't anything to say to this. I would rather be anywhere but here, bothering him. I stare at my lap, and am distantly surprised to see a tear splash on to my skirt. Belatedly I realise that the skirt ends shortly above my knee, and is thus utterly unsuitable to be seen in a yeshiva. Thank Ha-Shem I remembered to put a scarf over my head before coming in here.

Dov puts his hand on mine.

'If it is anyone's fault, Nathan, it is mine,' he says. For the first time I notice that Dov has lines round his eyes. He looks tired.

'You're always covering for her.' Nathan stands up. 'The dutiful younger brother.' He almost spits these words out, and points a shaking finger at me. 'You are taken in by her, Dov. She is not a good woman, she tempts people into doing the wrong thing. Your family were wrong to let her back into the fold, she is wanton and a liar and...'

Wanton?!

'Nathan, listen,' Dov says, and he stands too. 'It's my fault we're here. It's because of me that Aliza's daughter gained the misunderstanding. I was guilty of gossiping to my wife. My boy heard something, and he passed it on to Leah.'

'Still covering, Dov. It's admirable, but so foolish, too.' Nathan shakes his head. 'I hoped I would never have to see you again, Aliza.'

'I'm very sorry,' I say, wiping my eyes. 'But here I am.'

All these years, while I have been getting on with my life, my mostly happy life, Nathan has been nursing a grudge. Is he wrong to have done so? I don't suppose I will ever know how much I hurt him. But I sure as hell need to stop hurting him now.

In as steady a voice as I can manage, I say, 'I hope you won't take it the wrong way, Nathan, if I say that I didn't want to see you again, either. But my daughter has become convinced that you are connected to her, and she clearly hasn't let anything like sense or logistics stop her from doing what she wants.'

'Well, with a lack of sense, at least we know for definite that she's your daughter,' Nathan says.

I remember what a sharp tongue Nathan always had. And I also remember how to deal with it. 'Very good, Nathan,' I say. 'Touché.'

The man on reception calls Nathan over, and tells him there is a girl outside asking for him.

'I'm so popular today,' Nathan says drily. 'No visitors for two years, then three in one day.'

'That must be Leah,' Dov says, redundantly.

'Unless I have any other would-be children turning up today,' Nathan says. He nods to the man to let Leah in, and something about the portentous way he does it makes me think: you know what? He is slightly enjoying the drama of it all.

'Thank god she's all right,' I say. Dov puts his arm round me, and I hide my face against his shoulder. I'm ashamed of crying so much, and in front of Nathan, too.

I jump to my feet as I get my first glimpse of Leah. She is escorted by a huge security guard and looks childishly tiny next to him, tiny and exhausted. She's been travelling all day, had to find her way on to the right train or coach, then she must have despaired when she got to Nathan's house, expecting it to be the end of the road, only to have to move on again. How did she get here from Nathan's house, I wonder? She's pale, with black smudges of eyeliner and tiredness under her eyes, but she goes another shade paler on seeing me and Dov. She hesitates, but when I hold out my arms she runs into them.

Once she has stopped crying all over me – and me her – we sit. Nathan pulls his chair round so he's directly opposite her. She looks at him in silence, her eyes great big question marks.

'Leah, I know you've come here to find me,' he says. I'm astonished by how gentle his voice is, and impressed by how quickly he gets to the point. 'But I'm not your dad.'

'Are you sure?' she asks, in her smallest voice.

'I'm willing to do a DNA test if you wish, but it would be a waste of time. You look exactly like your father. You don't look like me.'

I don't think I have ever been so grateful to anyone in my life as I am right now, and what an odd person to be grateful to. I smile at Nathan, trying to send with it my complicated feelings of admiration and relief, but I doubt he gets it.

'I didn't know you knew my dad,' Leah says.

'I only saw him twice,' Nathan says, 'but I remember him clearly.' He stands up. 'Good to meet you, Leah. I hope you find the peace you're looking for.'

He shakes hands with Dov, then changes his mind, and hugs him. I get a grave nod, before he turns and walks towards the door. I know he won't like it, but I go after him.

'Nathan, thank you. Thank you so much.'

He turns, and though his face is calm and unemotional, his voice is not. 'We all did stupid things when we were young,' he says. He walks behind the reception desk and disappears through the door.

I return to my seat, and the three of us look at each other. It feels as if a whirlwind has passed through, leaving us shaken but unscathed.

'Can we go home now, Leah?' I ask.

'Yes,' she says meekly, like the child she once was. 'Sorry, Mum.'

'You believe that Dad is your dad now, do you?'

She leans limply against me. 'I do look like him, don't I? I look nothing like Nathan.'

I hand her my phone. 'Your poor father is going mad with worry. Why don't you call him?'

When she's spoken to Alex – from the noise coming out of the phone I'm guessing he is a lot crosser with her than I am – Dov pulls us out of our chairs, a hand each.

'Back we go,' he says. 'Back to our real lives.'

*

Leah is stretched across the passenger seat, her head on my lap. As if she has regressed to childhood, she asks me to tell her a story, and from somewhere deep in my memory, I begin, 'Once there was a little girl called Leah, who was very brave…'

Like Zaida's tales of Brave Aliza, thirty years ago, I weave truth and fiction together. I tell the story of Leah leaving home before her father is awake, taking her savings money and buying a train ticket, working out how to get from the station to an address in a city she doesn't know at all, so she can meet a king in a palace who turns out not to be a king after all.

She is asleep before Dov gets us out of the centre of Gateshead, long before the story gets to the yeshiva. I mean palace. The weight of her head on me, the softness of her hair under my fingers, moves me almost to tears. I think of her, aged about ten, saying 'It's been emotional,' in a cod American accent; it was something she'd heard on a TV show.

Dov glances at me in the rear-view mirror. 'Are you crying again?'

'Definitely not. A bit. I'm just so utterly relieved.'

'Me too. Everything's back to how it was.'

'Well, not quite everything.'

I wonder how Alex is feeling, and how long it will take him to forgive me for lying, or whether he will forgive me at all. I text him, holding my phone stiffly in the air so I don't disturb Leah, who emits adorable little baby snores and snuffles. I tell him that Leah is fine, and that Dov and I will drop her off at the house. Alex immediately replies, saying he wants me to come in too. I allow myself a moment to feel hopeful, then I text Deborah to update her.

'Dov,' I say, 'what do you think about what Nathan said? About how you're always covering up for me?'

'He was just trying to get at you.'

'I think maybe you did do a lot of covering up for me when we were younger.'

'Maybe a little.'

'All those weeks I was visiting Zaida at the home secretly, remember? And you never told anyone.'

'Of course not.'

'I still miss Zaida, do you?'

'Oh, *yes*. Think how much he would have loved our kids.'

Zaida did in fact get to see Leah, just about. She was only a few weeks old, but his face as he held her carefully in his arms was an absolute picture. I don't have to imagine it as I have an actual picture of it; Alex took one on his camera and it's in a frame on our bedroom wall. Zaida may not have known who she was – by that time he wasn't all that sure who I was – but in the photo he is beaming with delight. He knew she was somehow connected to him. I was glad I had the chance for them to see each other. Dov wasn't so lucky – Zaida died even before he married Ilana.

There was something I'd been wondering for a while, and there was probably never going to be a better time to ask.

'Dov?'

'Mmm?'

'You know the day I left with Alex?'

'Mmm?'

'I've always wondered why no one came after us.'

'Mmm?' I can only see the back of his head, but I can tell that he's smiling.

'Dad. Or Uri. I can't believe they let us get away. They were both so macho. Seems astonishing they didn't try and drag me back, don't you think?'

'Maybe they knew there was no point. That you were too *wanton* to listen to reason.'

I laugh at him using Nathan's word. I think of that last glimpse of Dov that day, as he asked which way we were going, then ran back towards my family. I lost sight of him after that, but now I follow him in my mind's eye. He is running back, not very fast, and when he reaches my father and Uri he breathlessly tells them that we turned left at the end of the road.

But we had turned right.

'Thanks, Dov,' I say.

'You're welcome.'

*

Leah doesn't wake until we're on the outskirts of London, then she uncurls herself from me and stretches, my baby giraffe, her hands scraping along the ceiling of the car, toes pointing out straight, far under the seat in front.

'Sorry you had to come all that way,' Leah says to me. 'Sorry, Uncle Dov.'

'It was a nice day for a drive,' Dov says, gamely.

'Mummy?'

'Yes?' I try but fail to hide my delight at her calling me that.

Her bottom lip wobbles. 'Is it my fault you and Daddy are cross with each other?'

'Hey now, come on. Of course it's not your fault.'

She starts crying. 'I just,' sob, 'wanted to be,' sob, 'Jewish!' she wails.

I catch Dov's eye in the rear-view mirror. He's grinning broadly, and I have to use all my willpower to stop myself from doing the same.

'Is that what all this has been about?' I say.

She nods, tears and snot rolling down her face. I give her a tissue.

Dov says, 'You *are* Jewish, Leah.'

'I want to do Jewish things.'

'You can do them with us,' he says, 'if your mum is OK with that.'

'I want to do them at home, with Mum and Dad.'

I'm about to make false promises, just to soothe her. But Dov steps in. Covers for me. As always. 'Leah, it wouldn't make sense for your parents to do that. They don't believe in it. It would make them hypocrites, and they are absolutely not that. They have always lived according to what they believe, and I don't think you should want them to be any other way.'

I wish I had always been able to be Dov's vision of me. I try and see myself through his eyes, and manage a fleeting glimpse in which I don't look quite so bad as I've always imagined.

'When your mum was a young woman,' Dov says to Leah, 'only nine years older than you are now, she realised she couldn't go through with a marriage to a man she didn't love. Even though all her family rejected her for it, she had the guts to leave. You wouldn't want her to pretend that she is someone different, would you?'

'No,' Leah says.

This interpretation makes me sound utterly heroic.

'So, Leah, you can come to us every Friday, and Saturday too, if you want, and celebrate Shabbos with us. And you can come for all the festivals. And if your mum wants to come too, and your dad, they would be more than welcome. How's that?'

'That's really good. Mummy, will you come to shul sometimes with me?'

'Sure, honey.'

'I don't mean you have to believe in it or anything. I just want to go with you.'

'I'd love to.' And I mean it, more or less. 'I'm sorry. I feel a lot of this is my fault, for denying you your heritage.' Something occurs to me. 'Why were you skipping your clubs after school?'

'Oh.' She looks embarrassed. 'So I could get clothes. I went to charity shops, I didn't spend all my birthday money.'

'You have lots of clothes.'

'Clothes for being Jewish in.'

I think of her bulging backpack in the boot of the car, presumably full of second-hand long skirts and turtle-neck tops. And I think of me, sixteen years ago, dragging my own heavy bag full of clothes between my life with Alex and my life with my family. I guess we aren't so different, Leah and me.

'Why couldn't you go clothes-shopping with your friends?'

'I didn't want to have to explain it. And sometimes I met Gidon to do planning.'

'It's a right old tangled web you've gone and woven, Leah. You made your friends worried about you.'

She shrugs. Let's face it, it's hard to think everything through to its logical conclusion when you're fourteen. Like Nathan said, we all did stupid things when we were young. It's hard enough to think everything through when you're twenty-three. And actually, was I doing so much better on this front even now, at thirty-nine?

Leah looks at her phone. 'Dad has sent me eleven texts,' she says.

'He really loves you, you know.'

'I know.'

'You are so like him.'

'How?'

I tick the similarities off my fingers. A new list. 'Even Nathan, who has barely ever seen your dad, recognises that you look just like him. You both have dark Italian hair and blue eyes and wonderful high cheekbones. You both have small earlobes and you can each do that weird double-jointed thing with your elbows. Until you became a teen, you both got up at the crack of dawn. You both like penguins, Terry Pratchett, and playing Frisbee.'

'Everyone likes penguins,' Leah says, smiling.

Dov drops us outside our house. 'Good luck,' he whispers to me.

'Do I still owe you?' I ask. 'I've lost track.'

'No,' he says, 'we are completely even.'

Leah and I walk up the path, and before we knock, Alex opens the door and flings his arms round both of us. He looks awful, as if he hasn't slept for a month. The quotation marks between his eyes are thick, permanent grooves. He pulls us inside, and closes the door. We are all back home.

Chapter Thirty-Three

Winter-Spring 2001

From: elizasymons

To: myfriendmarriedagoy

23 January

Dearest FBF,

Back, forth, back, forth. I can see you rolling your eyes, raising that famous eyebrow. 'If it's Tuesday it must be Brixton…' Don't worry, I'm done now. Done with dithering. I'm back with Alex, and it's for keeps. I have the best of all worlds. I have Alex, but I also have Mum, and Dov, and Zaida. I have everything (except Dad, though that's not a hardship. And Alex and I probably won't be hanging out with Uri and Esther any time soon, but you know – also not a hardship).

When I told you I was going back to Alex, you asked how was I sure this time. I told you how I'd gone to see him, and how overwhelmed I was, as if I was seeing him for the first time. He said he felt the same way, like starting again. I really love him. And I really want to live outside of our world, the one we have always lived in. I know it's for you, but it's not for me. And that's OK. I think I'll be allowed to move between the Real World and our world, as long as Mum is in charge, and that's as good as it gets, for me.

One thing I didn't tell you before I came back home, was that I'm pregnant. Roughly 18 weeks, apparently. I have an attractive round belly. I've actually bought my first pair of jeans – maternity jeans – and you should only see what my tuchas looks like in them, but I don't care. You should also see how huge the waist goes. I can't believe I'm going to get that big. Anyway, I've been wondering if we can somehow use this to distract Michael's mother from her surveillance of your womb. How about you borrow the baby when it arrives, and pretend to her that it's yours and you didn't gain any weight while pregnant. Worth it for the look on her face?

Thanks for your tough talking, Deb. I hated it at the time but you were right. You always are.

Aliza (GG) x

From: myfriendmarriedagoy

To: elizasymons

24 January

Dear GG

Wow, you sure know how to keep those revelations coming. Pregnant now, noch! Listen, I'm genuinely happy for you. It almost made me think I'd like to have a baby of my own soon, but then, nah. I'll wait till you really know what you're doing and can pass on a load of wisdom and hand-me-downs. You'll be a lovely mother. I look forward to meeting the new arrival, and the father of the new arrival too, at some point.

Love ya, Crazy Kid,

Deb-Who-Is-Always-Right xx

From: elizasymons

To: myfriendmarriedagoy

20 February

Dearest FBF,

Sorry for the email silence. But it was so good to see you and Michael the other day, and for you both to meet Alex. Thanks for not calling me 'Goy Girl' in front of him, though you could have – I'd warned him. He thought you were great, and he seems to think that he and Michael will be hanging out every weekend talking about whatever boysy stuff they talked about for all those hours.

Wow, if you were shocked when you saw the size of my bump, you should see it now. It seems to get bigger every day; by next week I might not be able to get through the front door. Which reminds me, we are looking for a new front door. Yes, the latest in Aliza's rollercoaster life events is that we are going to move house. Ideally before the baby comes.

Deb, I am so happy.

Valentine's Day this year was very different to my first one. I tried to put in Alex's card what he means to me. I don't know what Michael means to you, but I know that you love him with your whole self. I didn't feel exactly like that before about Alex, but I do now. What I tried to tell him in the card was, I chose him twice. I chose him first when I didn't know what I was doing, and my decision was clouded by needing to get away. The second time I chose him was completely different. I chose him not to be rebellious, not to be Crazy Kid, but because I couldn't do otherwise. I realised I loved him with my whole self. I wrote an essay in the card, trying to explain this. Then I put a line through it, and wrote, 'I choose you.'

When Alex gave me my card, it was blank inside, like the one I gave him last year. I said, 'You're supposed to write it in it!' and he said, 'Someone I know and love a great deal taught me that it's not always possible to put feelings into words.'

Well, I'm trying to put it into words now, for you. But I am failing. Thanks for everything, Deb. Thanks for always being there.

Eliza (GG), signing off with my Real World name x

We spent our weekends walking arm in arm round the streets of Ilford, being shown 'desirable properties' by spotty teenage estate agents. Alex's wish-list ran to just two items: a garden for the baby, and near a good school (also for the baby, obviously). Mine was a little longer, but it didn't take us long to find the one – a three-bedroom house in a quiet street near the park, a short walk from the town centre and a kosher deli. With a big bath.

Alex's flat sold quickly, so we were able to move in early April, and a week later, still surrounded by unpacked boxes, we hosted a small house-warming party-cum-Easter-Sunday dinner, with Dov, Sheila, Kim, Vicky, Holly and their new baby Freya. Dov brought along the words to 'Tradition', so he and Alex could do a duet. It was pretty bad, as Dov was, if anything, a worse singer than Alex. The rest of us were nearly sick laughing.

Alex and Dov were old friends by this time. Mind you, the first time they met, in the Brixton flat, it wasn't such a warm occasion, at least, not to start with. The two most important men in my life sat stiffly at the kitchen table eyeing each other, while I bustled about making tea and wittering inanely. For Dov, Alex was the outsider, the goyische stranger who'd stolen his sister away. And for Alex, Dov was still the boy he'd last seen the day we ran away together, a black-clad boy indistinguishable from all the others, who came after us and watched as we took the road to freedom.

I put their cups in front of them.

'I want to say thank you,' Alex said to Dov, unexpectedly.

'What for?'

'For always being there for Aliza. For not giving up on her.'

'She is my special person, always has been.'

'And,' Alex said, colouring slightly, 'she told me what you said to her. About how you thought she still loved me.'

'Ah,' Dov sat back and shrugged. 'She'd have worked that out eventually.'

'I've been thinking about it a lot,' Alex said. 'To your family, I must seem like the devil incarnate.'

'I wouldn't go that far!' I said, after a moment's pause that felt like an hour.

'Dov's silence is eloquent,' Alex said. 'No, it's OK. I know what they must think of me, and of the way that Eliza and I left. But despite that, despite what you must have been feeling, you helped get us back together.'

'But I knew you must be a good person,' Dov said quietly. 'Because Aliza wouldn't have chosen you otherwise.'

'Your faith in me is touching,' I said, using sarcasm to deflect the tears that were threatening. Alex put his hand on mine.

'I only want Aliza to be happy,' Dov said to Alex.

'And you think she's happy with me?'

'Well,' and Dov looked at me, witnessing my failure to stop the tears, 'Maybe not right at this moment. But yes. I think she has a better chance with you than with someone else.'

'Thanks, man,' Alex said, and if that was him wiping away a tear of his own, well, Dov and I were too polite to mention it.

Dov was now a big part of our lives, and he got on really well with Kim too – not surprisingly as they were quite similar in many ways, not least in the beard department. Dov was astonished by Vicky, and stared at her open-mouthed for most of the time, which she thankfully interpreted as admiration, and referred to him when he wasn't around as 'my young Jewish boyfriend'. At the house-warming party Vicky got rather drunk, and Dov told me she'd followed him round, backing him into a corner at one point while Alex and I were showing Sheila and Kim round the new place. She announced that she'd kissed every man in the house except him and what was he going to do about it. As the only men in the house were Kim and Alex, Dov cunningly sidestepped her main question by asking about the circumstances around her kissing Alex. She apparently became somewhat maudlin and said, 'I kissed him in Brighton but he said he didn't want to and pushed me away – not very gentlemanly, was it?'

I don't know how Dov managed to extricate himself from this scene without being ungentlemanly himself, though he assured me his honour was intact, but I realised that this put an end to the last traces of worry about Alex and Vicky that I had been carrying around. For this, and for so many other things, I was grateful to Dov.

Dov reckoned that Mum would be willing to see Alex after the baby came. My other siblings could meet him then too. I was happy to wait for that. But there were two people I didn't want to wait for.

I hadn't been to Hatton Garden for years, not since I was a child, and the sprawling streets were confusing to navigate. We found Dad's shop eventually; you had to buzz the door to be let in. I suppose the men behind the counter thought we were a couple in the market for an engagement ring, and quickly, given the size of the lady's tummy, as we were greeted with warmth and huge smiles. When I explained that we wanted to speak to Kap Bloom, the smiles switched off. I caught one of the men staring with horror at the Accessorise crystal ring on my finger and I put the offending hand in my pocket.

Dad came out from the back office, his expression as black as night. Before we had a chance to speak, the manager, a tall thin man with a goatee, followed him out and snapped, 'We can't have your family turning up whenever you like, Bloom.'

I expected Dad to explode at him – no one dared be that rude to Dad – but to my amazement he merely nodded and said, 'I'm sorry. It won't happen again.'

'It's not his fault,' Alex said. 'He didn't know we were coming.'

Dad frowned furiously at me, and shook his head. 'I'm sorry,' he said again.

Goatee said, 'Ten minutes, Bloom, take it off your lunch break.'

Dad stormed out without looking to see if we were coming, and marched up the street. We followed him, glancing at each other, wondering what he was going to do. He stopped on the pavement outside a café and turned on me.

'What in Ha-Shem's name are you playing at?'

'Sir,' Alex said, 'I'm sorry if we've caused you problems at work.'

'You've got some balls, boy, you know that?' Dad said, raising his voice. He looked at Alex for the first time. 'Some great big balls. First *her*.' He cocked his thumb at me. 'Then coming here. This isn't your territory, boy. There better be a good reason for this.'

Seeing these two men next to each other for the first time, I realised how small Dad was, how frail he was beginning to look, a tired old man. His thick black hair was receding at the hairline, his beard was speckled with silver. He still spoke like a dictator, but he didn't look like he could follow it through. I'd never seen him as vulnerable before.

I expected Alex to continue speaking for both of us. But he turned to me, and said, 'I think we do have a good reason, sir. My wife wants to tell you something important.'

Calling me 'my wife' to my father's face was a good way of showing Dad exactly how big Alex's balls were. I was never more proud of him.

'Well?' Dad folded his arms and frowned at me.

'You know we're having a baby, Dad.'

'That's nothing to do with me.' He said the words quickly, automatically, almost before I'd finished speaking. But there was something in his eyes that made me continue as if he hadn't said anything.

'We just wanted to tell you that, when the baby comes, we're going to name it after your father, Levi. Of course, I never knew him, but I wish I had, and the baby will carry his name: Lev if it's a boy, Leah if a girl.'

There was a long silence. I couldn't tell what Dad was thinking – for once, his expression was unreadable.

'Well, that's all we wanted to say,' I said. 'We'll let you get back to work.'

Alex and I started to move away, and we had taken a few steps when I heard my father murmur something. It sounded like, 'Thank you.'

I turned back, but he was already walking – scuttling, really – back towards the shop. Alex and I looked at each other.

'Did you hear that?' I said.

'I think so,' he said.

'We must have imagined it. I never heard my dad say "thank you" in my life.'

'Well, he definitely said, "*something* you",' Alex said, and smiled.

'I want to think it was "thank you".'

'Me too. I'm pretty sure that's what it was,' Alex said, and he reached for my hand. We both let out a breath.

*

Now there was only one person left who needed to meet Alex.

Zaida was going downhill rapidly, so time was pressing. One Sunday, a few weeks before we moved house, Alex and I visited him at Beis Israel. Alex held back as I went forward to Zaida's chair and gently woke him – he seemed to spend most of his time asleep now. He came to slowly, taking a few moments to focus on my face. Then he broke into his beautiful Zaida smile. 'My darling! My dear one!' It was some time now since he had been able to access my name.

I kissed him, and Alex and I sat on either side of him.

'Zaida,' I said, 'I want you to meet my lovely young fellow.'

Zaida turned to look at Alex. 'Hello,' he said.

'Hello, Moshe,' Alex replied.

Zaida turned back to me. 'A nice-looking fellow you found for yourself.'

'He is, isn't he? In fact, Zaida, I need to tell you something important. This man, Alex. Well, he's my husband.'

'Ah! Your husband! Mazeltov! I remember the wedding.'

He gently took Alex's hand, and mine, and joined them together across his chair. Alex and I sat, our hands clasped, Zaida's hand on top of ours. We were all linked.

I took a breath. 'Zaida, Alex has been my husband all along. Not that other fellow.'

Zaida looked at me, puzzled. He raised our hands to his lips, and kissed them.

'What other fellow?' he said.

Chapter Thirty-Four

May 2016

The carpet is new: a rich dark red, whereas the one I remember was beige and flecked with blue and pink spots. I spent a lot of time staring at that carpet when I was a child. But they certainly haven't replaced the chairs – they're the same uncomfortable hard-backed wooden chairs from my youth. I stretch out my legs so vigorously that I almost feel the muscles in my calves twang.

On one side of me, a woman in a mahogany-coloured sheitel wig is gossiping in a noisy whisper to the woman on her other side. 'You wouldn't believe it, would you? No discussion, no nothing, she says, "That's what I'm going to do", and who even cares if he doesn't like it.'

'What did he do?' the woman whisper-shouts back.

'What *could* he do?'

'Oy, I don't know what is going on these days, sometimes.'

'Then she has the cheek to come to me. "Mum," she says, "Mum, I know you're not going to like it but…"'

Troublesome daughters are everywhere. I really want to know what it was that the mum wasn't going to like, but Leah, who is slumped on my other side, puts her hand on my shoulder and whispers, 'How much longer?'

I sit forward and crane my neck to see the men praying below. 'I'm not sure, darling. Forty minutes? An hour?'

With a humpf, Leah flops back into her seat in a more or less horizontal position.

Alex just smiled when I told him that Leah and I would attend shul together.

'It's the right thing to do,' he said.

'I know. But it feels so hard, going there. Right back where I started.'

'But by choice, this time. For Leah's sake.'

'Do I hear my name?' Leah came in, wearing one of her long skirts. She must have grown a little recently because it wasn't quite as ankle-skimming as previously.

'Your mother is in philosophical mood,' Alex said, winking at me. 'I was telling her that going backwards is OK. We have both done plenty of going back.'

He was right, of course. I was a master of going back. I went back to my family after being married. Then I went back to Alex. Then I went back to my old life again just recently, staying with Deborah.

And then, finally, back again, to Alex, with Leah. A golden return I would often think of. Dov dropping Leah and me off, Alex opening the door and running outside to greet us, flinging his arms round both of us. I had come back, and he had taken me back.

'Sometimes you have to go back to go forwards,' Alex intoned solemnly.

'Isn't that complete bullshit, Dad?'

'No, it's a Buddhist thing.'

'We're doing Buddhism at school, actually. Ethan reckons he's a Buddhist now.'

So I take Leah to shul, and afterwards we go to Dov's for lunch, and she doesn't spend much time with Gidon, but instead hangs out with Chanah and Devora, the younger girls. And when we get home, she rings Macy and arranges to go into town to meet Ethan, and it's like old times.

Alex and I sit at our usual places at the kitchen table.

'Too early for wine?' he says.

'It's three thirty.'

'Wine it is, then.' He passes me our fancy new corkscrew, a 'glad you're back together' present from Dov. Alex knows I like using it.

'So,' he says, 'who's going first?'

'You better had. You're the one who threw me out,' I say levelly.

'Liza, I'm sorry.'

I slide the corkscrew over the bottle. 'Go on.'

He says, 'I saw my counsellor while you were staying at Deborah's.'

'Was she helpful?'

'She was really tough on me.'

The cork comes out with a satisfying pop. 'I thought she wasn't supposed to express an opinion.'

'She didn't at first. She was interested in why I was so angry.'

'Well, thank you for saying sorry. And I'm sorry too. Sorry that I didn't tell you what happened between Nathan and me.' It still feels awkward saying Nathan's name to Alex. Though it's starting to feel less awkward than it once did. I pour two glasses, and push one in front of him. 'But back then I didn't feel it was worth turning our new start upside down, with something that seemed so irrelevant. And I wasn't always great at speaking about my feelings. I was just thrilled we were back together, thrilled to be having a baby with you.'

'Can you believe how grown-up our baby is?'

'It feels like a few days ago that she was tiny,' I say, and we smile at each other. Ah, Alex's smile. We clink our glasses together.

'Well… I need to say some more.'

'Oh, sorry! Carry on.'

He shifts in his seat. 'The counsellor kept asking why I was so angry. I said it was because you had lied about Nathan. But she dug around, and it turns out that wasn't the only reason.'

I sip my wine. 'Because I committed adultery?'

'I love it when you go all biblical on my arse, Moses. Yes, of course, the breaking of the seventh commandment, that was a big part of it, too. But turns out there was more to it. I was jealous.'

'Of what?'

In a rush, he says, 'I was completely, irrationally jealous that you'd slept with Nathan.'

'But that's, I'm sorry Alex, that's… what?! I thought you were angry because I lied. Not because you were jealous. It was years ago! One time.'

Alex stares down into his glass. 'First I found out you'd slept with him all those years ago. Then I realised that the reason Leah found the pretend wedding photo was because you'd been looking at it recently. I couldn't think why you'd have kept it.' He looks up at me. 'Unless you still felt something for him.'

It was time – high time – to straighten this out. 'Al, I hadn't got the photo out to look at it. It was just in the box of things I was going through. I was actually trying to find something else.'

'What?'

'The Re-education book.'

His face softens. 'You still have that?'

'Of course I do! Every now and then I look through it and remember the things we did, the things we talked about, when I was newly arrived in the Real World.'

He leans across, his hands braced on the table, and kisses my lips. Him doing that hasn't made me physically jump for a long time.

But it still makes me jump inside.

'Oh god.' He sits back and says, 'My name is Alex Symons and I'm an idiot. It's been a few weeks since I was last a complete idiot.'

'Tell me something I don't know.'

'Believe me, I've not enjoyed hanging out with myself these last few weeks.'

'Nathan was only that one time, Alex. You and I were separated, and I thought we were finished. I was in complete turmoil. And when it did happen between me and him, it was a disaster. Do you want me to tell you how disastrous it was?'

'No, I'd be better off without the details. Here's the thing. I eventually worked out – or to be truthful, the counsellor did – that I was jealous because I wanted you to be just mine.'

'Oh sweetie, I *am* just yours.'

'I mean that I didn't want you to have been with anyone else, ever.'

'Err…'

'It's pretty embarrassing to realise,' and Alex coughs, stagily, 'that though I have always considered myself a feminist, it turns out that my position on my wife is the classic virgin-whore thing. My counsellor was super-tough on this. She said, "Was one of the attractions of marrying Eliza the fact that she was a virgin?"'

'And was it?'

A pause. Then: 'Yes.'

'God, Alex!' I gaze at him. Who *is* this person?

'I didn't realise it at the time, I swear.' He coughs again, and takes a slug of wine, spilling a bit on his shirt. He really is embarrassed. 'Basically, I always thought of you as pure.'

'I'm a person, not a bar of fucking soap!' These days, even *that* word trips off my tongue with ease.

'I know. I know! I'm a male chauvinist bastard even my grandfather's generation would be ashamed of.'

I'm suddenly furious. 'This is a bloody outrage, Alex!'

'I'm just trying to explain why I was irrationally angry.'

'You slept with *tons* of people before we met!'

'Well, not tons.'

'I've slept with two! And one of those was only once! Ask Vicky how many she's slept with! Or Kim's new girlfriend, what's her name, Sarah? Or anyone, really, who lives out here.'

'I know, Liza. God, I'm such an arse.'

I thought about Nathan calling me wanton. I would never have dreamed that my own husband thought the same.

'Jesus, Alex. Maybe it would have been better if you'd carried on letting me think this was all about me lying.'

He reaches across the table for my hand, which is clenched into a fist. He holds on to my lumpy, angry hand.

'The counsellor said I had a version of us in my head. A narrative, she called it. I was the worldly one, the leader, the teacher. You were the innocent, the pupil. But my version only worked if I was the only man you'd ever been with. When I found that wasn't true, maybe my whole world shifted on its axis. Everything I thought I knew was wrong.'

'Is this your counsellor saying this? Or you?'

'Me. Here's the thing, Liza. You came from such a different world. All the rules and traditions, your attitude, you were so incredibly interesting. You made me feel interesting too. I was the guy who won the girl from the hidden world. We were Romeo and Juliet. You let me show you all the things I knew. Do you remember when we first watched *Some Like It Hot* together? You laughed so hard I thought you'd break.'

'But I can't believe that you'd have such an old-fashioned belief! I fell in love with you partly because you were a modern man!'

'If you think you're disappointed in me, imagine how I feel.'

With my free hand, I take a gulp of wine. 'Really,' I say, 'I should have gone and slept with loads of men before we met, and then seen if you'd still wanted to marry me.' A thought occurs to me. 'Is this why you said that thing about Kim, too? Are you jealous because of my friendship with him?'

'No, honestly. I love that you are friends, I swear. But you know, he's always had a soft spot for you…'

'He has, I know. But he would never ever act on it, you know that. And neither would I.'

'I know. I really do know that. Believe me, I spent most of the Easter weekend trying to convince him that I'd trust him with my life. It was just a stupid thing that came out when I was angry, but later I realised that I've always felt more possessive of you than I should have. Even Kim's gentle interest in you unsettled me. I suppose it made me feel insecure.'

'I love Kim like a brother,' I say, my voice quiet, 'and it was lousy of you to embarrass him like that in public, and horrible to make him ashamed of his feelings.'

'Yes. I've been a complete arse. To him, and to you.'

He stares at the table, and I stare at him. His retro attitudes have shocked me, but they have shocked him too. And I have come a long way, because fifteen years ago, what he's saying wouldn't have shocked me at all. I would have accepted it as part of the deal of being female. You belong to your father, then you belong to your husband. Somewhere along the way, I have learned to think differently, have learned to value myself as a person in my own right. And here's the thing; the person who taught me to do that is sitting opposite me, telling me what a shit he is.

Without him, I wouldn't know that the things he is telling me are wrong.

'Let go of my hand, Alex,' I say, and he does, all hang-dog eyes.

I unclench my fist, and put my hand into his. 'Now you can hold it again,' I say.

Another Saturday morning. Alex goes to wake Leah. I'm almost looking forward to shul this time. Yes, there's a bit of a stir when I come in: the girl who married out is back! Bringing her no doubt wanton daughter with her! Some of the more hard-core ones look away, won't talk to me. Some of the others look at me with a smirking expression that says, 'So you couldn't find anything better on the outside, huh?'

I can handle it. The ones who are welcoming more than make up for it, and it's been surprisingly nice to see some long-forgotten faces from my childhood: the rabbi, looking about 102 years old, and his wife, who is so astonishingly unchanged that she is the source of much covert women's-gallery gossip on the topic of face-lifts. Mrs Benjamin, who used to reward my Hebrew learning at *chedar* with salty pretzels, a very effective technique, always smiles at me. The four Piller boys, who were kids then and now are grown men, almost identical, are each married with two or three kids of their own. Uncle Ben, still slightly smelly, has forgiven my transgressions, and hugs me warmly with the same 'welcome back to the fold' line each time.

'And oy, the pretty daughter,' he says, chucking Leah under the chin, regardless of – or because of? – the fact that she clearly hates it. I want to stop him, but I don't. Being chucked under the chin by well-meaning relatives never did me any harm. Or maybe it did. Who knows what I'd be like if they hadn't? Or if any of the other things that happened to me hadn't happened? I am the person I am now because of all the things that have influenced me, and all the things I have done, even the messes I have made.

The only thing I would change is that I wouldn't have said yes to Nathan. Either time. But nobody's perfect, as it says at the end of *Some Like It Hot*. You can only muddle through, doing your best.

I'm eating muesli, though it's early, and I don't feel like eating. I'm still half asleep. Alex comes downstairs, and I say, 'Is she in the shower?'

'She's gone back to sleep. Says she doesn't want to go to shul today.'

We smile at each other. Is this over already?

On Monday, when Leah comes down in the usual panicking flurry of school books, hockey socks and homework not finished, I notice she is wearing a tiny skirt again. I say nothing.

'Can I go to Ethan's after school?' she asks.

'Sure,' I say.

She pauses in the doorway, framed by it, a beautiful painting. 'I like Ethan,' she says.

'He's a nice chap,' I say. 'I hope he treats you nicely.'

'He's teaching me how to meditate. It's really helping me concentrate at school.'

'Oh, good.'

'Buddhism is cool, Mum.'

'Oh, good.'

'I might become a Buddhist, maybe.'

Oh, god.

A Letter from Beth

Thank you so much for reading *The Two Hearts of Eliza Bloom*. If you'd like to be kept up to date on my new releases, click on the link below to sign up for a newsletter. I promise to only contact you when I have a new book out, and I'll never share your email with anyone else.

www.bookouture.com/beth-miller

I hope you enjoyed reading *The Two Hearts of Eliza Bloom* as much as I enjoyed writing it, and I'd love to hear what you thought, so please leave a review. I adore reviews, and read them all: the brief, the long, the good, the… less good. Silence is the scariest review of all.

If you don't like leaving reviews but still want to tell me what you thought, or just say hello, you can get in touch on my Facebook page, through Twitter, or my website.

With thanks,
Beth Miller

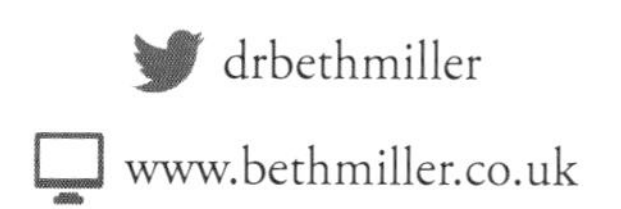

Acknowledgements

Books are like overflowing suitcases. Sometimes you need help folding things up neatly, and someone to tell you it's OK to leave a few items out. It's also great to have friends who'll sit on the lid with you to squash everything in. With boundless thanks then to the most brilliant folders, sifters and lid-sitters, my writing group: Liz Bahs, Jacq Molloy and Alice Owens. Really couldn't have managed without you.

Thanks also to my agent, Judith Murdoch, who suggested I re-work the entire chronology, the equivalent of getting me to start over with a rucksack: painful, but correct. And thanks to my special reader, Saskia Gent, who always says the right thing, and is a dab hand at capsule packing.

For guidance on various tricky aspects, thanks to Juliette Mitchell, David Seidel, and Ivor Silverman.

For useful writing chats and much-valued support from people who are going through it themselves, huge thanks to Melissa Bailey, Jo Bloom, Sharon Duggal, Lulah Ellender, Kerry Fisher, Abbie Headon, Ellie Knight, and Becca Mascull. And thanks to all the Prime Writers, a great group of talented authors who don't mind saying how it is.

For championing the book and telling me her favourite bits and being just lovely to work with, thank you to Maisie Lawrence, my sparkly publisher at Bookouture. And to everyone at Bookouture, particularly Kathryn Taussig, Kim Nash and Noelle Holten, thank you for making me feel so welcome.

Thanks to my children, for being funny and kind and supportive, and for giving me plenty of material for stroppy dialogue. Of course, all characters and incidents portrayed in this book are entirely fictitious. Finally, the biggest thanks of all to John, for never wavering in the encouragement he gives me to keep re-packing that damn suitcase for as long as it takes.